x

This book is dedicated to Saudi expatriates everywhere, especially

Juergen, Ginny, Debbie, Cockney Pete, Prince, Bryan, Paddy and all the others who did not survive to tell their story

I hope they will forgive me for my crude attempt to tell it for them

Contents

Chapter 1
TOUCHDOWN

<u>King Faisal was assassinated on 25 March 1975.</u>

It is a time of sadness mixed with great promise. Khaled Ibn Abdel Aziz has now been declared King of Saudi Arabia. His elder brother Mohammed has renounced his own accession to the throne and of his own free will, proclaimed Khaled the new King and Fahad his younger brother, as the new Crown Prince.

Gunned down by his nephew, Prince Faisal Bin Musaid, on 25th March 1975, the previous ruler, King Faisal, had already proved and exercised the power of the oil weapon. The price of crude has commenced its dizzying upward spiral, relentlessly drawing into the Middle East the vast industrial and commercial fortunes of the West. This economic diversion is well into development and thousands of workers, "Expats', flood into Saudi Arabia from every corner of the globe. The previously anonymous Kingdom has developed newfound credence in both geographic and geopolitical significance to the western world. The Kingdom of Saudi Arabia owns a twenty-five per cent share of the known, global oil reserves. Her economy is growing by approximately three hundred and fifty million dollars <u>PER DAY</u>. Prince Faisal would not be part of it, accused of assassination and pronounced sane, he was publicly beheaded in Deera Square in Riyadh.

As the Saudi economy booms, so do the population of foreigners. Thousands of hirelings arrive daily, amongst them the misfits, the tribe they called "Khowajas'. The foreigners arrived by modern-day jets; as for the misfits, they should have arrived by B-29, ejected from the belly of the "Enola Gay" - It would surely have been deemed, more appropriate.

1

CHAPTER 1   SAUDI STYLE   TOUCHDOWN

12 MAY 1975

I remember awakening, though I was still falling, falling through the dream, falling through the sky in a slow, controlled glide, helplessly lost in the hands of another, falling backwards through time, back to that fateful day when my present troubles began:

The great alloy bird commenced its slow descent, gliding down the escalator of air from eight miles high. As it fell earthward, it unfolded wing flaps and landing gear. They were cumbersome and awkward accessories, the unlikeliest possessions of a species of flight but our only hope, of reaching earth's rapidly ascending surface in one wholesome piece.

My ears began to ache - an internal pain where exploratory fingers could not probe. Forcing my jaw side to side and in a rapid chewing, motion delivered the pop of relief I had so earnestly been seeking. The great bird see-sawed its wings, first to the left and the whole cabin rolled over, followed by two quick dips to the right as the plane obeyed the computerized search for equilibrium, maintaining our glide path with stomach-Churning ease. Warning lights now flashed above my head,

"NO-SMOKING" and "FASTEN YOUR SEAT BELTS'.

Such icons meant nothing to me, a non-smoker, on his first real flight of any significance. My seat belt had remained tight for the duration of the flight, excluding the quick dash to relieve my bladder, followed by a rapid return down the aisle as I returned to my perch and the safety of my belt.

Even as the great bird fell from the sky, I noticed the fearless, female flight attendants flitting from passenger to passenger, clearing away the debris of the six-hour flight, checking that safety belts were secure and that all seats were back in an upright position.

"Does this mean they reclined?" I wondered feeling stupid, my back now aching from the six-hour sit-up-and-beg position that I had endured across the continents strapped into a tiny

2

airline seat. A beautiful young stewardess hovered by my side; she paused momentarily to check the belt. My spinal complications melted to insignificance, anaesthetized by the aromatic beauty of such unattainable, uniformed perfection. "Hope you enjoyed your flight, sir?" she purred, her Warm breath in my ear, her sultry intonations enhanced even further, by a pouty, wet-lipped smile.

"Yes". I lied a trifle embarrassed, "Very nice, thanks". She lingered for a moment, and then disappeared, I knew what she and the others of her intercontinental creed were thinking,

"New kid! Never been on a plane before! New Kid, he'd get the message".

Thinking back, we usually did - that was of course if we held our ground and made the grade. She would then have to fight us off with a stick, though with this one, from my point of view, she may not have to fight too hard. She emitted something different; I couldn't quite put my finger on it, but I knew; deep in my bones I knew, and the preternatural vibrations induced a delicious new tremble into my earlier state of embarrassment.

The overnight layovers in Dhahran were lonely, even for the "Stewies" as I learned they were tagged. Against airline rulebooks, they did not always decline invitations to dinner, from handsome young thoroughbreds of their personal choice. The Stewies knew full well, that it was almost impossible for their suitors to pursue a relationship further than a meal: time was too short. No guests were allowed in their Rooms and as several Stewies have told me, "They most certainly would not accept a ride back to expatriate digs like some common little harlot!" not unless they desired such an outcome anyway.

"New Kid," she thought and continued down the aisle with her work.

"Cabin staff to landing positions, please!"

The announcer's voice did nothing to reassure me. By now the Jumbo lurched and lumbered through the sky, initially side to side, before lumbering up and down in a constant adjustment, which although small, made me think the plane was out of control. The nose lifted and the giant bird floated a moment before a loud bang tore into the remnants of previously frayed nerves. A cacophony of thunderous clattering followed as numerous tyres bounced and squealed in protest at the crushing impact. The plane shuddered and shivered. It slued sideways as the engines screamed reverse thrust and when I was certain I was about to be thrown from my seat, the mechanical storm calmed and a soothing note dissolved the mayhem,

"This is your Captain speaking!" the authoritative voice announced. "Sorry about that ladies and gentlemen, seemed to be a spot of loose sand on the runway. We hope the sliding around didn't spoil your flight. Thank you for flying British Airways. We hope you enjoyed your journey with us, and we look forward to serving you again in the not-too-distant future".

The speaker crackled again, and the voice continued in guttural tones. I had no idea what the man was saying, presuming it to be an Arabic translation of the previous captaincy statement. The plane reached the end of the runway and began a smooth turn back towards the brightly lit terminal building. A new commotion filled the air as hundreds of passengers climbed onto their seats and snapped open the overhead lockers. All manner of cabin baggage spilled into the aisles of the plane. Excited chattering, broken by occasional laughter, swelled into the aluminium cylinder. The aisles were suddenly congested with bobbing, writhing passengers as they struggled with bundled belongings, pushed each other around and waited anxiously for the doors to disengage. They seemed desperate to disembark as if the plane were on fire. On the verge of panic, I scanned around the aircraft, to confirm that the plane's tail section wasn't burning and there was no immediate requirement to dive through the nearest emergency exit. I had never seen such impatience and, to my utter astonishment, the plane was still lumbering back down the runway, towards a distant off-loading point.

CHAPTER 1   SAUDI STYLE   TOUCHDOWN

"Sit down, please! Wait until the plane has come to a standstill. Sit down please!" The Stewie pleaded in vain. I sat and watched them in numbed disbelief, was it indiscipline, or was it ignorance? It was difficult to decide. Shortly, a young Stewie pushed through the mass of bodies and fell into the seat beside me, from where the previous Saudi occupant had ejected, grabbed his bag from the overhead locker and was now pushing his way to the exit.

'Is it always like this?" I inquired, forgetting to conceal my naiveté.

"You're new to this aren't you?" she smiled, confident with her statement, as a grin, faintly teased into the corners of her, freshly painted lips.

"Does it show that much?"

"Wait!" she replied, glancing around the cabin until her eyes alighted on their target.

"Look over there". She pointed a manicured finger, which I followed with increasing interest until I observed a calm, casually dressed man sitting alone. Just another human sardine waiting to disembark, not unlike myself, or so I thought at the time.

"So?" I questioned politely, "What makes him so different?"

She paused before replying, studying me thoughtfully. There it was again, that inner glow, the warmth rising upward from the pit of my stomach, drying my throat unwilling to allow me any further speech. She paused before continuing:

"Watch him carefully new kid, when you have the native term for such a man, you can take me out to dinner in Dhahran's finest because by then you will know, what this pantomime is all about".

I thought she was taking the piss, nobody ever offered to let me take them out like that before, so I tried to play it cool but not too cool to spoil any further progress.

The plane had come to a standstill. The doors slid upwards into the fuselage whereby the passengers, poured onto the landings and descended the mobile stairs outside. I studied the man she had singled out, watched him rise from his seat when the main throng had gone and followed him into the waiting night. Halfway down the stairs I paused and glanced back over my shoulder. Her wave was friendly, though her expression revealed something more. "She was right', I thought, "I was new here "The new kid", and in no position to achieve anything, other than a reprimand from someone who knew the game'. I returned her wave and, in an attempt, to appear indifferent, turned quickly, stumbled and almost fell, down the remaining stairs. I picked myself up from near disaster and hurriedly walked across the sand-sprinkled asphalt. Muffled laughter followed me; my cheeks were ablaze. I had a fairly good idea from where that laughter had emanated. My coolness melted with sheer embarrassment and I continued my walk to the terminal building, I had blown it with the flying beauty.

I began to wonder what magic had evolved aboard the plane. When we departed from London's Heathrow, I observed many business suits and exotic, fashionable, lady's wear; showing an ample collection of well-rounded, voluptuous, although covered, cleavage. Now there was nothing, no titillation at all, nothing but the night-gown-clad men with red tea towels on their heads, secured in place by a black rope in twin loops. The female species of Saudi had disappeared and all that remained were somber, shadowy figures, covered from head to foot in black flowing material. No bare flesh, nothing but the eyes, beautiful dark eyes, in total contrast to the cleavage and midi-skirted legs that I had encountered at the check-in desk for the flight to Dhahran. The sudden transformation had completely deceived me. I followed the man from the plane. What was it he carried about his person? which ingredient had God provided him with, that created obvious respect from the Stewies, it had generated some interest and it was an ingredient I wanted. Unlike me, the stranger carried no hand luggage, I now struggled with mine, as we crossed the heat waves radiating from the massive Rolls Royce engines. We walked beneath the

6

wing tips of the plane. My perspiration flowed freely; I carried my hand luggage with one arm and attempted to remove an excess of winter clothing with the other.

Advancing from the beached whale of a plane I immediately realised that the clammy heat wasn't from the engines,

"My God!" I remember thinking, "This is the heat of Saudi Arabia and it's after dark. The sun must have gone down hours ago". A strange, unknown excitement welled up within my body. This was great, a warm, dry evening. I savoured the balmy night air. It was much better than the damp, freezing, grey country I had left behind, even though it stank of jet fuel and urine. I attempted to remove my sweater and shirt. The stranger appeared beside me, observing my tangle and, to be of assistance, took hold of the bag with one swift movement of a tanned, well-muscled arm. I was now free to remove my excess clothing and immediately stripped to my undershirt, re-took possession of my hand luggage and stuffed the peeled skins of winter clothing inside it, I had a feeling it would be a long time before I needed such winter layers again.

"Thanks". I smiled at the stranger, secretly praying he wasn't gay, not that I believe there is anything wrong with gay people, it's just that - I'm not. and it's hard for me to imagine, why they, are. They're not interested in dating women and I'm not interested in dating men it's a simple fact I can live with.

"Sokay". returned the easy reply, followed by a friendly grin.

We continued walking together. The stranger's skin was golden brown, stretched tight across a well-developed, muscular frame. His clothing was simple, a cotton tee shirt with cut-off sleeves at the shoulder, casual jeans and comfortable-looking pair of well-worn training shoes. His neck was thick and clean- and around it hung a single, gold chain, which disappeared under his shirt and into the mat of hair below. The chain was too thick to appear feminine, yet it did not advertise great wealth. The tee shirt, however, looked strange; the sleeves had been hacked off and carefully remodelled to fit the top of the shoulder but did not drop down the arm. The man's face carried a worn, weather-beaten appearance, a neat Sinbad moustache sat above his top lip and his expression signalled a confident capability. As we waited in the immigration line, he seemed to mould into his surroundings as if he belonged. He did not appear to feel the heat, nor did he mind the wait; he was indifferent to his present location as if he had passed this way one million times before. I was sure he had a library of tales to tell, all of them exciting traveller's tales but I did not want to appear inquisitive, not just yet anyway.

The building awaiting our entrance was a complement to Arab architecture; great solid arches soared above us, blocked with stained glass, though the theme was barely visible in the evening light. The Saudi emblem of crossed swords below a well-leafed date palm hovered above the entrance. Electric fans hung from the high concrete canopy, but their frantic gyrations did nothing to cool the desert night air. Dressed in white nightgowns (Thobes) the Saudi men became the majority. An announcement cackled above the throng of passengers in barely discernible broken English,

"Welcome from UK flight 502, good evening and hope you have a nice flight, after passport desk, collect baggage; and buses and taxis waiting at your service". The message struggled with the acoustics, echoed around the domed roof and was finally lost to the night. I forced a smile but the stranger, who on catching this expression, offered me a few words of advice:

"Don't make fun of them, kid. They don't like it and you may find yourself departing Saudi on the plane you just came in on - after a night in airport jail, that is".

I felt my grin wane as the stranger's warning tone took hold.

"Here's some advice, for what it's worth. Take things easy, allow yourself to be accepted into their world and don't forget, this is their country. Don't try to force your standards on them, try to learn a little of the language. It can really help sometimes and if you're still here in two or three years, consider yourself settled. I didn't say accepted, I said settled. Do you understand?"

I nodded. The stranger knew his way around these parts and, as the Stewies had guessed, I was just a "New Kid".

The line moved forward, and we reached the immigration desk. A small, well-tanned, uniformed official sat behind the chest-level barrier. His hair was greased back, an important but bored, expression was glued to his face. Four ageing passports, bonded with a seal of authority, were poked under the glass screen, protecting the immigration official. The official spoke in Arabic and the stranger replied in a similar voice. Somewhat startled at the stranger's command of Arabic, the boredom disappeared and the official stamped the entry visa and handed the passports back accompanied by a genuine smile.

"Shukran" the immigration officer announced

"Afwan" the stranger replied courteously

The stranger moved to one side, now it was my turn.

I desked my shiny new passport, empty but for the single-entry visa into Saudi Arabia. My worldwide experience laid bare for all to see, "New Kid'. The official glanced at the passport with a thin smile of recognition. He scrutinised it, paying special attention to its silky sheen, then returned it under the screen, without stamping the customary entry visa.

"No!" he announced, "You are not allowed".

I was devastated, absolutely gob-smacked but before I could reach the desk to retrieve the worthless documents, the stranger intervened; conversing in a pleasant intonation, followed by a knowing smile that split his lips. The official, realising that his game with the new foreigner had failed, decided to stamp the visa and return it to me, I was more than just relieved to poke it back into my hand luggage.

"Shukran" I copied the stranger

"Afwan sadique" he smiled in response and I immediately learned something.

I smiled and I walked with the stranger through a gauntlet of airport guards, noticing, for the first time, the machine guns slung across their shoulders. I could almost feel their visual inspection but no attempt to refuse my progress was offered, some gave a few words such as "Welcome" and "Hello" as we passed them by, I offered "Thankyou" in English and Shukran, as my only reply. The stranger now held a small yellow card in his hand,

"Get your shots before you left?" he inquired.

"Of course!" I snapped back insulted by the question, I ain't stupid, Yellow Fever, Typhoid, Smallpox and Tetanus. I was sure that finally I had done something right.

"Roll up your sleeve," instructed the stranger, "You forgot one".

The stranger guided me to a straggled line of multi-racial misfits, who were waiting outside a small office door. A squiggle of Arabic hung outside on a cardboard sign.

"What's this?" I asked.

"Who?"

"Not who, what?" I pointed a finger at the Arabic sign.

"Oh, that? W. H. O". the stranger spelt it out, "World Health Organisation".

Before I could question my new friend further, a small, rotund man in a not-too-white, blood-specked jacket appeared from inside the office. He would have looked more at home in a butcher's shop, standing in front of a wooden block, chopping away at some animal carcass with a primitive, bloody axe, he exuded that flesh eater kind of aura. The man wiped the beaded sweat from his forehead with a small dirty cloth, which he placed between his lips as he collected the cards.

"Cards," he trilled through the cloth as he moved along the line of worried faces. "Cholera!" announced the butcher, gaily; "Everybody needs cholera".

He disappeared into the office and his voice trilled once more from inside,

"Sleeves! Everybody. Everybody roll up your sleeves".
This was followed by a translation into Arabic. He reappeared a moment later with a nasty-looking syringe. He aimed the needle at the ceiling and squirted an almost invisible jet of liquid that streamed into the air. I watched with stunned disbelief as the

10

butcher came down the line. I suddenly realised, to my horror, that the needle was not being changed and was about to protest this filthy practice. Although at that time, to the best of my knowledge, Aids had yet to become known to mere mortals like myself, what was about to happen was totally against any hygiene practices I had previously been taught and I motioned to leave the line.

"Forget it," whispered the stranger "You'll never get in without it".

The stab in the arm was quick but the pain lingered longer, too long for my liking.

"You can go". smiled the butcher.

"You were lucky," admonished the stranger.

"Ouch! You fat, dirty bastard!" was all I could think of as the pain flooded my deltoid muscle and began to throb like a toothache.

"Right gentlemen," announced the fat bastard, "The rest of you wait here until I fill this; the next injection is for typhoid. Won't be a minute".

"He's going to fill it again?" I asked incredulously.

"Again," grinned the stranger, waving his yellow card for emphasis. "Next time, get your shots done back home, generally speaking, it's worth it".

I rubbed my arm. It had begun to ache quite a bit now and a small patch of blood oozed into the cotton fibres of my shirtsleeve.

"The arm will be stiff for a couple of days," smiled the stranger, "Then the pain will disappear, it's better than a dose of cholera which can get you a ticket home".

"Home?" I asked, not understanding

"Yeah," grinned the stranger, "In a wooden overcoat".

The stranger bade me good luck and farewell and as he headed for the exit, I had to bawl after him,

"Hey! Haven't you forgotten something?" I shouted.

"Like what, kid?"

CHAPTER 1   SAUDI STYLE   TOUCHDOWN

"Your luggage," I offered, eager to do something in return for his assistance. The stranger tightened his lips and shook his head from side to side.

"You have me all wrong kid," he drawled, still shaking his head in a slow negative gesticulation. "What's your name, new kid?" he inquired.

"King, Bob King. Bob is what most people call me".

"Well, let me tell you, Bob. With a name like King, you should go far in Arabia, there are hundreds of Princes under your commanding name, but there's something you should have learned by now".

"What's that?" I quizzed hopefully.

The bronze muscular frame turned to leave but for my benefit, he turned as he walked away, looked me over once more and then spoke. The words spilt from the side of his mouth, over his rapidly departing shoulder.

"I ain't a bloody tourist, kid" he admonished, "I work here". He swept under the arch, out into the night and was gone. I suddenly remembered; I didn't even know the stranger's name, how rude and ignorant was that?.

I was alone once more but now more uncomfortable, one minute I had someone to converse with, but now I had to start all over again. I scanned the bustling arrivals concourse. Passengers were now departing with luggage, a constant stream of staggering, overloaded men. A few people, obviously the wealthy, hired porters who weaved through the throng with their home-built trolleys. Others simply dragged their baggage, skidding it across the marble floor until they reached their destination; or the suitcases burst open and deposited an amusing collection, of their most private possessions, unceremoniously in their wake. I weaved along in the opposite direction, until I discovered a human pyramid of passengers, frantically scaling a mountain of luggage. Even as baggage was retrieved, the conveyor belt continued to drop a selection of leather and plastic clothes containers, faster than they could be reclaimed. I sat down at the edge of the scrum; what was the hurry? I had no desire to climb the mountain and assumed it was better to wait until the main body of passengers had collected and departed, whilst making sure, from an advantageous position, that my baggage did not disappear along with them. Thirty minutes later, the frantic scramble had been reduced to a few bodies, milling amongst the debris of what had once been the luggage mountain. I spotted my suitcase, dragged it from the remnants of the mountain and headed for the door.

"Stop!" announced the voice, "Go back".

The guard blocked my exit; he repeated the same words once again. The guard commanded a limited vocabulary.

"Stop, go back!" the cry now almost a command. My eyes followed a second pointing finger and caught sight of a straggle of desks, on top of which, were suitcases of all sizes, during various stages of disembowelment,

"Customs," I remembered, "Of course you dopey git, you need to go through customs".

I dragged my case over to the scatter of tables, dropped it on the nearest available table and unlocked the lid. A Saudi man in a long white thobe approached me with an air of authority,

"Alcohol, pornography, drugs?" inquired the night-gowned inspector as he disembowelled my suitcase.

"No Sir" I assured him, "I have nothing that would break the law".

"Shukran, thank you," replied the inspector with a smile, closing the suitcase lid and chalking a large Arabic symbol on the topmost surface. The guard at the exit smiled as he remembered me, the new kid.

"Yes sir, now good, pass please and thank you".

"Shukran" I offered

"Afwan," he replied. I had learned my first and most important Arabic word, Shukran, Thankyou.

No sooner had I got through customs than a small boy grabbed the handle of my suitcase,

"I carry sadique, you my friend, I give you good carry".

CHAPTER 1   SAUDI STYLE   TOUCHDOWN

I wanted to say piss off but being outnumbered and almost certain there would be someone outside to pay him for his service, I reluctantly relinquished my baggage to the little pleader. The boy immediately headed over to the perimeter fence, where white-robed men were loitering.

He disappeared into the group, which immediately closed around him. I tried to follow but was delayed by the persistence of the loitering men offering, or should I say, almost forcing upon me, the service of their taxis.

"Taxi, sadique? Cheap price, give the best discount for you. You my friend, give you good discount".

"No thanks," I replied, having already been warned by interviewers, not to accept a taxi from the airport, unless I wanted to lose my belongings, or my life, or even worse in my tender young eyes, my anal virginity. The suitcase I had lovingly packed some hours before had now vanished, along with the boy, behind the haggling taxi drivers. I tried to push through without contact as politely as possible. When I finally broke through the scrum, my belongings had vanished without a trace.

"Shit!" I thought, "They warned me about that".

"Hey, Bob! Over here".

I immediately recognised the voice of the man who had conducted my interview. This man had also warned me of the tricks plied around the airport, to relieve new foreigners of their money and belongings. How was I going to explain that I had been suckered? I walked over in the direction of the voice with my head hung low and my confidence flushed down the tubes.

Scarborough Pete was a tall, well-built man in his late twenties. He sported a Mexican-style moustache. A worldly, well-travelled character and I had thought on our first meeting, that Scarborough Pete would have made the perfect model for Sinbad the Sailor. Scarborough Pete had described his adventures in Saudi Arabia. These tales had stirred my curiosity and drawn me like a magnet, to this barely known desert on the map of the world. I was twenty-odd years old, had toiled in the same drawing office since leaving school, inhabited the same

14

town all my life and often wondered what the world had to offer beyond the boundaries of the small South Yorkshire mining town of Barnsley, if there was nothing else to this world of ours, as far as I was concerned, I was in the shit but I knew in my mind, this could not possibly be the case, Could it?.

"Where's your luggage?" inquired Pete.

"Some kid-

"Don't tell me," He interrupted, "Some kid asked if he could carry your suitcase; you said yes, and you haven't seen him since?"

"Yes, I know," I sighed, "You told me so".

We didn't hang around, there was no point according to Pete, we would never see the suitcase or the kid again and if we did, we would have no chance of proving he had taken my luggage. There wasn't anything of any real value in there so, although extremely annoyed I made light of it and we headed across the tarmac to the car park. Besides, I didn't want to get a kid's right hand chopped off for a few pairs of jeans and a couple of shirts.

In the car park, which smelled of jet fuel and urine, Pete fired up an oversized American car and we headed towards the checkout gate. I quickly adjusted, to sitting on the right-hand side of the car and as Pete manoeuvered from the parking lot, I ran my finger across the small chrome logo, pinned to the glove compartment.

"Plymouth Fury," I mumbled with admiration, "Nice motor". The car was big, spacious and seemed to contain every luxury invented, for the sole purpose of travelling in style.

"Yeah," replied Pete, "We'll have you running around in one in no time".

Pete attempted to raise my spirits, though he noticed, that I wasn't too disturbed about the recent loss. There wasn't anything in the bags that was worth much anyway, just a few light-coloured clothes a couple of pairs of sandals and about ten year's supply of suntan oil, forced into the bag by my mum, God bless her, who had been collecting the stuff from Barnsley

market, for weeks. As we approached the pay booth, he allowed
a small minibus to cut across our path. Pete gazed enraptured,

"Just look at that," he whistled, in a meagre attempt to define
his appreciation. I followed his ecstatic, lusting gaze. The
minibus was chock full of Stewies, not more than an arm's length
away. Pete gasped as one of the young girls opened a nearside
window; he was even more amazed when an arm protruded in
our direction and waved in recognition. A uniformed girl thrust
out her head and shoulder and waved her arm towards his
passenger, me, the new kid. Gripped in her hand was a small
piece of paper. Pete turned to grab my arm but his passenger
had already jumped from the car and was receiving an
unexpected but promising message. The girl patted my head
and ruffled my hair, as the bus passed through the barrier. The
cars behind Pete began to blast their horns with frantic
impatience. I ran back to the fury and jumped in beside Pete and
we pulled away from the ticket booth. The note bore her name
and room telephone number. Pete wriggled in his seat,
desperate to see the note, which he hoped, would reveal more
information about the girl.

"Joined the Eight-Mile-High Club?" he laughed

"What's that?" I grinned; I knew what he meant but I wasn't
going to let him think I hadn't joined. I realised I could get
considerable mileage out of this, and I was going to screw it for
all it was worth.

"In layman's terms, Bob, did you bonk her on the plane?"

"What kind of a bloke do you think I am, Pete?"

"Well, you're here, Bob, and that only suggests one thing".

"What's that?"

"You'll find out soon enough Bob" that's for sure. Anyway,
what about the bit of paper?"

I nonchalantly studied the note and recounted her words to
Pete,

"Here's my name, hotel and room phone number, new kid,"
she had begun,

CHAPTER 1   SAUDI STYLE   TOUCHDOWN

"I don't usually hand them out so freely; this is the first time. I can see you look like you may need a few pointers. Give me a call, we can have dinner tonight, I don't want to eat alone".

"What did you say?" gasped Pete.

"What could I say, Pete? I've no luggage, my clothes have disappeared, I've no money, no car and no bloody idea where I am, so I told her I didn't think I'd be able to make it".

Pete goggled at me in disbelief, before he gunned the fury in the path of the minibus, which was already a good half a mile ahead. The distance between the Fury and the Harem on wheels closed quickly. He pulled alongside the window where the message had appeared and beeped the horn.

"Nod your head, Bob," he ordered.

"What for?"

"You have a date tonight".

A car now barreled towards us, hurtling along the road from the opposite direction, the distance was rapidly diminishing, Bob Seger pounded his music from the fury's tape deck the beat almost in tune with the Fury's progress, much too fucking fast .

"Nod your head to the girl," insisted Pete.

"Pete! the car!" I gasped, as the car raced towards us too fast to believe.

"Start nodding," ordered Pete.

I nodded to the Stewie, her smile rapidly fading to a shocked expression as the oncoming car horns screamed their warning. I sat and stared in horror as the distance between our two cars snapped shut like a trap, the on-coming car ploughing off the road onto the dark, desert shoulder, disappearing in a cloud of sand, dust and the diminishing wail of its overworked horn. Pete calmly accelerated the Fury and overtook the bus. I sat mortified; my only movement was to get the seatbelt around my frame and into its clasp as quickly as possible. My insides quivered with fear and my bowels hung on to their contents for dear life, I hummed a tune to the beat of the music to appear unruffled.

CHAPTER 1   SAUDI STYLE   TOUCHDOWN

"Jesus," I wondered, "What the hell am I doing here with a bunch of car-crazy loonies, who'll risk life and limb just to organise a date with a girl?"

"Relax," chimed Pete, as if reading my thoughts, "Happens all the time. The other guy will be OK. The roads here have flat deserts on both sides, and I saw him bounce back onto the highway in the rear mirrors. No problem".

"I'm not worried about the other car Pete, I'm worried about the date I just arranged, with no decent clothes, no car, no money and no chance of ever finding out where she's staying. She forgot to write her address".

"Bob," Pete began, a smile playing on his lips, "I paid the little Yemeni kid to steal your case. We do it to all the new guys. It's a kind of initiation ceremony, just to teach you new kids a lesson so that you won't get ripped off in the future. Believe me, Bob, it works. Bet you won't be handing over your case too lightly anymore, will you? Anyway, your suitcase is in the boot'

He assured me that he had money to spare, knew exactly where the Stewies layover and that I did not need to worry, everything would be taken care of.

I breathed easier. We grinned at each other for a moment, before I uttered my sincere and eternal thanks,

"You Bastard!"

When he had finished laughing at my distress, Pete explained:

"In this country, girls do not exist. You cannot show affection towards a woman in the street. If you are apprehended in a car with a woman, even during the day, say at the traffic lights and she is no relative or wife, it's eighty lashes, and a three-month prison sentence before deportation. If you even attempt to chat with a Saudi woman and she takes offence, they label it eve-teasing and that will get you eighty lashes plus three months then deportation. It is forbidden to even think about women. Do I make myself clear?" He waited for my affirmation before adding, "You must take every opportunity that comes along. Get cleaned up when we get home. Stewies layover at the Meridien Hotel; chances are she will have a friend with her, know what I mean?"

"What about the lashes?" I asked him, feeling uneasy about the situation,

"OOH! I hope so," grinned Pete, rubbing his crotch for effect, "I truly hope so".

I laughed along with Sinbad. I knew exactly what Sinbad had in mind. With the windows fully open, the hot desert air swelled into the car, Bob Seger yelled his message over the throbbing beat of the quad stereo. "Hollywood nights, Hollywood years". Strangely enough, it seemed to fit. I settled into the huge, padded leather passenger seat, to the rhythm of "Till it Shines" the beat soothed my composure and curiosity once more overtook my feelings of uncertainty. A warm glow of anticipation for the night ahead fueled my thoughts and I imagined the surprises that lay in wait in this alien landscape.

As he drove, Pete studied me, I asked him later in my apprenticeship, what he had been thinking and he told me. "Bob," he offered, "you blended into the picture as if you had been here all your life and not a stranger to open-windowed cars, racing along dark, desert highways". A wry smile crossed his features; "Perhaps" I remember thinking, finally, we had caught one at last!"

The buildings flashed by my open window, as if on fast-forward. Rope-tied, wooden scaffolding surrounded most. They appeared as if they were in the final stages of demolition, but we were on the outskirts of town and I discovered later, I was observing first-hand, the effects of the massive amounts of oil revenue now being utilised, building permanent homes for a nation of Bedouins. Burn-offs, waste methane gas flares, blazing over the well heads, constantly rippled and bathed the surrounding desert with an eerie, yellow glow, flickering and dancing on the spiralling thermal breeze. A new fragrance, not unlike burned engine oil, assailed my nostrils. The aroma, scooped into the Fury through the open windows, dominated my sense of smell and fired up my curiosity once more.

"Is that the engine overheating?" I inquired, more as a warning than a question.

"No, it's not the car, Bob. It's a billion-dollar perfume called money, the dollars from that single aroma are paying the OPEC boys their ransom and like you and me the bucks are coming from the west, but if I were you, I wouldn't make too much noise in protest. It also happens to be paying your fat salary".

The Fury sped on. There were no road lights and I marvelled at the star-spangled darkness, the stars seemed to stand out more in the Arabian sky as if you could reach out and scoop them from the heavens with your hand. Only the headlights scythed the inky blackness ahead of us and Pete drove as if he was trying to overtake his headlight beams. The car, unlike the Starship Enterprise, did not seem to hold enough power to make the jump to light speed but, that didn't stop Pete from trying. It was only my pride that prevented a request for a reduction in warp drive. I almost sighed with relief as we reached the outskirts of the city where Pete had no choice, but to slow down for the flashing amber lights at the crossroads.

"Have to be careful, Bob," He warned "Saudis give way to nobody. They think the traffic lights are only for foreigners. You should see the accidents during the day".

Although his intonation was serious, I could not help thinking that this was another of Pete's jokes; I had already tagged him as a master of the practical joker's club. Confirming my impression, we crossed various main roads without so much as a pause, carefully skidded into a side road that we followed for a mile or more, before entering an unlit sandy back alley in a place I later learned was named Thugbah, an old Saudi fishing village, where we finally parked the Fury.

I climbed and stretched from the vehicle into the sweltering heat, brushing from my body, the dust and sand that we had collected during the warp drive, Sand that now insisted on sticking to my clammy skin. A giant Jumbo whistled overhead, crawling down the glide path of final approach, to the runway we had just left behind. Crickets chirruped with perfect continuity, hidden somewhere amongst the surrounding sand.

"Sand is everywhere," I thought. It was as if we had been dumped onto the biggest building site in the entire world which; I would later learn, was exactly where we were. As the plane disappeared, along with its decibels, another sound probed my ears; a rumbling mumble of compressors, as thousands of air conditioners, attempted to force chilly air into the occupied rooms of neighbouring buildings.

"It's not so bad at night," Pete informed, "During the day, when the temperature gets above one hundred, that's when they start to work overtime and the noise is a little worse, but you don't have to worry, Bob. You won't be here. You'll be working and there are no air conditioners where you're going".

Pete fumbled in the boot, slammed the lid closed, circled the car and dumped my suitcase on top of my feet.

"Thanks, mate". I acknowledged, sarcastically.

"You're welcome," grinned Pete. "Follow me".

Pete pushed open a small metal gate that had been hacked into a perimeter wall as if an afterthought and we walked through into a courtyard. Ten gritty paces took us across sand-sprinkled terrazzo and we entered a small, pitch-dark passage. A few paces more and Pete opened a door. A click flashed me back from my otherwise imaginary surroundings to a new reality and I followed Pete into the room.

"This is the lounge," announced Pete, revealing all with one sweeping gesture of his arm. I gazed sadly at a broken sofa, one well-used, wooden coffee table with a sticky top, sporting three unusual types of home-made legs; and two chairs that resembled half-completed self-assembly kits, this was not the luxurious apartment I had been expecting.

"Seen some action this furniture, Bob".

"I'll say," I agreed with Pete, "By the looks of it, at least the first and second world wars".

CHAPTER 1   SAUDI STYLE   TOUCHDOWN

Pete headed down a small corridor off the lounge, turned right and disappeared into another room. I followed him, into a completely tiled room. None of the tiles matched. It could have resembled a colour scheme from Jacob's old jacket.

"Kitchen," I guessed without difficulty. One wall propped up a concrete sink with a single tap suspended over it. A cooker stood to attention beside the sink. I had my suspicions that it may have been used; the spilt and spattered contents of a million frying hours were glued to the surface, which I presumed to be enamel, but there was no way I could be sure without first using a chisel. I was starting to get downhearted when I opened the door of a wardrobe-sized refrigerator,

"The light's not working," I remarked.

"But it's brand new!" replied Pete, amazed, before realising his error, "Oh! now I remember, it's the wrong voltage. The fridge is two-twenty and the sockets are only one-ten, it needs a transformer".

"No wonder it hasn't been used," I groaned my enthusiasm waning.

I moved over to lean against the sink and something large leapt upwards from a half-full trough. I yelled and jumped backwards in shock, thinking the beast might be poisonous or worse.

"The sink needs unblocking as well," smiled Pete, choking on his moustache as he tried not to laugh.

"That's a Gecko," Pete pointed to the lizard, "They eat cockroaches, insects, ants and thankfully mosquitoes, and kill about all known household germs, dead! I've got one upstairs; I call it "Domestos'. They do more good than harm, Bob, so don't kill it".

"I'll try to remember that" I nodded, as the beast eyed me up and licked its eyes with a slimy tongue. I acknowledged the tap with a twist of the wrist,

"Cold or hot?" I inquired.

"Depends. If you get up early in the morning, you may find it cooler than usual, otherwise it's the usual warm temperature, growing warmer as the day goes by, but not enough to scald you. You see, Bob, the holding tanks are mounted on the roof and that's the advantage of living on the ground floor. The pressure in the shower is great, the water is always warm due to the solar heating of the fibreglass tanks and, of course, there are no stairs to climb".

"How come you don't live on the ground floor then?"

"I like you, Bob, you're learning fast". Pete grinned with appreciation, "But to answer your question, the dust and sand blow into the ground floor more than upstairs, but don't worry. As your time here increases, you'll get a raise, usually from the ground floor up".

We progressed from the kitchen along the corridor and through another doorway. Pete switched on the lights as we entered. Again, the entire room was tiled. A drain hole pierced the floor. High on one wall, a single tap thrust outward from the brilliant blue tiles. A toilet crouched immobile in one corner, immobile it may have been but it was certainly well used, it was bestowed with more Khaki stripes than a regimental sergeant major. A bidet, unconnected to any pipes whatsoever, sat uncomfortably above an eastern-style croucher toilet on the opposite wall. I pointed to the high tap in the wall,

"Shower!" I questioned Pete, with growing confidence.

"Right first time". replied Pete, verging on laughter.

On the opposite wall of the corridor, we entered another room, approximately four meters by four meters. A rough carpet attempted but failed to hide the uneven concrete floor. A hand-made wardrobe graced the wall and, without effort, I could see that the paint did not extend behind it. A rusting, army style, steel cot did not conjure up the image of a bed and atop the cot lay a small rectangle of foam rubber.

"My new pillow no doubt" I groaned.

I opened the wardrobe expecting the worst but it wasn't to be, inside there were bed sheets of all shapes and sizes. There were also pillowcases, though no two items matched, they were all garish to the extreme and all needed washing. Pete offered quick instructions on how to operate the air conditioner (a-c) and the ceiling fan. As they were expecting me, the room was already quite cool, a welcome relief from the muggy outdoors. I loaded the filthy bedding into the washing machine, which had been crammed into the utility room beside the kitchen. Pete disappeared for a few minutes and brought down his dirty washing and threw them in with mine,

"We have to save water" smiled Pete "This is the desert Bob after all" Pete threw in what seemed like half a box of washing powder and slammed the door closed.

As the washing machine burbled to life, I marched back to my "bedroom', hoisted my suitcase onto the bed and began to unpack.

"Come on, leave that, I'll introduce you upstairs".

Pete was in a hurry, so I followed him back along the corridor, across the lounge and out through the main doorway. Pete handed me the keys to my new home as we went. The flick of a switch revealed a previously unnoticed staircase and we ascended. Two flights later we entered the first-floor apartment wherein two men lolled around the furniture, clad only in skimpy underpants, now I was starting to get worried and it must have shown

"Keith, John, this is Robert King. But you can call him Bob".

"Don't mind us," said Keith reassuringly. "The fucking aircon has just packed up and we're trying to stay cool, we would have pinched yours but we didn't have the time". Keith, I realised, was deadly serious.

I pumped the customary handshakes of welcome, already fully understanding the need for such attire. Already the room was quite hot, habitable only in a state of near nakedness. I sat on a wonderfully new lounge suite, still in its wrapper, in front of a splendid oak coffee table and accepted a large bottle of ice cold, fizzy orange. Swap shop came to mind as it was obvious where the new furniture should have been, but hey ho that's life.

"Here, Bob, have a mars bar," the mars dropped onto the coffee table with a crack. I guzzled the ice-cold orange drink in one long pull and was immediately given a refill, I sucked on the mars bar for a while, I had to, it was frozen solid and no way could I get my teeth to bite off a chunk. I thanked the two men for their hospitality before I briefed them on my flight. They laughed on hearing that the baggage trick had worked, as usual, but before I could get comfortable, Pete broke into the conversation,

"Better get moving, Bob. We're going out, remember?"

The two men gawped at Pete but before any questions were asked, he waved them away. This was unusual, they told me later, most new guys suffered in their acclimatization. The jet lag, the heat, the mosquitoes; and were regularly observed, moaning and groaning, homesick in their beds. I did not feel that bad I had survived the initiation, got myself a date and still had no idea where I was or what I was doing here.

Pete showed me to the door,

"Half an hour, Bob," he instructed, "And I'll be down to pick you up".

The door did not quite close behind Pete and as I fumbled in the darkness for the light switch, I heard their lowered tones of conversation,

"Well, what do you think?" Keith began.

"Yeah," added John, "Do you think this guy is going to make it or is he going to run home to his mummy the first chance he gets?"

"Right, remember the last two guys? One of them couldn't even iron a shirt, hated housework, and ran home to his mum like a lost school kid".

"Listen," Pete interrupted. "Look, I'm sure this guy is going to make it. I'm certain Bob's going to settle in just fine".

"How can you be so positive?" Keith inquired.

Pete recounted my arrival story as far as he could remember,

"Well, he got through the immigration section with no trouble at all, hung around waiting for the rabble to clear the baggage hall like a real pro. He cleared customs without trouble and even took the butcher in his stride".

"He had the needle?" interrupted the two men in unison.

"Yeah, but he isn't making much noise about it, is he? When the other guys lost their suitcases, they were screaming blue murder. He accepted that it was his fault and barely mentioned it, oh! he wasn't too pleased about it, but then again, he didn't go berserk either-but there's one more thing,"

"What's that?" the two men were now showing a deepening interest.

"On our exit from the car park, a minibus full of Stewies pulls across in front of us, one of the side windows opens and out pops a beauty, handing her name and number to him".

"Jesus!" the two men chorused whilst laughing.

"So, the new kid walks over to the bus all casual and receives his message, but because he has no luggage, no money, no car in fact he has fuck all, he declines the invitation. As he turned away from the bus, she looked as if he'd disconnected her life support system. When he told me, I drove after the bus so they could arrange to meet later. I almost crapped my pants. We were alongside the bus and a raghead suicide pilot, travelling in the opposite direction, nearly wipes us off the road. Just as I'm expecting a coronary, I turn around to see the new kid, humming to Bob Seger on the tape deck and waving to his date. Later, he has a rendezvous with miss hot stuff. I'm assisting as a chauffeur on the off chance of spare and to the best of my knowledge, this is the first time any recruit has bonked a stewardess on his way in, got the butcher's old needle, arranged a date on his first night, lost his luggage, nearly got killed and not mentioned home once".

"Sounds like we may have one here," Keith and John agreed.

The three men viewed each other with raised eyebrows and a grin. Time alone would tell. They knew, that outside the walls of their building, awaited something far more testing than the misgivings of three expatriates. Their words were nothing compared to the external world, where the mid-day orb decided in a matter of minutes, the future and whom it concerned.

CHAPTER 1   SAUDI STYLE   TOUCHDOWN

"Sounds like we could have one here" announced Pete, proud of the fact; that it had been his choice of employee.

"Yeah, you could be right," agreed John.

"Takes more than a few days to make a Khowaja" admonished Keith.

"It's a good start though," Pete's tone was insistent.

"A Khowaja," Pete's voice trailed off as he disappeared into the shower, leaving the one word hanging as if all had been said,

"Khowaja".

I headed downstairs, the unfamiliar word turning over in my thoughts. I wondered what it meant and why the guys upstairs appeared to hold it in reverence. It sounded admirable and secretive. Whatever it was, I would find out, then I too could become "Khowaja', regardless of the deeds that would have to be performed to earn myself such a title.

I stretched my arms upward, pushing onto the balls of my feet whilst grasping the singular tap and attempting to turn it on. At first, it refused to move, then it gave way suddenly with a crack as if the metal had snapped in two, spinning me sideways and down onto my heels, with my forearms slapping against the tiled wall to retrieve lost balance. The tap hissed for a while, but nothing of a liquid nature came forth, nothing but the dry dust and plaster fragments of new construction. The tap had never been used, which was more than could be said for the toilet. Reaching up once more, I spun the tap wide open and was greeted by a louder hissing, followed by a gurgle and more dust. Evenly balanced and once more on the balls of my feet, I stared up into the redundant orifice.

"Something else that doesn't bloody work, Pete". I voiced my disappointment loudly.

A gurgle issued forth, followed by a snoring sound. The tap suddenly spat; filling my eyes with construction crap and I turned away cursing in what I hoped would be temporary blindness. The forceful flow smacked my shoulders. At first, it was quite cool but as the flow continued, the pipes were flushed through and the solar-heated water gushed forth. It cleared from a yellow colour to clear and warmed to a temperature not unsimilar to a baby's bath water, where it levelled at a pleasant thermal register. As Pete had previously explained, the flow was quite forceful from four stories above, where the holding tanks perched in direct sunlight high on the roof. The powerful flow almost massaged my skin from its bones. The temperature was just right, not at all unpleasant. I shampooed, shaved and scrubbed away the thoughts of home, that were already trying to sneak up and ensnare my vulnerable sentiment. The water massaged and cleansed completely. Once satisfied, I reached up and halted the flow as the last rivers of my body debris disappeared down the drain hole in the floor.

Fresh, was the only word to describe this invigorated spirit. I quickly dried myself with a towel; I thought I heard a bird twittering above the rumbling mechanics of the air conditioner. I hitched the towel around my waist and prowled around the Spartan apartment like an eager gun dog. It was minutes later and only when the birdcall was accompanied by Pete's voice, that I realised my mistake. The birdcall was in fact, a Saudi-style doorbell. I opened the door and Pete entered the apartment. A sly expression moulded to his features. It was obvious, that he too, had been fooled by the mysteriously stranded foul on his first acquaintance and he was hoping he could have made more of my ignorance. Pete said nothing, merely assembled an armchair and sat down - very carefully, to wait. I trod my way back to the bedroom to dress. It wasn't long before I was ready, shaved and smelling like a tart's handbag. They had told me to bring light-coloured clothing. I dressed in white canvas jeans with a white T-shirt and white trainers, Pete asked if Daz or Persil or somebody had sponsored my trip? and that he certainly wouldn't lose me in the dark. I had obviously overdone it on the light-coloured stuff, I changed my white trousers to Blue Jeans. It was ages before Pete stopped grinning at my Persil white predicament.

CHAPTER 1　　　SAUDI STYLE　　　TOUCHDOWN

Pete's grin was only removed, as we attempted to cross a downtown intersection and a yellow cab, driven by a rag head, as everyone called them, ran the red light and almost broadsided our vehicle. The sudden spurt of adrenaline charged my curiosity, awakening an appetite for knowledge, in short, I wanted to learn as much as possible before this crazy bastard killed me. Pete found himself buried under a landslide of pertinent questions and by the time the Fury entered the Meridien car park, I basked in an easy calm, developing by the minute as I soaked up the knowledge of this mysterious unfamiliar territory.

The Meridien Hotel was a luxurious testament to the recently acquired wealth of Saudi Arabia. Plush, deep pile, richly patterned Arabian style carpets, smothered most of the floor space, yet where carpets stopped short, brilliantly polished, deep burgundy marble exalted our steps. I thought the marble was too beautiful to be hidden beneath coloured cloth and fibres. Soft pattering fountains showered and rippled the otherwise mirror-like surfaces of ornate reflecting pools. The water music had a relaxing effect. Real palms swayed over an internal garden, with a selection of tropical plants, the likes of which I had never seen before. Plush, red leather Chesterfield upholstery was arranged in small, intimate family circles. I knew that it was real leather - I could smell it. The setting could have graced the pages of any top hotel brochure and, being brand new, Architectural Digest would have loved it. I searched for the small note as Pete hurriedly guided me to a phone.

"Give me some coins". I asked him for coins for the phone.

"It's in-house, Bob. It's free". Pete grinned continuously at my naiveté.

I dialled the number. It rang three times before the line clicked open.

"Hello, Flight Attendant Virginia Rogers speaking".

"Hello, Virginia. It's me, Bob, the new kid". I was nervous but tried not to let it show.

"Hello, new kid. So, you found me?"

"Yeah, it was easy," I lied through my teeth.

"Where are you?" she inquired.

"I'm in the lobby with a driver, I came to take you out to dinner".

"It's Khowaja, the guy is a Khowaja" I reminded her of her promise to go out to dinner if I could tell her what the guy on the plane was known as.

I was already taking a distinct liking to this girl; she had a soft voice and delicate mannerisms and it wasn't just my confidence that began to swell. The line muffled, I was sure I detected whispers. The line cleared once more,

"It's a deal, new kid. We'll be right out". Click.

Pete gawped in amazement. I hadn't uttered one syllable regarding the availability of my new best friend, the guy that had teased the crap out of me since I'd landed on this sandpit.

"I'm going to end up spare meat at a vegetarian banquet". Pete thought aloud.

"Well?" he gasped, "What did she say?"

"She'll be right out," I replied, allowing Pete to simmer in his own frustration.

"Is she coming alone?" quizzed Pete with some tone of urgency.

"I forgot to ask". my response with nonchalance.

"Great, Bob. You're a major help. A real expatriate pal,"

I gave Pete enough time to verbally extol about my more notable virtues and my cricket outfit and waited until his confidence totally waned, before cutting short his increasing frustration,

"She said, "they" will be right out, Pete. And unless I'm mistaken, she did not imply that she would be bringing her dad. You'll be OK, Pete. She's got a friend as she saw you driving and knew I would need a chauffeur.

"You arsehole, Bob. You knew all along!"

Pete thumped me in the shoulder and suddenly, I guessed from his expression, from now on we were mates.

CHAPTER 1   SAUDI STYLE   TOUCHDOWN

"That makes us even," I informed him, "Remember the suitcase?"

Pete remembered and he realised that I may not have been here long, but it was Pete who was now following my lead for a change and I could see he was hoping it was going to be a lead worth following.

You couldn't help but notice the new sparkle in Pete's eyes. We strolled around the perfectly positioned, indoor garden, sauntered by the soft, showering fountains and slumped into the sumptuous, red leather luxury of a lifestyle beyond our normal financial reach. Pete was in seventh heaven. He told me he had endured three months of miserable celibacy and he'd had to cover for the failings and hasty exits of the other new-kids and his eagerness was now beginning to show. Whilst we waited for the girls, he updated me with the local news and events. The minutes ticked slowly by and they got slower as more of them disappeared into history.

The Meridien was cool. So cool that the hot night air played against the windows, causing a misty condensation that obscured the dark, desert view.

After thirty minutes had elapsed, two girls appeared in the lobby area. I held up my arm and waved our presence, the girls clip-clopped their heels across the naked marble to join us, and I could hardly contain myself. Virginia spoke first,

"Hope you don't mind, Bob. I brought a friend".

"Me too," I responded and the standing introductions flowed.

We sat in a small, intimate family alcove and ordered non-alcoholic drinks. I had been told you couldn't order any other kind and was just finding out it was the truth, not another of Pete's pranks. Our initially nervous conversation slowly relaxed. Virginia's friend Pam took an instant liking to the Sinbad look-alike. She professed to remember seeing him previously on some outward-bound flight. Pete pretended to remember but then, I knew that tonight, Pete would have confessed to anything, including murder, to get closer to Pam's ample charms.

CHAPTER 1   SAUDI STYLE   TOUCHDOWN

The waiter hovered with large, red leather menus and when I saw what was on offer, I couldn't believe it; the delicacies available in this secluded desert location could have graced any cordon bleu magazine.

I couldn't help but notice the voluptuous shapes beneath my female partner's loose, silky clothing and beneath my clothing such uninhibited thoughts had begun to show. We chatted idly through prawn starters - prawns as big as bananas, more succulent than any such seafood I had ever seen, let alone tasted.

I got as close to Virginia as was decently possible and our two couples broke off into separate conversations. I listened with interest as Virginia recounted the more unusual aspects of the Stewie world, revolving around the chastity of certain members of her fellow crew. She told me that some passengers assumed, that the ticket purchased on the ground allowed access to everything in the air, not least the Stewies on duty.

"Creepy, horny perverts, they'd jump on anything in a dress that would lay still for a moment," she scowled with revulsion. I pretended to agree; though at this moment I fully sympathised with them and could understand on their behalf what had driven such desire but I did not, and would never condone their predatory ways.

As the main course was concluded, I recanted my own reasons for entering Saudi. A salary and conditions that defied belief and a burning desire to remove myself from the insulated capsule in which I was growing old.

Past loves were discussed - lost loves and new loves and I discovered that we were not unsimilar in likes and dislikes. By the time dessert arrived, it had become obvious, that one thing we both liked was each other and over the final dregs of coffee our pact was sealed.

"Had we really just met?" I wondered, "Or had we known each other for eons". It became more difficult to decide. Love, I had been forewarned, was the forbidden fruit of Saudi Arabia. Just as Adam and Eve had fallen, Virginia and I now trod that

32

similar path. In place of an apple, a chocolate sundae with extra chocolate sauce and to hell with the calories. I let my hand rove under the tablecloth and squeezed her hand with anticipation. Pete, meanwhile, floated over to reception where he booked a double room with twin beds, for the two of us. Virginia left with Pam, whispering with slight embarrassment. The two of us hung around like expectant fathers for a further fifteen minutes. Or what seemed to me like fifteen hours, before striding urgently to our room. I left Pete and disappeared down the myriad of silent corridors. I was frightened to death that at any moment I would be caught out, but hey, if you could have seen this girl, you would have agreed the risk was worth it. I knocked at what I had been led to believe was the "Stewies" door. Pam answered, tugged me inside and with one arm around my neck, kissed my cheek, before bidding a fond farewell and disappearing in search of Sinbad. Sorry, Pete, I almost dragged her back for a second tongue wrestle but courtesy, or naiveté got the better of me.

I walked around the standard hotel bedroom with twin beds, they could chuck one of those away for a start I thought, or at least I hoped. I was a little unsure of myself in these surroundings. Usually, for me, it was in the back of a car or on odd occasions an early evening romp when my parents and two sisters were all away from home, which wasn't that often. What the hell was I supposed to do now? I decided to be bold, what had I to lose, if she said no, fair enough, I wasn't a bloody predator and Ginny had instigated this union from the start. I enjoyed her company anyway but if she said yes! Wow! A gentle hissing issued from the bathroom. Steam drifted upwards along the ceiling and into the bedroom. My anticipation, like the steam, curled around my stomach. This was every young man's fantasy. These were the moments I would replay in my old age when memory was all I had left. Small fragments of time such as this I hoped would never be lost. Events such as these required a young man's utmost attention and I decided it would receive all the attention I could muster. I cleared my mind of all external thoughts, about home, Mum, Dad, Sisters, England whatever;

the next few hours would be mine to cherish and did I intend to cherish them well.

Gingerly, I knocked then opened the door and stepped into the bathroom. The shower hissed louder now and the steam swelled into a small, tiled room partially blocking my vision. I moved forward a few steps and caught sight of her, studying her form as she swayed and bobbed behind the misty, frosted glass. I wasn't sure about the next step, so as nothing came to mind, I knocked on the glass door containing the vision of loveliness, a moment of silent expectation, followed by desperation clawed at me as I prepared to sincerely apologise for such an unsolicited intrusion,

"Come in," Virginia acknowledged my presence. "It's not locked" she giggled

I tugged open the magnetic door above the bathtub and without pausing, climbed inside fully clothed for some sort of he-man effect. I reached out with my arms; I thought I could hide my embarrassment by squeezing my face into her chest but she tugged on my chin with her slender fingers and directed my lips to her own. A lingering tongue wrestle followed.

"Why didn't you undress?" she whispered as she turned to face me. I could have told her the truth but blurted out the only words available to me at that moment in time,

"Life's too short Virginia. Life's just too bloody short!"

I held her in my arms and she allowed me to savour the moment of fruits to be picked. Gently I pulled her closer before, eyes closed, head angled slightly, I pulled her mouth to my own. Our lips moulded to form an airtight seal. Tongues gently testing the intimate bond. she wrestled my shirt from my back; her eagerness matched my own. Our lip-locked seal remained unbroken as I kicked my trainers and sodden trousers free. Flesh against flesh, naked, we lost ourselves to the burning desires that dwelled within.

Our frantic, uninhibited struggle continued, charging uncontrollably, to the peaks of intimate, physical union, where we were lost to the procreative instincts that rule the race. Sometime later, finally satiated, and as the last spasms of ecstasy washed over us, we slumped into the bathtub.

Momentarily becalmed, the hot, misty spray played around our bodies. I slid underneath her body and, with her head on my chest, our legs playfully entwined in blissful contentment, apart from the odd escaped shirt buttons, which were now nipping the skin on my bum and causing slight pain but who cares at times like this? After a short while, Virginia arose, kissed my chest and tenderly pulled away.

"Bedtime" she smiled. I followed her from the tub and tenderly and sometimes rudely dried her with a soft, white towel before carrying her over to the bed. Her long brown hair spilled over her shoulders, sometimes hiding her nipples that peeped between her tresses like small cherries on her voluptuous well-formed breasts. Her long legs were supple and strong, certainly from the long-haul exercise of regular flight duty. Her feet were well-manicured. Red painted toenails signalled their tender care. I could hardly contain myself. It seemed like hours, before finally exhausted, we lapsed into each other's arms whispering small breathy endearments.

I couldn't sleep, or rather, I didn't want to sleep, preferring to gaze at her beauty, drinking my fill; for I knew deep inside, that there would be many a desert day to pass, if or before, I saw her again. By the time morning came our conversations had eroded all shyness and we were more than just acquaintances.

An hour or so before dawn, Pete settled the bill and knocked at our door, I dragged on my clothes that had dried in the night on the balcony, my jeans were still wet being thicker material but so what, it wasn't going to spoil anything was it? Secretly and regretfully, I left the beautiful young maiden in the room. I'm sure Pete did not hear her sleepy message as she whispered goodbye to her new kid love. I left by the back door and caught up with Pete in the car park.

CHAPTER 1   SAUDI STYLE   TOUCHDOWN

"Well, you certainly look like you enjoyed yourself," grinned Pete, as I squelched across the asphalt in wet trainers to the dew-sparkled fury,

"Yes, I did but I hate it" I remember sighing.

"Hate what?" exclaimed Pete in disbelief.

"Afterwards" I replied, "You know when you have to leave, I was really getting a feel for that girl. She was fabulous. I could have stayed with her forever".

As we drove away, Pete began to explain a few facts about Saudi life. He gabbled for fifteen minutes before he realised that I was a million miles away, lost between the time zones of worlds apart.

"Some bloody new kid," I heard Pete reflect, "Works like a bloody pro".

For the second time in as many hours, a magical phrase jogged to the fore of my sleep-sludged thoughts,

"Stick with it, new kid. We'll make a Khowaja out of you yet".

"Besides" continued Pete, "you owe me two hundred and fifty quid. Half the cost of tonight's extravagance".

I pretended not to hear the last statement, I was stunned at the expense of it all, back home, it was a few drinks and a bag of chips, out here it was a hotel, dinner and a bloody fortune but boy was it worth it. I hoped they were going to pay me as much as they said they would, otherwise Scarborough Pete was in for another screwing, one that he wouldn't enjoy as much as his last one.

The big Plymouth galloped along the early morning highways of Dhahran and returned to where it had begun the night's voyage. I slept in the front of the car. I wouldn't freeze in this country and if the truth were known, I would sleep better out here than I had ever done before. Fresh air, big fillet mignon steak, sex and no freezing cold draughts, bloody marvellous.

"Jesus!" mumbled Pete again, "With the exercise and prime steak you've had tonight, it'll be a miracle if you wake up at all!"

CHAPTER 1   SAUDI STYLE   TOUCHDOWN

It was the hot morning sun, dappling into my eyes that finally awoke me. Unsure of my whereabouts, I jogged my head upright. Slowly the realisation dawned, followed by acceptance. A lonely echo spiked my innermost thoughts. Three thousand of miles away now, my mother, my father, my sisters and my friends! I shrugged it away. A raging thirst burned in my throat and although I lay comfortable in Virginia's lingering, perfumed fragrance, her sweet scent only reminded me of the loneliness ahead. I didn't know if I would see her again, there was no phone contact in Saudi, in fact very little contact at all, you had to wing it every single day. At least four months would have to pass before I could escape from these present constricting boundaries and enter the real world once more. I had signed up for two years and I had no idea what I had let myself in for, even if I hated it, I was stuck for at least four months unless I wanted to cry myself home but that's not me, I could do this, I could do this standing on my head in a bucket of Shit, I kept telling myself I could but I knew this was only the beginning of a new style of life.

I clambered from the car, trod wearily to my room and threw the damp clothes to one side. I showered and dressed before falling asleep on the metal cot, remembering as an afterthought to hack the sleeves from a clean shirt. By the time the birds chirruped, I was ready. Keith and John voiced their approval of my new attire and ran a continual inquiry regarding last night's amorous encounter. Pete said nothing; he just smiled and languished in his memories. Keith blew a fuse after he had sat in the front passenger seat for a while and his arse got soaked from the bleed of my wet jeans,
'Fuckin hell, my fuckin seat's wet" he moaned like a baby all the way to work, we grinned as we tried to console his frustration between our own sniggers, giggles and explosive laughter. Despite their pressured enquiries, I did not reveal to any of them, why my pants had been wet when I left the Meridien, despite their chorus of curious interrogation, I thought it would be better for me, to leave them guessing, I was positive, that their own

fertile minds would invent something far more exciting than the truth.

"You rotten, secretive bastard, Bob," Pete cajoled in mock anger, as we headed out of the meagre habitation to the daily dramas of the Saudi Arabian workday, "You rotten secretive Bastard" I realized with a feeling of camaraderie, that despite my naivety, despite my initiation day, despite me being a complete new kid and despite Keith, STILL moaning about his pants, I had now been initiated into their tribal desert crew.

Chapter 2
STEEL

Constantly Interrupted by a sea of handshakes, my first days on the job at the Steel Plant blazed by, I remember them easily; they were burned into my memory by the heat. The overpowering all-day and particularly, noon-day sun dominated everything you planned, tried or thought. Pete remained at my side, guiding me through the routines, explaining that it was customary until I became accustomed and could manage alone. I suddenly realised; I was just a small cog in an extremely large machine. My first days on the job were more of a familiarisation or induction course. There were it seemed, a million safety procedures to be checked and performed. All regularly and I began to wonder if I had over-reached myself. I never questioned the safety routines when we were on site in the oilfields and refineries because, as Pete had already forewarned on our first site visit,

"There are decades of light crude and gas not that far below us, Bob, and if anything were to go wrong, Red Adair himself would piss his pants and faint with panic, at the thought of such a catastrophe. Millions of dollars" worth of construction equipment wasn't going to be turned over to a new kid in a matter of days. It was clear that I would have to play second fiddle for a while until I became proficient with the required standards. Then I could expect to be transferred to a new project, where my knowledge and experience could be built upon".

Just before lunch, Pete informed me about the safety alarms and became noticeably nervous when he broached one system.

"This is the baby," he instructed, "If you hear this sucker sound off, you'd better run for it".

'Run, Pete, run where?" I enquired; the desert seemed a big place to start running to somewhere, from the middle of nowhere.

CHAPTER 2　　　SAUDI STYLE　　　STEEL

"When boiling crude and gas are exploding into the sky, Bob. It doesn't matter where you run, just get as far away from the job as possible. Run like hell; if ignition occurs, the flames will spread low on the ground during the first blowout. If you're within range, you'll be fried alive. The safest action is to run like hell for a count of ten. That should get you at least fifty yards away. Then take a deep breath and bury your head in the sand".

"In the sand?" what the fuck was Pete was suggesting? but he was the boss and he was usually very sincere about on the job safety.

"Right! Bob. That way, if you don't get far enough from the crap, or the flames spread wider than normal, only your backside will be scorched and your pretty little features will be saved. Don't worry about it too much, although it's a good thing to remember. When that siren blows, it's too late for heroics. You have no choice other than to run, is that clear?"

I was undecided, Scarborough Pete was a tricky guy to understand at the best of times but he wouldn't lie about this, would he? This was serious and who was I to argue? I wanted to live for a while yet and it was for my own good, wasn't it?

Lunchtime arrived and we sat on the side of the structure, facing out across the desert, it was a fascination to me despite Pete's protestations that it was just a fucking desert. We sat on torn sections of cardboard that protected the cheeks of our arse from the solar hot steelwork. The protection didn't last long and the cardboard merely served as an acclimatiser so that your arse had time to acknowledge the raging heat in the steelwork. We munched our way through chicken sandwiches brought in by the company and washed them down with ice-water from the cooler. A raging thirst had plagued me all morning. Pete assured me that it was natural,

"Just keep drinking and stay in the shade as much as you can".
It would take my body a few days to adjust to the perspiration and rapid dehydration. Acclimatisation was the name of the game, some people were affected more than others were, and of

course Pete continued to inform me, some people never made the grade. I squinted through tightening eyelids; the brightness was almost unbearable. As far as I could see, out to infinity, no horizon existed on which I could focus. The boundary between land and sky remained invisible. Out there in the desert, the ragged line of infinity was continually washed away by the rippling haze.

"Mirages!" sighed Pete, as he shifted his weight from one burning buttock to the other, whilst at the same time interrupting my thoughts. "This place is full of em".

The site hummed and throbbed in the dusty thermal haze, huge cranes erected steel, which was lined and levelled to exact position. The smell of fresh anti corrosion paint intermingled, with the aroma of overworked diesel fumes. The sooty clouds pulsed, from the blackened exhausts, of the indefatigable generators, that powered the tools. The heat was just incredible. I can only describe the temperatures, as to being inside my mother's Sunday morning oven, moments before the Yorkshire pudding mixture was placed inside. Everything was hot to the touch, even in the shade. The heat conducted itself along every available thermal track, permeating everything and everywhere. Torn lumps of cardboard, supported on sticks, were used as primitive umbrellas and were carried by the labourers between the rare spots of shade. Even in the shadows, the heat was almost unbearable, but at least in the shade, the sun's rays could not radiate exposed flesh. The generators hummed monotonously and the occasional clank, from a carelessly dropped tool, where everyone prayed there were no errant sparks, the clangs punctuated the monotones of the rumbling site. Even the framework of the building itself creaked and groaned, as the structural steelwork expanded with the heat, straining and heaving, against the bolts and braces of its design. Flies settled on exposed flesh and were swatted away. They buzzed with discontent at their sudden ejection from hot and salty, sweaty skin. Occasional laughter could be heard, as the labourers went about their daily chores, joking with each other to break the monotony, but always the heat remained, rippling skyward from the desert anvil. It was as if below that burning sand, the furnace of hell scorched toward the surface and freedom. Freedom prevented by the sun, forcing back the furnace with a searing heat of its own. Day after day the struggle continued. Caught in-between that struggle were the mortals, skipping and hiding between sparse shadows, hoping that today at least, they would not be fried alive.

I had been lulled by my lunch into a dreamlike doze. Caught napping in the heat when my comfortable repose was shattered by the piercing shriek of the siren, the announcement of imminent disaster. Its sorrowful whines swelled from the bowels of the construction site and wailed across the desert, to warn of impending doom.

"Go! Go! Go!" screamed Pete, hurling himself without caution, over the side of the steelwork, plummeting into the drifting sand below and heading across the desert in a blind panic. The initial shock jerked me from dozing; I bolted from a seated position and set off across the desert like a bat out of hell, along with most of the surrounding employees. My feet were pounding into the soft sand; I ran as hard as I could, my arms pumping at my side, I quickly overtook Pete and was out in front. My heart felt as if it were pounding rocks in my chest and my leg muscles screamed as they were urged to greater achievement. A final cry exploded from Pete as the imminent eruption peaked.

"Down, Bob! Get Down Now! Here it comes, Aaaaaaaaaaagh!"

I dove forward in panic, thrusting my head into the sand with terrific force induced by a terrible fear of being fried alive. Just to be on the safe side I scooped the loose sand around my shoulders to provide as much protection from the explosion or flames or whatever catastrophe had occurred. Agonising seconds passed, I tried to hold my breath and keep the sand from my eyes, nostrils and ears. Anticipating the blazing froth, I prayed that I was far enough away, all the while, continuing to scoop the protective sand around my shoulders with the hand that wasn't being used to clamp my nostrils tight. I thought I was OK, I must have been far enough away because the searing heat never materialised. Unable to hold my breath much longer, I extracted my head with great caution, from the sand. I couldn't open my eyes immediately for fear of errant specks of grit, scraping beneath my eyelids and settling like boulders of granite. I had already learned; that this was a painful factor of desert life.

"Close your eyes" a new voice uttered.
A bucket of warm water smashed into my face, followed by a millisecond flash of blinding light.

"Nice gallop, Bob! Nice bloody gallop. Good at school sports, were we?"
The familiar tone I had now come to dread, was easily recognisable in Pete's mocking voice. A tape was already measuring the distance, from the site boundary to my feet. The polaroids were already being passed even before they had fully developed. I rose from my redundant, deathbed of sand, with as much feigned dignity as I could muster and suddenly, I was feeling very unwell.

"Hundred and thirty meters, Pete". a voice proclaimed.
"Sixteen seconds flat!" announced another.
"OK, guys," announced Pete, "You heard THE SIREN. Lunch break's over".

I burned inside and my cheeks must have been blood red. The siren of impending doom had signalled the end of lunchbreak. I followed Pete back onto the site where we approached a small wall-mounted cupboard. The doors were opened to reveal dozens of Polaroid photographs. Pete passed one over his shoulder,

"Just a small test," announced Pete, "Breaking in the new kid and all that".

My embarrassment melted, I had to laugh at the Polaroid and scanned the rest that included Pete himself with Keith and John.

"Jesus, I almost had a bloody heart attack".
I exclaimed, still panting from the exertions of the dash.

CHAPTER 2   SAUDI STYLE   STEEL

"Right," laughed Pete, "At least we know your heart's in sound working order. It's just a joke, Bob. Saves us a fortune in cardiology equipment and let's face it, if you can't take a joke you shouldn't join".

Pete pinned up the Polaroid and closed the doors. The labourers were back at work and they continued their duty without question. They were a friendly bunch and I admired their commitment to the company and fellow workers. I also noticed that Pete, knew all his co-workers by their first names. I made a mental note, that I too, would get to know them on a similar basis.

The day shift ended and the Fury sped home from the steel skeleton. It was a welcome relief to be under the high tap shower. The forceful flow was very soothing and the temperature exactly right. The red brands of the sun burned and prickled as I massaged my wet skin with the towel. I glanced at the mirror and a glowing red version of myself smiled back. There was now some time to kill. I borrowed a pair of scissors and hacked off the sleeves of all my shirts, sewing up the ragged edges with as much care as possible. Keith and John were employed at different project sites of the company and would not be seen again until Friday, the Holy Day, in Saudi Arabia. I worked into the night and by morning prayers had fallen asleep. A small, neatly folded pile of tee shirts sat at the bottom of the bed. On the floor, lay an even smaller pile of unwanted sleeves. The doorbell chirruped. I hastily scrubbed my teeth, gulped a glass of water and hurried to the car. The work cycle had begun and my recently discovered ambitions would never allow me to turn back now. I was introduced to Khalid Al Ocoma, one of the OCOMA Brothers; he was an absolute gem of a guy. He spoke excellent English, was very well-educated and well-mannered and if he asked me to go back and work for him tomorrow, I would be on the next plane out. It was an absolute pleasure to work for the Ocomas; they were one of the smartest outfits in Saudi based at their Dhahran HQ. They must have salted away considerable wealth, they owned the first licenced factory for air conditioners in Saudi and they were heavily into paint, food, Marine and general plastics. I was employed by their newly formed steel construction division which was obviously doing very well indeed. Yes, the Ocomas were switched on and it was obvious they were going places. Working for them made me even more determined to be successful, I knew they would look after me, so I got stuck in and grafted.

One rest day per week was all we were allowed. I counted the contract days as they slipped through my fingers. I watched my life relentlessly cascading through the choke of the hourglass. Suddenly, I had neither the energy nor the inclination to hold onto them. Workdays were just that. Very rarely did they ever reveal anything other than the workday routines. I suffered during my acclimatisation, alternating between severe migraine headaches and nosebleeds. Pete passed them off as typical, but then of Pete, that was typical too. I carried a couple of old shirtsleeves to the site every day, just in case the floodgates opened. For the migraines, I carried a bottle of aspirin and a prayer, a solemn prayer, that they would not be needed; migraines in Saudi were something else.

It was a humid, dusty day. The humidity constantly dampened the skin and the sand adhered to it. We were sat in the hundred and thirty-degree shade, our backsides, protected from the hot steel by rapidly scorching cardboard.

"Shit, we've got to get out of here for a while, Bob". Hissed Pete, as he wiped the perspiration from his forehead with the back of his hand.

"Get someone to look out for you. I'll do the same at this end and we'll see about getting you a driving licence". I immediately obliged and we were on our way.

Pete drove through the bowels of Dhahran. Eventually, we ended up in a small office at the local police station. The Spartan room we entered was dark, but for the sparse illumination poking through the wooden shutters, which hid dirty, cracked glass panes. An overworked "a-c" groaned on one wall. It failed miserably in its efforts, to blight the smothering heat. A police officer entered the confines of the poorly furnished room, he carried a white stick. At first, I thought he was blind.

"Stand on the line". he ordered curtly, pointing to a chalk stripe on the dusty concrete floor. I complied with his request whilst he walked over to the wall directly opposite the line, pointing with his white stick to an alphabetical chart and revealing the sweat stains beneath his armpits.

"Shoo Hada? What's that?" he enquired impatiently.

"Letter A". I replied, whilst turning to Pete and questioning him,

"That's what I was supposed to say, wasn't it?"

"And that?" Continued the officer

"Letter H". I began to wonder if this was another of Pete's tricks and was about to start reading wrong letters just for the hell of it. He called out the letters once, then once again, with me alternatively covering each eye as ordered.

"Good!" announced the officer. I couldn't see the point in all this; there were no other tests. This had nothing at all to do with my driving ability and Pete's record did nothing to encourage my confidence. I did not see the hundred-Riyal notes either, passed under the table by Pete. They too had nothing to do with my driving ability but were a pre-requisite if one needed a Saudi driving licence. I had a British Driving licence which was considered OK in Saudi, so it wasn't too much of a problem to get a Saudi licence. Saudi was still incredibly young; this was how all business was conducted since time had evolved. I was unaccustomed and found it disconcerting that anyone could get a driving licence for a few hundred Riyals and be on the same road as myself, whether they could drive or not. I acquired the licence without much trouble, but I knew there had to be a catch - and I soon discovered one, I had just been promoted to Pete's chauffeur.

I was not deterred. I enjoyed driving, especially the big, automatic American cars, with armchair-like seats. I soon learned something else. Driving in Saudi, consisted of a perpetual duel between the fearless and the brave. Anyone else proceeded nowhere. At major crossroads, with or without lights, the fearless always assumed it was their right of way. The braves attempted to prevent this and the lesser motorists sat around waiting patiently, until the fearless and brave wrecks, were towed away before they could proceed on their journey. The trip, to and from the site, took us over a railway crossing. The barriers, or what was left of them, swung down from the raised position to cover the traffic lanes. Barriers: that had previously been damaged and now afforded a good gap where a driver, could now zigzag between them to beat the train - and many drivers succeeded. We were travelling home one day, it was late in the afternoon, and as we drove back from the site, I approached the crossing with caution, as the bright red beach balls flashed their warning. A train was approaching. Its mournful wail sending out its warning. The Fury inched forward as each car in line zigzagged the barrier in front of me. Finally, the "Chicken" stopped the flow. I stopped the car, only three cars back from the chicken as the train thundered into view, crystallising to life from the rippling haze. The solid images of carriages were now bearing down on us. The siren still blaring its sorrowful moan, it was a certain, melancholy pre-requisite of impending doom. A small, family saloon of Japanese origin, shot by my open window and accelerated rapidly, showering my arm with dust and grit. Pete raised his head at the sound of the gravel peppering "his" car.

"Oh shit," he groaned, "He's not going to make it".

As the wheels of the on-rushing car locked solid, its momentum propelled it forward, the lunatic's tyres slid hopelessly on the loose gravel and sand in the centre of the road. Friction-burned rubber assailed my nostrils, as the tyres ripped at the asphalt in a final - and what could only be described - as a suicidal effort to claw back from disaster. The poor bastard had left it too late. With the train thundering forwards, the small car crunched like tinfoil, into and around the massive loco's, cast-steel bumper. Grinding metallic shrieks

47

spewed forth, train wheels squealed and sparks flew everywhere as the brakes took hold. Particles of the shattered windscreen, showered down like hailstones, peppering the bodywork and windscreen of the Fury. The remnants of the car were minced effortlessly along the track, like the silver wrapper from a chocolate bar. Gradually, the train slowed and finally stopped. The driver of the train jumped from his cab and was followed by dozens of passengers, who poured from their carriages onto the trackside gravel and hurried to the front of the Loco to view the wreckage.

"Thank heavens for small mercies!" Pete sighed with indifference.

"Why, what's happened?"

"The last car cleared the crossing. Look, we can go. Get moving, Bob or we'll be stuck here for ages".

"What about the car?" I gasped in horror.

"What car?"

"The car under the train".

"Oh! You want to take pictures?" sarcasm now bleeding into Pete's tone.

"No, I thought -" I didn't know what to think.

"Drive, Bob". ordered Pete, "Or we're going to be stuck here for hours, while those rubber neckers block the road". I dropped the Fury into drive and accelerated around the three cars ahead of us. As I zigzagged the crossing, I glanced back in the mirrors. Pete was right, as usual. We were, I discovered later, the only car to escape the jam. Every other vehicle was now blocked in by the raghead drivers, with blood and snot on their morbidly curious minds.

"Happens every time". drolled Pete, sliding back down into his comfortable position.

"What does?"

"That back there, Bob. They block the road because they want to see the ketchup and claret".

"Thank god for that". I said, "I thought you were talking about the accident". My composure was now returning.

48

"Don't be daft. That only occurs about once a week".

"Jesus!" I responded, although my exclamation held no religious intonation.

"Right!" Drolled Pete monotonously. "The will of Allah will take the responsibility for that little episode and the fact that boulder brains ran the light, jumped the barrier and refused to heed the train's warning, won't even enter the report".

The drive home continued in silence, with me still sickened by such an unpleasant experience and Pete dozing blissfully in careless slumber by my side.

Eventually, I grew accustomed to and relaxed into the new routine. I could not remember my last migraine and I no longer carried the shirtsleeves for nosebleeds. My skin had now peeled its damp, grey, cold climate layer and in its place, a bronze tan had developed. The physical effort of the work improved my muscle tone, and during these days I got to know every member of the team on a first-name basis. I had developed a calm, uninvolved attitude to the murderous traffic accidents that continued unabated. I wasn't particularly happy to do this but to get involved could also get you the blame, merely for being a foreigner in this country. So, I kept out of the way and got on with life the best I knew how. One accident generated my total disregard, an awful tragedy, which almost anaesthetised my pity and remorse.

A head-on crash had occurred between two estate car taxis. Thirteen people were killed. One body landed on the Fury's bonnet. I covered it with a totally inappropriate, brightly coloured beach blanket and awaited the police. I stood around for hours, until finally, satisfied with my innocence, much to their annoyance, as I had a feeling, they wanted me to take some blame, the police allowed me to leave the scene. Again, neither car had given way and the two Peugeot estate cars had become the death ships of thirteen people on life's final voyage. I did not yet understand such pride - their throwaway attitude to life itself. This was not my country - I was here to do a job. I could not help but think that they were people though, they had families and loved ones and why were they so careless with the precious gift of life? I hoped there was a paradise and I hoped eventually to get there, but I wasn't in the same hurry as the Saudis, just in case. I learned to detach myself from all manner of wasted life yet try to prevent it if I could. I tried to understand their culture. Most of all, I wanted to learn to communicate in their language. Under the circumstances, it was the least I could do; though I was beginning to feel that in this country, it would be all I could ever do.

The months passed. Pete left on vacation and never returned. I eventually received a card from Norway, to say that he had accepted a position there. The money was the same, but the place was more civilised. It may have been civilised but for me but it could never take the place of Saudi, Saudi was developing rapidly but still held the imagination, you never knew what would happen next in Saudi.

"Please stay in touch". he pleaded, "I want to know how my apprentice gets on".

It was a card of few words, but I immediately sensed in the wording, Pete's sorrow at letting go of stability and friendships. I too felt that sorrow. Pete was the man who had led me to Saudi. I couldn't help but recall the many jokes we had enjoyed at the other's expense. We shared some unbelievable experiences and developed an incredible bond of true friendship. We were pioneers or so I had come to think of us as such - though even as Pete had proved, our creed would always be searching for something different.

Now I took charge, moving about the various sites with well-practised ease. Excluding the odd Thursday evening, I rarely saw Keith or John. When we did get together, there was always something extraordinary to reveal. Bizarre occurrences had a strange habit of haunting our creed. I was engrossed in my work and the work suited me down to the bone. By the time my holiday came around, I was almost sorry to leave, even for the brief two-week period.

50

CHAPTER 2   SAUDI STYLE   STEEL

My first holiday was referred to as R & R (rest and relaxation) To the initiated it was known as F & F. Feasting and whatever pleasures young men in their prime encountered when released from months of solitary confinement and near celibacy. Not including, the stray stewardess or Nurse on rare, very rare occasions.

I decided to tour the Far East; I had heard so many wonderful stories about the place, that I decided to see it for myself. I was in no hurry to return home and felt that I needed to broaden my horizons. Broaden them I did. I fell in with a group of Kuwaiti expatriates and spent the entire two weeks drinking, partying and whatever else took my fancy. Call it third-world exploitation, call it what you will, but I was young, in need of some tender loving care and there were only a few places left in the world where you could get such luxuries without strings and I headed straight for them.

Sunbathing was outdated; Saudi expatriates never waste time lying around on a beach. There was enough sun and beach in Saudi to last a lifetime". But there were no women and officially no booze. To make up for such deficiencies, I wasted no time finding a female companion and a suitable bar in which to drink. We became night people. "Sleeping" through the day and partying through the nights. Another holiday romance ended but we parted on excellent terms and I boarded the plane for the journey back to the Middle East. In some respects, I returned with a broken heart and my first days back at the site, were pervaded by a new kind of loneliness.

The apartments were now empty. I discovered on my return that Keith and John had moved to different areas of the Saudi building site. Now I was alone with only the gecko lizard and the rusty red cockroaches to keep me company. The gecko would slide quickly up the wall on my approach, to hang, as if suspended by crazy glued feet, until I left the room or darkness concealed the gecko's movements, I let him be, my apartment was free of cockroaches, bugs and flies and I knew it was him I had to thank for that.

CHAPTER 2   SAUDI STYLE   STEEL

During the early weeks, on those warm sultry evenings when there was little else to do, we travelled to the pop stop in Dammam, where large crates of orange pop and Bebsi (Pepsi) were obtained. I soon learned that Coke was banned in Saudi Arabia due to its Jewish connections. My lips puckered to a smile as I recalled how, whilst awaiting the termination of prayers, we had enjoyed the gecko-baiting contests. We would flick the discarded bottle tops from our drinks, spinning them twenty metres across the night sky, aiming for the luckless creatures clinging to the wall opposite, forcing them to shed their tails. The geckos in the apartments brought back the memories of such trivia, but they could not bring back my friends. Now I had little or no choice, I drowned myself in my work once more, in a last desperate attempt, to brighten the shadows of the apartment's empty rooms.

Chapter 3

THE PUSH

There were no phones available, I answered the letters from home as I answered any other correspondence.

"Yes, I'm fine. Yes, I'm eating well. Yes, it is ridiculously hot. Yes, the pay is excellent, and I miss you all". I didn't really miss anyone, I was so busy with the desert and a total change in surroundings and culture, I hadn't really thought about life back home.

During my introduction to Saudi, I had written two or three times a week. This had later been reduced to two or three times a month. Now I was well into a routine and could barely remember posting my last letter home. I could at the time, however, remember the letter most recently received. It had arrived unexpectedly from the girl I had left behind - a girl I thought I could forget but it seemed I was wrong.

I knew in my heart, that I could not expect a beautiful, young girl in her prime to sit patiently by the fire and await my return from Saudi in triumph or disillusioned defeat. I really had no choice; I broke off the relationship. She was not the type to be caged like some fussed-over sparrow. Better the sparrow is released than confined to a prison of promised fidelity. Bearing this in mind, my sparrow had flown free. The pain of my subsequent regrets of this action, had mostly been anaesthetised during the early days of Saudi adventures and excitement but she, was the sister of one of my closest friends (RIP Brian) and I had loved her with a passion beyond my own belief. The trouble was, I only realised how much I loved her, when it was too late and it became a real pain in the arse, when the truth finally struck home.

The first few months in the desert clouded my thoughts. New sights, new work, new experiences, so many new discoveries. My past life lagged behind the new and absorbing Saudi lifestyle. A lifestyle coming of age and with the mellowing of the new adventures, came the unexpected letter, dragging in its wake a flood of memories that everyday experiences could no longer hide or disguise. Out of those small folds of paper, came the bitter taste of recognition, finally allowing acknowledgement, that my own actions had really broken my heart. The girl's haunting beauty shadowed me relentlessly, during the months that followed her letter, drawing me back, to those light blue, airmail pages, to taste the penned definitions of a lost love woe.

I learned sometime later that Lotty, as I had endearingly called her, had suffered after my departure, crying away the nights. She was barely consoled by the hopes of my imminent return, disillusioned with the desert and with a promise of forever, that would pack away wanderlust and eternally block the path, to an inquisitive search for adventure. Eventually, my sparrow acknowledged and tested her newfound freedom, including the rewards so freely available beyond her short-lived cage. She had always possessed a strong will and temperament and following my example, she had secured herself a position of employment abroad. Originally, I was only thankful that she had chosen the Isle of Wight and not Saudi Arabia, did I say thankful, I must have been verging on insanity.

Lotty embarked on her new career as a receptionist, at the Esplanade Hotel in Ryde, the island's capital. To some extent, this pleased me, though it failed to prepare me, for the dagger's blade, which was poised to pierce my heart. I learned that a relationship had blossomed between Lotty and the hotel proprietor's extremely pampered son. Compared to my wastrel rival's luxurious possessions and lifestyle, all I owned were the memories of our love. My lovely, nineteen-year-old Lotty, caught in the groping clutches of a spoiled son of a bitch from Ryde. Why it happened I don't know, but jealous anger raged within, encouraged by the lonely habitation, of a country so far away from home. I slammed my fist into the wardrobe, desperately searching for the physical pain of relief from the mental torture I

54

now endured. The inner bones of my wrist shattered, and the cheap plywood wardrobe disintegrated, along with my fading emotional restraint. I had to acknowledge, that the love I had so carelessly abandoned, had been lost to another. It was my fault entirely and I knew I had made a big mistake, bigger than I would ever realise. The spectre of Lotty's loveliness haunted me for months. And I thought at the time, they would scar my life forever. I could see at this point why some expatriates had packed up and gone home, this was the closest I had been to that unstable state of mind. It was a brain worm, once inside your head, it wouldn't go away and I remembered some of the times we had enjoyed together.

Lotty's father owned a well-known and much-frequented drinking establishment. From time to time, it served as a hotel. Usually when relatives came to visit, or when I was too drunk or too tired to drive home. Lotty would not allow me to drive home anyway until her cravings and appetites were completely satiated. At this time, I was employed by Davy International. A massive conglomerate, existing in the grimy, Northern, steel city which answered to the once adulated title of Sheffield. The home of quality cutlery, Iraqi super guns and the various British Steel spin-offs, still managing to survive during the industrial depression of the times. As a well-qualified engineer. being single and not of the alimonious species of male, I usually whiled away the hours, gracing one of the few nightspots my hometown of Barnsley had to offer. To be truthful, during this time, Barnsley had little to proclaim other than the biggest open market in the north. It's long since swallowed Barnsley Bitter and a football team bordering on relegation, not from the leagues, from the sport!

One Friday evening. As I leaned against the bar of the Birdcage, the infamous nightclub of Hoyland Common, where the sight of a traffic light changing, would have started more local headlines than a visitor from another planet. I sipped expensive cocktails I could ill afford, my British racing green,

Triumph GT6 sports car collecting envy stripes outside the main entrance. The perfect example, of a young man living beyond the means of not just his high street bank but probably the bank of England as well.

Lotty's elder brother arrived and as we conversed, Lotty, previously unnoticed in the dark crowded disco, appeared at our side, trying to squeeze a drink from her wealthier, elder brother. I was intoxicated by her presence; I was already aware of a personal strong affection for Lotty. Having noticed her on earlier occasions, whilst conversing with her family members, I did not push the issue, her brothers were mates of mine and, I presumed her to be quite a bit young for me to be tampering with. Lotty disappeared into the darkness, back to her friends. Leaving me with a strange sensation of wanting more. The evening progressed; dancing and careless attitudes accompanied the hits of the day. I espied Lotty across the room. I picked up my drink, bolstered my confidence by imagining possible winning scenarios and like a train on a track, squeezed across the dancefloor to what I thought would be my total rejection. The charged atmosphere dispelled all inhibitions. The music blared as I continued my threading walk. Some girls danced and chatted around small, handbag islands. Whisps of smoke teased my nostrils, I hated smokers, they were always accidentally burning your clothes or hands and would smile, as if that reveal of lipstick on teeth, were an acceptable apology. The alcohol must have fired up a collision course with destiny. I marched into her life, without a moment's hesitation and confidently announced my intentions,

"Fancy a dance chick?" my exact poetic proposal, I remember it like it was yesterday.

"Well, I- err- I," and finally, "Yes Ok, I do".

Lotty's words could have been, the "I do" of the wedding ceremony. From those two simple words, exploded a volatile relationship, which was about to kill me. In the literal sense of the word.

We danced apart for a while until the music slowed and I risked squeezing her to my frame. No hint of rejection appeared and Lotty replied with a grip as demanding as my own. Lotty returned to her circle of friends. Retrieved her belongings and apologised for her immediate absence. We sat together, almost cuddling, in a darkened corner alcove and, in the moments when our lips were not glued together, we both professed the same shared hope that ultimately, we would unite. We left in the small hours. I drove, with Lotty's prior approval, to a tiny, well-leafed country lane, where we whiled away the hours in a lovelock, only the triumph sports car engineers could have devised. I had known from that first dance, that this would be different. We were hooked or at least I can say I was, I was certain. As Brian Ferry would have proclaimed during the moment, "Love is the Drug" and we were both addicted. We spent many weekends in Scarborough. The north's easily available shore. A small gold ring, set with a single diamond, sealed our union. The rest would have been history. Marriage, kids and a two up two down in Barnsley, but for a burning desire for adventure and a series of events that threatened my very existence.

Event number one occurred during one of those sultry, lazy summer days, so often remembered but rarely re-captured. Lotty had decided to walk home from her place of employment. A short distance of pleasant greenery, covering a mile or so. A sky-blue summer evening held a promise of sunset, romance and a sweltering, sleepless night. As Lotty strolled beneath a row of apple trees in full scented bloom. An errant bee fell to her collar. Under the drowsy influence of nectar, the bee did not recognise the lovely Lotty and stung her fresh young neck. In great pain and some distress, she sought help from a local garage and repair shop. The owner of the establishment, a young man in his late twenties. Encouraged sweet Lotty into the rear of his premises, away from the heat and noise to a place where cool water could be obtained to soothe the painful swelling. Lotty allowed the kind man, to view the tender swollen flesh where the bee had laid its sting. She opened the top of her shirt and without revealing too much flesh, allowed the kind stranger to inspect the wound. Without another word, the kindly young man rose to his feet, pulled down his zipper and tried to show young Lotty a sting of his own, infinitely larger than the tiny sliver of bee bum now lodged in her neck.

Lotty screamed, bravely fighting his advances away. She barely escaped the premises with her clothes intact. Meanwhile, I decided to drive along her normal route home and surprise her with a lift home. I too had felt the evening's promise. Lotty's tearful description of her encounter enraged and infuriated me. A blind hatred erupted and I knew I was rapidly losing control of all reasoning. Lotty's sobs wound the coils of hatred tighter. I launched the sportscar in the direction of the evil deed. Fearing retribution, the perpetrator had flown. I brooded and smouldered all evening, with no way to vent the fires of revenge that were now insulting my male pride. As the gentleman protector of sweet Lotty's honour, I could not live peacefully with the attempted intrusion into our sacred bond, in my mind, the guy tried to rape her, he knew it, I knew it and I had no doubt the police would view it that way too, I could not let it rest. She had almost recovered as we kissed goodbye and I left for home. Lotty must have experienced a slight relief that we had not discovered the whereabouts of the would-be stinger. She had never seen me, in such a state of pre-violence.

Some hours after midnight when the entire world sleeps. Two glass milk bottles chinked in the darkness. They had been purloined, along with a small plastic tube, a length of cleaning rag and a desire for retribution of untested boundaries. The bottles were filled with the finest high octane, straight from the fuel tank of my second love. The rag was ripped in two and each piece was stuffed tightly into the bottlenecks. I positioned them carefully in the vehicle and drove back to the stinger's hive. I parked the car out of sight, removed the two bottles, assured myself of the lighter's presence and walked quickly and silently to the point of launch.

A moment passed as I considered the dirty deed or what might have been had Lotty failed to escape. My slender young lovely, writhing under the greasy overalls of an over-sexed, greasy ape. The thoughts rekindled the rage and the rags were ignited. Carrying the bottles at the bottom so as not to burn my wrists. I approached the target with my arms held away from my body. The glow from the flaming rags illuminated my path. I imagined once more, the tearing of clothes, the retracted zip, Lotty writhing underneath the bastard as she cried in vain for my help. My teeth ground together with an uncontrollable bite. The rage swelled inside and a hot flush burned against my cheeks. I could not hold on much longer. The first projectile arced over the ironwork fence. It smashed into the wooden sliding doors and flashed into a blazing inferno; eerie shadows now danced to life on the moonless night. Unhurried I scanned the premises once more. The glow now bathing my face and torso. The second cocktail soared higher. The sputtering flames, depositing a dingy trail of burning rag particles across the night sky. Crash!! - glass panes fragmented and the bottle disappeared through a skylight window. It bounced on the wooden framework and unbroken, it tumbled into the paint booth. The bottle shattered into splinters against a topless, fifty-gallon drum, that until a millisecond later, must have been used for the disposal of old paints and thinners.

The ensuing explosion lifted the roof, blasted the doors from their hinges and ejected every pane of glass from the window frames, before knocking me flat onto my back. Luckily, I wasn't injured but I was avenged. I brushed the dust from my pants and in no hurry, walked away. A short-whispered phrase issued tersely from my lips,

"Next time, bastard. You'll be in there". I must have been too young and too stupid, sometimes there seems to be only one solution and this to me was the right thing to do. Let's face it the police would have done nothing and this bastard would have denied it and jumped on the next girl who happened to turn his corner. He would get the message and now the choice was his, would he call the cops and risk them learning the reasons for the blaze? I can tell you that nothing happened and I never heard of him attacking anybody else. Whether I was right or wrong and the latter springs to mind, I'm sure it helped him temper his ways.

On my departure from the vicinity of the fire, an orange glow etched high into the night sky and could be seen for miles. I started up the car and was gone. Distant sirens broke the immediate silence, piercing across the townscape from the other side of Barnsley. I checked the mirrors for pursuers, there were none. Nothing behind now, nothing but the lust-light glow of retribution, signalling to warn the rapist, as far as Lotty is concerned - beware!

Later I started thinking, it was a miracle I had not been seen or even burned but the thought had never really crossed my mind. The attempted rape of Lotty blinded all fears. Lotty must have passed the garage the following morning, or what had been left of the garage. In its place were smouldering ashes where once had stood, a thriving though dilapidated enterprise. Two cars had been vaporised by the inferno. Three more were reduced to charred twisted metal. Fire engines and police were still present damping down and looking for suspects or evidence. Nothing remained of the garage but a perimeter fence of steel around a soggy ashen plot. Lotty hastened on her way. She knew I was crazy about her. When I phoned, she knew at once what had happened. She tried to chastise my actions but couldn't. Merely shedding a tear at the thought of such devotion. I bade my farewells; we would talk about it tonight. She wiped the tears from her eyes and laughed with her unknowing companions, both of us secretly wishing it were five o'clock.

Incident number two brought with it the realisation that despite her devotion, Lotty would not always tell me the truth.

CHAPTER 3   SAUDI STYLE   THE PUSH

Upon our first meeting, Lotty had confessed to smoking the odd cigarette. A habit, although I tolerated, I discreetly tried to break.

"Some women just don't lend themselves to cigarettes!" I would admonish, "Especially the beautiful ones! And I just want you to be safe".

Lotty smoked less and less in my presence. Until finally the habit disappeared and my lectures stopped. They were intended to save her health, her money and her life. I was certain of Lotty's abstinence and my success. Until that fateful night when I realised my painful mistake. Having returned from a party, the decision was made to stay at Lotty's place. It was late, but not too late to indulge in a bout of frenzied, muffled passion, lest the household catch the cry. I eventually crawled back to bed in a state of exhausted bliss. Drifting off to sleep as soon as my head brushed the pillow. Totally satiated and emotionally entangled, with the young girl across the hall.

I fell into a deep sleep and in my dreams; Lotty entered the room floating on a cloud. It seemed so real; I could even smell the SMOKE. An inbuilt alarm snapped me to my senses, bolting half-naked across the hall and into her room. A room that was rapidly filling with a choking, dirty black smog, which seemed to swell against the walls. Falling to the ground, a procedure I had learned somewhere. I crawled into her bedroom and coughed my way to her bedside. The mattress supporting her body smouldered. Occasionally, bright patches glowed as the slightest movement of air fanned the cindering fibres. I saw her move, thankfully she had not choked from smoke inhalation. I took a deep breath, grabbed her arms and yanked her from the bed. I dragged her limp body outside into the hall, closing the door behind us. By now she was wide-awake. Wracking convulses shook her body. I dashed down the hall, dragged the water hose from its reel, opened the valve and charged back into the room. It was over in seconds. The bed was destroyed and for safety's sake I dragged the mattress outside onto the roof, thankfully into the rain. Lotty's father arrived panting, her mother close behind.

Lotty coughed, sobbed and cried in the same breath. She admitted her dastardly deed, smoking in bed.

Her dad exercised the enraged father figure image, whilst her mum cradled her in her arms,

"Thank god, she's still alive". I shook my head in sorrowed disbelief. The thoughts of what might have been, swirling around my brain.

"You lied to Bob!" her father snapped, "I saw you smoking whenever he was away. Well explain this to him young lady! I wouldn't blame him if he walked out of the door and never came back. You're a bloody idiot, Lorraine, a silly idiot".

"Don't be too hard on her!"

Her mother pleaded as her father sloped angrily down the hall, certain that the fire had been extinguished and now returning to his bed, where he would be unable to hurt his daughter with the temper he restrained inside. Her mother soothed the highly charged situation. I saw no good in the deed. Everything stank of rancid smoke and later, Lotty was to discover, no matter how often she washed her clothes, they would have to be discarded, people were always asking her had she been to a barbecue? Lotty had just destroyed with one cigarette, her life's possessions to date. Thankfully, it was material junk, easily replaced. I began to think of Lotty the girl and not Lotty the bed burner. The rivers of tears that had flowed across her cheeks had eroded her mascara. Her hair straggled about her head. A tissue gripped tightly in her hand was pressed to her lips, in an unsuccessful effort to stem the sobs.

"Where am I going to sleep now, mum?" she sobbed.

Her mother glanced over in my direction; she wasn't stupid. She knew all about our love for each other and the discreet rendezvous such matters required,

"Well! if this young man still loves you, you had better jump in with him. We'll sort this lot out in the morning". A worldly smile crossed her lips, she must have remembered her own loves and she knew from experience, we would only be young once.

I eagerly accepted the offer with one single condition.

"What's that?" whispered Lotty, her mother's gesture slowing her sobs.

"No bloody cigarettes"

Locked together in each other's arms, we finally found sleep in the warmth of concerned tenderness. The following morning revealed a catastrophe. The proportions of which I was not unhappy to leave behind. I returned that evening to check on my love's condition. The previous night's inferno now commanded and directed, the tone of all conversation. Lotty revelled in her newfound fame. Perched high on a barstool, she related the details of her narrow escape. Whilst at the same time, much to my absolute disgust, she puffed on a chain of cigarettes.

Having sampled the opportunity of "Sati" as it is referred to in the Indian Dictionary, i.e.: throwing oneself into the funeral fire of lost love. I began to wonder, if not worry, where this present relationship was heading. I need not have bothered. Nature had her own system regarding my earthly enlightenment and as they say, up in Barnsley at least, "Disasters come in threes".

Lotty harboured a temper. To describe that temper as wild would have been no closer to the truth than the Equator is to the North Pole. One night, we were driving home from a secluded country tavern. Not directly home, as you must surely understand by now. More by way of a tiny, well concealed, leafy country lane. To where, on certain, smouldering, impatient occasions, the car almost had the inclination, to drive itself. After rolling around naked for hours and trying to wear out the car's suspension, finally, exhausted, we wrapped ourselves around each other and pulled the car blanket over our hot, entangled bodies. After a brief but breathy session of whispering terms of endearment. We decided to buy some Chinese refreshments from the all-night take-away. Lotty needed to call home first. A few womanly things had to be put straight.

Sufficiently straightened, Lotty borrowed the keys to her father's new Jaguar, complete with learner plates for her benefit. With a carefree wiggle of her rear, she enticed me to join her on a royal coach trip to the Chinese takeaway of our choice. I boarded the plush, real-leather passenger seat. The upholstery dictating its age by scent alone. I immediately relaxed and was sucked into the mass of Burgundy cowhide. Lotty was feeling confident. The Jag was an automatic and she steered from the premises with a smug expression, bettered only by the then Duchess of York's "I am the one" facial.

Five minutes and three elegant miles later, we placed an energy replenishing order with a promise to burn off the newly digested calories later. After collecting the brown, paper carrier bag, we walked to the Jag we had previously parked on the roadside. I offered to drive the vehicle home. My reasoning being the roads were full of drunks and I preferred to get us back in one piece. Lotty translated this statement as an affront to her driving ability and demanded the keys to her father's car. Lotty was losing the verbal argument and decided to pull rank on me, even though her dad had insured all his family, all drivers which included me, thanks Roy you were a great guy.

"This is my father's car and as you are no relation to the family, I demand the keys!"

Checkmate! I reluctantly handed over the keys and forced myself to accept her gracious offer of a lift back to her place.

"Where!" she informed me, "You can pick up your jumped-up sports car and bugger off home". I was sure of a change of heart. After all, we were on a promise later and a little verbal sparring stimulated the expectation. I climbed aboard with my pride in my pocket and mouth shut tight. Lotty jangled the keys. The new engine burbled to life with a sweet thrumming whine. She switched on the lights and indicated to pull away, pausing shortly, at my command, for a vehicle to overtake from behind. We waited for the vehicle to pass and then suddenly

BOOOOOM! Before we had even moved, the approaching vehicle rammed us. The aggressor tore into the rear wing. Scythed down both doors. Shattered the windows and showered us in particled glass. The force of the impact ejected the windscreen, almost threw Lotty into my lap and lifted the car three feet in the air. The cruise missile car continued its journey unabated, ripping open the front wing and dragging the bumper bar from its mounts and proceeded down the road with extreme effort. The blood swelled into my heart; adrenaline raced through my system. For the third time in as many weeks, my mind tipped into killing mode. I tossed Lotty back into her seat like a rag doll. Exploded through the opening where the windscreen had once sparkled and chased on foot, in pursuit of the obviously drunken driver, who was now trying to accelerate from the scene of devastation. The front tyres of the lunatic's car squealed against the mangled metal, which had been folded around them in the collision.

I tried to apprehend the departing vehicle, throwing everything that came to hand at the rear of the escaping car, including headlights, glass and lumps of twisted metal. Hopeless, the offending driver sped away, his car careering from left to right, as black rubber particles were shredded from his front wheels. He had not yet escaped. Burned into my memory was a number, PGW-81E; I was already on my way to a phone. Controlling the frustration at not being able to catch the bastard I marched back to the ex-new shiny Jag and was greeted by the hysterical cries of a woman possessed. Lotty cried and yelled in shock, probably brought on by the thought of paternal retribution. With a mild slap that could be heard a mile away, I had seen this in the movies somewhere, I reduced her to a sobbing, whimpering mass and offered the following comforting words,

"Shut up, Lotty! that bastard's going nowhere!"

The approaching sirens could be heard for miles, they were good in those days. Within minutes of arriving, the police traced the number and soon held the perpetrator in a squad car on his way to an overnight cell. He had denied all knowledge of the incident until a search was made of his garage. It revealed a battered vehicle with a tarpaulin stretched over the front end. The tarpaulin leaked smoke at the edges where the overheated engine steamed through. A hopelessly inadequate and drunken effort, to deny or repair a truth. He stood convinced of his innocence; his blood-spattered alcohol anaesthetised features declaring a firm denial,

"What accident, I never shaw an accident officer".

The die was cast and I decided to accept the position overseas. The previous delay had been nurtured by Lotty, whom I did not want to leave. Now I had no choice. At this rate, I would not live to marry her. When we met it was as if a fuse had been lit and we were now into the final stages of combustion before the explosions began. With the greatest of regrets, I informed her of my intentions to earn fantastic amounts of money abroad. The sparrow was reluctantly released. Lotty, still recovering from the sting, the fire and the crash said little but her expression burned deep into my memory. I pulled from her arms and turned toward the car. I did not have the courage to turn and look back, had I done so my I knew plans would have dissolved with her tears. I did not see her dash back inside and run upstairs to her room. Throwing herself across the bed that we had once so eagerly shared. Convulsing and shaken by the wracking sobs of grief. I did not see her shadow by the window, but I knew it would be there, crying as I drove away. I did not realise the love I had so carelessly tossed away until now, until this letter..........

Her letter ended with a casual goodbye. No love, no kisses, and no hint of recognition of the joy we had once shared. Nothing remained but the ice-water shock of a broken heart that had finally reared its head of unwanted recognition.

A fierce pain now burned in my wrist. I ignored the collapsed wardrobe, left the apartment and set out to the local company clinic where my wrist was immobilised with plaster of Paris. On my return to the apartment, I burned the letter in the confinements of painful solitude and vowed to reach the goal. This loss would be a sacrifice to the cause. A hardening of heart, to fend off the emotions that I had learned would only lead to pain.

66

Others noticed the change and sometimes mentioned their observations to my face but they never learned the rhyme or reason. I threw everything into my work, defied the desert heat and buried the secret anguish in the pit of my soul. I had acclimatised and finally arrived - and Saudi; despite my shortcomings, welcomed me with open arms.

Chapter 4
THE PULL

Moons, seasons, migrations - days, hours, and minutes. Increments that no longer held any meaning. Now I counted vacations, of which there had been many. Bangkok, Philippines, Hong Kong and Malaysia, to name a few. Intervals of four months sliced my life into segments. Splitting my working year into three. With each slice came the knowledge of travel and the experience of other worlds. Personal mental boundaries were expanded and a new awareness was reflected in my physical appearance. Monetary problems no longer existed - they had been solved by the monthly cash injections into various, swollen, offshore accounts. We were paid in cash, huge bundles of Saudi Riyals, no worries, nobody thought of stealing in Saudi the penalty was too severe. We took the cash to Al Rajhi the main money exchange outlet in Saudi, it was carefully counted by hand and then we were given a cheque for the same value. We posted the cheque to the bank of our choice and as usual, Saudi was brilliant, it was only when your transfer left Saudi that you prayed for its safe arrival and your return receipt a week later. I only ever had one problem, a cheque was lost in the post but it had enough definitive information on it to prove it had never been cashed and Al Rahji because I kept my receipt, cancelled the old cheque and gave me a new one. All things considered, Al Rajhi were excellent and honourable, never let me down once.

Junk mail signalled ascension to higher financial plateaux. Investments, gilt-edged securities, insurance policies, time deposits, peps and offshore funds. Sweetly concocted letters arrived from the same organisations that had recently threatened court proceedings unless I supplied funds to cover an account debit of mere single figure pounds. I filed all such mail - well shredded at the bottom of my dustbin. A rugged, deep complexion now signalled newfound health and my framework, through sheer demanding work, had been denied the accumulation of fat. Pleasantly intoxicated by my current rewards and, under the magnetic spell of the desert, I watched the new kids come and go. I helped them as much as I could but only a few of them endured the incumbent hardships and even fewer survived long term.

Having already tasted the bitter fruits of incarceration. Nothing too serious but enough to persuade me, that prison in the Middle East, was not to be recommended. Even to the rats, which I had heard during the night, scurrying around in the darkness. My problem had occurred on a site visit up the northern coast of Saudi

Jubail, where I had been sent, was a flourishing port, one hundred and fifty kilometres north of Dhahran. During my journey across the barren, desert landscape, traffic lights loomed ahead, climbing out of the haze on the dusty road and I slowed to a crawl. Although the light was red, the signal had remained so for some considerable time and I decided that the signal was out of order. As the road was clear, I went ahead through the traffic signal, which remained at red until it disappeared, swallowed by the constant rippling haze. A small black dot appeared in the centre of the road ahead and increased in size as my car thundered towards it. As I drew near, a uniformed figure appeared from the haze, signalling me to stop. The window slid into the door with a whine and the policeman poked his head inside.

"Where you go in such a hurry, mister?" he inquired, with an insincere smile and debatable breath.

"Jubail". I noticed that the officer had a gun and that his companion, who leaned against their car concealed at the side of the road was also armed. The car that had been hidden from view by a small dune, fashioned by a bulldozer for such a purpose as this. The Saudi police sported black berets, tilted to the side of their heads. Both men wore outdated, black leather, platform shoes. The leather was dry, cracked and scrubbed by the careless shuffling of their feet through dusty, windblown sand. The badly worn heels caused their ankles to lean outward as they walked, bow-legged as if they had ridden up on a horse.

"Iqama!" demanded the officer.

I fumbled through my pocket and produced my work permit.

"Roxa!"

Fumbling in my pocket again, I produced my driving licence.

"Taal!" snapped the officer as he walked away with my papers. I was obliged to follow the policeman, without these documents I was an illegal immigrant, destined for jail before deportation home. The two of them conversed in Arabic; before they jumped into their car and beckoned, I should follow. I decided that if they left the main road and headed down a dirt track, I would not follow them. Instead, I would immediately race away and head for the nearest OCOMA site. I had heard that in Saudi, members of the public, especially foreigners, had a peculiar habit of disappearing in the strangest of circumstances. I assumed this to be scaremongering nonsense but I wasn't taking any chances. I followed the green-striped police car, the uncertainty tightening in my stomach. I followed them for three or four miles, until a small, concrete box of a building, rippled into view by the roadside. The police car pulled up outside and I followed them into the outpost. Once inside the small building, I was led to a desk and motioned to sit. Flies buzzed around the desk, disturbed from their search for sugar that had crystallised on the sides of dirty, unwashed, small, glass cups. An air conditioner groaned to life at the flick of a switch, as if conscious of the impossible task ahead. An ancient black phone was placed before me and I dialled HQ, sighing with relief as the ringing tone ceased and a polite voice answered.

"Marhabba, Sheriqua Al Ocoma, Naam?"

"This is Bob. Please get me Ahmad, the boss. I'm at a police station on Jubail road. I went through a red light. It wasn't my fault. It was broken. Get me, Ahmad. Hurry!"

They realised what sort of a state I was in from the tone of my voice.

CHAPTER 5   SAUDI STYLE   PULL THE PLUG

I related my story to Ahmad, who listened carefully, though I was sure I detected some amusement in Ahmad's voice as he relayed my predicament to his staff. I re-cradled the receiver. Ahmad was on his way. I needn't worry; everything would be taken care of. Three months in prison, I thought dismally, was the usual penalty for running a red light in the city. But today I was out in the wilderness, alone and entirely at the mercy of two men and I had no idea what they were planning for me. Neither of them spoke any English and maybe they were tossing a coin at this very moment, to decide, who would take first turn at this virginal delicacy, of white male flesh. Sometimes in situations like this, your imagination tends to get the better of you, but only because you've heard that such occurrences happen. A cup was placed before me, still unwashed but full of hot tea, plenty of sugar but according to custom, without milk.

"Maybe they weren't so bad after all," I thought, "Or the tea was drugged. They were going to drug me first before continuing with whatever they had in mind". But they had already allowed a phone call, my team knew I was alive, so I wasn't too worried

My imagination worked frantically on the possibilities. I sat in worried silence. I studied the police and the police studied me. No attempt to communicate was made. An hour or so passed, and when I became sure, that they were about to make a move against me, I heard a car draw up in the gravel outside. Relief ran through my body when the familiar figure of Ahmad, popped through the doorway and strolled up to my side. Ahmad wore the traditional thobe and headdress - a long, almost night-gown-style garment of pure white cotton. On his head, a gutra; a red and white tea towel style of cloth, held in place by a black rope in twin loops. Ahmad's hawkish features surveyed the surrounding building. He shook his head in disapproval before turning to me.

"Mafi Mushkela, Mr Bob" he smiled, "Don't worry, we'll sort everything out as quickly as possible".

Ahmad and the police argued for at 30 minutes. Occasionally Ahmad looked worried and my heart sank. Sometimes when Ahmad smiled, I felt much better. Finally, after considerable shouting and hand waving, Ahmad stood up and walked to my side. He smiled.

"Don't worry, everything is Ok," Ahmad's words did not sound as certain as his smile.

"What about the three months in prison?" I whimpered.

"Not necessary!" replied Ahmad, with a shrug.

I sighed with relief,

"Thanks, Ahmad, I thought I was in trouble there. You were great. I really appreciate this. I knew you would come through and help me, you're a real mate Ahmad, thanks so much. How on earth did you manage it?"

"Simple, Mr Bob, you won't have to spend three months in prison because they've agreed to let you off with eighty lashes instead".

'Whaaaat?" I wailed in disbelief.

"Believe me, it will be easier for you and they've agreed to carry out the sentence now',

Inwardly panicking, I began to imagine all types of lashings, the cat-o-nine tails, the flesh ripped from my back, with salty sand rubbed into the wound for good measure. I was sweating with the fear of the unknown. They led me outside, ordered me to face the wall and lean forward until my forehead, pressed against the warm, plaster rendering. I was about to panic when the officer in charge walked toward me with a cane. A simple schoolboy thrasher of a cane, six feet in length with a diameter of half an inch. The officer tucked a copy of the Koran, wrapped in a pure white cloth, under his armpit, the armpit of the hand that wielded the dreaded rod, before lining up the length of the cane against my naked back. I listened in terror as Ahmad informed me, that the officer was not allowed to drop the Koran from under his arm, which makes it almost impossible to swing the cane with any real force. If he did drop the Koran, it was considered a foul shot, he got the red card and I got off with whatever lashes he'd given me to up to that point. Anyway, he warmed up with a few slashes at in air and then got on with the task, Ahmad was smiling, did he know something I didn't?

72

CHAPTER 5   SAUDI STYLE   PULL THE PLUG

The pain did not match my expectations. The rod struck me across the back in rapid succession from my shoulders to my buttocks. The blows rained quickly, approximately four per second. I wanted to laugh with relief but decided against it. Accepting my punishment, I shook hands with the police and apologised for my careless mistake. The Police and Ahmad had obviously made a game out of it and although they were quite jovial and pleasant, my back suddenly began to burn.

I suffered in silence on the drive back to Dhahran, my back a mass of red, slightly swollen, stripes of discomfort.

Ahmad had been right," it was certainly better than three months in prison and left only a severe stinging pain that would last for a day or so. The humiliation was the hardest part, though as Ahmad informed me after the lashing,

"Out in the desert was one thing, Mr Bob, out in the City Square after Friday afternoon prayers, with crowds of people watching the spectacle and cheering the blows, was a totally different concept".

I vowed that I would never cross a red light again without first stopping; climbing out of the car and, for the benefit of would-be observers, thoroughly searching the horizons for approaching vehicles.

The Wahabbis, or religious teachers, had also left their mark on my person. One evening whilst out shopping during the Holy month of Ramadan. I stood outside a shop in the gold souk. Whilst gazing in wonderment, at the hundreds of thousands of pounds worth of gold, on the other side of the glass, I had an unexpected encounter. It was prayer time and all good Muslims were praying furiously in the mosque, whilst the other, less fervent members of the immigrant community, hung around outside the shops, ogling the western women and staring them into embarrassment with their lust-filled eyes. Small crowds chatted idly as the prayers hummed simultaneously around the city. This was a peaceful time and although it curtailed your lifestyle, I enjoyed the spiritual break from modern life. As if by magic, a hand suddenly grabbed me by the hair and yanked me down to the floor. Thinking that I was the victim of a mugger, I struggled against the attacker and was about to strike back when I realised my mistake. It wasn't a mugger who held me, but the Wahabbi, a beady-eyed, wizened old man with a long grey chin beard who knew that I couldn't strike back. These men travelled around the city enforcing prayers. They made certain, all stores were closed and that the faithful were at prayer. They carried long canes for beating offenders, but more than this; they were escorted by policemen bearing the standard weaponry – sub machine guns. Scissors appeared from nowhere, hovering menacingly above my head before swooping down and hacking off a lump of my hair. I had known it was too long and had intended to get it cut shorter, but now it was too late, my bloody fault again. The Wahabbi threw my hair to the ground and trampled it with his sandal.

"Mamnooah!" he yelled, whilst waving his cane under my nose. "It is forbidden!" he whacked me with the long cane, before continuing his way, to check shop doors were locked and to remind the faithful, with his big stick, of their duty to pray.

I was helped to my feet by casual bystanders. I thanked them and was just about to ask if they spoke English, when one of the men pre-empted my question,

"Ignore him". whispered one of the men of African origin, "They are fanatics you know. Old men, too old to enjoy life but not too old to make everyone else miserable". The speaker grinned and I shook his hand in customary fashion. Though I made no comment, just in case they were all working as a team. Smiling, I moved on into the night. The air hung heavy with the smell of diesel fumes, urine and roast chicken, regularly interrupted by the foul smell of a broken or blocked sewer. Hawkers trilled out the special discounts for their wares and vehicles squeezed through the jabbering crowds The incessant heat caused the sweat to dribble a line down my temple but now, long since accustomed, I had learned to enjoy it. It was preferable to the cold, damp climate of my native country. I continued my journey, weaving among the bustling crowds until

74

finally, I ducked into an alleyway. Prayer time was over; shutters were pushed upward from the front of shop windows and the crowds swelled once more as they were joined by the faithful, who poured from the mosques into the bustling throng. Gabbled conversations laughter and shouts continued all around. Hawkers tried desperately to catch my eye; offering bargains and promises that they had no intention of keeping. I passed them by; I had other things, of an extremely urgent nature, on my mind.

The young man smiled and immediately recognised my plight,

"Sit here, sir. We'll tidy up your hair in no time. Why do they do this? This Wahabbi man is crazy, he is always doing this to foreigners". Then he smiled, "Lucky for me, eh?" I got the impression he was the Wahabbi's favourite son and he loved his dad's marketing plan.

I did not say anything, the Wahabi could have been his dad for all I knew and this was just one of their ploys to boost trade. I just smiled back, as the barber began to trim my hair, to match the length of the stubble that remained, where the earlier locks had been hacked off. I made no fuss; I was growing accustomed to these games. Every day was an education and I learned my lessons silently, but well.

Fridays alone almost bored me to death. To relieve the boredom, caused mostly by inactivity. I bought a second-hand desert bike. A weird-looking machine to say the least. Its single seat was perched high above the knobbly rear tyre. A two hundred and fifty cc air-cooled engine was slung in a single tubular frame. The handlebars held the clutch and front brake lever. The rear brake was operated by a pedal under the metal foot pegs located on either side of the engine, which was slung in a steel cradle between the front and rear wheels. Sparse comfort remained for the rider, a total contrast to I previous road machines back home.

"Just like a camel" I thought, "Looks like nothing on earth, but it's perfect for the desert'. Indeed, I discovered it was. Friday mornings, the bike would be thrown into the boot of the now battered Fury. Unable to be fully closed, the boot lid would be secured with expanding straps. I would drive out of town to the rolling desert dunes. Complete with packed sandwiches and enough water to drown an army. Petrol would be siphoned from the car into a twenty-litre container and mixed with one-part oil to twenty parts petrol. Then it was slopped into the bike's plastic fuel tank via a plastic funnel. The bike may have looked weird on first inspection but, once crackling across the sand, I realised that the machine was in tune with the desert itself. My confidence increased the more I rode this beast. Sometimes I raced up the windward side of the dunes on the firm, well-packed sand where the bike would crest the knife-edged ridge and sail out into space as if heading for the stars. Rooster-tails of sand sprayed skyward in a giant particled fan and as the rear wheel broke free, unhindered by the dune, which now fell away behind, the bike would hang almost stationary in mid-flight before sliding back to earth pillowing into the soft, loose sand of the leeward slope which tried to suck the roaring beast to a sand-swamped stop.

The spinning wheels threw up loose dust and sand, which caked my exposed skin. Where the sweat ran in rivulets, it washed the sand away to creep into crevices that could only be described as intimate. Sandy biscuits formed as the sand adhered to my sweat-soaked clothes. Many times, I had to stop, to quench my burning gullet with litres of clear, melted ice water. The exhilaration of release as the bike soared skyward from the razor-edge peaks became addictive to my senses. Driving the loneliness to the back of my mind vanquished once more to an easily forgotten shelf.

I now anticipated Fridays with an eager expectancy. The rapidly alternating emotions of fear and wild excitement became addictive to my senses. The desperate need for the bike to hold its true course and not twist from my control and fall on top of me. Crushing me into the sand, unconscious and burned by the broiling, overworked engine. The extra strain of endurance wasted the spare flesh from my body. Increasing my stamina, toughening my guts from within and, with the guaranteed pain of mistakes, a swelling confidence of desert riding was born. Fridays had suddenly become an exhaustive ritual.

The construction site shimmered in the midsummer heat. Flies buzzed incessantly around my face. I dodged from shade to shade, carefully avoiding the guardrails; they would have been solar heated, well above the tolerance of mortal man. The desert haze rippled all around, reflecting the sky on its silvery waves, alikening the site to a desert island, cast adrift in a silvery sea.

A welcome silence becalmed the huge metal structure. A large Oil Pipe manufacturing facility for Ameron. A routine safety inspection and break period would extend the silence for at least an hour. I gazed outward in a futile effort to fix the horizon but the rippling haze pushed back my efforts and created unsteadiness. This apparition must have been the vision of water, responsible for driving the early desert travellers to insanity, as they chased off in search of an imaginary ocean or drink. The truth lay bare before me. As the imaginary sea glistened all around and the sun burned my neck between the shade, I went ahead to the site cabin, where I gulped a full litre of ice melt from the cooler. A sudden blinding headache tried to prod my eyes from their sockets and the ice melt numbed and froze my throat. I screwed my facial muscles into a wild straining gesture, held it for a second, and when I relaxed, the ice bite ache had gone and a new sound invaded my ears.

Rotor blades battered the afternoon heat, distant yet rapidly drawing near. The approach of galloping wind born approaching the site with speed. The humidity disguised the approach, throwing a false direction to the incoming craft. All around me, hands shaded eyes then finally their arms poked skyward. Out there, off to the left, a small white dot against the blaze blue sky. Within seconds the helicopter cruised around the site. We lost sight of him as; he crossed the blazing orb. Once more the white

CHAPTER 5   SAUDI STYLE   PULL THE PLUG

helicopter appeared from the glare, circling the site, before it pitched away from the structure, hovered momentarily, before its engine cut dead. The flying machine floated to the ground like a careless autumn leaf.

"Auto rotation," I had heard of such a manoeuvre but never actually saw the event, until now. The helicopter settled, into the tornado of dust whipped up by the rotor blades and the landing floats bumped into the wind-rippled sand. I observed the visitation from a cardboard, insulated perch on the exposed steelwork. A rugged figure dropped from the bulb of perspex encapsulating the cockpit. As the pilot strode toward us, I inspected him closely. He was physically in decent shape and strode as if with great purpose. A cap rode his head, dark blue in colour, with a pleated black band across the brow. The cap band nestled above a small trim peak. Yesterday's stubble had not been wiped with a blade and black sunglasses shielded his eyes, denying any real means of identification. I strode to the ladder-top to meet him. As the pilot's bearded features poked above the deck, I opened the conversation.

"That was some landing. Auto rotation, wasn't it?"

"Got to keep in practise". grinned the pilot, "Besides, with all the heat you guys put up with down here, I figured the last thing you needed was a sandstorm; blown up by the food mixer blades over there". he stabbed an arm in my general direction,

"Hangar!" he announced, "Jerry Hangar".

I returned the handshake,

"Bob King. Call me Bob, most people do".

We exchanged Saudi grins and I led the way back to the quiet coolness of the air-conditioned cabin. I wondered what the OCOMA chopper was doing out here. It wasn't long before we entered the site cabin.

"Cold beer?" I offered.

"Whaaat!" exclaimed Hangar with a grin.

"Sorry, I'll re-phrase that. How would you like a non-alcoholic beer?"

78

CHAPTER 5   SAUDI STYLE   PULL THE PLUG

"That's better," grinned Hangar, "For a minute I thought you were trying to corrupt an innocent young man, like myself, into drinking that sinful concoction, normally associated with the wicked western influence".

I threw him the beer and watched as Hangar removed his cap and rolled the frosted can across his forehead. It was a useless attempt to ward off the melting heat.

"What are you here for, Jerry?"
I wasted no time, curiosity rapidly overtaking dwindling patience.

"Patience Bob, haven't you learned yetI must take you with me. A dozen people over at headquarters want a word in your ear. It can only be one of two things, either you're about to get fired or you're on the move up, they seem to think you're project management skills are making the grade so far. The fact that they sent me and not a Dear John can only be a good sign. If I were you, I'd start to get excited right about now".

"Right about now?" I gasped as a surge of excitement flooded my body.

Hangar continued "Well, we could chat for a while, but that bird over there on the sand tends to get extremely hot when she's left out in the sun all alone and if we wait much longer, I'm going to need asbestos gloves to fly her back. You hear what I'm saying, Bob?"

"Loud and clear, Jerry. Let's go. Give me a minute to hand over and check out and I'll be right with you".

The last of the beer was unceremoniously thrown down the back of our throats, I organised cover for my absence and it wasn't long before we strode across the steel decking, down the ladder and across the anvil to the helicopter. I had previously flown in a commercial helicopter, but that in no way prepared me for what I was about to experience.

"Seatbelt!" commanded Hangar as the turbines whined into life. The rotor blades were already accelerating to invisibility, as my seatbelt clicked into place. The helicopter rose upward as if signalled by the click, lurching forward at a sickening angle. I double-checked my belt. I had a feeling that this was going to be no ordinary flight. I could only stare into the sand as it flashed across the front of the bubble screen. The helicopter accelerated and I was forced into my seat. The pressure only eased when the machine levelled to a more normal position of flight. Rotor blades lifting us skyward, not dragging the chopper forwards across the sand. Hangar fumbled in the canvas flying jacket carelessly tossed across the back of his seat.

"You like music?" he yelled, loud enough to be heard above the teeth-rattling vibrations. I nodded still staring out of the perspex canopy. I wondered if Hangar had a licence to fly the thing, - or had he just stolen it? The chopper slued around the sky, out of control whilst Hangar fumbled a cassette into the tape deck,

"Isn't that illegal Hanger?" I yelled above the din.

"Yeah it is!" admitted Hangar, unconcerned.

I recognised the music from the first clash of guitars, Jailbreak, by the Irish band Thin Lizzy. The music boomed into my ears, drowning out surrounding noise until victorious in its quest for our utmost attention.

> Tonight, there's going to be a jailbreak
> Somewhere in this town
> Tonight, there's going to be a jailbreak
> So don't you be around.

Thundering across the desert in the fragile perspex bubble of a helicopter added a special ingredient to the music. The chopper skipped low across the glaze of the sun-bleached sand, power-swerving around obstacles in our crow flight path. Hanging by an invisible chord of whirlwind air. A distant glint caught my eye. It pulsed closer with every beat of the music and raced toward us with the throw of the swirling blades. Recognition choked in my throat, where fear had already lain the dry chords of silence. My words tumbled erratically in a desperate whisper,

CHAPTER 5   SAUDI STYLE   PULL THE PLUG

"Pylons! Hangar the pylons! Watch out for the cables!" The music drowned my cries as I stared at the on-rushing cables with sickening disbelief. My eyes must have bulged wide in Hangar's direction, pleading for some sort of recognition, of our plight. Finally, it came as Hangar yawned lethargically, as if unaware of impending disaster, turning to my terror-stricken features with a lazy, almost unconcerned smile. I froze in shocked anticipation of the certain body-mangling crunch.

"Tonight, there's going to be a jailbreak". screamed the stereo.

"Somewhere in this town". Hangar joined in, lunging the cyclic stick forward and plunging the chopper under the lowest cable by an arm length. Then he heaved the cyclic backward, the chopper instantly obeyed, climbing straight up the elevator of airspace on the far side of the cables. I squirmed in my seat, totally disorientated only managing to recover my bearings, as the chopper reached the peak of its climb and stood on its tail, almost motionless in the sky. Suddenly, its tail spun upward and behind us. We plummeted downwards once more, tracing our earlier parabola, back under the cables and clawing against nothing up the opposite side of the cables, before Hanger flicked the cyclic forward, levelling the chopper's lean and launched it across the top of the cables, accelerating rapidly as it dragged us back, to our previously selected flight path.

"Bloody hell!" I yelped, to myself. The music drowned the engine, and both strangled my voice. I pulled myself up in my seat and disengaged my panic-stricken grip from the alloy framework of the seat support.

"What's wrong?" grinned Hangar, "Never flown in a chopper before?"

Now Hangar power-swerved the chopper around a lonely desert oil rig and the blades frantically chopped at the sky, clawing for a hold. Pure adrenaline surged through my veins, as the G-force crashed me further into my seat. Hangar threw the chopper from the gyroscopic grip and we catapulted away at speed, the rig rapidly diminishing behind us.

CHAPTER 5   SAUDI STYLE   PULL THE PLUG

"Wow, this is great!" I yelled, the adrenaline finally taking hold. The release became addictive as the chopper air-ripped into a valley between huge golden dunes. Blasting skyward a dust storm that could have been seen for miles. My exhilaration could scarcely be contained as we exploded from the valley and power-turned in a G-force wrenching radius, pointing us towards the city in a blaze of shimmering dust and noise. The strains of Thin Lizzy faded in our wake as the desert returned once more, to a more normal tone of existence.

"So, Bob we decided to give you first refusal"
"Why me?"
"Look, Bob, you have been with the company for a respectable number of years now. It would be easy for us, to offer this position to college kids with degrees, but let's be honest. How long would they last? A week? A month? Even a year. We need somebody with experience who will be in at the beginning, but what's more important, still plugging away at the end. This is going to be a lengthy project, with five years to completion and full production. We're going to suck crude out of the ground and refine it right here in Saudi before it goes anywhere. We need a refinery built right here, tangled, structural steel by us and pipework crackers and storage tanks by the refinery companies, purifying our oil. More outlay, but a hell of a lot more profit. We need someone like you. You're professionally qualified, speak a good deal of the language, have a good man-management background and, hell Bob! We think you're the man for the job".

"I don't really know what to say". I struggled with the words, almost embarrassed by the praise now being thrust upon me.

"If I were you, I'd accept". growled Hangar from the back of the room, his voice laced with a congratulatory tone.

I looked around at the three OCOMA executives who were awaiting my reply. The Ocomas had commented on my staying power. Most foreigners, they had always believed, wanted money and out, never taking the time to learn any of the language or customs. I was familiar with the most intricate of customs and spoke a good deal of Arabic with good intonation. The Ocomas knew me well and hoped that I would accept this post.

I swayed, with the formidable responsibility now being offered. Project Engineer, one of many, but I would manage all mechanical and structural work constructed at the new refinery to be built in Jeddah on the Red Sea coast of Saudi Arabia.

I pondered the situation; I understood that, during this time, the Iranians were causing major problems. If the Arabian gulf were to come under Iranian fire and major sea lanes were closed, Saudi would have no way of loading oil into the cavernous bellies of the super tankers of Europe. A major plan was now underway. A pipeline would cross the desert, East to West, for more than one thousand miles. In case the Arabian Gulf is closed to shipping, Saudi could pump her oil cross-country and continue reaping the revenues unabated. Additionally, huge refineries and storage depots would be built at Jeddah and Yanbu on the Red Sea Coast. The crude would be processed and shipped in its finished form as gas, chemicals, or differing grades of processed oil. Increasing the profitability of Saudi crude and reducing wasted by-products, which could be stored and sold in the required quantities. Saudi could afford to take a few financial knocks now. She had twenty five percent of the world's known oil reserves. She was not about to sink without trace - not while America and most of Europe depended on her oil. She was the jewel of the Middle East and her Sunni stand against the fanatics in Shiite Iran, more than enamoured her with her sucklings in the west. Such globally important decisions were made by the powers beyond the shores of Saudi, wherever that may be. Third parties always seemed to make Middle Eastern decisions. This time, I would have to decide of my own. The world's oil market was not holding its breath for my reply, but for me, it was a decision of significant importance.

Finally, I delivered my answer,

CHAPTER 5   SAUDI STYLE   PULL THE PLUG

"OK, thank you, I accept," I grinned as the friendly handshakes and back-slapping ensued. I left the office with a broad smile that must have illuminated my features.

"Let's go," announced Hangar I've been instructed to show you over a similar site in Dhahran, to give you an idea of the size involved. Do I call you Chief or Sir?" enquired Hangar, sarcasm lacing his voice.

"You can call me a whole lot wealthier and salute me if you like, I don't really care". I grinned.

We were soaked as we left the air-conditioned offices of OCOMA and stepped out into the steam bath of the midday desert. Condensation immediately fogged our sunglasses beyond immediate use. They would have to rise to the external temperature before they could be worn to any effect. As my seatbelt clicked, the chopper once more leaped into the ever-blue sky.

"When did you start flying?" I asked the simple question and Hangar almost froze, before melting back to reality to utter my reply,

"Vietnam". Hangar paused for what seemed like an age before he continued with our conversation,

"I was just a kid, Bob. I was in love with flying helicopters. I wanted to fly them so bad I joined the army. Next minute I'm in Nam, sitting above a steel plate to stop my balls being blasted to bits and wondering what I was doing there. Oh, I knew, believe me, I knew. I was having a ball - the guys on the ground had it rough, but me, I loved it. Flying by the skin of my teeth, shooting shit out of the enemy. Problem is when you come home from maximum excitement to nothing but plain old life. I couldn't cope. Like most vets, I almost went crazy until I got this job. Now here I am flying for all sorts of people'

"But why here?"

"Mostly the freedom, try pulling the stunts we did earlier and in any other country, with all their poxy regulations we would have been grounded before our feet had hit the airport asphalt.

Out here, nobody gives a shit, so I'm free for the occasional boogie. Know what I mean chief?"

The chopper swooped low over the dunes and I watched for the grin as it sliced Hangar's features.

"Here's a man". I thought, "Here's a man who loves his job, enjoys the work and probably wouldn't do anything else if they paid him his weight in gold".

"You're right!" grinned Hangar as if able to read my thoughts.

I did not reply. I understood the smile completely. Self-contentment, the watchwords of life. I tried to relax but the chopper's shadow hurtling erratically across the dunes, barely meters below me, didn't quite allow it.

The journey catapulted us over a huge flatland. Bulldozers and bucket trucks were already levelling the great mounds of sand and gouging the earth for the massive concrete rafts that would soon be poured into existence.

"Take a good look!" ordered Hangar, "In a few months" time, that beachy bit of real estate will be over-run by men and machinery building the biggest, most technologically advanced refinery that small piece of scrubland will hold. You, Bob King, will have a similar plot in South Jeddah, three times the size of this one".

A new emotion swept over me. A feeling of belonging, interlaced with the fear of the unknown. The chopper scudded low over Dhahran and from my advantageous perch I saw the real extent of the construction. It had been fuelled by the billions of dollars pruned from western economies, in payment for that once worthless black sludge known as crude. Half-completed hotels littered the landscape. Their scaffolding reached skyward to meet us, spider webs of timber, reaching up to ensnare our mechanical fly. Massive earthmovers crawled across the desert below - monstrous mechanical dinosaurs, had been reborn, to shape the earth that had once destroyed them. Everywhere the criss-cross of black asphalt with silver lamp standards, bristling like spines on the black snake's back. Once, on my arrival, I had thought that Saudi Arabia was one big building site, the sand merely awaiting the arrival of the water and cement. The Saudis were trying to assemble, in a few years, the major city infrastructures that had taken the West years to develop and perfect. From where I sat now, the Saudis were going to succeed and I had nothing but sincere admiration for them. The vision of development below awed me with a new respect.

The tour was all too quickly over. The chopper vibrated back to my operation zone.

"What are you doing on Friday, Bob".

"Well, normally I take my bike into the desert, to scare away the work-day blues with a stint of exhilarating manoeuvres but after this little trip, I think I'm going to be wasting my time. Riding a bike will never be the same again".

Hangar smiled with appreciation at the unveiled compliment to my flying abilities.

"You dive?" Hangar enquired

"Skydive?" I queried. Surely this could be the only form of diving my bird of the skies had in mind.

"No, Bob, I mean Scuba diving. Saudi has some of the best reefs in the world, especially over on the West Coast where you're headed. You ought to consider learning to dive".

"Who's going to teach me? I don't know any diving instructors".

"You do now," grinned Hangar, I'm a better diver than a pilot. I could teach you the basics in a weekend. In a couple of Fridays, you'll be scubaring like a pro".

I accepted the offer. Two weeks later I was gliding through the waters of the Gulf as if born under the sea. I picked up the skill with a natural ease. Hangar was a good teacher and loaned me a myriad of books from his personal library. Within two months I had been assessed for proficiency in a pool and thrust to the depths of the Gulf and taught to pop up to the surface like a cork. A manoeuvre described as "free ascent" in diver's jargon. I was grilled in a classroom for over two hours before finally being labelled proficient, awarded an open water diving certificate and adding a new string to my bow of Saudi accomplishments. It never failed to amaze me; the way foreigners went out of their way to help each other in an alien land, despite their differing and sometimes warring nationalities.

I left Dhahran with a certain measure of sadness. The old apartment and my old colleagues including the company football team were all gone now and I left nothing behind but the small family of Geckos and the memories of those early days. It was some years later when I learned that one member of the football team made himself famous for all the wrong reasons and it came as a real shock. The OCOMA team for which I played, played against Binladen Concrete, and the son of Binladen, who loved to win and was a lousy loser, turned out to be Osama Bin Laden. He was just a normal gangly kid playing football in the yard with the rest of us, Ocoma vs Binladen. He didn't like to be tackled but he loved to trip you and we had some real ding dong games. He often threatened to kill me for "stealing his ball" but it was all in good fun and we all enjoyed a Vimto and a shawarma after the game. So, what happened there then? Something or somebody got to him and really did a job on his psyche, thank God they didn't get to him during his football years, stealing "his" ball may have been a big No - No. Anyway, I was moving on, but I had not given up on the goal. I learned the lessons well. I was already speaking a good deal of the language and now I prepared myself for the mysteries of Jeddah that lay ahead.

It didn't take long, Jeddah cast her veil around me like spilled liquid on a glass surface, ever spreading and expanding, growing every day. The refinery steelwork poked upward from the foundations and infrastructure and the massive, skeletal structures began to take shape. Fresh-faced new foreigners arrived. Some left in such haste that no one even got to know their names. They were unprepared for the desert Kingdom's ways. A few survived and managed to stay a while longer, some even finished their contracts. Some, for the fabulous fortunes that could be earned. Some, to get away from previous marital mistakes. A few, like myself, were held in the desert's strange grip and it was unlikely that such a powerful grasp would easily be broken, Saudi was changing fast, so fast, the city of Jeddah could outshine many of the European cities with the commercial enterprises now clammering to be part of the big game.

Chapter 5
PULL THE PLUG

Tuesday 20th November 1979.

On Tuesday 20th November 1979, the telephone, fax and all other forms of communication with the world outside Saudi Arabia were dead. Reports were scant and whispers on the jungle telegraph were rife, incredible rumours reporting the same story, Islamic fanatics had captured the Holy City of Makkah.

Today was a special date for the Muslim faith, the beginning of the Islamic year 1400. It was the time of the Mahdi or the new Islamic Messiah, conveniently proclaimed to appear at the start of the new century, starting today.

Fearful undercurrents rumbled through Jeddah as the whole city held its breath in anticipation of a new Islamic uprising, following in the footsteps of the Iranian affair, after the late Ayatollah Khomeini's return to power from exile in France.

The perpetrators sealed off the prophet's mosque. The leader of the uprising claimed to be the Mahdi's brother, Juhayman. All immediate resistance to Juhayman's claims was stamped out and the Gates of the Prophet's mosque were sealed. In modern terminology, the Prophet's mosque had been hijacked. When the late Ayatollah Khomeini of Iran, heard the news, he immediately announced to his followers, that it was the work of the Zionists and Americans and released the wrath of the global Muslim community on the Embassies and Consulates of all the nations allegedly involved. As usual, the Americans and the Israelis got more than their fair share of flag burning and fanatical protests.

Saudi Arabia shuddered under the conflict. The Saudi Army and National Guard jumped to red alert. Roadblocks barred all entry and exit points to Saudi cities and in the struggle to regain control of the runaway firestorm, the Kingdom gritted her teeth and began to fight back, the only way she knew how, with absolute determination, smeared with heroic blood and guts. The hijackers were estimated to be two or three hundred strong and armed with AK-47 assault rifles. Juhayman broadcasting his demands from the minarets of the Prophet's mosque, announced that his followers were there, to clean up the corrupted Princes. He singled out Prince Fawwaz for special attention, citing the prince's love for whisky, pornography and gambling. Juhayman certainly had a knack for winning friends and influencing people.

At that time, Prince Fawwaz was the Governor of Makkah, the Holy City. Juhayman had hoped that many of the worshippers in Makkah would support him but wisely, the Kingdom's citizens did not heed his call. Juhayman had already been marketed as a madman, homosexual, drug addict and drunkard. It became increasingly clear to all expatriates, that Juhayman was heading for a fall and it was unlikely he would be bouncing back from it. He had one chance, if he were the new Messiah, he could win this fight with no problem but I didn't rush down to Ladbrooks to place a bet, there were no bookies in Saudi and I would have backed the Saudis every single time.

King Khaled called the religious leaders to audience. What action, he demanded, could his forces take to recapture the Holy Mosque? Was it lawful to take life under the present emergency circumstances? His reply was an absolute affirmative. The Saudi rulers could not demolish the Prophet's mosque with bombs, rockets, mortars and grenades. Already the eyes of the world and the global Muslim faith were upon them; they had to act quickly and cleanly and success was an absolute minimum requirement.

Some Saudi troops were unhappy about fighting in the house of God, the very house they had worshipped and cherished since birth. Eventually, a course of action was agreed upon. The building would have to be taken by the infantry; shot by shot, step by step, death by death. The Saudis had to regain control of the Mosque. They were the protectors of the Holy City; it was their battle and their battle alone. More rumours circulated to the expatriate community, based on various levels of assistance from the British SAS, the French Foreign Legion and a few lesser-known military establishments from around the globe.

The Saudis used tear gas, percussion grenades, and above all, a giant slice of their fierce, unfaltering pride. By the time the hostilities had ended, more than eight days had passed but the Prophet's mosque was back in the hands of its protectors. Of the government forces involved in the assault, 127 Saudi soldiers were dead and martyred, 461 injured and blessed and 117 rebels had been killed, along with several worshippers caught up in the crossfire. Despite the rumours, not one foreign soldier was mentioned on the casualty listings. It became clear to most observers, that the Saudis had crushed the terrorists with their own hands.

As the Royal Saudi Forces took back control, the lines of communication to the outside world opened once more and were immediately flooded to near collapse by thousands of calls. The die-hard rebels had been flushed from the warren-like cellars under the Prophet's mosque. Amongst them was Juhayman. His brother, the so-called Mahdi, he had been shot dead after only four days of the siege - proof beyond any doubt, of his false claims to be the divine one.

The perpetrators were severely dealt with. Sixty-three were beheaded in small groups of half a dozen or so, at various locations throughout the Kingdom, usually in the car parks next to the main mosque of the town or city chosen. Finally, the Kingdom of Saudi Arabia exhaled, though nervously once more and the press popularly similarly described the incident to the Jim Jones cult, with the mass suicide of the divine one's followers.

As foreigners, we would never really be sure of what had taken place, only that the incident had ended and it had been a bloody affair. I had suddenly become certain of one fact, if you messed around with Saudi Arabia and broke her laws, don't start to complain when Saudi Arabia got around to messing about with you.

Prince Fawwaz resigned his position as the Governor of Makkah and existing Governors in outer regions were replaced by King Khaled's younger brothers. A complete tightening of the Kingdom's security policies was carefully, if not secretly, undertaken and any would-be Juhaymans had been warned, think twice before you lose your head.

Important meetings were taking place in every corner of the vast landscape of Saudi Arabia. A few weeks after the incident another meeting was to take place - a meeting of total insignificance to any of the ruling powers of Saudi, at least for the time being anyway.

Chapter 6
HIRELINGS

Vandyke eyed every step as I strode toward him along the hot metal catwalk, the tempo of my gait in tune with the refinery humming around me. The confidence must have radiated from my body like the beam from a fresh batteried torch. I felt good today, and things were going extremely well, the project was nearing completion, my experience was still growing every day and the team I had around me was brilliant. Peter Vandyke had tried and failed previously to secure a meeting with me. He told me later that everyone had presented him with the same advice, "Speak to Bob, He's your man". Now Vandyke had cornered his elusive prey, I had previously avoided him, my excuse always being the same, too busy. But now an easing of schedules and workload had opened the door.

"Bob King!" I extended my arm in customary greeting.

"Peter Vandyke!" Taking the outstretched hand and pumping, passing his business card over with the left hand. I immediately realised that Vandyke was not acquainted with Middle Eastern ways. You never hand over anything with your left hand, it was considered extremely bad manners, this was the hand you saved for wiping your arse, but unperturbed I let it pass, his hand looked clean anyway.

I quickly appraised my visitor; Vandyke was a straight-looking sort of person, dark and handsome, but quite short for his looks to be of any promotional help. Short dark and handsome was a term that neatly packaged his appearance. A typical salesman, collar and tie, docksider's leather shoes, and an imitation leather briefcase completed the mould. His tie had been loosened for effect. Sunglasses by Carrera and his bullshit by some sales cloning agency in the North Americas. I had time to spare and I decided to give the guy a hearing. I also had the inner gut feeling that we might have something in common. I opened the conversation,

"We'll go to the office. Follow me, Pete. It should be much more comfortable and at least we'll be able to hear ourselves speak".

Pete followed me along the maze-like catwalk trail. He mentioned the respect between my fellow employees and me. I was on first-name terms with everybody, according to his impressions. I constantly advised and instructed as I led Vandyke back to the office, trying not to take too much notice of his sales patter. The refinery had steamed into operation three months ago. Peter informed me he was sure that somewhere in this metalloid monster, his company's products could be used to a maximum.

Peter Vandyke was a French Canadian, representing a chemical company from the States, supplying all manner of coatings and paints to the steel-related industries of the Middle East. He specialised in protective oil field coatings, travelling the length and breadth of Saudi, where it had been assumed that his perfect French would have been put to beneficial use. he had conversed in French just once since his arrival three years ago, ordering coffee in the Meridien Hotel on the old Makkah Road, it was wasted, they only spoke Arabic or English. Since then, he had lost all hope of ever speaking French again, other than to himself, he informed me later, when the loneliness of his work overtook him.

By the time we reached the cabin, I had conversed with at least five men, each time using their first names. Peter commented on the tremendous team spirit that hung about the complex. Most of the five had received a smile and a few words of encouragement and, not one man had any complaints. Peter Vandyke said he felt strangely at ease here compared to some of the laxer sites he had visited previously. I held the cabin door open for my visitor and we entered the insulated cabin. An oversized aircon thundered away in one corner, blasting in chilly air with such force, that it almost pressurised the tiny building. I

94

knocked off the power to the ac and the calm was almost blissful. The office was small and neat and I tried to keep it well-organised. I scribbled notes on a desk pad, held three phone conversations, one in Arabic, before finally opening the statutory refrigerator.

"Cold beer, Pete?"

"What, the real stuff?"

"Sorry!" cold non-alcoholic beer"

"That's better," responded my guest, "For a minute there I thought you were offering me a can of that obnoxious liquid, normally associated with the wicked western influence".

I slumped into a chair and I waved Vandyke into a seat, a broad smile now brightening his features.

"Please, Robert, call me Pete, everybody else does".

"And everybody else calls me Bob". We settled back and relaxed now that the inhibiting formalities had been dispensed with.

"Did I say something funny, Bob?"

I related my first meeting with Hangar, who had used the same words at the offer of a beer and had then tried to kill me in a helicopter. Pete sat and listened with interest, partly because he was paid for doing such things and mainly because he was genuinely amused by the tale. The ring pull snapped back and Pete guzzled the contents of his beer without pause.

"Hits the spot," he sighed, following with a hand-smothered burp, which he excused with a broad grin.

"OK! Pete, what have you got in the little bag that I should be begging you to sell Ocoma?"

Pete reached inside his briefcase, passing a selection of glossy brochures across my desk, samples and a current price list, which would be specially discounted - for me, of course. I knew the rules of the game. Pete was not the only sales clone who had fed me the baited hook and line.

I gave the loss leaders a cursory glance and toyed with the samples before disinterest forced me to speak,

'Hey look, Pete. We just got this baby online, everything in this place is top dollar brand new, we pump light Saudi crude in one end and nothing short of ladies" cosmetics are coming out of the other. Personally, I'm not a chemical engineer, but I have some reports here on the corrosive nature of this area, I'll get copies of these items for you to run alongside your coatings. When you can produce ironclad solutions backed by guarantees and insurance certificates, I'll personally introduce you to the paintwork chiefs. Till then I'm not about to allow a bunch of toilet brush jockeys anywhere near my pride and joy. I hope that sounds fair enough to you".

Pete scanned the charts for a moment before replying.

"This is great, Bob. It may take a while to decipher this lot but as soon as I have all the answers, I'll be back to see you".

"You won't, you'll be back to see the refinery's chemical engineers; if they say your products are OK, I'll sign for the orders, with iron clad guarantees. Till then it's up to you - and, you won't be the only company bidding for business, so if I were you, I'd sharpen your pencil. Those are some of the most expensive prices I've seen".

Pete tucked the papers into his briefcase, obviously appreciating my no-nonsense approach and realising he had a tough task ahead. Pete did not bother me with the standard sales pitch. Instead, he decided to find out more about his fish on a hook.

I sensed the visual inspection and as Pete opened his mouth, I pre-empted his question before he uttered a single syllable,

"England'.

Pete wanted to open his inquiry further but once more I answered before he had verbalised his question from thought,

"Five years!" I added, predicting the next question. I grinned at Pete's bewilderment.

"Diving in the sea and dirt biking in the desert, I've been known to sneak around Saudi with the occasional Stewie or nurse sometimes, but those indulgements are unfortunately few and far between".

"How do you do it?" laughed Pete, all his questions had been answered before they had been asked. I had to tell him the truth

"Look, Pete, since I've been here, somebody like yourself comes through that door every other day, scattering their bait. Eventually, they realise I'm not biting, so they get down to the more personal side of living in Saudi. It's always the same questions - where are you from? How long have you been here? What do you do in your spare time? Believe me, I've heard those questions a million times before. The first time some chap comes in here with originality, I'm buying. Believe me, I'm buying".

"Three years," began Pete, "Toronto, Ontario, Canada, certified diver and desert biker".

He removed a pile of Photographs from his briefcase. Bikes in the desert, beach pictures complete with tanks and lumps of newly pillaged coral reef. I scanned them all with interest. This was my kind of entertainment.

"How about this weekend?" Pete must have hoped for a positive response. His sales targets for the year depended on it.

"I'll check my diary, Pete," I closed my eyes, face pointing to the ceiling for emphasis, "No parties, no barbecues, no discos, no night-clubs, no women," and after a brief pause added, "What a boring life, looks like I'm going biking in the desert with you. I hope you can ride because I certainly don't want to babysit

The verbal gauntlet had been thrown in Pete's face. The time and the place were quickly arranged. It would be a duel to the death. Friday's dawning would signal the start of that duel. The phone jangled urgently above the humming refinery, shattering our immediate cocoon of calm; I grabbed the red phone.

"Bob here!" I barked, "What! - Oh shit! - Right! don't let anybody within a mile of that place with a cigarette. I'm on my way". I dropped the receiver into the cradle and dashed outside. A millisecond later, I stabbed my head back around the door leaf, gabbling apologies,

"Sorry, Pete finish your beer, help yourself to another and make yourself at home. If I don't see you later, I'll see you Friday as arranged. Bye".

Pete threw the final contents of his can to the back of his throat. It had been a good meeting and I could tell he was more than pleased. I could not put my finger on why, but I liked this guy. There was something about him that you couldn't help but like. On Friday I would pick up the gauntlet, drive Peter the painter into the desert and claim my title. No quarter given; no mercy metered out. Pete would have to drive me into submission if he wanted to claim his sale and to hell with his discounts.

I decided to rest on the Thursday evening prior to the duel, I had to, as far as I was concerned, Stewies were becoming an endangered species. There had also been a clampdown at the hospital. European nursing staff had been warned to be extremely careful about sharing body fluids with members of the opposite sex. Such practices could result in extreme suffering followed by deportation in shame. I smiled to myself as I lolled on the sofa; a "Sid" clenched in my hand. The ice cubes clinking against the side of the glass were music to my ears. This was Saudi where alcohol was forbidden in any form, a bone-dry territory in every sense of the word. Foreigners caught indulging in such heinous crimes suffered a degrading public flogging, followed by a prison term of not less than three months, which would end in deportation. Funny I mused, how the Saudis flew to Bangkok, Manila, London and other fun cities of the world to drink, mess around and generally get pissed out of their skulls, whilst at the same time, managing in the process to make a thorough nuisance of themselves but let's face it, they weren't doing it in Saudi and they were obeying the laws of their destination countries so who could complain? The colour of their money saved them from the usual bouncy exits from the nightclubs. They would return to Saudi with the same holierthan-thou attitude, mocking and jeering the foreigners who had the misfortune to get caught whilst downing a drop of the hard stuff. A colleague of mine, who had been caught recently, had eighty litres of homemade wine in his apartment. Having already downed a litre or two, he decided that the wine was too good to pour down the toilet before the religious fanatics got there. So as the police banged at his door, he continued his drunken attempt to drink eighty litres of wine before the door was smashed from its hinges. When the police finally got to him, he was out cold. Even the police laughed, as they helped themselves to a drink, before bundling him into the black van on his journey to the cells. His sentence was nine months in prison and eighty lashes for manufacturing that evil potion, which had been immediately confiscated by various members of the arresting staff.

I remembered a news article that told of some Saudis applying for a drink license at one of their exclusive London clubs. I could not remember the outcome, which was usually a quiet acceptance. The memory managed to bring forth the usual silent judgment to my well-lubricated lips; "Hypocrites!" I knew that although alcohol was banned in Saudi Arabia for religious reasons, I was sure this was not strictly correct. I had read somewhere. How did that story go? Ah yes, I remembered now,

A cocktail party at the British embassy or consulate was in progress. Certain members of the Saudi hierarchy were invited. It was well known that even to this day at such functions, the drinks flowed faster than the ornamental fountains, in the luxurious well-manicured grounds. One Saudi, having reached that stage of consumption where the world and its inhabitants assume a different guise, decided to proposition a female member of the embassy staff. Unfortunately for him, she was married. However, his blatant grope of her body was discreetly rebuffed, with a slap across his face that brought immediate silence from the surrounding crowd. Losing face was one thing in Saudi, losing face to a woman was a completely different matter. The perpetrator slunk away in ridiculed embarrassment, warned off by the husband of the sobbing, well-groped plaintiff.

CHAPTER 6   SAUDI STYLE   HIRELINGS

The incident however was far from over; the Saudi promptly returned and shot the husband dead at point-blank range. Unfortunately, there were many witnesses and action had to be taken at once, despite attempts to cover up and smother the facts. Being attached to the Royal Family, the shootist escaped execution and is still in some sort of Royal incarceration to this day. Since that Royal Saudi finger squeezed that small metal trigger, alcohol to this present day is banned in Saudi, on purely "religious" grounds.

This does not necessarily mean a drink cannot be obtained. It simply means, that if you drink do not get caught; a hangover will be the least of your worries.

"SID" is a local brew consisting of pure alcohol, locally manufactured by remarkably interesting but carefully mysterious men. Practised brewers have been known to produce and market certain concoctions that enjoyed the honoured distinction of resembling the real thing, right down to colour and taste. Less practised brewers have been known to blind their eager customers and demolish apartments containing their illicit stills, in thunderous, roaring explosions, sending pieces of their brewing equipment into a better orbit than the space shuttle, at a fraction of the cost. "Sid is usually diluted - "Cut" to the initiated, with equal parts of water before a further dilution with a mixer of the indulger's choice, usually lemonade, tonic or Pepsi, not coke, which is also forbidden in Saudi, due to its Jewish connections.

To impress some hardened Scots personnel. I once drank myself into a "straight" sid stupor. I remained bedridden for a week, with an illness that I presumed curable only by my lingering death. Tomorrow I would be giving Mr Vandyke the biking lessons of his life. Thursday night binges had been responsible for ruining many a Friday pastime, be it beach visits, sporting events or Nurse and Stewie impressing. Tomorrow would be different. I had a job to do and certainly, it was a job to be done well. I thought for a second and then disregarded the warning before swaying into the kitchen for another refill.

100

CHAPTER 6   SAUDI STYLE   HIRELINGS

We met on time at the pre-arranged location. When both bikes had been carefully mounted and strapped onto my trailer, we headed south for the open desert. I wanted to explore the massive dunes that I had encountered on a previous helicopter trip but had not dared to explore alone. Biking accidents in this territory usually preceded a lingering death from dehydration if help was not quickly at hand. Jerry Hangar, currently on vacation, did not ride a bike. So, I had bided my time until today, for a chance to conquer the dunes. It took thirty minutes before we arrived at the Holy City checkpoint. This was not a work permit check; this was a religion segregator. Non-Muslims were not allowed to enter the Holy City of Makkah. This stop would divert us around Makkah and down onto the Jizan road that headed south for at least two thousand miles before it hit the Yemen border. To the Christians, the Holy City would remain a mystery until we either changed our religion or Saudi Arabia did. One of these, as unlikely as a snowstorm in the one-hundred-and-forty-degree summer heat.

I turned in the direction of Taif a small-town nestling atop a meandering escarpment. A few miles further on I turned once more, back onto the southbound Jizan road, famous for its murderous accident death rates and the carcasses of camels, which had been hit by massive Mercedes trucks which never bothered to stop, the drivers growing tired of this all too familiar accident, which was why mounted up front, the trucks sported large metal crash cages that minced the camels into leather bags of flesh and bone, before flinging them unceremoniously to the side of the road. From the number of dried-out carcasses evident, it was a wonder there were any camels left in Saudi at all. The mountainous escarpment followed our progress south. A barrier of rock three thousand feet above sea level. The wind had tried to blow the sand over this natural barrier but had only succeeded in drifting the sand against it and forming the giant, constantly shifting, sun-baked dunes, which we hoped we would soon be conquering. I told Pete the tale of the American engineer detained in Makkah. Pete was obviously relieved we had passed the turn-off to Makkah in the opposite direction, as I unfolded my grisly tale.

"The American was under extreme duress, one of his building projects in Makkah, a few meters within the boundary of the holy city, was progressing at a pace slightly faster than stop. The engineer took it upon himself to pay an unannounced visit to the site to find out why the job was taking so much time. Despite the fact it was forbidden, he dressed in Saudi garments, passed the checkpoint without so much as a glance and was furious when upon his arrival he discovered his Egyptian Foreman asleep in the site cabin while the workers lazed around in the shade. He fired the Egyptian at once, a fatal mistake. The foreman trudged from the site, only to return thirty minutes later accompanied by all manner of Saudi officialdom, responsible for protecting the Holy City and God's house against undesirable aliens, terrorist groups and defamation of any kind from any imaginable source. Including the late Ruhollah Ayatollah Khomeini, who at that time was a constant thorn in the Saudi side. Within minutes the American was enjoying the hospitality of the Saudi prison cells. Some say, he may still be there to this day. Of course, the Saudis being a generous race, have explained he can leave whenever he likes, at his own personal leisure in fact but a small condition was attached".

"What's the condition?" interrupted Pete.

"Simple really," I replied, "He can leave the holy city but he has to leave behind the feet that soiled the Holy ground which will be burned to dust after the Friday afternoon prayers".

"UUUGH!" shivered Pete and after the shakes enquired, "What would you do, Bob?"

I thought for a second before revealing my answer.

"I would probably be mounted on roller skates for the rest of my unnatural life, I certainly wouldn't like to be imprisoned here, where none of my family or friends could visit me unless they changed their religion".

"UUUUGH!" Pete shrugged again; "I guess you're right". I could see Pete's mind working overtime, pitying the unfortunate man and the sheer brutality of the decision he would have to make.

The road now sliced between the towering rock face of the escarpment some thirty miles to the West, and the long flat plain to the East, which would ultimately run down to the Red Sea. Brief glimpses of the turquoise waters occasionally flashed into view between the scrubland debris of the rolling desert.

"Not far now". I announced, mostly to myself, as Pete still pondered life without feet.

We caught sight of them instantaneously. The twisting peaks of the huge dunes, rising from the shimmering haze that disguised and disfigured their lower bulk. Landlocked sandbergs, with only their tips revealed above the shimmering silver slivers. Pete whistled his appreciation,

"They're huge!" he spat with amazement.

"Not bad at all, Pete," I returned. The excitement and expectation of the realised challenge stunned us both to silence and the rivalry between us reared up and announced its calling.

Pete now scanned the desert as it streamed by his window to the right. The sand was hard-packed, with a thick crusty capping and a heavy deposit of salt. The plains had been flattened by the winds. The airborne salt spray had been carried inland from the white-tipped waves. It occurred during the winter months when the temperature dropped to as low as seventy degrees Fahrenheit and the wind blew stronger than usual in excited gusts. "Shamel" was the term used by desert dwellers to describe this phenomenon. "Bloody nuisance" it had been labelled by the foreigners, who sat on the beach, clinging to their umbrellas and crunching through their grit-sprinkled sandwiches. The surface of the sand had been cured by the broiling orb's heat. When walked upon, the baked crust gave way to the softer sand below; the foot would continue downward, the jagged edges of the crust peeling the skin from around the ankle bone, rubbing the salt deep into the stinging wound. An eye-popping sensation followed that had reduced grown men to tears. Reaching Phenomenal temperatures during the day, it was impossible to traverse the sand pack in bare feet. Temperatures of one hundred and fifty degrees had been recorded. Even the hardiest of the nomads hopped, skipped and swore when a sandal fell free and an unprotected foot was carelessly pressed into the salty fire. Pete turned and spilled his concern at the thought of a crash into such a furnace of pain, even if their bones were unbroken, the lacerations would be enough to drive a man bananas with the salt-stinging pain. At worst they would receive one, "Exit only" visa - a small slip of paper, placed in a plastic envelope before being nailed to the side of their wooden overcoat. Pete, I could tell by his expression, experienced unease as reality washed over him. It was dispelled and replaced by sudden impulsive laughter as I uttered my contemptuous response to his reservations in solid upper-crust English, "What a bloody Pussy!" I exclaimed and the ensuing laughter carried us for miles.

I pulled over to the side of the road. The giant dunes beckoned a few miles to our left. From bitter experience, I parked the car away from the road, where no raghead would ram it in his daydreaming blindness. Having first assured myself the ground was firm before finally braking, I did not want the wheels to sink into soft sand, causing great hardship later when we would have to dig the vehicle free. The Fury settled on the hard-compact ground. As the engine stopped, a boisterous, competitive spirit exploded between the two of us. A smothering charge surrounded the Fury. Although invisible, I am sure we both felt its presence; I had sensed this aura previously, mostly on competitive occasions throughout my life. It was the burning desire to conquer, to stay out in front at all costs, to triumph in glory, or face the cold wind of defeat as it blew away your pride.

"I'll be waiting for you at the top of the big one, Bob".

CHAPTER 6   SAUDI STYLE   HIRELINGS

"What do you mean, you pussy? by the time you get to the
bottom of that dune you'll be seeing hundreds of tracks ripped
up the side by the wheels of my bike".

The banter continued as we changed into our protective gear.
Tight leather gloves with skin breathing holes. Sturdy boots to
protect ankles from the slashing spines of the desert scrub
brush. Heavy denim jeans to protect our legs. A slim line tee
shirt over which was folded the neoprene plastic body armour -
modern day replica of the knights of old. A tight, six-inch-deep
kidney belt reduced the bend of the lower back, protecting the
kidneys from damage by fall, or from being battered to a pulp by
the rapid-fire bouncing of the rear wheel, as it fought for grip
over the troughs and valleys of rippling sand. Pete laughed when
he saw my shirt, across the front was a message in bold black
letters against the red cloth, "I ain't a bloody tourist, I work here".
Pete commented on my bare arms, in a fit of macho bravado, I
had torn the armour from the sides of the chest and back
protection. This allowed my arms to hang free with no protection
at all, my bronzed manipulators of measured might, or so I liked
to believe. Pete said I was either crazy or a super confident
rider. The no-protection ploy worked, Pete must have realised,
not without apprehension, that he was about to find out. Our
machines were almost identical in power and size. Both sported
five hundred cc engines. They had the same Spartan design and
even the same fifteen pounds per square inch air pressure that
was needed to inflate the same knobbly tyres. Both machines, in
the right hands, could exceed one hundred miles per hour
across the lunar-like desert terrain. A fall at this speed, out here,
would deliver a savage injury. A body could be damaged beyond
repair, if not devoid of life. Unpleasant facts, that the two of us
were now trying to ignore, particularly myself, as I silently
regretted removing my arm protection. I swung my leg over the
big red Honda and jabbed at the kick-start to flood the
carburettor. Next, I closed the choke lever and jabbed again and
the big red beast howled to life. The rapidly popping exhaust
shattered the silent desert haze. Seconds later Pete's yellow

Suzuki screamed from its earlier coma, both engines now harmonised, producing a solid frenzy of two-stroke howling. The pulsing, aluminium heartbeats quickly warmed to the required running temperature, not too difficult a task, as the ground temperature was already one hundred and thirty degrees and yet, we had not even begun to work.

The warmup would prevent seizure and hopefully prevent the bloody, limb-ravaged consequences of such occurrences. Our bikes cackled like caged beasts, each impatient to assess the other, just like Pete and myself. Blue curling plumes of sweet-scented, two-stroke exhaust fumes, announced a powerful intention, blasting from tiny tubular exits and fuelling an urgent desire. Our faces were now concealed behind neoprene plastic, gladiator-like facemasks. Heavily padded helmets covered all but the glint of a steely, throttle-drugged gaze. I thumbed the choke lever back to normal running and Pete followed my lead. We stood motionless for a while, each mentally appraising the other. I fumbled a glove peeled hand to the fins of my engine in a final temperature check. With the glove quickly replaced, I was ready. A moments pause followed the glove, then came our voiceless, single-nod exchange of accepted challenge, our engines revved to power and our two ultra-technological stallions, dragged their modern-day Knights out onto the merciless, rolling tundra, where fear knows no shame unless you forgot to bring a clean pair of underpants for the journey home.

Side by side, we ploughed into the savage terrain, bouncing and weaving across unfamiliar track. Rooster tails of fine powdered sand spattered skyward from our rear wheels as we skidded and spun to achieve maximum purchase. The speed now increased, neither rider singularly guilty, both of us, under the circumstances, were lost to a different beast that dwelled within. The bikes now lurched forward with the quickening pace but remained parallel. The scrub brush whipped our legs as the unfortunate limbs flashed by. A further increase in velocity occurred but neither of us gave way. The bikes were bouncing heavily as sand ripples threw up the wheels. In tandem, we instantly transferred weight to the rear wheel to settle the bounce and achieve maximum grip, I could see from his stature, Pete had ridden before. The sudden thrust of the added weight powered us forward. Our body weight was now thrown over the front wheels, which had started to slide precariously, before finding bite and the two machines powered sideways around the larger desert obstacles, which we could not batter down.

We were screaming along in top gear now, eighty miles per hour and increasing, the fierce, red-hot, speed wind tearing at our bodies, now constantly grit blasted by the furiously spinning wheels. Muscles were stretched and crushed as the bikes bucked and tossed for supremacy across the alien terrain. Neck and neck, though four meters apart, the gap fashioned by the obstacles on our crow flight path. We surged forward faster now, maximum torque was wrung from our engines, which screamed and howled in a vibration of protest, as every millisecond bounce of piston to charge cracked and spilt the turbid air. A sudden shrieking cry and the rear wheels lost grip, the desert unexpectedly vanishing beneath us, both our bikes hurtled across the sky in a controlled though desperate, seventy mile per hour death glide, into a fall of unknown space and immediate consequence. I gasped with shock, kept my grip and sailed downward in a controlled panic.

A Wadi or dried-up riverbed had snared our progress. The steep bank facing away from our erratic path had concealed the yawning ravine, forty meters across and five meters deep. The two bikes continued, as if in slow motion, across that seemingly endless space. Our engines screamed in protest at the vicious gyrations of the unchained rear wheel. A loss of traction had occurred which now over-revved the piston to a danger limit pulse. The alloy stallions plummeted earthwards, their wheels biting and gouging the rubble strewn wadi bed as gas shock absorbers collapsed, viciously slamming our buttocks into the Spartan saddles. With the breath smashed from my lungs, I had to gulp in as much air as I could; we now hurtled towards a wall of mud-packed sand now barring our progress. The remaining meters of safety snapped shut like a trap. No quarter could be given and our suicidal throttles remained fully open, as the bikes slammed into the sloping wall of hard-packed, windward dune sand. The front shock absorbers bottomed with a terrific jarring thud and deflected our momentum skyward. My arms smashed into their shoulder sockets, to the point of collapse, but I managed to hold firm as the bikes ascended the wall of mud-packed flotsam at a furious scrambling pace, which launched us for the second time into the clear blue sky. At this point I flicked my head sideways and caught a quick glimpse of Pete; there he was, right by my side, level and true like a multicoloured shadow, what a guy, what a bastard. "Shit!" I spat, the little bastard could ride and the exhilaration was too much to hold as our skyward climb continued. Triumphant war cries of victorious release, exploded from behind our facemasks, bellowing loudly above the howling engines. The realisation of the conquered near catastrophe, firing our spirits and nerves, slamming us ever closer to the dune's rapidly approaching wall. Our rear wheels tore into the landing zone, slamming us forward to within meters of the massive dune. Front shock absorbers bottomed once more. The force rammed into my arms punished my shoulder sockets, I was sure, my shoulder sockets were on the verge of dislocation. The suspension springs recovered and launched the front wheel skyward, where it remained, well above the ground, pumped into the air by the powering torque of the rear wheel. The rear tyre power scythed the dune, gouging a single track all the way up to the cresting peak, where, to avoid the over-run down the opposite side of the dune, the throttle was wiped. Our bikes dropped forward onto both wheels, simultaneously and a sudden, all-conquering moment of victory overcame my inhibitions, my emotions ran wild with the overwhelming sense of achievement.

The bikes fell silent and the desert calm returned once more. We tore the helmets from our heads. My sweat-soaked hair spiked upwards from a sodden scalp, almost punk style. A

108

sudden burst of exaltation and nervous laughter exploded as we savoured our triumphant, death-defying voyage. It was quickly followed by a sudden silence as we reflected on what could have been. Absolute silence but for the pinking of overworked alloy engines, trying to rid their innards of massive accumulations of heat. Pete could hold back no more,

"Wowee! That was some ride, Bob!"

"Absolutely amazing, Pete!"

"What about those wheelies up the side?"

"I wish somebody had that on film, what a shot?"

"And I thought you were full of hot air". grinned Pete.

"You thought wrong, arsehole, eh?"

'Not bad, Bob, not bad at all".

I held both arms in the air and screamed out across the desert, loosing pent-up emotions were that bursting to be free. The sound carried for a second or so before echoing away from us, across the emptiness where it was swallowed into the massive barren void. I bent forward and shook my head violently. My hair whipped outward throwing off sand, sweat and dust in a circular arcing spray.

"So that's what holds your ears apart?" chimed Pete.

"Yes!" I replied, "Do you want some?"

"No thanks, I've got my own". Pete bent in a similar pose and thrashed his head in wild gyrations, showering the dune and me with droplets of sweat. The pair of us dropped to our knees in the sand for a moment's rest, and thoughtfully traced our ascending path, with pointing fingers and exhaled pride. The wadi was now in plain view, slashing and scarring the desert plain below us, its high undercut bank now facing our position and sombre in defeat.

"I have a confession". offered Pete.

"Let's hear it," I returned.

"I was shit scared when we dropped over the edge of the wadi, I thought we were dead meat for sure".

"Why did you keep going then?"

"You know why" replied Pete, "I thought, if he's going over then so am I, he's not going to beat me".

"I wasn't scared at all". I lied

"Whaaaat!" yelled Pete in disbelief.

"I was bloody terrified". I cut back without hesitation.

We broke into a knowing grin, no words needed to be exchanged about such a near disaster, and the relief was amply evident.

'How did you feel when you blasted into the sky at the other side?" Pete continued.

"The closest thing to an orgasm without sex".

"Right on the money," he agreed,

"Absolutely smack on the nose".

The two of us enjoyed the view from our lofty perch. Then suddenly Pete pointed his arm away towards the coast.

"There, you see it, Bob?"

"Yeah, I can see it,"

The massive, metal cylinder thundered down the Jizan road far to the west. Its wheels were hidden by the heat haze, which supported the dust, boiling skyward from the tanker's rear. Normally observed in petrol stations filling their tanks. The torpedo-shaped, grey vessel, hovering along on the haze was easily distinguishable by the huge blue letters emblazoned along its side, OCOMA.

"Maybe they're looking for you, Bob?"

"Wouldn't surprise me, an important man like myself".

Pete scooped up his helmet and launched it on a trajectory that would surely strike my arm, until I dodged out of its path and the helmet sped past, rolling and tumbling down the wall of the dune with an ever-increasing velocity.

"Bloody hell, Bob why didn't you stop it?"

I grinned as Pete leapt to his feet and chased the helmet, now careering down the dune like a giant boiled egg.

"See you later" I laughed, as Pete sprinted by my shoulder, bumping into me with mock anger.

Halfway down the dune, Pete gave up the chase, we watched entranced, as the white sphere bounced and rolled in erratic flight for what seemed like hours, until it finally came to rest amongst the scrub brush, way below us at the foot of the dune. A goat, probably a stray from a Bedouin herd, appeared from nowhere and casually strolled over to inspect the sphere, then smelling something of interest it sank its teeth into the exposed inner lining.

I couldn't help but laugh, as Pete scrambled to his bike in a hurried attempt to prevent his only helmet from becoming the lunch of a starving goat. I replaced my own helmet and facemask and joined Pete in the frantic charge down the dune where we were enveloped by a flurry of sand and dust. The terrified goat pranced away in a mad panic, it obviously wasn't that hungry, but still managed to chew a large chunk of protective lining from the inside of the helmet. Pete chased after the goat, cursing in French. I sat aboard my bike laughing at the ridiculous spectacle before me. Pete gave up, retrieved his helmet and crawled back up the dune to his bike. We headed back towards the Fury, a desert thirst, already cracking the lining of our desert dried throats.

The timeless morning passed by and the midday sun began a final assault on the remnants of any remaining stamina. The sun's rays burned deep into the flesh of our exposed necks. The inside of my helmet became hot, wet and soggy. Salty sweat flicked from straggled wisps of hair, stinging and blinding, when it splashed my eyes. Finally, after a mad chase across the tundra, followed by a wild leap into space as we traversed the wadi. A near mid-air collision brought us literally down to earth; enough was enough, we both agreed. The bikes were loaded onto the trailer and we bounced across the Bedouin track towards the beach road, where the turquoise waters of the Red Sea beckoned, warm and inviting.

The Red Sea, a miracle of creation, the very waters parted by God as he prepared the way for Moses and the children of Israel on their flight from Pharaoh Ramses, the cruel ruler of Egypt.

Moses and his followers crossed the seabed unharmed, while the massive rush of water crushed their Egyptian persecutors as the sea returned to its normal state. The Red Sea steeped in History since the dawn of man. A treasure trove of biblical events that had been seen by the waves but were unable to be replayed and what stories they could have told. At the shoreline, the knee-deep water whispered onto white, sandy beaches. This minor depth extended for two or three hundred meters from the beach; at this point, the seabed would drop clean away, to a depth of fifty meters or more. A myriad of brilliantly coloured, coral species inhabited the wall created by the drop-off. The coral was constantly patrolled by millions of sparkling fish of every colour; size and species known to man and more than likely, some that were unknown to man. The fish graced and inhabited the living wall of colours. A jewel of vibrant life, constantly shifting with the moods and momentum of the rolling swell. Jacques Cousteau, the famous explorer of the deep and magical marine biologist, had himself admitted, that his most endearing discoveries took place amongst the fabulous reefs of this very sea. Tribute indeed from such a widely travelled ocean explorer.

Every man did not regard the Red Sea with such esteem. Many captains had met with disaster on those same beautiful testimonies to God's creative prowess. If Sinbad the sailor really existed and was not the figment of some storyteller's imagination, he too would have passed this way with immeasurable care, the possibility of wrecking one's vessel, torn apart and shredded on the razor-like reefs could never be ignored. Thousands of ghostly wrecks littered the Red Seabed. I retold the tale of a cargo vessel, abandoned to her fate after she had struck the reef.

"Her cargo had been livestock, Pete. Hundreds of luckless goats on an ill-fated voyage. The captain had tried unsuccessfully to force his ship the "Jeddah', from the vice-like grip of the reef. Finally, the Jeddah and her live cargo were abandoned to their fate. Some goats jumped overboard, their wild thrashing bodies telegraphing to the nearby sharks, of their available meaty presence. Within minutes the white-tipped monsters were devouring goat meat by the pound, as it fell into their jaws from the upper decks. Some goats

died on board, after wandering around for days in a fruitless search for food and more desperately, water. Some pitiful beasts survived a month or more, cannibalising the bodies of their own kin, that now littered the ship in rotting stinking heaps. Finally, all that remained were the sun-bleached goat bones on that ship of terrible grief.

The Jeddah remains on the reef to this day, Pete. Just south of the naval base. Constantly battered by the unrelenting sea, the perfect spot for shark fishing and diving. Behind the Jeddah, on the seabed lays the "Medinah" another victim of the reef, completely submerged, both ships a twin testimony to the reef's unaltered charms and the seafarers' well-founded fears".

"What do you think, Pete? do you want to dive the Medinah next week? have a look at those goat-eating sharks?"

"Ready when you are, Bob," Pete replied at once, displaying no fear of the sharks. It was a deal. The following Friday we would dive the Medinah. Another challenge, another chance to discover the weakness in opposing armour. But for now, we would sample the Red Sea, washing away the caked dust and sweat from our burning skin and bathing in those cool, saline waters.

Tennis shoes accompanied our swim trunks as we entered the crystal waters. The shoes would protect the soles of our feet against the small but razor-sharp coral and rock formations which abounded in the shallow water. Another reason existed for the footwear too, the dreaded Stone Fish. One bare foot, carelessly placed onto the upraised spines of this ugly little brute, could kill a man within twenty-four hours unless he received the antidote The warm salty water of the shallows refreshed us as it cleansed our hard-worked bodies. Ultraviolet radiated our skin unnoticed, magnified by the sea spray lens. Regrets were sighed at having to leave such a place but tomorrow was another day and the treadmill would not be denied.

"There's always next week," I consoled.

"I suppose so". groaned Pete.

The drive back to town seemed endless; it was only made pleasurable by the setting sun as she bleached the canvas landscape with her spilled orange hues. As the orb dipped below the horizon, we reached the edge of town, just in time for the call to evening prayer. All around shutters were pulled down over shop windows. Would be patrons were milling around outside the closed supermarkets and everywhere the Muslims were bending and kneeling, in humble worship to the one true God. The cry of "Allaaaaaaah owoo Akhbar!" echoing across the evening, "God is truly great!"

"What about dinner, Bob?"

"What have you got in mind?"

"Well, I know this little Hotel on the outskirts of town where the Stewies layover, we could eat there, and at least have a look at the beautiful girls walking around the place".

"Sounds ok to me, Pete".

"Ok, Bob you unload the bikes at the compound get cleaned up and pick me up at seven, see you later".

"Thanks for the help chum," I shot back sarcastically

"Sokay, you're welcome, see you later," Pete was gone.

"Maasalama" I offered the Arabic farewell before I headed home.

I showered and changed quickly, by seven o'clock I was already crunching across the gravel at Pete's compound. A touch of nostalgia flooded my soul as I pressed the doorbell to Pete's flat and the doorbell chirruped my arrival. It had been a long time since I had heard such a bird. Pete immediately bounced through the doorway - showered, refreshed and starving. The two of us boarded the Fury,

"Where to, sir?" I asked, imitating the perfect English chauffeur.

"Meridien Hotel, driver!" returned Pete, with a sickly aristocratic voice of doubtful breeding.

I was having trouble understanding this moment in time. It was as if the new Canadian Pete, were a re-incarnation of the old Scarborough Pete, the door chirrup and now the Meridien Hotel, only that it would be in Jeddah this time and not Dhahran, but when you had seen one Meridien, you had seen them all, especially out here. I began to remember that first night.

"What's wrong with your face, driver, why are you smirking?"

"Nothing sir, just happy that's all".

"Don't be so bloody stupid man, this is Saudi Arabia, a foreigner can be imprisoned for being happy, stop that smiling at once and get on with your driving".

"Yes Sir!" I snapped back mockingly and gunned the Fury in the direction of the Meridien Hotel.

The fountains, the marble and most things were just the same, an exact architectural replica of the Meridien in Dhahran. The red leather furniture wasn't looking too new these days, but that worn look added a certain homely comfort to the general appeal. Pete led to an alcove and flopped into a chair. By some strange quirk, this was my favourite alcove too. A waiter hovered with a menu,

"Good evening, Mr Bob the waiter welcomed us.

"Good evening, Alex. How are you this evening?"

Pete's mouth fell open, he had not expected this, and he had no idea I patronised the Meridien.

"The usual drinks, sir?"

"Yes please, Alex. That will be fine".

The waiter strode away leaving me studying the menu and Pete studying his guest.

"What did you order?" inquired Pete.

"Saudi champagne," I replied. "A mixture of apple juice and Perrier water in equal parts, the closest you will ever get to drinking sparkling wine in a Saudi Hotel. It usually arrives chilled in a large glass decanter with a choice of tropical fruits floating on the surface".

The decanter arrived as I had promised and we gulped a glass down before refilling and studying the menu.

"Pheeeeew! will you look at that honey?" whistled Pete in rapturous appreciation. A young Stewie had entered the lobby and was checking in for the night. She was obviously from some international flight by the look of her uniform and her confident "Been here, done it all before" mannerisms.

I rose from my seat,

"Where are you off to?" quizzed Pete with a mocking tone.

"Not too far, I'm gonna chat her up," I did not turn around, instead I headed straight for the young Stewie and my words had to flow over my shoulder to Pete.

"Forget it, Bob. You've got no chance". he advised me.

"You wanna bet?" I offered, turning to face Pete now with a losing look on my face.

"Loser pays for tonight's dinner," Pete grinned, I already looked like a loser as far as he was concerned. We shook hands on the deal and as our hands parted, I allowed my expression to change and the losing look was gone, a confident smile, followed by a laugh instantly replaced it. I continued back to the target and stood alongside the young girl as she signed the register. I casually picked up her overnight bag, like a well-rehearsed porter. The young girl turned, and instantaneous recognition flooded her expression,

"Bob!" she squealed with surprise.

"Hello, Ginny,"

"New Kid!" she snapped pointing her finger at my stomach.

"How did you know I was here? I was about to give you a call".

She tenderly placed a kiss on my cheek, Pete's eyes roamed the room for the police, he was more than likely certain, that at any moment the shit would hit the fan. What he saw instead probably bewildered him, the hotel staff present were smiling, some even looked the other way.

Pete now knew, only one question remained. I watched him take out his wallet and check his funds, something warned him, if I was as hungry as he was, it was going to be an expensive evening.

Virginia showered, dressed and quickly rejoined us. The three of us ate together, Virginia insisted on revealing to Pete, how she had met the new kid,

"My goodness how he had changed over the years. He was a real desert fox now; she continued her appraisal and wasn't Bob handsome with his tan, his lean rugged looks, his neatly trimmed moustache and his....................!

Pete boarded his taxi; I would need the car later, if I ever got out of bed that is. The taxi rattled to life in the warm sultry night. Pete recounted later that he had become more than a little envious of my secretive lifestyle.

"Shit!" he hissed, mostly to himself with a smile but I caught the last words of his exclamation, "Shit! I just spent a week's pay feeding that animal. Shit who the hell is this guy?"

I leaned backward against the door, after covertly following Virginia into her room. The door closed and locked with a reassuring click. Virginia immediately flung her arms around my neck, pulling my lips to her own in a fierce crushing embrace. I quickly responded to her attention, my own arms encircled her, squeezing the breath from her body. Virginia struggled free and gasped an urgent breath. Our relationship had been continually interrupted since onset, by frequent absence. Virginia circling the globe in aluminium tubes and myself unavailable at some unexpected site emergency. Those same interruptions now magnified a mutual urgent desire, exploding to life as a burning prickling fire within my blood. Virginia stepped away from me,

"I've missed you, New kid," her voice was soft, riddled with the passion of her words.

"Not many nights have gone by when I didn't think of you, Ginny"

"I have something for you, new kid," Virginia's tone lowered further, husky with desire, tinged with slight embarrassment. She unfastened her dress at the collar and quickly moved her arms around her back. As the zipper peeled open, she wiggled the

117

garment seductively down her body. First, she revealed her bra, followed by her trim waistline. Then the material avalanched over her buttocks and she allowed it to cascade down her long and slender, stocking-clad pillars of sheer ecstasy, where it pooled into sensuous ripples at her feet. I yearned for her perfection. Ginny, my personal living centrefold, now offering her heavenly body adorned with the skimpy black silk bra and the tiniest briefs I had ever seen.

"Didn't she know what she was doing to me?" I thought, "Of course she does," I answered my own thoughts as a wide smile spread across my lips.

I almost ripped my shirt from my body and eagerly danced from my pants, nearly falling over as one foot caught in a legging. Recovering from the tumble, I moved toward her. My excitement must have shown, again, we kissed, lightly at first but the static between our naked torsos fuelled the urgency as it crept upon us. I slid my arms around her, flicked the tiny, alloy fastener between finger and thumb, before gently sliding her bra down her arms. Ginny whispered passionately, as my hands slid down her waist and tenderly sneaked, into her tiny silken briefs. My hands guided her briefs down her long, shapely legs, down to her feet. My body - that same tortured body, that only hours before had been drained of strength by the desert, now swelled with the blood of rampant desire. All aches and pains were anaesthetised by the adrenalined lusty glow. She kneeled before me, tugging away the final obstructing garment sliding it down my legs and slipping it from around my ankles, lifting herself up my framework and raising her pouty lips to my own. The fire now raged beyond control. I scooped her into my arms and strode eagerly over to the bed, where I allowed our unified bodies to fall. Ginny's body was crushed deep into the quilting as my own body weight followed in her turbulence. Tongue tips darted quickly, probing the boundaries of oral extremities. I did not care about breath, and at this moment in time, I did not care about life, this was the moment that breath and life were one and the same. Her body shuddered as she tried to control her

118

eagerness. She tightened her limbs around my own, squeezing and holding tight but with no effect, the time span of our abstinence had been eight days too long, to allow her or myself any real control. Now she was mine and her body pulses resonated with unashamed delight. Her muffled cries of ecstasy were drowned into my neck. Moments later, her own frenzied struggle had fuelled my own desire. Now I lost all control, releasing the primal instincts that I sometimes feared to own and finally as the last remnants of her control surrendered, We incited breathy tributes of mutual satisfaction and desire. Hugging and twisting among the sheets, writhing and struggling till we could endure no more and finally collapsed into the tangle of the white linen bed covers. Slowly our senses returned. I was where I always wanted to be. The night was still young and besides, I thought to myself, I too had a present for Virginia and I knew she would receive it as freely as she had given hers. Now we communicated by small, spasmodic, muscular pulses from deep within. Ginny's schedule matched with my own would keep us apart for the weeks ahead but it could do nothing to inhibit our fiery union, over the following hours.

This was Saudi, this was dangerous, and this was illegal but how sweet were the fruits of forbidden desire?

The phone jangled in my ear abruptly jarring me from my studious concentration, I grabbed the receiver without looking,

"Hello, Bob here".

"Hey, Bob, it's me, Pete. Just calling to see if you're Ok for our dive tomorrow?"

"What! Oh Yeah! Jesus, is it Thursday already? I thought it was Wednesday; I'm still in the middle of the week. I've been so busy these last few days I haven't had time to crap".

"Yeah! I tried your office a few times but could never get a hold of you. I thought Virginia had laid you to rest?"

"Smart arse" I gruffed at the implication.

"Hey, come round to my place tonight for a dinner with uncle "SID" we'll plan tomorrow from there unless you're otherwise engaged of course?"

"No, I'm not, Pete. Ginny is out of town for a while so I'll drop by your place around eight, is that OK?"

"OK, eight is fine, Mr Busy body". Pete's sarcasm was warmly obviously feigned.

"Maasalama Ibn charmouta!"

"What's that supposed to mean?" Pete still struggled with his Arabic.

"I said bye you son of a bitch".

"Charming way to address your host!" Pete cut the line dead allowing me no chance of a smart retort.

Saudi time held few boundaries; Fridays sliced each month into four. Saturday and Sunday just became another working day and once accustomed to the routine, they were rarely missed. Fridays were the key to sanity; biking or the beach, preferably with female company, as far away from the humid gasoline smog of downtown Jeddah as was physically possible.

Pete unlocked the door without hesitation, he knew, that it could only be me constantly pressing the chirrup. I dashed by Pete into the living room and immediately switched on the television.

"What's wrong?" snapped Pete, startled by my urgency.

"Listen to the news," I replied.

The Saudi news had just begun, the reader announcing the departure of the British Ambassador to Saudi following the release, on British television of the documentary entitled "Death of a Princess'.

"It's all over the place, the Saudis have taken extreme offence and are pondering further measures aimed at the British Expatriates.

"What can they do to us?" snorted Pete unconcerned, forgetting he was a French Canadian and in no trouble at all

"Send us all packing for a start!" my tone was serious.

"No chance, Bob. The whole of Saudi would suffer, the Hospitals, the airports and everything under British supervision would disappear down the tubes. Just about every company in Jeddah would feel the impact. Shit! the refinery construction would halt for a start if you left, or so you're always telling me".

"Of course!" I agreed without conviction, "But these guys don't think about things like that, Pete. They won't accept any criticism, they cannot be seen to lose face, even if it means cutting off their own nose to spite that very same face".

We both sat glued to the screen, carefully listening to the possible actions that may have meant my sudden departure - King Khaled was considering further measures but nothing was immediately clear as was customary in Saudi. The Saudis never let anybody know anything unless they themselves were ready. The only obvious fact was that the Saudis were incensed about the whole episode. Nothing was final but under consideration was the deportation of all Brits. They were also considering cutting all ties with the UK, including arms deals, oil deals and everything associated with the United Kingdom, suddenly, I felt very: Jewish, was the only word that sprang to mind and it wasn't an easy feeling I switched off the TV. I did not want to watch the ancient cartoons, which was all the Saudi TV offered the expats at this time, excluding the news which was something else I wasn't keen on watching in view of the latest black storm brewing. All other programmes involved attempted brainwashing of the viewers into believing they were living in paradise-on-earth, here in Saudi.

"All because of a TV movie". Pete broke into my state of shock.

"Yeah!" I replied, "Are these guys paranoid or what?"

"It's all the bullshit they are being fed by the west; the Saudis are starting to believe it all. I was in an office the other day; Bob and a Saudi began lecturing me on the Muslim faith and how the Saudis were the closest race to God and everybody else was scum".

"Listen, Pete. Some of these boys come close to getting all the way up there with some of the stupid auto antics they pull out on the roads. For two pins I'd get out of my car and punch a few of them out. Arrogant little rich kids, with no manners or courtesy, sometimes they make me want to quit this place".

"I know exactly what you mean, Bob, exactly".

"Listen, Pete. I know a couple of nurses who are in prison, just because they held a small Sunday afternoon prayer meeting, in their own apartment with close personal friends".

"Jesus!" gawped Pete.

"Exactly! they're building mosques in our gardens back home and we're getting thrown in jail for possession of a bible. Something is definitely wrong here and personally, I don't think it is going to get any better".

"When do the girls get out?"

"Nobody seems to know, Pete. Like everything else out here they'll be made to suffer a while to repent their ghastly sins and maybe they'll be set free. One thing is for certain, the Embassies in this place won't lift a finger to help them, no matter which country is involved, they're too worried about oil embargoes and arms sales to worry about the rights of a few human beings".

"I hear you, Bob, loud and bloody clear!"

"What's for dinner?" I enquired; the political discussion had obviously ended.

"L'escargot, petit poisson and how do you English say, le pomme de terre cut in bits".

"Fish chips and snails?" I howled

"Yeah, Bob. We eat them all the time in Canada".

"Bloody French Canadians". I sighed, "No wonder you're all so short, your legs are receding and your backsides will soon be excreting slime, you are what you eat or so they say".

"OK wise guy, you can have the fish, chips and peas, I'll take the snails, and I knew you Brits wouldn't appreciate fine cuisine anyway".

"Alhamdullilah!" I thanked God.

I enjoyed the meal. Pete was a reasonable cook, or at least he hadn't burned the chips. I even managed to down a few snails but as I informed Pete immediately afterwards, rubbery food had never been my Forte. Especially when it crawled around on a pillow of slime before you ate it. The two of us settled down with a couple of "Sids" to merely relax. The hours slid by unnoticed, old tales of adventure helping us on our way. Midnight struck the clock and I excused myself and prepared to leave.

"Goodnight, Cinderella!" grinned Pete. "Thanks for the ball and don't bother to leave your slippers on the way out, I won't be looking for a filthy desert rat like you".

I replied with a silent, well-practised flash of my middle finger, a universal language, the courteous farewell clearly understood by Pete and all expats.

"I'll be here at nine in the morning, Pete. I'll drive, I've got something I want to show you".

"Nude pictures of Virginia I hope?" beamed Pete.

"Just be ready for action dummy," I hissed as we bid our censurable goodnights.

"Nice guy" I thought, "Pity about the snails".

"Hope he dives as well as he bikes, we could become a good team for some weekend action".

I arrived at my place, forgot to set the alarm and bottomed out into a deep slumber. I was eventually awoken by Pete swinging on the door chimes.

"What happened to nine o'clock?" growled Pete in mock anger; "Uncle Sid knocked you out cold did he?"

"Forgot to set the alarm," I replied through the foaming toothpaste and rapidly scrubbing toothbrush.

"Coffee?" hollered Pete from the kitchen.

I popped my head around the bathroom door and nodded, my mouth, now too full to voice acceptance. Pete poured two coffees and sat on the living room couch, by the time I'd finished with the bathroom,

"I won't bother to shower, hardly seems worthwhile if we're going to the bottom of the Red Sea in a few minutes".

"Jesus, Bob, you mean I have to sit beside you all the way to the beach with you stinking like that?"

I threw the soggy towel and knocked Pete's coffee over.

"OH! thanks for ruining my carpet, Pete".

"Sorry, Mr Hygiene". Pete apologised.

"Get another coffee, I'll add it to your cleaning bill".

Pete mopped up the mess and poured himself another coffee, just in time to leave it behind as we loaded Pete's gear into the Fury

"What have you got to show me?"

"Curiosity killed the cat!" I responded to Pete's inquisition.

"Yeah, but it manages to get all the pussy," grinned Pete.

"Wait and see, Mr pervert, just you wait and see".

I drove to North creek. Within forty minutes we were scrutinising the Friday windsurfers and European bathing beauties, we were just as bad as everyone, as the Fury ran along the coastal road, parallel to the beach. We were probably worse than the Saudis when we were amongst the females and always ready for a quick glance at some gorgeous young lady in a skimpy bikini. The creek was busy; my late arising had thrown us into the midst of the rush hour traffic of Friday's family excursions, usually between ten and eleven o'clock in the morning. Thursday afternoons were also popular but did not have the same congestion. The Europeans had to work Thursdays and so only the Saudis ventured to the creek during the late afternoon. Pete whistled his appreciation at the quayside yachts and motorboats, they obviously belonged to the wealthier Saudis and boy did the wealthier Saudis have some cash.

"Pheeew!" Pete exclaimed pointing his finger, "Just look at that beast"

Pete's attention had been grabbed by a slick, black, power boat, black, but for the red eye blazing from her bow that added a certain menacing appearance to her racy profile. Pete scanned her structure as we approached; when we were almost close enough, he read aloud the license number,

"CR-30-Shark! now that's what I call a boat!"

"Yes sir!" I agreed, "That's my girl".

"Whaaat!" hollered Pete in disbelief.

"Well, she's not strictly mine; I'm the only guy who takes care of her. She was originally brought here for the bosses but they seldom use her: too much heat old chap what? They're the dicks that chose the colour, Black, in the middle of the desert, Black, what a bunch of amateurs I must give her a run now and again to keep the engines in shape. Virginia loves this old crate, know what I mean?"

I parked the Fury alongside Shark's mooring jetty. Pete reserved doubts and expected me to turn away at any moment; obviously, he thought that this was just another of my pranks. Pete pulled his diving gear from the car with little enthusiasm, he remained unconvinced. I climbed aboard but Pete refused to follow me, hesitating at the foot of the boarding ladder. I noticed Pete's unease and stepped forward to the control panel. I stuffed the ignition key into the exposed console, turned once for power and inspected the fuel, oil and charging gauges. A second twist of the key ignited the mighty, marine engines housed below. The powerhouse, unused for a while, coughed once or twice before burbling to a sweet mellow symphony of rampant raw power.

"Permission!" squealed Pete, "Granted" I replied

Pete scrambled up the boarding ladder unable to contain his excitement. I loaded the diving gear as quickly as possible, itching to get underway on this almost sensual ocean craft. Shark's engines now throbbed with a tempered but contained force. I pulled off my T-shirt, blew the dust from my sunglasses with a sharp blast of spittle-free breath and took hold of the wheel,

"Cast off the lines, shipmate!" I commanded.

"Aye-Aye, Sir" replied Pete, his voice laced with excitement as he dashed to the bow and released the mooring line, which recoiled into the keeper. With the rear line disengaged, Shark

125

drifted from the jetty and was now free. Pete joined me on the pilot deck. I palmed the chrome throttle levers forward. Shark bucked underneath our feet and with a surge of power from below, she spewed spray from the stern, Pete recognised the signs immediately,

"Holy shit!" he cried, "Jet boat"

I allowed the boat to cruise forward from the jetty, swinging her out into the centre of the creek, holding the wheel with my knee as I adjusted my Sunglasses and palmed the throttles back.

"I knew it! we're taking her back now, aren't we?" sighed Pete.

Pulling into the side of the creek, I waved to the coast guard whilst passing courtesies in Arabic. The coast guard logged the registration and took our work permits, and then he waved us away without fuss. Friday was a busy day; he was in no mind to check everybody on the creek, especially the polite foreigners, who spoke the language, regularly tipped him and were well-known on the waterway. The boat, now released from official scrutiny, burbled forward once more. I checked the gauges: fuel-almost full, temperature- normal, battery- charging, oil pressure-normal, Pete; well and truly awe-struck.

"Are you ready, Pete?" I inquired,

"You bet!" replied Pete like a kid with a birthday present.

I stroked the chrome throttles forward in a single smooth action. The engines shrieked with a new unconstrained howl and Shark lifted her belly from the fluid grip of the creek, accelerating forward at a sudden, rapidly accelerating velocity. Shark skimmed down the creek and out of the inlet to the open sea, almost as if aware of her unrestrained freedom. Pete uttered a few choice words as he picked himself up from his backside. He had been purposely deposited on his arse on the deck by the incredible velocity of the acceleration and now he steadied himself in anticipation of further shocks, as shark roared down the coastline amidst rainbows of sun danced spray. I handed Pete the control wheel in apology for my dirty deed.

126

"This is absolutely fan-bleedin-tastic!" Pete was ecstatic and forgot his anger.

"Yeah! I remember my first trip, certainly grabs you by the balls, doesn't it?"

"You said it, Bob. You said it!"

The refinery rushed by to our left, I took a polite bow as we broadsided. The burn-offs rippling our vision with the wasted thermal heat. We exercised great caution at the mooring jetties, where huge supertankers were at berth, dwarfing the Shark to obscurity; despite the fact, we were only allowed around the perimeter barrage. The tankers were like newborns, suckling at mother earth's teats, feeding the West's insatiable desire for oil. I pointed at the container vessels queuing outside the port. Merchant seamen waved a greeting as the Shark flashed by their commercial Armada.

"Over there" I yelled, stabbing my finger in a new direction

Pete turned shark into a slow curve, following the direction of my arm. A small, grey cigar against the clear blue sky jutted above the rippling horizon. As Shark neared, Pete must have realised this was the goat boat. His thoughts were confirmed, when he noticed that the goat boat was rammed high onto the reef. I moved to his side and eased back the throttles until Shark assumed a more leisurely speed. Within a hundred meters of the goat boat, I killed the power, throwing shark into a slow, leisurely turn and halting our forward motion.

"Come on, Pete, let's have a look".

"Where?"

I was already disappearing below and Pete followed my lead. I removed an upraised part of the lower deck. Turning a crank set into the solid hull and watching expectantly as before our very eyes, a section of Shark's belly opened revealing a clear perspex screen, now void of the hull's protection, and beyond the screen, unfolding into view, the miracle depths of the Red Sea.

A large eroding vessel lay below us, derelict and silent as if still in mourning of her terrible fate. She lay on her side, the

127

corroding, metal skeleton of a long dead species. Myriads of fish swam around her, some performing acrobatics as if aware of silent observers. The great shadowy hull loomed toward us. We both studied the tragedy in silent mournful wonder. What of her past journeys? what of her passengers and crew? was she now haunted by their lost souls? I couldn't help but wonder.

"Are you ready?" My whisper was in harmony with the ghostly vision.

"Ready when you are," Pete returned the solemn intonation.

We wore T-shirts to prevent the tank straps chaffing our shoulders. Air pressures were checked and double-checked. Operational checks were conducted on all our equipment, especially the breathing regulators. In this game, we were both aware; you paid for mistakes with a high price, usually your life. Pete swilled anti-fog into his dive mask, offering the same to me. We each carried a sharp, stainless-steel knife, strapped to our legs. Compulsory depth gauges were secured to our wrists. Finally, clutching our facemasks with our flippers gripped in our free hand, we allowed ourselves to fall over the side. I immediately pulled on my flippers, as I surfaced amongst the frothing bubbles and grabbed Shark's anchor line that I had dropped over the side before the jump. I offered the OK signal that Pete returned and we opened the valves in our buoyancy vests. As the air hissed free, we slowly descended into the silent azure depths.

I pinched my nostrils between finger and thumb whilst expelling air into my nasal passageways, pressurising my inner ear, that the piercing, ear pain of descent to greater pressure would not strike. At a depth of fifteen meters, I tied off the anchor line to the bow rail of the sunken vessel. Assured of its security I thumbed the valve on my buoyancy vest until the wheeze of air swelled the pocket cavities. Slowly I began to rise. I opened the release valve sending a stream of pearl-like bubbles rushing to the surface. Two more, minute adjustments were made to the air pockets and my ascent ceased. Now I hung motionless in neutral buoyancy, the weightlessness of space right here on earth, a special sensation that never failed to amaze me.

Pete followed the example, now both of us hung motionless at a depth of ten meters. Ghostly silence reigned, but for the whirr and click of our regulators, delivering sweet pure air. I checked depth and pressure gauges, and then checked my watch, all working perfectly. At this depth we were allowed forty minutes down time, adjustable respectively as we increased or decreased our depth. These minute details were imperative, unless of course you were preparing to die.

We swam in proximity, gracefully gliding around our surroundings. Known as the buddy system in diving terms, this procedure ensured that in case of unexpected mishap, we could help each other within seconds of any unforeseen emergency. Now we drifted along the side of the ship, peering into portholes, nervously glancing across the fluid, particled space to each other, both of us must have been wondering what lay in store. Deadly silence but for the whirr and click of the regulators and the exhaled bubbles The occasional melancholy metallic moan as the ship rolled in the swell of her protracted nightmare. We approached the stern; two huge propellers loomed out of the particled greyness. I grasped Pete's arm and pointed ahead. Pete followed my stretched arm with his gaze, what he saw caused him to bite down on his regulator and suck in a heavy comforting breath. Ahead of us, cruised two large reef sharks, their white-tipped dorsal fins almost glowing in the gloom. Pete signalled his unwilling acknowledgement. We would have to keep a wary eye on those two creatures or become their dinner. The choice was ours. The slow-motion thrusting of our flippers propelled us slowly forward. Now we traced the handrail from the stern back to the bow. Curiosity finally winning over our initial fears. We turned from the handrail and headed to the captain's bridge. Above us and to one side, the sharks circled and harried the ascending columns of exhaust bubbles. The door to the bridge was propped open by a small shaft of wood. Pete eased his shoulders into the door space and pulled himself inside. He kicked with his flippers when his arms ran out of leverage; he forgot the awkward length of his flippers and his kick dislodged the timber prop holding open the door. The prop fell away and the heavy steel door began a slow yawn, back into its frame.

Within seconds, I grabbed the handle but to no avail, the weight of the door merely pulled me along as the massive steel clam groaned shut. I relinquished my hold and swam around the cabin side; the only other doorway was wedged tight against the coral reef and the windows were far too small for a man's shoulders with an airtank to pass through. I kicked back to the entombing door. Pete's worried face acknowledged my arrival. Signalling by hand, we agreed to combine our efforts. Pete would push from inside as I heaved against the outside. We assumed the position and by tapping a count of three with a knife; we heaved in unison against the metal lid. Twice, three times we tried but the lid remained tight. I noticed the unease now flooding into Pete's mask, I couldn't blame him, and it was him who was canned up like spam for the sharks, not me. I grasped the small wooden prop; we did not have too much time. On land this would have been a huge joke, me taking my time to clown around between unconcerned attempts to free Pete. Down here it was different, the increasing tempo of Pete's bubble columns now signalled the urgency. Together we strained and I used the wooden prop as a lever, success. The door began to rise, until the prop broke and the door returned to its seal. Our air would be used much faster under tense, industrious circumstances. We were both aware of this and tried to breathe with some normality. I cursed the door and checked my watch; already thirty minutes had elapsed. Our time was running low. I removed the tank from my back pushing it through the porthole in the door. The tight fit scraped yellow paint from the tank as it slid inside. I signalled to Pete, who unhooked my regulator and as the regulator came free, I headed for the surface in free ascent. The air in my lungs expanded as I rose. Staying behind my bubbles, I exhaled slowly as my lungs expanded with the reducing pressure on their contents, a necessary action to prevent them bursting. I broke the surface and immediately swam to shark with urgent purpose. Once on board, I dragged two tanks from the lower deck locker, only one was full. Cursing my luck, attached the regulator and grabbed the sand anchor from the stow rack. Gripping the anchor to my chest I leapt over the side and as the anchor dragged me downward, I noticed Pete's bubbles, a New Testament to his hurried, nervous breathing. That wasn't all; the sharks were now showing more than a keen interest in the proceedings. They had obviously sensed the vibrations of alarm and now they circled the cabin. Flicking their tails and widening the radius of their encirclement as I approached. I tried not to think about them, the Red Sea was full of food for them, why would they want to eat me? Pete was already sucking on the second tank of air as I peered into the porthole. I plunged the anchor tip between the door and jamb and on the tap of three, we heaved in unison, again the door eased open but the anchor did not have the leverage length to raise it more than six inches. Too small for Pete to escape and too dangerous to try lifting in case fingers were trapped and broken, an unthinkable reduction in manpower. I twisted the anchor in all positions but it was no use, then I remembered the wooden prop. As I leaned over to lift the prop, Pete's hand grabbed me by the shoulder pulling me back against the door, just in time to see the shark almost nuzzle against my chest. My heart somersaulted in my ribcage, I gulped on my air supply, almost choking on the regulator and the taste of oily silicone rubber, flavoured my immediate, sickening fear. Pete's eyes bulged from their sockets, almost luminous inside the perspex facemask. I pressed my back against the door as the shark, now gaining confidence, tried what I assumed would be another pass. My heart almost froze as the shark turned and pulsed forward at a terrific speed its snout thrown back and jaws wide open, revealing a ferocious flash of ripsaw arranged teeth. Instinctively I raised my arm to protect my face and I'm sorry to say, I was screaming as I did so, though I can't remember what words if anything coherent escaped my lips. The shark battered

into my body but here; at the bottom of the sea, I could not
outrun the perfect hunter killer species, even though I wanted to.
I heard the metallic thud as the anchor's eye smacked into the
cabin door with a tremendous force. The shark furiously
gyrating, slapping my body against the door. I felt no pain; I
knew for sure I was dead meat. Strange how my blood smoked
into the water around me, eerie that the massive lacerations had
caused me no pain. Dreamlike, the frenzied body of the shark
juddered against my flesh. I still gripped the knife I had
previously used for signalling but it was useless now. All I could
see, were the thick, smoky blood clouds, swirling around me,
shading my eyes from the horrible death I was suffering, a death
I had desire to see. Now I got mad, this fucking fish was not
going to get away with this, if I were to die, so was he. I began
stabbing the bastard for all I was worth, stabbing and stabbing at
its chest and underbelly, the only place where my knife would
penetrate. I was so mad I started to scream at the shark, yell into
my regulator at how I was going to slice it to pieces and rip its
fucking belly open. The force of the gyrations sent shock waves
into the cabin, stunning Pete to a previously unknown level of
fear. Blood blossomed everywhere around him; it flowed in
through the portholes obscuring his view. Pete did not wish to
see, he assumed he knew what terrible vision lay beyond the
door.

   All Pete had to do now was wait, until the air in his tank ran
out or the sharks found their way in and finished him off for
dessert. He told me later that he wanted to cry and scream and
shout in his impotence, all impossible underwater. Instead, he
forced himself to the porthole and peered outside. The sight he
said, brought tears to his eyes. He wriggled back in horror as a
bloody, lifeless corpse, floated down across the porthole. It
slowly dawned it was the shark, a huge beast with the anchor
wedged deep into its throat. The curved sand spade had forced
its mouth so wide; it had ripped open the corners revealing pink
torn flesh, from which the smaller fish were now tearing
mouthfuls. Pete stared in amazement, as the handle of my

diving knife came into view; the blade plunged deep into the shark's eyeball socket. A vapour trail of blood traced twitching body as it descended nose first, dragged downwards, by the weight of the anchor, passed the bridge gantry and onto the deck below. The soupy, water began to clear and within the blood cumulus, he saw me tying the anchor line from the handrail to the door handle. I turned, thrust my fist into the cabin grabbed Pete by the hand and signalled for him to hold onto the porthole, then I heaved up the anchor line to the surface. Pete's immense surge of gratitude fizzled quickly, "Jesus Christ" was his last gasping words, as the air tank emptied and ended his life support.

I broke the surface and turned to inspect the sunken Medinah, I could see that bubbles no longer issued from the cabin. Pete had run out of air. I leapt aboard the Shark almost falling over my flippers. Shark's mighty engines, still warm, fired up on the second attempt. I slammed the chrome throttles to full speed and Shark obeyed my command, surging forward, with huge spuming jets fanning her rear as the anchor line tightened and tried to restrain her. Shark bucked and strained at the line until she shot forward in sudden release. I reigned her in, spun her around to her earlier position and immediately jumped overboard. The line had broken; the door remained shut tight. I screamed into the regulator at the unfairness of it all. Flippering down to the cabin with wild thrashing anguish. I gripped the door handle and braced my legs against the cabin side. I took a deep breath and heaved, the muscles in my back screamed in protest yet I continued to strain, the blood was flooding my head and swelling into my brain. I heaved with a strength I was sure I did not own. My heart must have been pumping pure adrenaline. I felt the door tremble and it began to rise, slowly upwards, from the rotten, rubber seals. I felt the movement that encouraged me to strain even more, until, with one final, blood-vessel bursting effort, I screamed into the regulator and with a muscle-popping strain, I pushed the door open and rolled it onto its back. I stabbed my head inside but Pete was nowhere to be seen, it was as if he had vanished. I immediately searched around the bridgehead, before turning my head to the surface where I caught sight of Pete, now waving frantically from the stern of Shark. I ascended slowly; my body felt like a limp sack of burning muscles. Pete dragged me aboard and we collapsed into the pilot's deck. I spat out my regulator before delivering my gasping words.

"I thought you were a gonner!"

"I was a gonner, Bob, What the hell happened?"

I sucked in deep heavy breaths of pure sweet Saudi air before relating my tale.

"The shark came at me so fast. I just lifted my arm to protect my face. I thought I was a dead man. I didn't realise what had happened until I writhed away from the smothering, clouds of what I thought was my own blood and I saw the bastard for the first time. He'd forced himself onto the anchor; I knew I had to nail him quick, so I stabbed my knife repeatedly. I couldn't get the knife through his thick skin so; wallop I stuck it in his belly a few times before I smashed it straight into his eye. In his rage, he bit the anchor point through the top of his mouth; it stopped him dead in his tracks. I don't mind admitting, Pete. I pissed myself when I thought he had me. Jesus, I thought I was going to die. How did you get out?" I asked him as we lay on the deck, soaking up the sun.

"The line pulled the door open, I got out of there double quick, before, smack, the line broke and the door shut fast again. I didn't have any air so I couldn't wait to explain I did the only thing I could, I headed for the surface like a rocket, trouble is I think I swallowed a couple of gallons of the Red Sea. Anyway, why didn't you just open the door in the first place? it would have saved us a lot of trouble?"

"The hinges must have been bent, Pete. When the line heaved the door open, it straightened the hinge pins enough to allow me to open the door, Jesus I thought we were both fish food there, bloody hell, I can't believe we got away with it".

134

The two of us lay in the heat, soaking up the unusually welcome sunshine and gulping sweet breaths of fresh sea air, finally, I sat up, tested my regulator and headed for the side,

"Where are you going now?"

"I just remembered - that dirty bastard's still got my knife".

With a huge plume of spray, I was gone, I returned in moments with my knife and the sand anchor,

"Better get the tanks, Pete. Before the other sharks start forming a line to eat the one down there".

Pete pulled the tanks aboard using the anchor line that I had tied around them on my excursion for the knife. When all the gear was aboard the two of us relaxed, before stuffing sandwiches into our mouths and washing them down with ice cold, non-alcoholic beer. The conversation full of the previous events and the nervous relief flowing through our bones.

The sandwiches were quickly demolished

"Is your stomach settled Pete?"

"Yeah, I'm ok now why?"

I fired up the engines edging Shark in the direction of the "Jeddah" until she drew up alongside and nudged the metal sidewalls of the stricken ship. A mouldy rope ladder reached down into the sea, Pete heaved once or twice against the ladder. Certain of its fastness and strength, he hoisted himself upwards rung by rung carefully testing as he progressed. I reversed Shark clear of the ladder bottom.

"Where are you going?"

"I'm moving the boat, Pete. If you fall, I don't want you to hit her she may get damaged if you come down headfirst".

"Thanks for the vote of confidence".

"You're welcome, and by the way".

"What now?" moaned Pete.

"Stay away from any doors that may have been propped open".

Pete reached the top of the ladder and craned his head over the sides of the ship. His stomach heaved at the vision before him,

"Uuuuuuuuugh!" he cried with revulsion as he was greeted by thousands of teeth, bleached white by the sun, grinning in disconnected lower jawbones. Pete shivered at the pitiful sight. I knew what he was looking at; the rusty steel decking was littered with bones. The bleached white, half-skinned skeletons of goats, their decapitated skulls returned his stare through empty sockets of woe. Pete shivered at the thought of the suffering they must have endured and the lingering, protracted death of starvation and thirst.

"Well?" yelled I from below.

"I've only got one thing to say". Pete barely able to breathe lest the vile, evil before him should enter his body.

"What's that?"

"They booked the wrong cruise".

Pete's yell startled me and I looked up in time to catch sight of Pete as he cannon balled into the water, still grasping the rope ladder and disappearing into the sea, vanishing behind a curtain of foaming spray. I smirked, Pete would be OK, the water was at least three meters deep. I cruised alongside and hoisted Pete aboard.

"Shit!" spat Pete, noticing he had not completely escaped unscathed. As I hoisted him aboard, the blood ran down Pete's arm to his wrist, a small gash had been torn into his upper arm and now the blood pumped freely. It wasn't a serious wound but would require stitching. We wrapped a compression cloth, tightly around the wound before Shark began her rapid return to the creek.

Shark was quickly unloaded and we left her as we had found her. I gunned the fury back into town. Serious or not, in these climes, infections were difficult to contain and had a nasty habit of souring even the simplest of scratches. The wound was inspected at the King Abdel Aziz University Hospital, just off the Makkah expressway. Pete's arm was stitched by a Sudanese Doctor who insisted on more injections to quell any infections. The Doctor left the cubicle and a young Saudi Nurse entered with a syringe,

136

"Where Injection?" mimed Pete.

"Buttock!" She replied, pointing to Pete's backside.

Pete dropped his pants without a moment's hesitation and the nurse dashed away in a wild, giggling Panic.

"What are you doing?" the hurriedly returning doctor enquired.

"I thought she wanted to give me an injection in my bum, so I dropped my pants, that's the normal procedure, isn't it?"

"Not here!" announced the Doctor, "Saudi Nurses are not allowed to touch male patients, let alone inject them in the buttocks".

"What if I'm about to die?" Pete queried incredulously.

"You die!" replied the Doctor.

"Whaaaat!" cried Pete in disbelief.

"It is forbidden". grinned the Doctor finally deciding to join Pete's mirth. "Saudi Nurses are not allowed to touch any male body other than their husbands, so as far as nursing is concerned it's a tricky area which they haven't yet got to grips with".

"I don't believe it". chuckled Pete.

"Believe it," the Doctor fixed Pete with his eyes, "It's true!"

We both chuckled in disbelief as we left the Hospital still amazed at such an unbelievable revelation. Saudi Nurses were not allowed to touch male patients. The new knowledge became the topic of the journey home and the life and death struggle with the shark was forgotten in the light of such a futile and crazy law. Modesty before urgent treatment and as far as we were concerned it seemed like Saudi Nurses weren't allowed to be nurses at all, just glorified waitresses, no wonder they need so many foreign Nursing staff.

"It is forbidden!" we announced in unison, the mirth carrying us back to my apartment.

It was late; we had showered and enjoyed a barbecue of steaks, sausages, huge succulent shrimps, jacket potatoes and a side salad that must have wiped out a small market garden. All had been washed down with a healthy dose of Sid. As I walked Pete back to his car, he seemed pre-disposed,

"Bob, I owe you one," he began,

"Bugger off Pete, you would have done the same for me, forget it. it was just one of those things".

"No, I won't forget it, I'll never forget it, you don't know what it was like being trapped down there, and then seeing you risking life and limb to get me out".

"Suit yourself arsehole but you don't know what it's like seeing your mate in trouble, you would have done the same for me if not more". I was lost for any other words and tried to cover my embarrassment with a grin.

"Goodnight Bob'. Pete's words were almost a thank you, as he boarded his car. Pete drove away and as I remembered his words, the realisation dawned on me, what I had done during the day's dive. I was almost sick, when the events replayed in my mind, how close we had come to a total disaster.

The friendship between the two of us thrived. Pete listened with amazement when I revealed home and Saudi stories from my past. Although Pete must have known, I never really opened my heart about my feelings for Lotty and the family I had left behind. Pete had his own experiences to relate and a strikingly familiar pattern emerged, leading both of us to believe that we had been drawn to Saudi by the same strange lure. We engaged in a search for something that may not even exist, driven by a burning desire for knowledge of our shrinking planet. We wanted more than an ordinary life, probably as everybody else does and we were prepared to do something about it, regardless of the risks that such a quest would ultimately involve.

138

Chapter 7
THE TEMPERING

As the bond between the two of us grew, so flourished the city of Jeddah. This major Petropolis had once survived as an obscure Arabian fishing village, held together by the catch of the fishermen and traders who plied the waters of the Red Sea. When the Americans came to search for oil, almost a decade after Lawrence had routed the Ottoman Turks, the promise of wealth offered to King Saud by the Americans, proved to be an offer too good to refuse.

Who could have imagined during such an impoverished age that the Saudis would find themselves one of the richest and most commercially powerful nations in the world? They were sitting, quite comfortably above one-fourth of the world's known oil reserves. In 1981 the oil revenue flooding into Saudi's coffers peaked out in the region of one hundred and thirteen billion dollars per year. Saudi - as the world's strongest producer was pumping in the region of ten million barrels of light crude per day. A magical output. The revenues of which allowed them to spend close to six hundred billion dollars on the re-design of their cities, modernisation of their infrastructure and the commencement of major projects, which were quite simply, beyond the belief of the more basic inhabitants of the Saudi desert plains. More than one Bedouin had flown in panic across the desert on his camel. Scared out of his wits, as the new F-16 fighters of the Royal Saudi Air force, practised low-level manoeuvres over the empty wastelands and barren desert voids.

Thousands of foreigners flocked to the desert Kingdom, in search of salaries and standards of living, as much as six times their normal earning capacity back in their home country. Saudi became a melting pot of Nationalities. American oil field workers, British engineers, Canadians, French, West Germans and all manner of skilled technicians correlated within the bounteous market. Labourers flooded in from the poorer countries of the world, India, Pakistan, Thailand and the Philippines. They arrived on the promise of pay which at first seemed small but often exceeded six or seven times their earning capacity back home.

Jeddah flourished and blossomed into the ultra-modern, cosmopolitan commercial centre of Saudi. A city where at the time, Rolls Royce managed thirty percent of their Middle Eastern business and it was a very good business.

I remember when Jeddah International Markets opened in the early 80's, I needed some film for my camera and thought I'd be able to get special offers at the opening of this huge shopping centre. The Nikon store was on the second floor alongside the coffee house, outside of which a group of extremely well-dressed men loitered. As the wall of bodies parted, there right in front of me sat Mohammed Ali the Boxer. I ordered coffee and sat down at the table opposite, he looked straight at me and smiled

"Hey man how are you doing, you look like you're in the wrong country" he smiled and waved me over, I took my coffee. His huge hand swallowed my own and we exchanged courtesies. He asked what I was doing in Saudi, we discussed the country and its progress, I think my eyes were wide and my mouth was open from start to finish, I tried not to faint, grovel or cry in his presence but it was absolutely awesome. Not many Saudis knew who he was due to the lack of sports and world news on TV at the time but I knew who he was and I had just had coffee with one of the most famous sportsmen in world history. I had been to a meeting and wore a shirt and tie at the time, I think the Saudis thought I was part of his entourage and no one asked me to leave. I told him I had followed him since he beat Sonny Liston when I was just a child and kept reminding myself not to fawn, he thanked me, we smiled a lot until the owner of the shopping centre asked me who I was, I told him I was a big fan and congratulated him on his opening.

140

CHAPTER 7   SAUDI STYLE   THE TEMPERING

"He's OK" said Mohammed Ali, as if we were friends and the owner smiled, motioned for Mohammed to rise as they were leaving. He again shook my hand with his own massive appendages, was swallowed into the people of importance crowd and was just about to disappear before he turned and spoke,

"Take care Bob, enjoy your life, good luck"
Mohammed Ali spoke to me, I lifted my fists in a fighter pose and announced,

"You're the Greatest Mohammed and you always will be"
Suddenly he was gone, I sat down to finish my coffee and tears sprang to my eyes, it was just so emotional and so fulfilling, I just couldn't stop the tears, what the hell was wrong with me?

Saudi Nationals were well protected by their government. Social services, health programmes and interest-free housing loans were provided to the tune of one hundred thousand dollars per man, these were in the form of generous loans - loans that in most cases would never need to be repaid. Basic food items such as bread, cereals and milk, were all heavily subsidised and it would be difficult to imagine that any Saudi National could possibly ask for more.

The Saudi government certainly cared for its people. Originally the ruling authorities had iterated the desire to bequeath each male citizen, one million Saudi Riyals, at an exchange rate of five Riyals to one pound, which would mean two hundred thousand pounds per male head. The folly of this idea quickly came to light, not because of the lack of funds, but because of their plans for industrialisation. It would have served small purpose, to attempt to industrialise a nation of Riyal millionaires. But that did not remove any of the smaller packages of benefits. The Saudi Government even offered to pay the dowries, required by the parents of potential Saudi Brides, so that the young men could marry and hopefully, rapidly increase the relatively small Saudi population. Conditions were included, the men had to be of good religious and learned standing; a set of terms not too difficult to fulfil as far as the young Saudi males were concerned. The government took a pride in their country's development and was regularly hailed as achievers of miracles by the outside world, which needed oil. Nothing was ever mentioned about the foreigners who managed to transpose the Saudi government's wildest dreams into reality. Though one comment had to be made of the nation as a whole - The Saudis certainly looked after their own.

The newly constructed port became the heart of the city and every beat of that heart pulsed millions of tons of goods and equipment along its vast commercial arteries. Thousands of arc lamps turned the port darkness into twenty-four-hour daylight. A halo of light beamed into the desert night sky. A beacon of industry that could be seen far across the Red Sea. A halo, which guided many a captain to this Petropolis of wealth. Millions of petro-dollars had bought the most modern equipment available and combined it within months, with the experience that had been cultivated by the west over hundreds of years. The port was a model of success and any country in the world would have been proud to boast of the miraculous achievements carried out by the port of Jeddah. Regularly complimented on its performance and unmatched for its turn-around of shipping. The port became one of the proudest areas of development the Saudis could advertise. Regular trips were arranged for visiting dignitaries, in order that they could marvel at the wonder of the age. Every day, a small armada of vessels could be seen, anchored at the entrance to the port, awaiting permission to dock and disgorge their kaleidoscope of cargoes.

Although the port was a major achievement, it never managed to clear the backlog of vessels, continuously steaming into Jeddah's waters from all corners of the globe. Millions of cars flooded in from America, Japan, Germany and the world's great auto builders. Special terminals were designed and constructed for livestock, Sheep from Australia, Cattle from the great dairy herds of Denmark, Poultry from France. All manner

142

of livestock came to Jeddah and if the great Arc of Noah himself
had docked; he would have found little room for complaint.

This was Saudi; her only exports were oil and the Islamic
religion but the wealth, generated by the oil, allowed the Saudis
to purchase any commodity that money could buy. A scheme
had even been put forward to tow an iceberg from the Polar
Regions, in a bid to quench the desert dwellers' massive thirst.
The berg theory was never put into practice. Desalination plants
were coming online. Producing in the region of four hundred and
eighty-one million gallons of potable water per day. The iceberg
theory lost its charm but the cost factors involved were
irrelevant. It was merely a fact, that Saudi, through the process
of osmosis, had now begun to suck the Red Sea dry.

A new airport had been constructed to the north of the city. A
credit to the masters of its design. Although the airport was set
far to the north of the city, the indefatigable construction turned
in its direction and, brick by brick, the Petropolis of Jeddah
began crawling towards the giant, sprawling, multi-billion-dollar
terminals. The airport would not be the orphan in the north for
long. The pilgrim transit terminal, or "Haj tent" as it was known,
won dozens of awards before it had even been completed. Great
tented roofs of a special fibreglass composition were hung from
stainless, alloy wires, which were in turn suspended from
towering columns of steel. It would offer shade to the many
pilgrims on a spiritual journey to the holy cities of Makkah and
Medinah, as they paid homage to God and his Prophet
Mohammed. Under the fibreglass canopies, giant transit buses,
capable of carrying planeloads of passengers, were dwarfed by
the immensity of the structure, as it hovered in the sunlight,
hundreds of meters above them. The fibreglass had been
specially designed. It would shade the terminals from the sun's
midday ferocity and its special composition filtered the damaging
rays from the orb's intense light. The shaded area below was
pleasantly cooled by the natural airflow that had been created by
the design team. During the night, that very same airflow pulled

in the warmth that had been stored in the desert, producing a pleasantly warm temperature for the in-transit occupants in transit.

On first arrival, a visitor would be awe-struck by the immensity of the project. Considerable hours would be spent discussing the fantasy building with fellow passengers. Until after an hour or so, it would become a memory, along with the multi-million-dollar fortune it had cost to build. The main airport terminals for foreign airlines were huge monuments to Arabian architecture. Acres of the finest Italian marble and tons of stainless steel were cleaned and buffed to perfection by the hundreds of Filipino and Thai workers who had been imported specifically for such a purpose. Automatic doors connected to the finest air conditioning systems money could buy, were installed in the buildings to supply comfort to all creeds. An incoming jumbo, loaded with Eskimos in full winter clothing, could have easily been accommodated without the use of artificial winds. Those chaps could have built igloos in the chilliest climate this far south. Hailed as the airport of this century and beyond, the Saudis basked in this new accomplishment, though any well-travelled being would have spotted the deliberate mistake on his immediate arrival. A de-planed passenger was herded aboard a bus, which then took some fifteen minutes or more to travel from the plane to the terminal. Whilst the rest of the world were busy converting to walk on walk off jetways, the Saudis had settled for the bus trip mode of transfer, totally out of sync with the modern-day airports scattered around the shrinking globe. The marble and polished stainless-steel interiors exuded wealth and created a truly medicinal sight to a weary traveller's eyes.

The customs officers were not really a flaw, more of a nuisance as they were at any airport if they chose you for special treatment; they disembowelled your baggage and searched for alcohol, drugs or pornographic material. Including videos - which were quickly scanned on fast forward for incriminating evidence. Fanatical officials embarked on a frantic search for the forbidden

144

fruit. Magazines were confiscated, doubtful reading material shredded and any picture of a girl with naked legs or arms were classed as unhealthy for the Saudi Nationals. Anything remotely relating to any religion other than Islam, such as the Bible, Buddha and other artefacts were immediately destroyed without discussion and woe betides any protester. The extreme lengths to which these men voyaged on a discovery of filth had to be witnessed to be believed. After an efficient turnover of personal effects, a small cross, chalked on the baggage after inspection enabled the passenger to pass on his way. Despite the multi-billion Riyal investment in the airport, these upstanding citizens, could turn a well-scheduled flight into a major delay, depending upon their personal whims and fancies. The officials endured a thankless task, it did not come as a surprise to me, when I learned, that at the end of a gruelling day they enjoyed nothing better than to go home to a good old-fashioned shot of whisky and watch their personally purloined video of dubious rating.

All offers of unregistered taxi rides should be refused. Such rides have been known to provide the customer with night tours of the desert, interrupted by attempted rape and ravishing and if an enthusiastic driver got carried away, murder. Single ladies, Ignore such advice at your peril, anywhere in the world.

Between the airport and the seaport, run the many highways and byways that slash across the constantly shifting surface of Jeddah. The most interesting of these roads is the Cornice. Situated on the partly reclaimed shores of the Red Sea. This stretch of road provided Thursday night entertainment for thousands of Saudis, as they sat on the pavement, watching portable TVs and smoking their hubble-bubble water pipes. Sculptures and monuments costing millions, adorn this stretch of road, extending from the port to the airport. It is a wondrous place to behold if you can ignore the party leftovers continually strewn around by some uncaring patrons that often included the meatless carcass and offal of a recently slaughtered goat.

CHAPTER 7   SAUDI STYLE   THE TEMPERING

Halfway along the Corniche dwells the humongous, twin-towered desalination plant. Millions of gallons of potable water per day pour from this metalloid monster of tangled steel and pipework. The massive twin towers dominate the skyline for miles, providing an easy point of reference for the many commercial airline pilots, as they swing over from the coastline on their final glide path approach to the airport. The desalination plant is heavily protected and surrounded by carefully concealed batteries of anti-aircraft missiles. If the enemy knocked out this fountain of life, the only available drinking water in Jeddah would be the bottled variety. Washing clothes and taking showers would be a luxury of the past, until such time came when the plant was repaired or the once famous water bowser trucks could be hurriedly returned to service. Destruction by design or accident would constitute a disaster that would be sampled by every member of the community regardless of religion, creed or financial standing.

The Cornice extended for approximately thirty-five kilometres. Apart from the desalt plant, the only other visible signs of industry were the various amusement parks for females and children only and of course the Hotels, not least the Albilad, famous for its sporting facilities, Thursday night barbecues and non-interference from its staff into the marital status of the regular visiting couples.

The early days of the boom had seen a shortage of quality hotels. This situation had rapidly been brought under control. Members of the greatest hotel chains in the world now competed eagerly for the patronage of visiting businessmen and dignitaries alike. As the Intercontinental neared completion, a new King graced the Saudi throne - King Fahad. King Khaled the previous ruler, who had succeeded the assassinated Faisal had died suddenly of natural causes and was buried in Makkah and mourned by thousands of hysterical, weeping Nationals. It was the basic Muslim ceremony without elaborate ritual - they chucked his shroud-clad body into a hole and filled it with rocks and sand. Goodbye Khaled, Hello King Fahad. Fahad - the new

King inhabited a small, man-made iIsland, one kilometre or so from mainland Saudi. Unfortunately, the Intercontinental had grown to a great height and now overshadowed his Island retreat. Fahad immediately bought the Intercontinental and converted it into his own personal guest palace. It stands to this day, fully staffed and ready for the occasional visits by Presidents and Royalty. It was here that Prince Charles and the late Princess Diana would stay on their whirlwind tour of the Middle East in November 1986. I was there, I said hello to Diana and hoped they were enjoying Jeddah, she thanked me and asked if I was enjoying my stay, she wasn't aware of my situation and was just lovely, God bless her.

During that same month occurred the opening of the Saudi-Bahraini causeway. A twenty-five-kilometre link bridge between the tiny island of Bahrain and the massive deserts of Saudi Arabia. Costing a mere one hundred thousand million Riyals, (twenty thousand million pounds) it had been constructed, so that the Saudis and everyone with an Exit Re-Entry visa, could drive over to Bahrain to play around and have a few bears. That; is one expensive way to travel to nightclubs. So, the causeway and the Intercontinental stand as monuments to the power of petro-dollars. The King enjoys his private island retreat and the causeway is now officially known - in Saudi at least, as the King Fahad Causeway. Before the causeway, I crossed the Gulf on Dhows, the Arabian single-sail ship, very cultural, very interesting and with very diverse passengers a great melting pot of conversation and smiles.

Other hotels not sought after by the King were experiencing a sudden downward trend in business, a downward trend that was soon to be felt throughout the commercial establishments of the Kingdom of Saudi Arabia.

During the seventies, OPEC had ridden along on the crest of European misery. A misery that had been forced on the western world, by the continued and unabated rise in the price of crude oil. Incredible amounts of capital changed hands, most of it on a one-way journey to the Middle East. Many nations did not relish the thought of continual subordination to the whims of OPEC and alternative sources of supply were earnestly being sought. Energy conservation began to take its toll. Saudi realised what was happening and warned the cartel of future problems. The cartel did not heed her call, continuing instead to increase prices. Eventually, exploration of the world's oceans for oil became a workable alternative to the forty-dollar barrels of oil that were now on the spot market. Floating on an ocean of petrodollars the cartel refused to heed the call by Saudi to moderate and for the moment, the price of oil continued to rise, despite the best efforts of Saudi to moderate.

Britain and Norway began to suck oil from the bed of the North Sea. Originally, such a practice had been considered too expensive for established oil markets. North Sea oil had become comparably profitable with the prices now being squeezed from customers by OPEC. Then Mexico announced a massive oil field deep beneath her strata. Other nations joined in the search and as the plentiful flow increased the price of crude oil was forced downward by the market glut. By the eighties, oil shortages no longer posed a threat to the economies of the West and although still in big demand, sources of oil were plentiful. The rot had set in; price-cutting procedures were prising open the oil market and as the thin end of the wedge slid home, unwelcome cutbacks in production started. The Saudi Arabian oil minister - Yamani, continued the call for moderation and still, his words were ignored and, inevitably the cartel began the unpreventable slide to over-production and near financial ruin.

The major cartel members had invested heavily in the development of their country's resources and labour. Billions had been poured into their armed forces. Air and naval bases had been constructed, at great expense to their host nations. Most were immensely oversized, in proportion to the country they were supposed to defend. Payments for the upkeep and maintenance of such services had to be kept and all were connected to the fortunes of oil revenues. Some cartel members would go to any lengths to ensure their balance of payments was covered but they could see the problems now looming before them. The rot quickly developed and from the euphoric monetary highs, once reached by the Cartel it was a long and bumpy descent down the pyramid. Saudi, despite her willingness to moderate, now found herself in a similar position, though through no fault of her own. At that time, the Iran-Iraq war continued as the late Ayatollah pushed his people forward in a suicidal effort to crush the Iraqi regime of Saddam Hussein. Iraq was secretly supported by members of the cartel, not least Kuwait, which, considering recent events, gives some idea of the loyalties in the region. The war continued to devour a huge feast of men and machinery. The support had been promised and was easily budgeted during the boom years. Now it had to be continued, to prevent a major loss of face and more concernedly to prevent the Iranian revolution from swallowing up any other countries, in particular, Kuwait which, seemed constantly under threat due to its small size and accessibility. To lose face on such a scale was to lose all, which is one of the reasons the war raged on; neither side was prepared to lose that all-important face. And so, the war continued, sucking in the wealth of the surrounding but supportive nations.

The previous exchange of wealth slowed dramatically as the West began to rebuild its economies. Now it was the turn of OPEC to feel the pinch of commercial constraints and the folly of their earlier intransigence came home to roost. The early months of eighty-five were a disaster, with agreement after agreement being broken by various members of the cartel. All manner of weird and wonderful oil deals were on offer to entice and attract the wary western conglomerates. The price of oil continued to plummet. So rapidly did the price fall, that deals were arranged on a netback system, you paid the price of oil at delivery not on order, as the oil could have fallen in price by a few dollars a barrel by the time the tankers had reached their destination. Accusing fingers were pointed during meetings, blind eyes were turned and for a while, chaos ruled where the once mighty cartel reigned supreme. Something would have to give way and as most economists feared; it was only a matter of time.

On the surface, Jeddah still prospered, and everything moved according to the Government's present five-year plan. Slowly the cutbacks infiltrated the scheme of things. Projects were delayed and spread over a greater period. Contractors had to wait for delayed payments. Major projects were shelved. Hospitals, Airports, roads and major construction were abeyanced or cancelled until further notice. The cutbacks were hard on businesses and more than a few companies went to the wall. Some disappeared overnight, their management and staff fleeing the country in one mass exodus, rather than get involved with the Saudi Law Courts which tended to favour the Saudi sponsor every time. In Saudi, every business had to have a Saudi Sponsor, which usually meant a sleeping partner. The Saudis took a cut of the profit and the company took the rest. If there was any problem, the Saudi took his leave and the company took the blame. These problems were handed down the line and eventually reached the company pawns. The workers who built the country but never received acclaim now reaped their own bitter harvest. When their usefulness was considered too expensive, contracts were re-written without negotiation. Salaries were slashed and benefits denied. A few chose to stand up for their rights and when the threats and abuse began, a new breed of foreigner was born. Somewhere amongst this breed were the Khowajas. Decades and the desert had not broken but merely tempered their spirit, they were proven, survivors. An old Arabic proverb suggests, "Treat the desert dwellers with respect, one day you may need a drink'. It seemed that under the present circumstances the proverb could be forgotten as a matter of convenience and in the drought of respect that followed, the Khowajas would endure their ultimate test.

Chapter 8

REVELATIONS

The swollen orb of liquid fire fell steadily, descending into the desert haze that rippled above the horizon to disfigure its creator. The sandscape constantly changed colour, from the white fire brilliance of midday to the softer, amber hues of evening's dusky glow. An eerie light now tinted the plains and not least, the sprawling majestic dunes that stood back from the sea, towering as if straining to keep the desert's creator in sight, lest it fail to reappear, dawn-bringer at their backs. The natural monolith centurion of tempered granite was the lone guardsman, who had prevented the dunes from their windborne march inland. The last fingers of daylight released their grip on the heavens and retreated from the advancing shroud as if drawn to the horizon by the weight of the descending orb. The horizon glowed like bright embers, with occasional flames of luminous gold and red, scorching the sandscape with the last remnants of perpetual fire. Now the land smouldered as it reflected the burning sky, blanketing the earth with a deep, warm orange, scarred only, by the approaching shadows of the swollen dunes. As dusk slowly cloaked us, the dunes took on a different guise, the dark side unearthly, with little or no perspective, where unknown creatures could lurk with intent. A razor-sharp line split the dunes in half, the contrast emphasised at the peaks, where the golden sands tripped and fell, into the darkness of the shadowy void. When the sun vanished completely, so the wailing would begin, signalling the Muslims of Saudi Arabia to present themselves to God in prayer. As the orb's tip dissolved into the haze, an absolute silence reigned. A deathly silence, almost as if the evening were mourning the demise of the day.

A savage screaming howl scythed the tranquil air as two desert bikes previously swallowed by a deep trough crested the massive dune. The bikes soared into the blood-red sky before gravity took hold and threw them back down the dune into the burning sand. The shrieking cackle of two-stroke engines reverberated between the dunes, peeling back the silence as if challenging it to intervene. We lunged into a sliding power turn, the rear wheels flaying the desert, clawing and biting for purchase. A sudden grip flung us forward to gouge two scarring lines, up the wind-packed sand of the mountainous wall. Our progress was traced by twin ribbons of blue, two-stroke mist, spitting furiously from tiny exhaust ports, I did not turn to see him, I knew he would be there but I had no time to turn my head. The two of us crested the dune, reigned the bikes in and cut the engines, the silence victorious once more.

"Listen!" I whispered, my voice barely a breath.

With helmets removed we adjusted our auditory senses from blocking the previous cackle of the bikes and attuned them to the pervading silence. From a distant place, echoed a slight but melodious wail, wafting toward us on the warm breeze, caressing the silence and moulding the night into a new mode of tranquillity.

"Allaaaaaaah Akbar'

God is Great, he truly is

"Prayer time". whispered Pete, unwilling to disturb the lullaby of dusk.

A covering of loose sand and dust was glued to our bodies by the perspiration of maximum endurance. Garments once clean and fresh, were now soggy and biscuit-like in appearance.

"They're playing our tune". I grinned.

"Yeah, ours and the millions of Muslims who inhabit this unforgiving landscape".

Sweat coursed down my temples, mixing with the sand already encrusted on an unshaven jaw. I blew through pursed lips, shaking my head in wild gyrations, which threw a plume of sand and dust into the air.

"Is that coming from inside or outside your head?" questioned Pete.

CHAPTER 8   SAUDI STYLE   REVELATIONS

"Why do you always ask me the same old question?" I spat my response,

"Every time I take my helmet off it's the same old routine, is your needle stuck in a groove or what?"

Pete shook his head in the same manner and his accumulated dirt spattered all over me,

"There!" he announced, "Looks like we're even".

By now we knew exactly what was meant by the terminology of the word even.

During the last five years, we had endured a fierce personal rivalry on the battlefield of bruising sports. Neither had mastered the other, yet we existed almost as brothers, totally at ease with each other's company. Many men had entered our friendship but few had stayed the course, discovering the intense pace of the rivalry too difficult to contain. Our relationship was based on mutual respect and the knowledge, that when involved together in some physically testing sport, neither would yield any advantage, no matter what such a sacrifice entailed, including severe pain.

We had been burned bronze by dwelling for many years in the land of no winters. All excess fat had been burned from our bones. Two similar bodies toughened by the brutalising effort required piloting a motocross bike across the desert at unrestricted velocity. A method of transport slowed only by fear. In short, we had achieved a fitness rarely found in men outside of uniform. When I reflect on these times, I cannot remember a day when I felt fitter.

The final strains of prayer call retreated from our ears and above us now, a new invasion, as the great bulk of a jumbo jet, grumbled overhead on its way to the airport. As it flew over our crest it opened its metal belly to reveal black rubber wheels, slowly unfolding outward and locking into place with a slight hydraulic squeal. Essential preparation for the tire-squealing conclusion of that gentle fall to earth.

"Must be a good pilot". I announced with sarcasm.

"How do you know?" Pete asked.

CHAPTER 8   SAUDI STYLE   REVELATIONS

"He remembered to get the wheels down before landing".

I still harboured a deeply rooted pain regarding Saudi Pilots and Saudia Airlines in general, and my thoughts returned to the source of the heartache.

It was rumoured that many corners had been cut, to get the Saudi pilots into the air. In most other countries, years of experience had to be logged as a senior member of the flight crew before moving on to co-pilot. Finally, after the stiffest medical inspection in the world, impeccable qualifications and extensive flight experience at all levels, a co-pilot, of many years, may just manage the jump to captain and was able to take command of the massive Jumbos that now crowded the skies. Not so with Saudi - they were out to prove they were immediately as good, if not better than the world's best. Saudia did everything possible to get her pilots into the air in the shortest possible time span. So much so, that in many countries of the world, Saudi pilots were not allowed to land the massive passenger planes at non-Saudi airports. They had to be accompanied by qualified national pilots of the countries being visited. Rumours of accidents and near disasters were rife. Rumours that could not be confirmed but still put the fear of God into the Europeans, who had to fly on the national airline between the desert Kingdom's major cities.

Only one disaster had so far been recorded; three hundred people had perished. A Tri-Star flight 163 had taken off from the capital city of Riyadh to continue its journey from Karachi to Jeddah. A fire had developed on board but the plane managed to return to Riyadh, perform an emergency landing and taxi down the runway. A near perfect landing, yet something had gone horribly wrong, the doors wouldn't open and a planeload of passengers, unable to evacuate had been incinerated.

As usual, rumours flooded the country; it proved difficult to lay the blame. Saudi had been numbed along with the aviation world. The accident started a re-design of the Tri-Star's doors, which probably exonerated the pilot who had come into many controversies. The tragedy haunted for months. The whole of

CHAPTER 8   SAUDI STYLE   REVELATIONS

Saudi mourned until finally the disaster was laid to rest as God's will. The nagging doubt remained and it was doubtful the actual results of the enquiry would ever be made public.

I had been sickened by the tragedy but like most foreigners I pushed the incident to the back of my mind, dwelling upon such incidents had driven men insane and in Saudi, the possibility was heightened, by the lack of an outlet for such painful emotions. There was nothing else that could be done, such was life. It was some weeks later when my grief was rekindled and burned away at my very soul. A letter had arrived at my desk, a simple, sterile white envelope addressed to myself, in Jeddah, Saudi Arabia. Inside the envelope a simple but devastating note,

> Robert,
>
> It is with deep regret that I must inform you of Virginia's passing aboard the ill-fated Tri-Star in the Riyadh disaster. We found your address amongst her recently returned personal effects and felt the need to contact you personally. Her funeral took place...................

Silent tears coursed down my cheeks; I continually wiped them away to decipher the parental grief in the unwanted note. In all my life to date, I had never felt such pain. Such stomach-turning, hopeless, helpless grief. I raged at the unfairness of the selection and unconstrained, smashed my fists into the blameless, concrete wall that surrounded me, searching for the physical pain of relief from the unbearable mental torture that now boiled up from within.

I took emergency compassionate leave. Three days later placing a wreath at her graveside, one arm enclosed in a sheaf of sterilised, white plaster, the other clutching the flowers for my tragically terminated love. I spent the weekend with her parents reliving the past through old snapshots I had collated in her memory. The trips aboard Shark, underwater shots of Ginny, diving in the Red Sea and the countless party pictures of dancing and happiness. Now Ginny was gone and the loneliness returned, with a vengeance that ravaged my heart once more.

I shrugged away the distant memory and like the Jumbo above, it disappeared into the night. Our relationship thrived on the absence caused by our respective employment. This absence had almost anaesthetised me during the following months, providing me with an easy belief that I would see Ginny very soon. Any day now she would phone the office and we would cement the bond once more. I felt the pain once more, Ginny had never phoned and deep within my soul, I knew that just like Lotty, I would never see her again. I remembered our first date and the shower incident, "Life's too short Virginia. Life's just too bloody short!"

I signalled to Pete and we donned our helmets, the bikes were hoisted from the soft, sucking grip of the sand. A sudden flash of headlights danced across the plain below us. Hawkeye, our new companion, was waiting. He knew we would be searching for the truck in the fading light and had decided to signal his position. The headlights of the truck would slice a reference point in the rapidly darkening landscape.

Hawkeye had begun the day riding with the two of us but like the others before him, he had been unable to match the indefatigable pace, spurned by our intense rivalry. Falling behind, he had toured the desert at his own speed, knowing, that we would have to return to the truck eventually, indeed our lives depended on it. Once more he signalled his position to the two, what to him would be, tiny shadows atop the darkening mass of the dune. A wild cackle tickled the silence, and probably caused a smile to spread across Hawkeye's straining features.

"We're coming Hawkeye," I grinned to myself, "lookout Hawkeye; here we come".

Atop the dune, visors were pulled into place as a final check-over was completed. The two of us straddled our machines side by side. Then a slight nod of acceptance pre-empted a shrieking charge down the dune. Descending rapidly, we disappeared into

156

the darkness, where the afterglow no longer caressed the massive pile of sand. It was more difficult to drive now, everywhere there were shadows and it was difficult to tell where the dark ruts started and the shadows ended. We drove at full speed and as usual, probably trusting a little too much to chance.

It must have been obvious to Hawkeye, that contest still raged. Hawkeye always questioned where we found such stamina and what earthly phenomenon had created such a fierce rivalry between us. Hawkeye clambered aboard the truck, it was almost dark and he had no wish to be standing in the path of our incoming two-wheeled missiles, which were now homing in on his headlight signal at approximately seventy miles per hour. The two-stroke cackle smothered every other sound as our bikes thundered past the truck, over-running the vehicle by some fifty meters or more, to skid sideways and disappear, braking into an avalanche of swirling sand and dust, before returning to the vehicle at an almost leisurely pace. We lined up the machines at the rear of the truck, a silent nod sent Pete up the plank ramp and into the back of the pickup. Pete had barely dismounted his machine before I bullied alongside, laughing aloud as I almost knocked him over the side. The three bikes were firmly roped down in the pickup. Only then was the body armour removed and the slowing of the adrenaline pump allowed brief but coherent conversation. Our dusty dishevelled features grinned in the gloom,

"Well?" I quizzed Hawkeye; "Did I beat him or what?"

"No chance! I was miles ahead!" spat Pete.

"Dead heat". announced Hawkeye, knowing the consequence of entering the endless argument.

Mumbles of ridicule and laughter were all that remained as the three of us boarded the pickup. Hawkeye drove, me and Pete guzzled litres of cool water, almost choking on the liquid torrent as it coursed down parched throats and shirt fronts. Only then, as the excitement of the day's events receded, did the verbal chatter slow. Hawkeye scrambled the small truck up the

157

side of the verge and onto the empty main road. Minutes later we accelerated to cruising speed and headed in the direction of the silver bronze halo heralding the city of Jeddah, the Bride of the Red Sea. No longer the humble fishing village of years gone by. Even Hawkeye had seen the latter part of the growth which, even in his short expatriate years, had been nothing short of phenomenal.

Hawkeye was a slightly different species to the two men now guzzling water by his side. He was considerably older and whereas we were charging full steam ahead into a lifestyle that had been sculpted by our own hands, Hawkeye had run from a previous lifestyle sadly removed from his control. He had entered Saudi almost four years previous, the new guy, willing to work hard and determined to scrape together a new life for his wife and two cherished daughters back home. A family nothing short of his pride and joy. The photographs regularly made the rounds on meeting new acquaintances. He was employed in the transport department of the refinery, managing the day-to-day schedules and journeys of the various tankers, which could be seen all over the city. Delivering cheap petrol, diesel and oil, to a multitude of end-users. Days before his first R & R he was busy shopping for the family back home; he carried a pile of presents that would themselves require a truck for delivery. Gold, jewellery, Saudi souvenirs, radios and cameras, typical purchases for that first trip home. Pete and I carried his excess baggage to the airport and waved bon voyage to this standard measure of solid family life. Wide grins and well-pumped handshakes delivered him to the departure lounge. I experienced a more than slight envy at the thought of the welcome, awaiting Hawkeye at the other end of this journey.

Hawkeye had burned his skin sore, grown a moustache and tried because of his age, to be the father figure to Pete and myself. Hawkeye finally surrendered to the fact, that it was us who were fostering him and at the same time realising, it wasn't a father figure we needed, it was a Gunnery Sergeant Major.

CHAPTER 8   SAUDI STYLE   REVELATIONS

I collected Hawkeye at the airport some weeks later his return. Hawkeye carried a worried expression on his lean and sickly, unshaven face. My first words said it all,

"Jesus! Hawkeye. What the fuck happened to you?"

Hawkeye hardly spoke; he finally broke down when we arrived back at the apartment exposing a heart-breaking situation. The very first week after Hawkeye's departure, his wife had installed her boyfriend in his place. By the time Hawkeye arrived back home, he was met by his wife, who informed him of her action and that his presence was no longer required. The children had given up on him as a father and he could only arrange to see them at weekends. He could collect his personal belongings from the garage and deposit them at his mother's house, where his wife had no doubts; it was better for him to stay. Hawkeye had been too stunned to react; he had done nothing to deserve such crap.

I couldn't believe it,

"So! what did you do?" I asked him impatiently.

"I wanted to kill the other guy. I wanted to kill her. I wanted to steal the kids. I don't know, Bob. I don't even know why I came back; I may as well hand in my resignation, go back home and try to sort out the whole mess, divorce, custody, house, everything".

I had seen it all before, Saudi had wrecked more marriages than the proverbial other woman. Most men went home to divorce or separation, or they found themselves a nurse or Stewie that they assumed they couldn't possibly live without. It was a factor of the territory, the loneliness, the laws and the lack of entertainment. They were the victims of a world where most major forms of entertainment were forbidden. I did not consider myself old enough or qualified to give advice. Hawkeye was an employee of Ocoma, somewhat under Pete's jurisdiction and we had no desire to sit back and watch a good friend go under.

"I've seen this thing many times before, mate" I began,

"I don't feel you should be listening to me; I can only tell you what's happened in the past. Some guys charged back home, resigned their position out here and tried to patch things up. It rarely worked, too much water under the bridge and all that, from what I've seen before there's only one way out".

"What's that?" Hawkeye was at least listening.

"Here's where you earn your money, Hawkeye. Right?"

"Yeah" Hawkeye responded without heart.

"So, if you go running back, you'll lose your family AND your livelihood. You'll lose your money and probably any respect you have left in the eyes of that woman, if you go crawling on hands and knees, you'll only prove to be the assumed loser she left, right?"

"Yeah, I can see that," agreed Hawkeye.

"So, for a start, I'd make my nest here, continue earning and saving the big lumps of cash. With all the taxes back home, that guy can't possibly be earning anywhere near the sums of money you're stashing away unless he's the Chairman of Barclay's Bank. He isn't the Chairman of Barclay's Bank is he, Hawkeye?"

Hawkeye looked up and I thought he almost smiled.

"So now you're single you can go to all the parties with the lads. You can travel to some of the loveliest places in the world and I'm not talking about sightseeing and doing all those things you used to dream of but didn't want to spoil your marriage. Well, Hawkeye, she's had her turn now it's yours. When that guy realises how much it costs to keep a family of four, he's going to forget about his little bit of excitement every night. Shit! in twelve months" time he'll be wondering what the hell he's done and there's sure to be problems. Meantime you'll be seen around your hometown, bronze, handsome, loaded and available. Your missus is going to be so sick she'll be threatening you with every lawyer in town for more money".

The thought almost cheered Hawkeye.

"So, Hawkeye, bugger it man, make the best of an unpleasant situation and don't go thinking you can change it, because from where I'm standing it looks a hopeless case. Sorry mate but that's just my opinion. It's easy for me to talk but the only alternative is you going home and OCOMA through no fault

of their own, refusing your application to return in six weeks"
time. Believe me, I've seen it so many times before, and all the
sob story letters in the world won't get you back out here if you
renege on your contract".

I really didn't know what else to say, I was always asked for
an opinion on these matters but I had no real idea of what to tell
these guys. I just spouted the first reasonable arguments that
came into my head. Most took notice, most ended up OK but
some finished up in a right old state, no chance of a
reconciliation and no chance of returning to Saudi. What a mess
and I was the poor sucker that had to read their begging letters
to come back or assist them in finding a new job, which was
almost impossible. It took a while for Hawkeye to come to terms
with the facts, at first, he said he would think about it. I kept him
busy, so he wouldn't have too much time to think and eventually
the urge to go home must have faded. We worked hard to keep
him in one piece and Hawkeye's smile had returned as his
vacation drew near. As Hawkeye boarded the plane for the Far
East, we were sure he was going to be OK. But were we
mistaken? Hawkeye never arrived at the airport on his stated
return date. Two weeks after his due return date, Hawkeye
finally arrived at the apartment in the early hours of the morning.
A beaming grin on his face and a million words per minute
spilling from his mouth. He had fallen in love with a dozen
beautiful acquaintances. Now he was rebuilding his life. He was
going to open a hotel in Spain, install a wife of Asiatic beauty
and live happily ever after on a sea of romance and dreams. His
only worry now was - which girl to marry.

It had been done before; many foreigners chose to live
abroad after trying and failing to settle down in England or their
home countries. Hawkeye was a changed man, grins and
smiles, winks and nods. He had taken and developed
photographs that would have had him sentenced to fifty years
plus life had he been caught smuggling them into the country.
Yes, Hawkeye was a changed man all right, right down to the
small, white penicillin tablets he had been prescribed on his

return, to rid his body of a gift given freely, during one of his nights with Venus.

Pete now worked for Sharief. I had switched companies and informed Pete of a vacancy in the construction department. Pete was not an engineer but then neither was anybody else who worked there. Pete's speciality was paint, metal coatings and finishings. He breezed into the opening as if he had worked there all his life, never once suspecting - though secretly hoping, for a helping hand from me. I had been offered the position by the Shariefs since OCOMA built the Shariefs massive auto dealerships throughout the Kingdom. The Shariefs were into everything, putting up buildings all over the place. They were into turnkey projects, which meant doing everything from concrete foundations to wallpapering the walls. I joined them because the scope for personal achievement was immense. The Shariefs were not quite as big as Ocoma but it was sometimes better to be a big fish in a small pond than a small fish in a big pond, or so I thought at the time. The three of us were often seen together, during lunch breaks, or often on Fridays, out on the desert plains where the sand runs on forever and the swollen orb of liquid fire reigns supreme.

The pick-up's heavy sand tyres rumbled along the river of asphalt. The warm night air blasted in through the open windows and twisted our hair into mops of impossible entanglement. Mike Oldfield's soothing music was dissected by loose conversation as we threw jokes and innuendoes at the motocross ability of the present company. It was pitch black by this time, only our headlights scythed through the darkness. Mike Oldfield finished his musical wanderings and the mood turned to silent reflection, verging on sleep until,

"You're going to what!" gasped Pete.

"I'm going to quit," I announced for the second time.

"You have got to be joking, Bob?"

"I've had it," I continued, "I'm sick of the petty restrictions and the harassment we put up with while we're helping these guys build their country. They do everything they warn us not to do, drinking, partying, screwing around, to tell you the truth it's starting to get on top of me".

"No shit!" spat Pete, "After all these years you suddenly decide you don't like it; you could have fooled me, Bob, you could have fooled me".

"It's just recently, Pete", I offered in consolation. "Have you noticed how many contracts we've signed up? Well, I'll tell you, Pete. Two, during the last week. This place has had it, man. Every Tom, Dick and Abdullah is undercutting the price of crude. The boom has finished, it's over, and this place is going down the tubes faster than anyone wants to believe. Shit, they can't agree on where to have the next meeting to decide where the next meeting's going to be. When they finally decide, the moment backs are turned it's every man for himself. Britain and Norway are hindering the OPEC boys left right and centre. Just think about that, ten years ago they were kissing backsides to get the oil and now their causing the cartel more grief than they dare admit. The cartel is getting a taste of its own medicine and the bastards don't like it. Nah! this place has had its Heyday, the oil bubble has burst for the time being, and I'm off. I can't stay any longer with restrictions up to my neck. Let them have their oil and hypocrisy, they deserve each other".

Pete and Hawkeye sat in stunned disbelief; finally, Pete opened with an obvious question,

"So, what are you going to do?"

"Pete. I've got a job in the Emirates". I told him.

"Doing what?" Pete was not going to let go.

"Weapons systems, sales and marketing of weapons systems".

"What the hell do you know about weapons systems?"

"At the moment, not much more than I learned in the Terries and training with the US Embassy Protection Squad whilst we were building their transit tunnels under the grounds of the Embassy but I know the people, I speak the language and I'm no stranger to dealing with the big wigs, Saudis or otherwise. I also have a sympathetic approach to the political overtones of the

Middle Eastern territories. In fact, according to the interviewer, after a few months of training, on the various weapons systems and their applications on the modern battlefield, I'll be in decent shape".

"Sounds like a brilliant job; maybe they'll even let you demonstrate some of the systems, perhaps massacre a few peasant villages?" grinned Hawkeye.

"Yeah, for sure!" spat Pete, "Right on the Iran- Iraq border, or maybe in the Arab Israeli war zone!"

Pete, hurt by the sudden unexpected revelation, barraged me with jovial ridicule to mask his disappointment and obvious concern for my previously unannounced but now imminent departure.

"Weapon systems," grumbled Pete, "The only weapon you've ever held is the one you point at the porcelain and that's not much of a weapon from what I've been told".

I laughed along with the two of them, the jest releasing the tension of the surprise announcement.

"I know a lot about man's basic weapon system," I joined in.

"Yeah! like what?" quizzed Pete.

"These two lumps of bone and gristle at the ends of my arms that are going to bust your ribs".

The truck veered and lurched on the deserted road as Hawkeye fought to control direction whilst at the same time, protect himself from the wild thrashing scramble of the two of us. It was nothing new, a release of fired-up emotions, the daily insults and restrictions we suffered, plus the arrogance of the some of the uneducated foreigners. It could not be bottled up forever. We had fought this battle before. The rules were simple, face and genitals were not to be targeted but the rest of the body could be mercilessly pounded until one man was hurt, which was rare, or both of us collapsed to the ground exhausted. Hawkeye flung the truck to the side of the road, as Pete and I struggled for an advantageous hold. Hawkeye strolled unhurried around the front of the cab, opened the passenger door and we fell from the vehicle in a tangled heap of grappling arms and legs. I tore

164

Pete's shirt from his back with my teeth; Hawkeye checked his watch, before announcing his thoughts,

"Be quick you dozy bastards, somebody break a bone or something then we can get home, it's nearly prayer time and we'll miss the teatime shopping".

Vicious punches thumped into torsos. To the outsider we were genuinely trying to maim each other; grunts, squeals and mock acknowledgement of pain broke the silence. So involved were we, we did not see the approaching car. As the vehicle drew closer it swerved suddenly to the side of the road throwing up a cloud of dust and sand as the wheels slid onto the verging desert. Too late, the problem materialised all too quickly, as two Saudi police jumped out, their pistols drawn in anticipation,

"Aish hada!" What's all this they yelled.

We rolled around almost unconcerned by the arrival of the police,

"Wrestling!" yawned Hawkeye,

"Like on TV, sadique. Hulk Hogan, wrestling', Hawkeye's Arabic was getting us nowhere.

It was a fact; wrestling was extremely popular on Saudi television, despite the almost naked appearance of the contestants. You could be arrested in Jeddah for wearing shorts but they ignored the scantily clad men on TV. The police caught on and relaxed as I gave a running blow-by-blow, hold-by-hold commentary in Arabic, laughing and joking with the two policemen as I did so.

Pete and I rolled around for a further five minutes, executing various throws, blows and tongue-ejecting strangleholds, which had the police laughing and shouting encouragement. Eventually exhausted, the bout has concluded a draw. The two of us stood there, covered in sand, sweat and dust. The police re-holstered their weapons and declared me the winner, by a technical knockout; my Arabic was obviously much better than Pete's. Now they wanted to exchange courtesies. One officer studied us with extreme interest, slapping his hand on his compatriot's shoulder and motioning to leave, but not before uttering a few words that were almost a symphony to my ears,

"KHOWAJA!" he announced, "No point taking the trouble to arrest them, they'll talk their way out of everything, cause us headaches and paperwork and give us a hard time by translating the other prisoners" complaints. It's no use, we'll let these guys go, we don't need the hassle".

"Maasalaama, Khowaja, mafi mushkella, arref inta?"

"Goodbye foreigners, don't go causing trouble, you hear?"

I acknowledged the appointment loud and clear; I had just crossed the border onto hallowed ground. I had finally achieved the goal and it had been bestowed by of all people, the police. On the announcement of my departure, they had recognised my creed. It had been a long time coming but how sweet that simple word rang between my ears. The three of us stood waving in silence until the police car disappeared.

"Had enough Pete?" I asked.

"Yeah, I wouldn't want to hurt you Khowaja," he grinned.

"KHOWAJA!" I rolled the expression through my mind.

"What's that?" Hawkeye interrupted my thoughts.

"Means they respect us, Hawkeye". Pete answered before I could climb down from my newfound heights of accomplishment.

"Great!" announced Hawkeye sarcastically, "Just what I've always wanted, does this mean we get a pay rise, can I put it on my CV, can we have letters after our names, great, just what we've always wanted?"

Pete and I knew that the terminology was now a rarity; in fact, Khowajas were becoming an endangered species. Foreigners were no longer the same breed. Nowadays, Jeddah was full of supermarkets, shopping centres, fast food outlets, music centres and everything a foreigner could purchase in his homeland. They lived in luxurious compounds, and drove air-conditioned cars, from air-conditioned homes to air-conditioned offices. They were pampered to excess. I would laugh aloud when I met them at parties and they were heard to remark,

166

CHAPTER 8   SAUDI STYLE   REVELATIONS

"What a tough life we're having out here in the Saudi desert".

Sometimes I would politely agree with the women, just in case they fancied me for a leg-over later, but mostly I laughed, telling them they should have been here years ago when men were men and the women couldn't resist us.

"Yes, it really is a hard life, isn't it? why, only the other day I ran out of Eau-de-cologne and caviar".

I could remember my steel cot. The square of foam rubber and my appendectomy performed by candlelight during a blackout, half in and out of consciousness. I had become so bored with the hospital, all the nurses were blokes from the Far East, and not strictly male. I checked out after two days of lying around with nothing. I got the hell out and got back to what I knew best, work. I even played squash at the weekend, about five days after the op. I took it easy, it was OK and I reckon anything was better than being holed up in bed with a bunch of male nurses ready to jump on your bones. I was frightened to death of being drugged and shagged whilst I slept. No thanks, sadique. I was out of there in a flash.

I knew the new kids well, they had arrived, and they were special. They were unable to find employment back home, they were unfortunates. Why else would they desert their home country for salaries that were now so low they equalled the same pay rates back home but were not taxable and the only other benefit was the constant sunshine? I knew them very well; they were one of the reasons I had decided to leave. The challenge had disappeared; the Khowajas had anaesthetised the bitter struggle. These days everything was oh-so-easy and I longed for something more than a comfortable, air-conditioned existence. China was promised to be the next boom territory but I would wait a while longer yet. The commies were still in control, killing students and preparing to gobble up Hong Kong. No; I decided, I would wait - but at the same time I would wait in the Middle East, where there was still some danger or adventure, a new land, a new territory, a new destiny, as far away as possible from boring old farts and the same routine.

We were rapidly approaching the outskirts of the city, now we had connected with the floodlit dual carriageway and in some respects appeared to have crossed a time zone back into daylight and the real world.

"Weapons systems" sighed Pete, the three of us sniggered insults as the lights ahead turned to red and Hawkeye shifted down the gears, slowing to a crawl before pulling to a halt at the signals.

A car pulled alongside our truck, it carried a pretty, young woman, I got the impression they were new arrivals, her white complexion signalled her disposition. Although Saudi women had white arms, they did not display them in public, unless they needed a coat of matt black spray paint, which is what the police used to cover exposed arms when the women were caught displaying such erotica. The Saudi women displayed eyes only, which in some cases were the most beautiful eyes in the world and which occasionally fluttered more than once at the muscular, bare-armed Europeans. To be honest, trifling with Saudi women was not to be recommended. Headless men do not discuss their sexual prowess with such creatures, cassation being the ultimate penalty for adultery. My eyes appraised the driver in front. It was the custom for women to ride in the rear, as they were not allowed to drive and were considered second-class citizens. I realised the folly of my thoughts; the young woman was cradling a newborn baby. I smiled to myself at the picture of family life, being careful not to offend by my careful observation of the passengers of the car. I held an affinity with the young couple, there was myself, or so I hoped, in a year or so. The lights changed to green and the car alongside pulled away. Hawkeye fumbled carelessly with the oversized gear shifter.

The sickening crunch snatched our attention, from Hawkeye's clumsy attempts to shift into first gear. A yellow taxi ran the red light. A large yellow American-style vehicle had suddenly rammed into the side of the young couple's car. Glass chips sprayed everywhere. The taxi driver was already jumping from his car and screaming at the foreigner in Arabic. The baby howled a pitiful cry and the mother began to sob hysterically. The taxi driver spat in the foreigner's face as the foreigner pulled himself from the wreckage of his car. Splintered fragments of red and orange glass sparkled amongst the windscreen chips, glistening in the sodium glare of the overhead streetlights. The foreigner stood helpless; lost in a world he had only just entered. His wife sobbing, his baby crying, all around him was painful woe and chaos. He had no idea where to turn and was verging on panic. He understood nothing of what was being screamed into his blood-drained face.

"It was green!" Begged the foreigner, "It was green!"

He pointed a shaky finger at the taxi driver,

"You came through on red, it was your fault".

The taxi driver, offended by the pointing finger, slapped the foreigner hard across the face. Surrounded by Saudis, the foreigner could do nothing. He was cornered; there was nothing he could do.

"It was your fault!" he announced once more, his voice choked with emotion, as he pointed an accusing finger in the direction of the taxi driver. The taxi driver, to deflect the blame raised his arm once more to strike. By this time, I had seen enough,

"Bob! Stop! - Bob! Wait! Oh shit!" I heard Pete exclaim as Hawkeye's mouth dropped open and his eyes blinked wide in disbelief.

I saw the foreigner close his eyes in anticipation of the slap. A loud smack exploded directly in front of him yet he did not feel the pain. The taxi driver dropped to the ground as if hit by a bullet, his legs melting away beneath him. The foreigner opened his eyes, unprepared for the immediate vision. The taxi driver lay on the ground unconscious, over his body stood what he must have presumed to be a crazy, beast of a man, filthy hair everywhere and covered head to toe in loose dirty sand. My

169

clothes were dishevelled and torn, bright eyes blazed from
behind a ragged, unshaven face, or so he told me later.

My thump in the chops put the taxi driver into a comfortable
stupor on his backside. I took the foreigner's arm and led him
back through the surprised gathering to his own car.

"It wasn't my fault," he began to explain.

"Relax!" I comforted him as much as possible "We saw it all,
you've got witnesses, don't worry, we'll take care of things until
the police get here".

The foreigner stared at his unlikely saviour,

"But who are you?" he inquired, politely, just in case.

I thought for a while before replying and the single-word
response rolled across my tongue as I remembered my newly
acquired title,

"KHOWAJA!" I replied, and I strode around the wrecked car
and stuck my head through the shattered window,

"Are you OK love?" I enquired of the young woman's present
health.

The young woman opened her mouth to speak; left it open
and soundlessly nodded her reply, her sobs slowed and the
baby stopped screaming with fright.

Pete had already begun to direct the traffic around the
carnage; he made sure as many witnesses as possible were
available for statements. The Saudis tried to park next to the
wrecks to see what was going on, some kindly offered
assistance, they weren't all bad in Saudi, it was just the ignorant
that caused problems. Pete moved them on wherever he could
but as usual, some of them weren't going to be moved away
from something as exciting as this. Hawkeye had the emergency
lights on full beam across the immediate area and the red strobe
lights flashed above the cab for full effect. Everything was under
control. The traffic began to move again, I went back to the
woman in the car.

"We'll have you out in a minute, love. Are you or the baby
hurt?"

170

She did not speak, merely shaking her head. I wedged my boot against the door and bent the twisted metal away from the frame. I assisted her from the car and escorted her to the side of the pickup. Hawkeye pulled out a beach chair from the rear and sat her down with her baby. The husband now joined them, offering his thanks.

I waved away the gratitude and feeling somewhat embarrassed, walked back to check on Pete. Approaching police sirens warbled closer across the city. It would be a while before they arrived; they too would be locked in the lengthening traffic tailback. Pete directed traffic like a professional; he sighed as I approached,

"The woman and kid, OK?" he asked.

"Shook up a bit but fine, Pete". I replied.

I took some water from our bottles, made a path through the crowd and back to the stunned driver of the taxi. I offered him water and a few careful words he drank and shook his head from side to side. A car passed by full of English expats, poking their heads from every window,

"Nice swat man, about time somebody stuck up for us".

I waved them on; they were just what I didn't need at this moment in time.

"Shoo Hada? what happened?" enquired the driver.

I replied in comforting Arabic, "You had an accident, it was entirely your fault, you went through a red light, smashed into a car carrying a woman and," I paused for maximum effect, "A baby! There are witnesses, better for you if you own up, it may save you a great deal of trouble".

The taxi driver, despite the fact I was a foreigner, knew he was in trouble, he would have to pay dearly if anything happened to the woman or the child. Maybe with his life if the foreign infidel husband so desired.

"Are woman and baby, OK?" his voice trembled with fear and his concern forced me to ease off,

"They're ok, shocked but not hurt badly, Alhamdulillah, thanks to God".

"Alhamdulillah! thanks to God," replied the taxi driver, climbing to his shaky legs and walking over to his ruined livelihood.

When the police arrived several statements were taken, thankfully from the good side of Saudi, I had some difficulty explaining why I had slapped the driver but all the evidence pointed to him being at fault and trying to pass the blame on an innocent family. The taxi driver knew he was going nowhere with his protestations, and admitted he ran the light, and that it was his entire fault except of course that foreigners shouldn't be in his country. The police made an immediate judgement, fifty-fifty. Fifty percent the foreigner's fault, fifty percent the taxi driver's fault, which was the best the foreigner, could hope for. After all, if he hadn't been in this country, he wouldn't have caused the accident, would he? which is one of the laws they fail to mention in the interviews. The foreigner was about to protest, I took him to one side and explained this was the best deal he would ever get and his company would know he was blameless. Better to accept this than stay in prison until the courts decide who is to blame which could take months or even years. The foreigner immediately signed the release papers along with the taxi driver, now they were both free to go. The wrecks (one fearless and one unwitting participant) were removed from the road and towed to the police compound for safety. Their owners could pick them up at their leisure. The foreigner hailed a taxi, gingerly climbed inside with his wife and child and after expressing more thanks than I really cared to receive departed the scene. The police even thanked the three of us for our help.

"Some things never change!" I groaned after they left.

"Bloody typical!" spat Pete, "I ask you, fifty-fifty".

"I'll never understand them," began Hawkeye,

"All because they refuse to give way, just for the sake of pride or a bit of face, somebody could have been killed back there. The woman, the baby, either or both drivers. I just can't understand it".

"Better get used to it," I warned Hawkeye. "This is their country,"

"Yeah!" Pete agreed with my sentiment, "And their laws!"

"Yeah! and THEIR oil!" Hawkeye added,

"Otherwise…

"YEAH!" chorused the three of us in unison.

The traffic was almost back to normal as we drove away from the scene of the accident. Hawkeye dropped me off first; I no longer lived in the single man's accommodation. I was now a married man with a place of my own and I shared it with my wife Lyn, how did all this happen, well it's a long story but I'll shorten it as much as I can.

In Saudi, male and female may not travel alone in the same car together unless they are brother and sister or more correctly, husband and wife. Foreigners have been imprisoned for up to three months for the simple crime of travelling with a member of the opposite sex to whom they had no marital or family ties. I had believed, when I first arrived, I would find no available females in Saudi and certainly no alcohol. Now I had a wife waiting for me at my apartment and come to think of it, there was at least half a bottle of Sid in the fridge. Life just wasn't so bad after all.

My late arrival had probably worried Lyn. I was usually punctual and in Saudi, being extremely late usually preceded problems with the police, traffic, religious, civil, special, military or otherwise. Being a nurse Lyn displayed concern as I unfolded the tale of the accident. I mixed myself a drink and slumped into the sofa and as it was Lyn's turn to prepare the evening meal, I recalled our first encounter.

I had no desire to venture out on that night; I would much rather have stayed indoors, listened to some music or watched a video. However, I was a man of my word. Ed was a new kid, a Filipino engineer. Ed had no driving licence, no car and no idea of his surrounding territory, but he had managed to secure an invite to a party, and, seeing something of myself in Ed, I promised to deliver him to the venue at the right time, guaranteeing to pick him up some hours later.

I showered, shaved and slipped into my casuals. Ed's chirrup was not long in coming, this was his first invite of any significance and he smelled like a tart's handbag. When we reached the required destination, and after a good deal of persuasion from Ed, I reluctantly followed him into the venue for one small drink.

I was about to discover the real meaning of the word hospitality. As a total outsider, I held no affiliation with the people inside the apartment by nationality colour or creed, which was why I was at first, reluctant to attend. I was welcomed amongst them and literally forced to eat all manner of delicacies, before finally allowing myself to be dragged onto the dance floor and persuaded to dance by some of the most beautiful girls I had ever had the good fortune to lay my eyes upon. The gathering could have led one to believe - that laughter and happiness were the national pastimes of the Philippine race. I thoroughly enjoyed myself and realised without surprise - not one drop of alcohol had been consumed. My eyes were opened to a world that could not possibly, legally exist in Jeddah. And yet, even as I tried to leave, I was prevented from doing so until I had eaten some more food, or at least tried the dessert, or how about another dance.

After dancing myself to a frazzle, I collapsed in a corner with Ed, the patrons still trying to force more food and drink into my hand. The door opened and in trooped a party of girls, Ed explained, this was the afternoon shift from the hospital, that's why they were late. I was stunned by my good fortune and watched with increasing interest, as the nubile, young female bodies wiggled over to a few empty chairs, where they sat down and began chatting, smiling and mingling with the other patrons of this marvellous venue. When my eyes met hers, "Trouble" was the only word I could think of. I knew that from the moment I saw her, this girl could ruin my single status and to be honest, I don't think I would have any regrets at all. She was the girl a man dreams about but very rarely meets.

Her liquid black hair sprayed around her shoulders, enhancing her natural golden complexion. Her eyes were like deep pools of mystery that tugged at my inner soul. Some Chinese blood was evident, the epicanthal fold caused her eyes to smile, such a sensual wicked smile. She turned to face me and her lips smiled, her eyes smiled, her whole body smiled. I was smitten. I could never leave this place without at least knowing her name. My eyes would not release such a magnetic beauty; it was as if they feared they would never alight on such a vision again. I wanted to walk up to her side but my legs were paralysed. Her legs mocked my own. Strong ankles supported the finest combination of dimensional sensuality I had ever seen. Well-defined buttocks supported a trim waist which eventually gave way to those well formed breasts, which now jiggled invitingly below her fresh, cool clothing. My animal instincts were making themselves known. It was Ed, who finally broke the spell,

"OK!, Bob, I Ready to go if you are".

How could I leave? I thought. I had only just arrived. Ed caught my gaze and recognised the problem.

"Hey! just go over and introduce yourself, no point sitting here staring, which could upset her. Go on, Bob. She can only say NO!"

I remembered my grandfather's favourite saying,

"Faint heart never won fair maiden". or something like that but maybe with a touch of pork in there somewhere.

I raised myself from the seat, strode over to the girl and almost melted at her feet,

"Hello, I, err, I just noticed you arrive, how come you're so late?"

"I just finished my shift at the hospital," she smiled and I almost died.

"Do you always work so late?"

"No, one week in four on rota, mornings, afternoons, evenings and nights, I like mornings better, but I don't mind, nursing's like that". Again, she smiled. I felt as if the whole room was watching my every move, ready to burst into laughter at my first mistake or when she turned down my advances flat.

"What's your name?" I enquired expecting to be rebuffed.

"Lyn, why do you ask?"

"Well, Lyn. I just came here tonight to deliver a friend, now he wants to go home. I'd really like to see you again; may I ask you out? here's my card, I'd really like to stay but I must go".

I felt sheepish, some girls giggled in the background and I wanted to turn and run. Lyn automatically took the card, scanned it quickly and placed it inside her purse.

"I'll think about it". She hit me once more with the smiling eyes and body routine and her voice was so low, I hardly heard a word, now I loved that voice, along with her smiling everythings.

"I have to go I announced if it's OK I'll give you a call?"

I turned and walked away wondering how much of my body had been left at her feet. Suddenly I felt like such a complete idiot. At least I had made the move; at least I did not have to wonder what she would have said - if. She had taken my card, spoken a few precious words and completely ruined what remained of my confirmed bachelor life, what a first meeting.

During the weeks that followed, I did not see the dream girl but Hawkeye and Pete carried a perfect verbal picture of her, hammered into their minds by my continuous and now monotonous appraisal. I saw her friends in the supermarkets, shopping centres and fast-food restaurants, much to my embarrassment. I continually sent back messages that I would like to see her again. I tried telephoning the hospital but as usual, the Saudi, male switchboard operators, treated the girls as their own property and were loath to transfer inquiries, especially into the whereabouts of the beautiful young nurses whom they thought they were saving for themselves. I warned them it was a matter of life and death, which increasingly, it was. Still, they cut me off, nothing seemed to work and I was rapidly losing hope. Pete ribbed me about my obvious state of mind. The sickness was beginning to show, even in my motocross.

Some weeks later, I suffered a massive head-over-heels tumble from the bike. Seventy miles per hour to zero across the largest sheet of sandpaper in the entire world. Pete told me he had been surprised to see me stand, let alone immediately get back onto the bike and head back to the truck. Blood seeped through my shirt, my elbows were badly grazed and across my shoulder blades, which had taken the full impact of the fall, massive bruises bloomed. Back at the truck, we joked away the pain, washing the salt-scraped wounds with ice meltwater. I danced around like a crazy man. I did not know which was worse - the wounds, or the shock of the ice water. My eyebrow had burst open on impact with the handlebars, showering blood all over my filthy clothing but the flow was now slowing, as the ice water compress tightened the capillaries. My wrist burned inside, I knew what had happened, I had experienced this sort of pain before. The nearest hospital was fifteen minutes drive from our present location. One hour later as instructed by me, we steered the truck into the carpark at the New Jeddah Clinic. I headed for the emergency room, dusty, bloody and sand trailing in my wake. My T-shirt was shredded, but I carried a grin on my face as big as a banana. She gasped with surprise when I entered her emergency room domain.

"Fell off the bike!" I beamed; shyness now abandoned.

"Oh, my goodness" she sighed, betraying a slight familiarity not normally associated with patient-nurse relationships. Perhaps it had been the flowers. Or maybe the Swiss chocolates. Or maybe the card on her birthday. Whatever it was, her shield had begun to fall and I intended to prevent her from raising such an impenetrable barricade again.

"I think I've broken my neck," I began, "Here have a look at my eye. Ouch! be careful, that hurts. Hey, mind my wrist, yaaah! that stings nurse".

Lyn was obviously sorry to see me in such a state and I used my injuries to achieve maximum effect. She sutured my eye, washed away the dirt and tenderly patched up any wounds before she herded me off for an X-ray where she enquired if there was anything else.

"Have a look at my heart, Lynlyn". I sighed,

"I think it's broken - not by the crash," I added quickly,

"It's been giving me tremendous pain since we met at that party a few weeks ago".

She squirmed but said nothing as she marched me down to the X-ray department.

"Is this for my arm or my heart?" I enquired.

Finally, she smiled, before slapping my leg with the large brown X-ray envelope in chastisement. I was sure I was winning through.

"Be quiet and behave yourself," she admonished.

The X-ray revealed nothing.

"It's just a sprain!" she announced.

"Are you sure?" I questioned her professional judgement; I was sure it was broken. It had felt like this before as if the bones were grating together in my wrist. I ignored the pain, partly anaesthetised by the luscious Lyn in her sparkling white uniform. I was now cleaned, sutured, disinfected and struck down with a sickness I had never known before.

Outside of the hospital. Pete was probably wondering if I had lapsed into a coma. What was taking so long? If he had known, he would have gone home for his dinner and returned later to collect me. After what seemed like hours, I finally appeared. Pete almost whistled when the lovely Lyn passed him by.

"Come back in two weeks". she ordered with cool professional efficiency.

"What about dinner?" I almost pleaded as I sensed the barricades climbing skywards to block my emotional appeals.

"I'm thinking about it," She smiled and disappeared back to her duties.

"So that's the famous Lyn who's had you running around like a lost dog, is it?" grinned Pete.

"That's the one and only". I sighed.

178

"No doubt about it, I. She's a real winner but you've got a big problem now boy".

"What's that?"

"Next week I'm going to break my leg and she's going to be all mine for the taking, Bob. All mine".

Pete laughed at my overdone expression of hurt. The two of us left the hospital, verbally threatening how we would incapacitate each other to win the hand of Lyn. Pete did not push the subject too far. I had already shown more than just the usual interest in this girl. Something inside probably told him - this girl could be the start of my move to married accommodation and I hadn't even taken the girl out yet.

Pete had never seen me in such a determined state regarding the affections of the opposite sex. I toyed with the thoughts now circling my brain. Pete began to quiz me about the accident. How come you fell off Bob? there was nothing to fall over. I had never fallen during the whole time Pete had ridden with me and we had ridden over far more treacherous surfaces than flat sand. I had ridden across that track a hundred times before. There could be no plausible reason in Pete's eyes for me to dump the bike the way I did - Unless,

"You sly fox," mumbled Pete.

"What's that?" I responded.

"Nothing, Bob, just thinking aloud".

We returned the bikes to the camp another Friday had disappeared, for me, it had been a painful day and I secretly hoped that the Pain had not been wasted.

The week following the bike crash could only be described as burning agony. I could barely sleep. Even the thought of grasping an object, set my wrist aflame with searing pain. I returned to the emergency department knowing she would be on duty, explaining in slow careful and minute detail, the grief I was presently suffering. Lyn was not in a sympathetic frame of mind,

"Look! big baby. It's just a sprain. I know it's painful, sprains usually are but you'll feel fine when the pain has eased".

I protested and offered to pay for the X-ray out of my own pocket just for my own peace of mind. I was sure it was broken and nothing was going to change my mind.

"OK! - Mr King. Here is the deal; if your wrist is broken, I'll personally take you out for the finest meal in Jeddah. If it's sprained, I can assure you, it is! I don't want to see you in here again for at least two weeks for a check-up!"

"You've got a deal!" announced I, wondering how I could smash my wrist before we got down to X-ray. I need not have bothered; the new X-rays revealed a badly broken scaphoid.

"There you are, Mr King". the doctor traced his pen along the fine white line revealing the break.

"Great Doc, so it's definitely broken?" I asked enthusiastically.

"Absolutely, more than once and all quite recently by the looks of the calcium deposits around this particular area".

The doctor couldn't understand my delight upon the discovery of broken bones; he had no idea of the relevance of such a lucky "break'.

Two days later, I lolled on the beach with Pete, Hangar and Juergen - a German national who had recently joined the clan. I covered my wrist with a plastic bag; I did not want to get it wet as I windsurfed. My sunglasses disguised an extra special glint in my eye. It wasn't until later, as the group drove home, did I reveal the reason for such careless exuberance.

"I won't be dining with you tonight, guys. Tonight, I am going out to dinner with the best-looking nurse in Saudi. To the best restaurant in Jeddah and, best of all, she'll be paying the bill".

"I hope she has plenty of money". sighed Pete, "You eat like a bloody horse".

"Yah das ist true". Juergen agreed.

"It's not that he's got a date that he's so happy about, it's because he doesn't have to pay the bill". Pete groaned with derision.

I suffered the brunt of the jovial attack on my manhood all the way back to Jeddah. I was about to embark on a first date I would never forget.

Lyn arrived thirty minutes late, accompanied by two of her friends. I was on the verge of ending the long wait, when she arrived with the two chaperones, as was the custom in the Philippines. She was also, I found out later, a devout practising Catholic. She did, however, foot the bill, even though I offered to pay. We arranged, after much cajoling on my part, to meet again and Lyn, continually arrived on these dates, accompanied by the two chaperones. I was losing my hopes, not to mention a large slice of my spending money; dinner for a foursome can be expensive, especially in some of the best restaurants in Jeddah. Finally, after four months of dating Cinderella and her two "sisters", they weren't ugly, as I had tagged the threesome. She finally turned up alone and thus began the romance that two years later led to marriage and a shared hope that our union would last forever, Shit! it would have to, I discovered later, divorce wasn't allowed within the Catholic Church.

"What are you smiling at?"

Lyn's voice intruded into my nostalgic grin.

"I was just thinking about how we met. Now look at us, I find it hard to believe my luck sometimes".

"I told everybody I would never get married," Lyn teased, "Then you walked into emergency that day and I was so upset and I couldn't understand why, I hardly knew you?"

"Were you really upset when I walked in that day, Lyn?"

"No!" Lyn snapped back, "I was upset when I realised, I had to pay for your dinner, you ate like a horse".

Lyn laughed aloud, I jumped up from the sofa and chased her squealing into the Kitchen, where the gas cooker was placed on slow and the hugging and kissing commenced.

During the week following my decision to quit Saudi, Pete and Hawkeye visited my office on many occasions with the hope of a change of heart. I appreciated their efforts and concern and I discovered that since Pete and Hawkeye had also considered the possibility of moving on. The three of us arranged a pact. I would be a scout in the fresh territory. I would stay connected and keep them informed of any suitable employment prospects.

If the openings were reasonably distanced from areas of conflagration and free of the irksome restrictions of Saudi, then we would join forces once more, a fitting tribute to our close friendship. The plan was welcomed by the three men. Now I would begin the task of disentanglement from Sharief. My contract expired shortly and with the years of service I had registered, I hoped to leave with a golden handshake of sizeable proportions. It was important that the correct procedures were followed, the Saudis had recently developed a bad habit of sliding out of signed and sealed gentlemanly agreements.

I finally managed to tie Sharief down to a meeting. The Sharief had moved me up the ladder to big wheel status. All personnel above a certain management level had to deal with him. The meeting was arranged during the first week of September 1985 at the end of which month, my contract would finally end and require renewal or termination depending upon our mutual agreement.

The day arrived and I professed my regrets as I slid the white envelope containing a notice of my intention not to renew, across the desk to the Sharief. I expressed my sorrow at leaving the company but had decided that now was the time to move on. The Company was fully operational, my task was completed and a change was required in my lifestyle. I hoped Sharief understood my reasons for not wishing to renew the contract. My contract was carefully worded. The Sharief held a business degree from the states, although I had never seen it. I was sure Sharief would understand the simple message regretting my decision not to re-new our contract.
I was owed somewhere in the region of one hundred and fifty thousand Saudi Riyals, a sum of money not to be sneezed at in any man's language.

I again expressed my regrets; after all, I had practically built the company from scratch and had never experienced cause for complaint with my work. Sharief took the notice and sighed. He expressed deep sorrow at my decision and promised to take care of all my entitlements personally. We discussed old times and held a friendly conversation before we shook each other warmly by the hand and parted.

"So far so good," I explained to Pete when we met later that same evening. "Everything seems to be in order".

September dragged slowly by; Lyn spent most of her spare time packing the sentimental junk we had acquired on our travels together since we had taken the oath. Only her appetite for our comfort matched Lyn's giant appetite for souvenirs. She resigned from her post at the hospital and together we prepared for the new adventures that lay ahead. For some reason, I never managed to catch Sharief at his desk, though I did try, more as an act of courtesy than anything, but I did try. The departure date loomed closer and I finally contacted Sharief. During our meeting, I approached the subject of my benefits and entitlements with extreme care; I had no desire to rock the boat.

"What rights?" quizzed the Sharief, almost with contempt," These were cancelled long ago when the company was Saudi-ised, did you not receive my memo? The Sharief passed me a conveniently positioned memo. It instructed higher management that due to falling levels of business, certain gratuities would have to be cancelled from all employment contracts. The memo was dated almost two years earlier, conveniently a week or so AFTER I had signed up for another two-year contract. I had never seen this document before, and I was sure, neither had anybody else. I would have certainly been aware of the ill feeling it would have caused around the company. I expressed my thoughts to Sharief and informed him of my disappointment at not being told about this amendment personally.

"I'm sorry, I. But I thought you'd been informed', apologised the Sharief "However, you are a long-standing member of the company and I have some good news for you here".

I was still sure they would pay out what was contractually owed; it was illegal to do anything else wasn't it?

"According to our records and including the additional one thousand US dollars for excellent performance, we owe you two thousand US dollars and two round-trip tickets to the place of your origin".

"There must be some mistake," I was shocked, they were going to screw me and I knew it, I approached this attempt with as much reserve as possible

"But Sharief, I have a signed and sealed legal contract, you have no documentation stating I accepted you're changing the terms of the contract, nor do you have my signature of agreement to such an act. I have never seen this document before. All I require is that you reconsider this position and complete your obligations to me regarding our signed contract, please don't forget the years of service I have put into this company, this has been my life's work to date".

"Come now, Bob. These are tough times for us all, the company cannot afford to go around paying the end-of-service benefits you are talking about, why we'd be broke in a few months".

The Sharief smiled his sickly smile. Unknown to me, he himself had devised this illegal method of cutback. Yet he had informed none of his superiors about the questionable methods. He was out on his own and didn't need any hassle.

"I have a signed contract," I pleaded with him to be reasonable, "My papers are in order, I never saw that memo before, neither do you have proof of my agreeing to it. I am sure that I am legally entitled to my rights so I will have to investigate this matter with a legal office before I agree to accept, what to me after all this time is a grossly insulting offer".

I shook Sharief's hand dispassionately; I picked up my papers and left the room. As the door closed behind me, I heard Sharief sneer at my exit. I knew what he was thinking; he would fix this foreigner, who was he to threaten legal action? He would have to fix me good; to make sure everyone else did not follow my path down to the legal institutions of Saudi Arabia. I now had to bear the unwelcome news and it was not a task I relished,

"This is horseshit!" stormed Pete.

"He's trying to screw us". Injected Hawkeye.

None of our staff had ever seen the memo before but it had sickened us all. We stood to lose a fortune in hard-earned benefits. The three of us began to discuss in earnest, what could be done to prevent the loss of perfectly, legal entitlements.

"Tomorrow, I'm going to see a lawyer friend of mine, he speaks fluent Arabic, knows the labour law inside out and I'm sure I can show us the way out of this mess". I tried to appear confident but I had already heard some very distressing stories of a remarkably similar nature.

We agreed to combine our efforts, something had to be done. Surely Sharief could not do this to us after all the years of service we had contributed to the company.

Two days later we met again.

"We're in the clear!" I announced with a smile, "They can't do this to us if we have signed contracts and, if none of us agreed to the cutbacks by signing any other documents, we can fight for our rights and we're sure to win. I have an appointment with the labour court at the end of the month, my friend reckons it may take a month or so but, when I get my rights, it means the Sharief will also have to pay yours. There will be no way he can cheat you. My action will set up a company precedent, he'll have no choice but to pay up".

The fact that the immediate problem belonged to me meant nothing, we had agreed to stick together. If I lost my case, they would surely lose theirs and at this moment in time, they were not prepared to accept one Riyal less than they were legally entitled to.

Lyn was agreeable; she could spend more time with me when she left the hospital, knowing she would have to comfort my boiling though constrained temper. The end of the month drew near. Bolstered by my black-and-white evidence and the legal help from various sources, I was fully prepared,

"We have to win this one". I warned Pete.

Hawkeye and the other employees of the Sharief were now in a similar position. All the men involved in the dispute witnessed my resolve I was told later, they were all of the same

185

opinion - most agreed in unison, the overlord Sharief couldn't have made a worse decision, in their opinion, the mighty Sharief had chosen - The wrong guy to fuck with".

Chapter 9
SHOOTING THE BREEZE

This visit would not be an official court hearing. Merely a
meeting of minds between the two parties concerned. An
attempt to settle the dispute without taking the case to trial.
Arbitration through communication was the name of the game
and personally speaking, I was all for it. A settlement would save
the courts a great deal of time and trouble. I rehearsed my lines
well; I wanted to put my side of the story to the authorities.
Before the hearing, I found it difficult to sleep. The questions
would roll around in my head. I would answer them as quickly
and accurately as possible - in Arabic. I would have to be quick.
The meetings would be short and I was not allowed to enter the
court without an Arabic translator just in case words were thrown
around totally alien to me. A ploy used by some unscrupulous
employers to outwit their employees.

The meeting was scheduled for eight am. I was awake and
showered by seven. After three cups of coffee, I kissed Lyn on
the cheek and set out to do battle. It didn't seem long before I
entered the office of the Directorate of the Western Region for
Labour affairs. An elongated, two-story building of uninspired,
block work architecture, which lay in wait behind the Jeddah,
Sheraton Hotel, for the unsuspecting, inexperienced foreigners.
When I arrived, the place was almost empty but for one solitary
figure, whom I presumed to be a guard.

"What time does this place open, sir?" I enquired in my best
Arabic.

"Tamaneah, eight!" snapped the guard, annoyed at the
intrusion.

I opened my briefcase and began to read the notes I had
penned from a direct translation of the Saudi labour law. Eight
fifteen crawled into existence and still no one else had entered
the building. The guard slept soundly. I decided not to disturb

him again, I had enough adversaries, and I didn't need to cultivate any more. Outside the building, people began to mill around in the hot morning sunshine. I watched them through the small, half-shuttered window. Pakistanis, Indians, Sudanese, Philippinos, all manner of nationality, carrying all sorts of files and papers. All, I decided - from their obvious look of disdain, victims of Saudi, in one way or another.

Occasionally two or three of the wandering paper carriers entered the office where I sat; they scrutinised me, flashed their eyeballs across the empty desks and disappeared. This was repeated until eight thirty when a solitary Saudi entered the room, his long white thobe crisp and fresh.

"What time does this place open, sir?"

"Eight O'clock, Inshallah," replied the Saudi, falling into his thickly padded swivel chair. He opened a very official-looking briefcase and took out a newspaper and an egg and ground beef sandwich. (They are delicious) The briefcase was now empty. He had purchased the sandwich at one of the small kiosks, which flourished wherever Saudi Officialdom placed its authoritative seat. The vendors were blatantly aware of excellent business, where bureaucratic boundaries knew not the meaning of the word - "time".

"What time do the other employees start, sir?" I excused myself politely before interrupting the Saudi.

"Eight O'clock!" mumbled the irritated Saudi through his egg and ground beef sandwich. It was already long past eight-thirty. I had heard of such dereliction of duty but until now, I had regarded them as just one of the frustrations of turning a nation of Bedouins into an industrialised and professional workforce.

"Is it prayer time?" I excused myself once more.

"Not yet!" replied the Saudi with a stern glance, bits of egg and beef falling from his mouth onto the open newspaper.

"Then, if I may ask Sir, where is everybody?" my question held a polite tone.

188

"Khamsa dageega Inshallah - Five minutes, God willing," replied the Saudi.

"That's it then," I thought to myself, I was well-schooled in Arabic terms,

"Khamsa dageega Inshallah" was a span of time somewhere between five minutes and a few hours of a patience-tempering endurance test, punctuated by hundreds of small, glass cups of sweet, milkless tea. By nine o'clock, the Saudi had ceased the visual display of his teeth ravaging a sandwich. Swilled the tea around his mouth and set down in earnest to read his favourite morning daily. More wanderers without hope entered the room. Some stayed. Some left. All carried woeful expressions, the mirror image of how I felt - sick to the teeth. I was about to give up and go home when an assemblage of various Saudis entered the room followed by hundreds of would-be petitioners. The Saudis sat down, and copied the exact actions of the early bird, whom - I had decided, must have wet the bed to be up so early. Which was probably the reason for the crisp fresh thobe.

I relaxed. I had an idea this was going to be a long day. Ten o'clock came and went and still no sign of the Sharief or his representative. At ten thirty the whole room emptied leaving me wondering what I had done to deserve such anonymity.

Prayer time had arrived and pushed me back to square one. I was alone once more with the sleeping guard. A normal prayer time could be considered a fifteen-minute ceremony. At eleven o'clock the assemblage filed lethargically back into the room. Prayer times were sacred; nothing could be done or said about the length of time utilised, to do so would have delivered dire consequences to the complainant. God deserved more attention than the fingers of a watch or clock. Suddenly a voice called out,

"Mr Robert King, Sheriqa Sharief" I marched over to the piece of paper waving above the heads of the crowd and swirling the dense cigarette smog.

"Sit here please," requested my saviour.

A small demitasse of hot, sweet, milkless tea was placed at my elbow. I welcomed the drink and its sweet flow of revitalisation, probably due to the six or seven spoons of sugar. Time marched and at twelve O'clock I was presented with a small slip of paper, and it read,

"Sharief representative did not attend, new appointment in thirty days", or words to that effect. The next hearing will be October thirty".

"Another month," I sighed, "Just like that".

"Can't you make it any earlier please?" I pleaded.

"Sorry, we are very busy at the moment," drolled the less than uninterested reply.

"Yeah! I can see that Sir". I replied, sweeping my eyes around the suddenly crowded room.

"Nnnngh!" the Saudi grunted and threw the paper across the desk where it dropped over the side and down to my feet.

"Shukran sadique" I retrieved the paper, slipped it into my briefcase and headed toward the door. I caught sight of the early bird, still reading the paper and champing his teeth into another sandwich.

"Be quick!" I thought, "It will soon be time for lunch".

The following day I received a telephone call during my coffee break. The Sharief could not conceal his extremely bad temper.

"King!" he yelled wildly, "What do you think you are doing? Why did you go to the labour court? Why do you want to cause trouble? Let me warn you now. We have friends at the labour court, we have friends in the police force, we have friends who are Princes and, the King is a personal friend of my family. We will keep you here in the courts forever and we'll never let you go home, then we'll see who's right"

"No shit, Sharief". I replied. But as I cradled the receiver, a sickly sensation caught in my heart. Now I had officially received threats and there could be no turning back. The Sharief had played his hand and not being satisfied with cheating me, he had warned of his intention to use every trick in the book, including family connections, to deny my legal entitlements. I knew I had a

190

fight on my hands. The Sharief was nothing on his own, but he was hiding behind the skirts of his noble family connections. I knew now that I would have to take this all the way. I would have much rather settled this amicably but the Sharief needed a lesson and I decided, unfortunately, it was myself who had been chosen and I would do my best to give him one. I had no choice; the rest of the workforce were relying on me. I did not care now if the Sharief was in league with the devil himself, the threats had been made and with a strange sickness rising in my stomach, I prepared myself for the worst.

I remembered Skip, an American citizen, employed by Sharief for fifteen months. Skip was a bearded giant of a man; roughneck was his middle name. Skip worked a distant area of the refinery territory and was rarely seen through the week but always noticed as he raised a little hell on a Friday, the Kingdom's Holy Day. Skip was promoted the day before the Sharief left for the States on a business trip. Skip, thrilled with his new position, threw everything into his work with new energy. Suddenly skip was everywhere and regularly around the refinery. The maintenance department even sent a letter of commendation for his efforts and a whole area of the refinery was bustling under the auspicious management of Mr Skip.

Skip was sacked on Sharief's return; the whole workforce was shocked by such an unqualified, callous action. Skip had to leave the company but he did not leave Jeddah. He registered a complaint with the labour board and dug in for the long-awaited trial.

Skip spent most of his redundant days, inhabiting a small beach cabin rented by some of his American friends. Skip was having the time of his life but it was not to last. Tuesday and Wednesday of most weeks Skip would return to the Sharief accommodation to collect mail and check for messages. Come Thursday he would leave once more, a big banana grin on his face and enough food to feed an army, off to the beach, where he would laze away the days – fishing, windsurfing and partying the nights away until dawn. Sharief's spies were watching carefully and early one Wednesday morning, around two am, the Sharief arrived at the staff residence. Faleh Muteiri and members of the local police force went with him. Skip was dragged out of bed and promptly bundled off to police headquarters for "questioning'. Johnny Land, his neighbour saw Skip's hurried departure. A heck of a racket thundered from the rear of the police van as it drove away into the night. The van rocking from side to side as if some great unstable load were rolling around its interior. Skip was obviously being "restrained". The Sharief presented some cock and bull story to the effect that Skip, had stolen a hefty sum of money and jumped his work permit to escape the country and of course Saudi justice. The captain in charge, Faleh Muteiri, a very dignified Saudi officer, in my opinion, had allowed Skip the courtesy to reveal his own side of the story. Skip produced his receipt from the labour court, proving it was himself, who had a case against the Sharief, which of course the Sharief had failed to mention to Captain Muteiri. The leg irons and handcuffs were immediately removed. The captain apologised to skip asking if he would like to file a complaint. Skip declined while he was ahead of the game. The Sharief was forced to apologise to Skip who was later driven home in the captain's personal limo. Much to the chagrin of the two corporals who, acting on instructions and a fat bribe from the Sharief, had attempted to beat skip to a pulp in the back of the arresting van. Sadly, they were in a terrible state, skip had left no tell-tale marks but as Johnny reported later, they were having trouble breathing, let alone walking when they brought skip home.

The Sharief had been lucky; Skip had not filed charges against the police for wrongful arrest. Had Sharief not been a close friend of the captain, he would surely have been thrown in prison. The captain ordered Sharief to pay skip all his dues plus a payment for "inconvenience" and get Skip out of the country fast - before the American changed his mind. The yank was just too big a guy for his men to manage and, he carried a valid, registered complaint. The last time I saw Skip was when he boarded the Pan-Am Jumbo for America. Skip's healthy, sun-tanned framework supporting his well-rested features. He also carried a pocket full of dollars and a grin the size of a banana.

I remembered the Skip episode well and I promised myself, never to get caught out in such a situation. I copied all my documents in triplicate - one for myself, one for the British Embassy and one copy for Pete to hang on to. The originals I hid in my apartment where I felt sure no intruder would search - in the toilet header tank. Saudis loathed such things, they used crouchers and these were alien to most of them. Wrapped in a waterproof diver's bag, they were well concealed and, I hoped, out of the reach of intruding alien hands. I made one copy of the labour court receipt and pinned it to the outside of my door and wall, if the police did try to enter my apartment, they would be the first things, they clamped eyes on.

I positioned my aluminium baseball bat by the door, placed my razor-sharp diver's knife with an eight-inch blade by my bed and my rice flail, a souvenir from the Philippines; I placed beneath the refrigerator. If the intruders carried a warrant, I could do nothing, but if they weren't from official sources, let the games begin, then I was ready and if anything happened to Lyn, I would not be responsible for my actions.

I was evicted from the company with a cowardly note, delivered by the hands of a messenger boy but nothing else happened. Pete and Hawkeye visited regularly and left before midnight. Everything appeared to be OK. Then one night, the doorbell chirruped and disturbed Lyn and myself from slumber. I opened the door and there before me stood the Sharief, I glanced at my watch, it was two o'clock in the morning.

"We have come for the car," gloated Sharief

"At two in the morning?" I tried to appear calm.

"It's a company car and we want it now!" ordered the Sharief.

"Forget it!" I warned him, "You're completely out of order; this is illegal harassment and you know it; you can't change the terms of my contract until arbitration is completed".

"This is our vehicle and we want it now!" sneered Sharief.

I quoted the labour law; I knew Sharief was illegally harassing me. It was two in the morning; he had no right to be here at such a time and this action constituted undue pressure and illegal harassment, punishable by Saudi law.

"Don't quote the labour law to me, King. I'm a Saudi, I am above such laws, these laws are here for the likes of corrupt westerners not for the Saudis, now give me the car keys!"

"No way!" I announced. "This is illegal and you know it, why else would you come around here at two in the morning?"

"Where are the keys?" demanded Sharief with such menace in his voice that Lyn released a worried sigh behind me,

"If you don't give me the keys now, we are going to come inside and take them".

The Sharief motioned to the two cronies he had brought with him, not for their intelligence, that much was obvious. Lyn released a worried cry. The fear grew in my bones, why was Sharief doing this, I thought. Why was he getting away with it, I didn't want this sort of trouble, I was no street fighter. I wanted to give Sharief his keys and hope they would leave us alone. What would I tell Pete? I wasn't going to tell him I chickened out, that's for sure. I did not want to let them down. Again, Lyn caught her breath, as the two men stepped forward. The blood flushed to my cheeks fear or no fear, they were causing Lyn grief, the two men advanced further. I slid my arm behind the door leaf and my fingers curled around the warm aluminium baseball bat. Suddenly, I wriggled my shirtless body around the door and quickly closed it behind me locking Lyn inside. The fury welled up inside, smothering my previous fear. I swung the bat under the noses of the two men, stopping them dead in their tracks. If they had been about to jump me, they had suddenly changed their minds and now they were back-pedalling into the elevator leaving Sharief, standing alone before the foreigner, whom they had just realised was in a vey bad mood.

"Go away, little man!" I waved the bat in front of Sharief's face; the hasty retreat of the henchmen and the worried stare of my adversary boosted my confidence,

194

"Go away, I don't want any trouble. The courts will settle our differences but if you wish to take it outside the courts and make it a personal issue. Then somebody is likely to get hurt and I guarantee you Sharief, eventually, that somebody, is going to be you".

I pushed into the Sharief's chest with the bat, the Sharief stumbled backwards into the open elevator, the door slid shut, its safety locks fastened with a reassuring click, the lift whirred and descended. I could see Sharief's furious expression through the glass door panels. He had lost face before two hired flunkies and the hatred blazed from his eyes. I chirruped the doorbell and Lyn opened the door. Once inside she closed the door and threw her arms around me,

"Oh! Bob" she cried, "I'm scared. I really am scared. He's crazy that man, he's evil, let's get away, let's just get away from here".

I held her close; sorry for the pain I was now causing her. I would never let them hurt her, not Lyn. I assumed the car issue was over but I was mistaken.

The heavy throbbing diesel engines warned me of their mischievous intention; I grabbed a camera, lunged through the door and headed up to the roof, hoping I was wrong. Even as I sprinted barefoot across the warm terrazzo, the tow truck from the Auto Dealership, Jeddah Automobiles, had already hooked onto the back bumper of my car. A wry smile must have crossed my worried features. I wondered if they would notice before it was too late. My answer was not long in coming. As the tow truck moved away, the American saloon lurched sideways, shuddering violently as it battered into the car standing to its right. I had an idea either Sharief or some of his cronies may try to repossess the vehicle and so I took, what I thought, were the only precautions available to me at the time. I had locked the wheels in a full left turn and now the two cars squealed in protest as they were rubbed together by the force of the tow truck. The friction crunched their body panels and savagely scored the paintwork, as the side mirrors were torn free and mangled between the two vehicles. I activated my flashgun; below me, Sharief was in a panic, wondering what had happened. The Sharief was down on his hands and knees checking the underside of the car when a blinding flash lit up the night. Sharief leaped upwards in shock, a second flash caught him in mid-flight, with an expression like that of a surprised squirrel, milliseconds before it turns into a blob of squashed fur on a major city highway. I grinned; I was enjoying this. The Sharief looked upward; a new blazing expression revealed all. I held my palms to the sky,

"Evidence!" I announced, "So that when you inform the police that I stole the car, I'll have photos of the real thief".

With that small explanation, I evacuated the charge in the flash, and once again the whole area was bathed in brilliant electronic daylight. I turned and walked from the parapet. The Sharief did not see me leave; the Sharief could not see anything, other than the bright orange spots that must have been dancing in front of his eyes.

I rented a car, I had no choice, my mobility was vital, and I had to collect the necessary documents and paperwork that were essential to my case. It was no great length of time before the Sharief's next illegal act surfaced. I had to admit it would have been a good move had the Sharief not made earlier enemies, forcing an old Arabian proverb, and my sanctity, to mind.

"Mine enemy's enemy is my friend".

Sharief sent a letter to the landlord of my apartment, basically translated it read,

Sir,

It is our duty to inform you, Robert E King is no longer under the sponsorship of Sharief. Henceforth no rent or service claims will be accepted after the date shown on this communication.

Sharief.

196

CHAPTER 10   SAUDI STYLE   AMBUSH

Fortunately, Sharief had failed to authorise payment to the landlord for the previous nine months and despite many requests from my landlord, Sharief refused to discuss the matter. The Landlord knew Sharief was a crook and that something was amiss. His first action was making direct contact with me for my version of events - mine enemy's enemy is my friend. The landlord had been educated in England. I had met the man previously and we had discussed several topics in and around the UK as well as Saudi. The landlord had been well pleased with my knowledge of the Arabic language and their customs and courtesies and decided to give me a full hearing. When I produced the photos of Sharief stealing the car, the landlord was a happy man. He shrieked with delight at Sharief's expression and I was made to promise I would supply copies for the Landlord to show his friends. Before I left, the landlord promised, I could stay for free, if I were fighting the case. As the landlord left the apartment, I knew I had at least one Saudi ally. If he reads this I want him to know I am extremely grateful for another Saudi friend.

I had not expected proceedings to take the increasingly protracted course, on which they were now headed. Lyn had resigned from the hospital and had begun the role of housewife. I was still troubled. Sharief had proved to be a vindictive person. I did not relish the thought of Lyn being in the apartment alone while I was out on business, or at court. I could not take her with me everywhere I went. Women were not allowed in the male bastions of Saudi, in fact, they were rarely allowed to go anywhere in Saudi other than shopping, or to visit friends and relatives. Women were not allowed to drive, never went out alone and when they did venture out, they did so in family groups, or with their husbands, who usually insisted on them wearing the smothering black chador, leaving only their eyes to view, revealing nothing to the foreigners other than a few, smouldering, what sometimes seemed like wistful glances to

Western freedoms. Women, at this time, had one key role in
Saudi, that of a wife and baby maker. In most cases, they had
no real choice, even on whom they could marry. That question
was decided for them, sometimes as early as infancy by their
well-meaning parents. A fair amount of choice however was
given to the prospective husband - yes or no, which was all the
choice he would need. It was not unusual for a girl to be married
at thirteen or even younger. Sometimes her menstrual onslaught
decided for her. If her periods appeared earlier than her teens,
then she was considered marrying age. The prospective
husband could be of any age. He could already be the proud
owner of a trio of wives back home, with an untold number of
offspring and in fact, be the father of eligible daughters himself.
In certain cases, it was said that when a young girl began her
menstrual cycle, some fathers would hoist a green Saudi flag
atop the roof of his house. This was a sign to friends and
relatives that his daughter(s) were available and ready for
marriage, to any prospective husband, with the financial backing
needed for the purchasing dowry. Of course, a father's paternal
instincts and love for his daughter would not allow her to be
mated up with any old Tom, Dick or Abdullah, but his greater
love for massive sums of money, from very well-to-do Saudis,
could sometimes get the better of him. It appeared that this was
just the Saudi way but there was more to it than that, it wasn't
such a mercenary act but most foreigners would never get close
enough to a family to find out.

Cousins and other peripheral family members were also
allowed to marry. This locked the families involved, into a close-
knit tribe or community and sometimes produced the
accompanying genetic complications, associated with such
close-blood entanglements. Shotgun weddings occurred in
Saudi too. The families had a choice in this matter - marry the
concerned parties or have them face a cruel punishment, usually
stoning, unless the parents of the girl cried rape and then the
man, if there was enough evidence, was conveniently beheaded,
especially if he was a foreigner. The lid was tightly closed on

198

scandalous behaviour, the penalties severe indeed and it was many a marriage that saved the neck of the known perpetrators.

Married upon menstrual onslaught, it was not unusual for a girl to conceive shortly after the wedding as birth control was frowned upon and the Saudis wanted to increase the population and as they were, in some cases paying the dowry, who were the happy couple to complain. Proof of virginity would be proved on the wedding night, the bloodstained white cotton sheets passed around female family members for all to see and the dowry subsequently handed over. By the age of fourteen, a Saudi girl could expect to have or be carrying at least one child. By her late teens, she would have delivered a fine brood of kids, following a waddling state of constant pregnancy. She was now probably of large proportions and spent her days eating and gabbling with her friends, or more usual, her husband's other three wives. Her husband, having taken the best years of her childhood, if he had the money and was so inclined, would be searching for more wives or, if he already held a full house of four, he would be searching the cities of the world in search of that wicked western influence he so heartily despised back home.

The daughters of wealthy families were more fortunate. They had the opportunity of travel and education abroad. They would board the plane in Saudi smothered head to foot in black chadors. When they reached the airspace of their destination, some would disappear for a few minutes, to return to their seats in the most up-to-date modest fashions that money could buy. Beautiful clothing that would raise more than a man's eye. Having been unable to see their faces earlier, it would have been difficult to point the finger of recognition, but one thing remained certain, young and wealthy Saudi females in black chadors, rarely deplaned in the cosmopolitan cities of the western world. These fortunate young ladies enjoyed life to the full, including the tribal rituals of the wicked western influence, commonly referred to in cosier circles as copulation of the co-eds. These wealthy young bloods attended hospital a few weeks before their arranged wedding where, a few well-placed stitches would camouflage any past indiscretions, and on their wedding night; behold, the chastity and purity of blessed restraint held aloft for all to see. Such was the life of the Saudi women, schoolgirl, baby maker and early retirement.

I decided it would be safer for all concerned if Lyn left the country. I could not imagine the dire consequences had I returned home to find her abused in any way. That act would pre-empt the bloodiest retribution the Sharief would ever witness before finding his God.

It had not been an easy task. Lyn fielded a fierce and convincing opposition to the idea but finally accepted when I explained - she could begin the search for a house of our own and window shop for the furniture to go with it.

On the night of her departure, a smouldering tense atmosphere blazed into a tearful screaming row. Lyn wanted to stay with her husband. I had tricked her, I was trying to get rid of her. I was on the verge of slapping her hysterical outburst but I knew it was her way of loving me, and her desire to stand by me, no matter what the consequence. I could never slap her, instead, I threw my arms around her and we fell to the floor in a wild passionate struggle, burning our pent-up, frustrated emotions, to a smouldering, white ash of compliance.

Lyn boarded the flight and I watched the plane as it disappeared into the early morning sky. I was suddenly alone once more; my spirit was only bolstered by the fact, that if the Sharief interfered on a personal level now, there remained no one to attack but me and, I promised myself, I would be well and truly prepared.

I got rid of the hire car - after all, I had nowhere to go and was in no hurry to get there. Now I could walk, it would do me good.

Another directive was issued from the head office of Sharief, henceforth all mail would be sent to employees through Sharief's office, to ensure safe delivery to the addressees. I knew exactly why such a statement had been issued. During Skip's altercation with Sharief. Skip had often mentioned, how he had not received any mail from home, sometimes for months at a time. I had already directed my mail to the postal address of a close associate. If any mail did get through it would be of little importance, and the Sharief was welcome to it. I penned a letter to myself, a scathing attack on Sharief's moral values and despicable principles. I quoted verses from the Koran that dealt with such matters. I included the Sharief's refinery nickname, "The poison dwarf". If Sharief did read the letter, it would surely set his fury ablaze, he would have to retaliate and I would know for sure he was receiving my mail. I addressed the letter to myself and photocopied the envelope for evidence. I personally inserted the letter into the Sharief post office box. The next stop from here was the Sharief. Although I mailed many letters of this nature to myself, I never received any of them. When I had collected a stack of deposit slips from the post office. I paid a visit to the Sharief. The Sharief refused to see me. I left behind a message and photocopies of the letters, adding that I would like an explanation of their whereabouts during the next court hearing. I did not see the sickened features of Sharief as he read the note, but I knew my evidence was growing into a sharpening sword of justice that would eventually, at least I hoped, cut down Sharief to less than normal size.

I began receiving wake-up calls at all hours of the morning. I did not need to guess the culprit or the intention of the calls. The voices were disguised but made the same old threats to which I was becoming accustomed. I wracked my brains for a better than obvious solution to the problem, it came to me one night as I read the notes in my diary. There before my eyes was the address and telephone number of Sharief's London residence. It was normally habited by the Sharief's mother and had been passed to me freely as an act of bravado, as the Sharief boasted of his international wealth.

"This is our place in London," he had crowed, "My mother usually stays there; feel free to call for help. You can also leave messages if you need urgent communication or wish to contact us out here".

The telephone number was sweet music to my ears and in the depths of my mind, a plan began to form. Now I longed for the early morning caller to wake me from my dreams. As usual, I did not have to wait long. Four nights later, an excellent opportunity arose. It was three in the morning when I was shocked from my sleep. I gave the caller time to gloat as I prepared the recording, lifted the receiver and switched on the tape,

"Hello, Sharief residence!" That was all I had been able to tape, but it was all I needed. The Sharief must have thought he had pressed the wrong button on his telephone's memory system and the automatic dialler had dialled his mother's number in London.

"Hello mother!" he began, his cheery voice full of apology at the early morning call, launching into a conversation about his mistake with the phone. No reply came from his mother.

"Hello! Hello!" sang Sharief.

I waited for the appropriate moment.

"Are you OK, mother?" the Sharief meekly inquired his voice trailing off to a silent suspicion.

"Yeah, she's here Sharief but she can't talk right now she's kinda busy, and hey, she's a really nice lady Sharief".

I caught the choking sounds at the other end of the line, a millisecond before it cut dead. I had seen Sharief's mother, another case of young girl marriage and at her forty-odd years of age, she would have given any of the beautiful soap stars a run for their money. I lay in bed a grin beaming from ear to ear as I imagined Sharief's present state of mind. Meanwhile, Sharief must have been pounding his fists into his pillow,

"I'm going to get you for this," I could imagine him shouting, "I'm going to destroy you for what you've just done!"

I rolled over to try and get some sleep, unaware of the Sharief's real anger but certain, that from now on, I would have to be incredibly careful indeed.

202

CHAPTER 10   SAUDI STYLE   AMBUSH

A week later my phone was mysteriously disconnected. At the telephone office I was assured it was entirely due to non-payment of bills and no intervention from third parties. That was impossible the engineers assured me. I quickly worked it out; Sharief was withholding my mail. That would include bills - I could not pay what I did not receive, score one point to the Sharief.

I strode into the accounting offices of Sharief to register a complaint, merely to record the illegal acts, now being waged against my person. The staff having been warned of my crimes tried to block my entry. I waded through them and their verbal insults, but the expected folly of physical attack never materialised. With a stab of my arm, I recognised and snatched my phone bill from the accounts tray. I was lucky, I had never expected to see the bill again but now I held it aloft for all to see. It was addressed to me. It had been opened; someone in this office was a thief. Red faces surrounded me. Theft in Saudi is a serious crime, punishable by the sword as it chopped off the right hand after Friday noon prayers.

I could see their furtive little minds working on finger-pointing excuses and denials. Sharief would surely explode when he heard of my new evidence. I knew what they were thinking - How they wished they did not have to bring this matter to Sharief's attention, how they wished they had been out of the office during my arrival and how they wished, I am sure, the country could be rid of these damn Khowajas.

I did not pay the bill; instead, I used it as evidence for the court, to prove beyond doubt that Sharief was refusing to pass on my mail. After all, Sharief had declared himself responsible for the mail and it was, therefore, his explanation that would be required in court as to how my mail was undelivered or stopped and opened at Sharief's office. With the phone cut off, I slept without interruption and I was sure, it would be Sharief who also endured many sleepless nights from now on.

October 30th - Labour Court Day

CHAPTER 10   SAUDI STYLE   AMBUSH

The court procedure followed the same pattern as my previous visit. I hung around the labour court all morning until the call to midday prayers. After prayers, I was duly informed of Sharief's representative's non-attendance. The arbiters were apologetic but could not understand my displeasure when they requested, I return in one month's time.

I left the court with a heavy heart. I had spent many minutes on the telephone, listening to Lyn's tearful exclamations of loneliness. She wanted me home, to hell with the Sharief, just come home. I wanted to heed her call, but something inside refused to yield and my resolve once more, turned to stone. I spent many nights with Pete and Hawkeye comparing notes, filling in details and exchanging ideas. The discussions bolstered my spirit and willed me forward - after all, it couldn't go on that much longer, could it? I continued to use my own apartment. I was legally entitled to do so, and the Sharief would have to foot the bill eventually. The more I burdened the Sharief, the happier I felt. Weekdays I spent walking and exploring Jeddah from a pedestrian point of view. I met various local Saudi characters during these walks and I got to know them all very well. They got to know me too and I became quite a well-known visitor myself. My Arabic improved greatly during these frequent excursions and chats with the local populace who were all really decent Saudi citizens, the guys anyway, as I didn't want to be labelled an Eve Teaser for obvious reasons and never conversed with the ladies.

The walking improved my appetite and sent me to bed exhausted, destroying all opportunity for thoughts of revenge that were apt to creep across my mind. I continued with the motocross and beach visits. Some mornings, as the sun rose and bleached the sky red, I ran the roads of Jeddah. Initially, my body ached but after a few weeks, the ache was swallowed by the body's acceptance of my new routine. In the clear light of dawn, I ran the empty streets, my stamina continually increasing. Pete and Hawkeye continued their work at the refinery,

204

completing enough tasks to get them through the day and not raising any suspicions. Neither was in any mood to exert themselves. They supported me without reservation. My fight was their own and if I lost so would they and they were not going to let me down.

As I read the newspaper, I couldn't believe my eyes; there I was for the whole world to see, the second page of the Jeddah daily. It was almost a wanted poster. The Sharief was obviously behind the advertisement and the object was clear, to defame my character and cause maximum embarrassment.

THE SHARIEF WOULD LIKE TO ANNOUNCE THAT HE HAS TERMINATED THE SERVICES OF MR ROBERT E KING. HE WILL BE ISSUED WITH A FINAL EXIT VISA AND HIS WORK PERMIT WILL NOT BE TRANSFERRED TO ANY THIRD PARTY. THIS COMPANY WARNS ALL AGAINST HAVING ANY DEALS WITH THIS MAN. ANY PERSON HAVING CLAIMS ON THE ABOVE-MENTIONED PERSON SHOULD CONTACT THE SHARIEF AT THE FOLLOWING TELEPHONE NUMBERS WITHIN A WEEK OF THIS NOTIFICATION DATE.

I burned with hate; fuelled by the embarrassment the Sharief had now caused me. Pete and Hawkeye joked with me, after all, I was now famous and anybody, who knew Sharief, would know he was just being an arsehole, which was his usual position in life. I grinned at the insulting publication but it wasn't easy to forget.

A lone woman on the streets of Saudi would be classed as a whore, subsequently falling prey to the basic instincts of most of the passing male population. They would pass her by in their limos at walking speed, commenting on her situation whilst offering her sums of money and trying everything they knew to get her inside their vehicles. How could they be blamed, with the laws as they were, women were in short supply, whores were in big demand and I often wondered, how many women must have accumulated an absolute fortune from the seemingly limitless finances of the sex-starved males living in Saudi Arabia. These men owned no prizes for originality in their solicitous vocabulary.

"Jig-Jig, Miss?"

"How much, Miss?" they enquired.

"Hey, Miss. Do you want a ride home?"

The men often travelled in pairs on such occasions. They were probably terrified of dealing with the opposite sex alone. In closed societies, relationships with unrelated women were a rare occurrence. It was not surprising, therefore, that as I walked around Jeddah I received some attention myself,

"Jig-Jig, Mister?"

"How much, Mister?"

"Hey, Mister, do you want a ride home?"

I knew such things existed but to me, honestly, such practices held no appeal. I could never understand why a man would want to poke his penis up another man's bum, something had to be wired up wrong somewhere, I don't apologise or condone, I believe in live and let live, these are just my own feelings on the subject. To the inhabitants, temporary or otherwise, it appeared to be a way of life. They had no women to court, extraordinarily little, or no chance of a sexual encounter with the opposite sex out of wedlock, and so their location and its laws forced them into acts that some people regarded as normal. In 1986 the Saudi government ordered all new foreigners to provide proof of their freedom from the AIDS virus before they were allowed into the country. A lot of the expatriate donor countries were furious at the insinuation but most obliged, for obvious commercial reasons and were reduced to humbled apologies. One thing was certain, with the number of kerb crawlers pestering me for sexual favours, I was sure, that if AIDS did get a grip in the Kingdom, without condoms, which you never saw or even heard could be purchased, the foreign and local inhabitants were in deep shit and to call them an endangered species would be the understatement of the millennium. I am glad to report, it never did and they're fine

During one of my walking sessions, Sharief's Mercedes, an expensive, customised special with a TV and cocktail cabinet in the rear, drew up alongside me. The dark tinted passenger window whined down into the door revealing Sharief's grinning features,

"Give it up, King. You can never win; we will keep you here forever; why even our friends from the labour court had dinner with us last night and assured me your case is hopeless'

I did not believe him. The Sharief was a habitual liar and antagoniser. This was merely an attempt to destroy my resolve, the Sharief continued with his verbal insults.

"Why are you walking, King? walking is for the poor people, why do you embarrass yourself in this manner? have you no decency? where is your self-respect, lost in the mail perhaps?"

The final remark almost burned through my restraint, though I steeled myself against the provocation. I knew it would serve no purpose to attack this man; it would be a sign of weakness. If I spilt the blood of a Saudi, I could expect at least two years in prison. He was well protected by Saudi law and he would maximise its potential. I had to be very careful, I spoke, quietly but confidently,

"Listen, Sharief. We all have friends. You say you have powerful friends all over Saudi, well let me explain why I'm walking, it's like this, every time I walk, I get stronger, whilst you sit on your fat backside and get weaker. Any day now I'm going to beat you in the Saudi court. Then I'm going home to England and with this new strength I'm going to legally take your place apart, brick by brick until you come to England for your dues, or your family is forced to leave my country".

"You should be more careful with your mouth, King. We have friends..................

"Listen, Sharief. I have a lot of friends too and they're watching your mother's place in England right now, and if anything happens to me while I'm out here, there won't be enough left of your house or its occupants to put in an envelope and post out here to you. So, take your threats Sharief and shove them up your arse!"

I spat the last words with a malice I couldn't contain. The Sharief did not reply. His features paled and he scowled to disguise his loss of face. A knot of hatred crossed his brow; the tinted glass returned to its former, upright position and the Mercedes sped away.

30th November - Labour Court

Again, the Sharief did not appear at the hearing but the Sharief had sent a messenger, who informed those present,

"They had not received their summons in time to prepare their case. They were briefing a lawyer and Sharief would attend the next hearing without any doubt, Inshallah".

"Another month?" I sighed in disbelief.

"Another month!" announced the court with no consolatory gesture. I noticed they seemed to think it was quite a joke as if Sharief's words were correct. I was upset. For three months now I had wasted my time trying to bring Sharief to justice and nobody seemed to be interested in the slightest. All I wanted were my legal entitlements and to leave, couldn't they see that? I had completed my contract to the letter and done nothing wrong. Maybe Sharief did have these people in his pocket. It was a possibility but at this moment, I refused to believe it. A Muslim was supposed to be good to his word and a law-abiding citizen. It was only Sharief and individuals like him, that ruined the reputation of everybody else. I headed back to my apartment,

"Another month!" I thought, "God give me strength". I could pray too.

It was later, as I entered my apartment that the realisation swept over me. Another month would be December the thirtieth, as I ringed the date on my wall calendar, it triggered uncontrollable anger. Another month meant I would have to stay here for Christmas, no wife, no family, nothing but the thought of visiting the court again five days after Christmas day. A silent promise entered my heart,

"Sharief is going to pay for this," I vowed, "Sharief will pay for every day that he keeps me in this country, I swear he is going to pay".

Pete and Hawkeye did their best to console me, though sometimes I would drift off, deep in thought, mentally carving the Sharief into shark fishing bait.

My morning runs continued, faster and farther than before; I ran until my feet bled through torn and blistered skin, almost unnoticed to my troubled mind. Hawkeye and Pete noticed the change. I became a fanatic, I gave up eating junk food and I only ate fresh fruit, between protein-packed meals of barbecued giant shrimps and fillet steak. They could not even tempt me to drink the thick chocolate milkshakes I had once so enjoyed. What a liar I had become.

As the month rolled by, I would have to break the news to Lyn. Pete and Hawkeye sat outside their apartment as I revealed the news that could only lead to pain. Lyn cried bitter sobbing tears at the thought of spending Christmas apart. Finally, the sobbing subsided and her fierce Warrai Pride, burned through the shell of her inconsolable disappointment.

The Warrai lived in the Samar province of the Southern Philippines; they were a fearsome, fearless breed. Nature's natural hunter-survivors and one of the last communities to join civilisation, not counting the recently discovered Tasedai tribe, which the entire world now knows, was a hoax concocted by the late President Marcos of the Philippines. During the war, the Warrai had instilled a deep-rooted fear in the occupying Japanese forces, originally attacking with nothing but knives, spears, bows and arrows, sticks and stones until they had amassed a large armoury of weapons, which they had torn from the hands of the dying Japanese soldiers. Once armed they behaved like demons, intoxicated by the power of the weapons

209

they now controlled. Small hunting packs of three or more Warrai would charge into the Japanese encampments in the dead of night, blasting away at everything that moved until finally, nothing moved or the Warrai were shot dead in the firefight. They were driven by a screaming wild fury, born of the denial of their peaceful island homes and the personal knowledge of the atrocities committed by the Japs against their men, not to mention the womenfolk. Acknowledged as the fiercest band of guerrillas the Philippines had ever spawned. General McArthur himself had mentioned the tribe in despatches,

"A merciless fighting machine who harboured no concept of fear and on occasions had to be restrained from charging the enemy through their own artillery bombardments". The Japanese were finally conquered and the Philippines liberated. The Warrai returned to their peaceful Island existence, the grandparents included, of my wife Lyn, who now released her woeful cry of vengeance.

"So!" she cried, "The Sharief has decided to ruin our Christmas and he's going to try to ruin our marriage if not our lives, his intentions are clear, Bob". Her voice trailed away before returning with venom I had never heard before,

"Whatever happens I'll wait for you, Bob. You just do what you must do. I'll wait here until it's all over and finished with, just promise me one thing,"

"Anything, Lyn. What is it?"

"Burn that Sharief so bad he's sorry he was ever born, hurt him, make him feel the pain we're feeling now and if you can't get to him out there, come home. He must leave Saudi eventually, our friends will keep an eye on him and when we see him, we'll pay him back with overdue interest, that's all I really want, whatever happens".

My heart swelled in my chest; my pride soared to heights I had never experienced. Now I had received an open ticket. Lyn was going to be OK; she was going to wait for me. I had no need to worry about her. All I had to do now was take care of Sharief

210

and return home to my wife in that order, approved by the stamp of burning hatred from Lyn. I kissed my good-byes and re cradled the receiver. Pete and Hawkeye returned from the patio at my signal. They expected to find me depressed as on previous occasions when I had spoken to Lyn. This time I was different. Gone was the heavy heart and bland expression. I was actually smiling. Hawkeye sensed it and so did Pete; there was a fire in my belly and behind these eyes, a bright but controlled fire of hope. Pete had only one singular thought, he told me later, The Jeddah fire service should embark on some serious practise sessions, just in case that fire got out of control.

The hearing was two weeks distant, when, despite my phone being disconnected I received the call,

"King!" snapped the Sharief, "Still here I see".

"Of course, I'm still here," I replied matter of factly, amazed at the Sharief's telephone "connections".

"Just wanted to let you know, King. I'll be going to England for my Christmas holiday. I wondered if you have any messages I could pass or deliver to that cute little wife of yours. I'd love to be able to" the Sharief paused for effect, "See her!"

I felt the sickness in my stomach and the burning rage flow forth from within. I struggled to prevent myself from blurting out my desire to kill Sharief; I knew he was probably taping this conversation. The fuse to my temper was burning shorter as the weeks went by and, at times like this, I found it difficult to control.

"You don't have to worry about my wife, Sharief. And it won't be necessary for you to visit her, she'll be visiting you with a proposition".

"Really?" breathed Sharief, mounting interest in his voice, "You mean she's going to make me an offer to let you go? I'll be looking forward to it, King. Maybe we can come to an arrangement over dinner?"

"You'll need enough money for four persons, Sharief".

"What do you mean?" Sharief was taken aback.

"It's customary for a Filipina to be chaperoned on her dates with new acquaintances and my brothers will be coming with her, they're in the British army, Sharief. They're on leave for Christmas and it seems they've got a present for you and...... Click!

The line cut dead; I knew Sharief would now go to England with a permanent crook in his neck as he continually glanced over his shoulder to see if he was being followed. As for paying a visit to Lyn, Sharief would not have the balls to leave London if he left his home at all. I had no brothers, but Sharief didn't know that and I was sure, Sharief certainly wouldn't try to find out.

Christmas came and went mostly unnoticed, as it usually did in Saudi. Most Christian foreigners returned to their own country for the celebrations and the ones left behind did not like to be reminded of the fact. Christmas was illegal in Saudi and little fuss was made if any at all. I was accustomed to the non-existence but I was not accustomed to the tearful phone call made by Lyn. Still determined and sorry I was not at her side but she promised she would be thinking of me which was all I needed. To block out the memories of Christmas past, I concentrated on my preparation for the court hearing. It would be a good opportunity to finish my task; Sharief's representative would be present by promise to the court and I knew they could not now withdraw, without forfeiting the case.

DECEMBER 30 - Labour court

Sharief's legal advisor sat smugly and confident in the court. I had seen this man many times before, at five-foot-tall he was short but very fat with the features of the doughboy on the bread wrappers, which is how he came by the nickname.

"So, you see honoured justices, Mr King was informed of the changes in policy, regarding the contractual benefits, that were once standard procedure with Sharief and have since been cancelled by the circulation of this memo, submitted in evidence here. We therefore propose he be paid the amount as specified and deported on an exit only visa to be blocked against re-entry into the Kingdom. We ask this due to the nature of the vital company information he could pass on to our competitors thus damaging our current market position".

A smug satisfaction crossed the doughboy's face.

"Did he really think it would be that easy? Did he not realise how many days and nights I've studied my position? Had he no idea of the determination involved, not to mention the regulations in the labour laws? I wasn't fighting for my job, like him, I was fighting for my life"

The judges requested evidence that I had seen the memo, in cases of change of contract before expiry, a signature was needed from the employee, on the re-written contract, no signature was evident and the memo was insufficient, that could have been typed anywhere and at any time, the judges wanted more.

"I'm sorry, I didn't realise". the doughboy sputtered, he had no such evidence and he knew it, I knew it and now the judges asked me to comment.

I stood and paused until all the judges were listening to me and not the continuing protestations by the doughboy or distracted by other matters involving ground beef and egg. The court was a simple affair; a few well-placed desks separated four or five officials in black robes, from the occupying plaintiffs. All the officials were, and had to be, devout Muslims. They all sported goatee type chin beards and moustaches and being of the same elderly disposition they all looked strangely alike, as if cloned from some central, legal collection of authority.

"Your honours," I began, "The documents presented here today by this man are false. Neither I, nor any of my colleagues have seen such a notice before. I ask that irrefutable proof to be presented here today, as you have already stated, by the way of signatures or initials, as was the company procedure before this claim. Sharief has falsified documents before, I can prove this beyond doubt".

"Lies!" guffawed the doughboy, "All lies!"

The judge waved the doughboy to silence and spoke to me personally,

"This is a very serious allegation, Mr King. I hope you can substantiate your words, or you could be in serious trouble, but nevertheless, please continue".

"How long have you been employed by the Sharief?" I looked down at the doughboy.

"One year and eight months!" a confident response.

"During which time you claim never to have falsified documents?"

"That is correct, and I deeply resent the accusation".

"You have entered this court today as an employee of the Sharief, to represent the Sharief and you say you have never seen or utilised false documentation?"

"Of course not!" the fat boy grinned to the intently interested Judges.

"Would you swear before the court on that statement?"

The doughboy paused before replying; suddenly he became suspicious,

"I swear before the honoured Judges of this court". The doughboy grinned as if to hide his dawning inner fears.

"Good, can I see your work permit?"

The realisation hit the doughboy like a sledgehammer between the eyes. He turned red as if about to choke, stuttering and lost for words, blind panic flashed across his pug-like features and sweat popped up on his brow,

"I don't have it with me". he lied again.

"Did you register with the court?"

"I did" replied the dough boy, now going under for the third time, now he had to produce his permit, I knew, the judges knew and he knew, you could not get past the guards without one.

"Slowly the elusive document was produced. I took the document in my hand, I had no need to read the Arabic, permits carried English wording and the company stamp for good measure, I increased the volume of my voice for effect.

"Can you explain to the judges why your permit is registered under United Arab Trading Agencies?"

"Whaaat!" exclaimed one of the judges.

214

"Mr Sama came here today under the pretence of being employed by the Sharief his permit is not registered with the Sharief group, nor is it registered with the Sharief family. I therefore charge him with entering this courtroom under false pretences and lying under oath. He signed into the court as Sharief employee and presented a false work permit, with false documentation to back up his case".

I sat down as the judges inspected the work permit. One of the judges peered over the top of his reading glasses and spoke directly to Mr Sama,

"Mr Sama you have two days to return to this court with your papers in order. If you succeed no action will be taken against you regarding your immediate deportation, but I do not, and I repeat, I do not want to see your face in this legal establishment again, is that understood?"

The doughboy nodded, he could never get his permit organised in such a brief time and had effectively received an instant deportation order. He was just another casualty to the dishonest procedures of the Sharief. I had known all along. The doughboy had revealed the information to me on an earlier occasion. He had not wanted to change his work permit, as he did not yet trust Sharief. With this permit, he could work for Sharief and, when it suited him, he could return to Egypt without Sharief's knowledge or permission. Now he was going back to Egypt in two days, he had better get home to his wife. He had a lot of explaining, packing and preparation to do. The court was adjourned until February 2nd. I sighed at the additional month's wait, comforted only, by the doughboy's hasty, but anguished departure from the court, the country and the fact that I had crushed the opposition's first attempts to cheat me.

I tried not to think of the illegal clutches of the Sharief that were now holding me in the country. By law, the Sharief was entitled to hold my passport during my stay in Saudi. This ensured protection of the employers and prevented some foreigners fleeing back to their own country with huge sums of money, payrolls and payments that were supposed to be under their care. Sharief held my passport and it burned me to think what Sharief might do with it if things turned sour for him. I settled back into my usual routines, running at dawn, walking during the days, mostly backward and forward to the Sharief residence where Pete and Hawkeye lived.

I lost weight, my body carried little fat to start with but I slimmed down from a thirty-four waist to a thirty and lost eight Kilos in the process. It was a gradual loss and only my loose-fitting pants alerted me to the fact. One evening I was reading the Jeddah Daily, there was to be a marathon the following day, forty kilometres of running up and down the Cornice. I fancied my chances. I walked six kilometres to the start of the race, registered on the day, ran continually for three hours and fifteen minutes and despite my physical atonement, I only managed seventh place.

"Must be out of condition" I thought, as I walked the six kilometres back to my apartment. In the same Hush Puppy shoes, I had run the race in as I forgot my trainers. (photos available)

FEBRUARY 2ND - LABOUR COURT

The Sharief attended the hearing along with a rather smart looking lawyer, obviously appointed since the deportation of the doughboy. I hardly spoke. The Sharief introduced himself and his Lawyer and then tried to pile a myriad of documents before the judges - supposedly pertaining to the theft and misappropriation of funds by one Robert E King.

I could not believe it, there were masses of paper and documents. The Sharief sat with a sickly smirk during the whole of the proceedings. It took two hours for the court to register the supposed evidence. I felt demoralised. The court hung on to every word from the Sharief but I was hardly allowed to speak. Sharief's lawyer looked down his nose at me like I was some poisonous insect he was about to step on and squash. The court

216

was adjourned until March 15th, I left the court with some distress, and I failed to see the point of it all.

I contacted my lawyer associate. I informed him, he could not represent me, only a Saudi could, but he knew of somebody with an excellent reputation in Jeddah and suggested I go to see him. I did not have to be told twice.

It had to be a Saudi lawyer, which was stated in the Saudi laws too. All lawyers attending court had to be of good Saudi origin, and no foreigners were allowed. The Saudi lawyer laughed at the case before him. It was a piece of cake. I need worry no more, in fact with a power of attorney. I could go home and my lawyer would take care of everything.

It was too good to be true; I prepared the power of attorney for the lawyer. It was stamped and authorised by the British Embassy and I delivered the document back to the lawyer just two days after my hearing.

The Sharief vehemently refused to hand over my passport. Suddenly he had a massive claim against me about stolen money and announced he had every right to hold the passport until my proven innocence dictated release. I almost blew my top. The Saudi lawyer calmed me down,

"We'll get your passport at the next hearing on March 15th. Don't worry, King. Everything is crystal clear; you'll soon be on your way home".

I boiled inside for a few days and then finally resigned myself to my lawyer's advice. Mohammed Mansouri, God bless him, was no teacake and I felt sure I was in good, safe hands. Mansouri was another Saudi I would genuinely trust with my life, a proper Saudi Gentleman with no prejudice whatsoever.

Pete and Hawkeye were also upset. What power did the Sharief control, which enabled him to detain people without charge or cause? They argued along with me. All three of us agreed it was unfair, it seemed the Saudi law was specifically designed to protect Saudis and to hell with the foreigners. Whatever the three of us thought, Saudi law was paramount and

217

the only thing we could do was to comply. To do otherwise would have caused more problems than we needed and we already had more than enough problems to cope with. For the time being the Saudi Law reigned supreme and Pete, Hawkeye, and myself, nor anybody else for that matter, could do anything about it but with Mohammed Mansouri on my case I at least felt safer than I had done before. He was another genuine Saudi with honour and dignity that I hoped would prevail.

Chapter 10
AMBUSH

MARCH 15th - LABOUR COURT.

Sharief attended the court, with his ever-present lawyer constantly buzzing and whispering at his side. More bundles of irrelevant papers were once again submitted to the court. My lawyer objected but the objection was overruled and the presentation of hundreds of hand-written documents I had never seen before commenced. It took the best part of two hours to register the documents, leaving no time to discuss the case and a further date was set for the next hearing. The judge warned the Sharief that no new evidence would now be accepted; the Sharief glanced over to me and grinned,

"It's OK", he began to smile, "We have enough evidence here to keep things moving for a long time yet".

I chilled at the words; I inquired about the charges of stolen mail, harassment and abuse. When would the court act on my evidence? Were the judges going to do anything about that? What about his evidence presented to the court on day one of the hearings? Why, weren't they doing anything about that? I wanted a simple answer, why couldn't they give me a simple answer?

"Mr King," began the judge, "The simple answer is, Saudis - just don't do these things".

"That's right," smiled the Sharief, "We don't".

"What!" I exclaimed, in stunned disbelief, "What about my evidence, what about my stolen mail, this man is a thief and I can prove it". I was losing my cool.

"It's OK!" my lawyer took my arm to console me, "We can take care of this later, don't worry Bob. Everything is under control. He's digging a deep hole for himself from which there will be no escape. He can't present more evidence because he has no evidence. It's just a stalling tactic. The judges will throw

219

out all this nonsense at the next hearing. You'll see. Please calm down and take it easy, don't upset or insult the judge's intelligence, they are more aware of what is going on than you may think".

The court was adjourned and I left the room as calmly as possible, desperately craving to punch Sharief on the nose. Another month wasted, just like that. What about my black and white evidence, were they really going to look the other way?

Pete and Hawkeye could hardly believe the news. Black and white evidence was completely ignored.

"Saudis don't do these things" what sort of court utters a statement like that? I may just as well resign myself, to the fact that I was wasting my time, if the judges were already saying that Sharief, was not capable of crime simply because he was a Saudi, what was the point of it all? It was a week, before I had settled down from the sheer frustration of the event and rid my system of the burning hatred now carried in my bones for the Sharief, but it wasn't long before the rage flooded back with a vengeance.

I walked the distance of six kilometres from the Sharief apartments. I preferred to walk. It allowed me time to cool down and burn up any spare energy before I retired to bed. It was the only way I could guarantee a good night's sleep, provided the Sharief or his cronies did not come calling. I had walked this route so often that I could have done it blindfolded, which was almost my undoing. One evening, I walked briskly homeward, the music from my Walkman stereo numbed the efforts of my walk and drowned out surrounding noise. A small untidy saloon car overtook me, continued for a distance and stopped fifty meters ahead of my position. As I neared the parked vehicle, I saw two Sudanese men climb out and disappear under the bonnet, the car looked like it had broken down, and they were obviously having some sort of engine trouble, I would give them a hand I thought. As I drew level with the car, one of the Sudanese guys surfaced from under the bonnet and blocked my path. I pulled the tiny earphones from my ears,

220

"Scuse me," I apologised and tried to walk around but the Sudanese guy moved quickly and blocked my route. Now his partner appeared from under the bonnet with a large wooden shaft in his hand. We were on a lonely, unlit, sparsely inhabited, back street. I walked this route to avoid trouble; hardly anyone ever came this way, no traffic, no pedestrians and hopefully no Sharief. It was obvious what these guys wanted. I wanted to shout for help but there was no point. These two guys looked like two shaven gorillas. Big, black and just the sort of guys you wouldn't want to meet on a darkened back street in Jeddah, Saudi Arabia. My brain worked overtime on the scenario, me lying in the street, a pool of blood, life oozing away from my body, bashed to death, murdered, mugged. I couldn't help the hopeless sick feeling as it washed over me. I tried to think of a way of escaping the inevitable. It was now impossible to run, their car blocked one side parallel to this was a pile of construction debris from the road works, too soft to climb over with any speed and now one of the men was in front and the man with the club came up behind me.

"We gotta message for you, Mista".

I couldn't speak; sheer terror had me by the throat.

"Drop the case and leave the country or else".

"The gorilla in front with the wooden shaft did the talking; his confident voice was riddled with malice.

"What happens if I don't drop the case?" I knew the answer, I just couldn't think of anything else to say, other than begging for mercy and I wasn't prepared to do that just yet.

"If you don't drop the case, we have been told to drop you, Mista. So, do us all a favour and go home, we hate to hurt you shiny, new, white boy, new kids, you squeal so loudly you wake up the peace-loving folk of Saudi". They flashed each other a brilliant white grin and sniggered, almost as if they were school kids who had been naughty and knew they weren't going to be punished for their minor deed.

I wound the earphone wires around the Walkman and thrust the small cassette player deep into my pocket.

"Hey, don't put that away, I've always wanted a Walkman". He was obviously the leader and now he had made his intentions clear, they were going to fuck me over for Sharief and rob me for themselves. I wanted to cry out, beg them to leave me alone and tell them I would do whatever they asked. Then I remembered Lyn and my two friends Pete and Hawkeye. I felt a little better, this fight was for them as well, and I would have to be brave. I swallowed my fear and said nothing; maybe they would just warn me and go away.

"Well, what's it going to be, Mista?"

"I have no choice". I almost whispered, "You really give me no alternative. What chance do I have against the Sharief and his connections, especially gentlemen of your breeding? I just can't give up the case, not now, it's already too late to do that"

I could see them gearing up for their attack, nodding to each other, making sure they were both well prepared. I was getting fed up, why don't they just bash me over the head and get it over with, I knew it was coming, why don't they just get on with it, let's just get the whole thing finished! I thought I was going to break down, maybe even cry for mercy but then a small voice whispered in my ear, one small anonymous voice with a single encouraging word, "Khowaja'. It was like an electronic signal, a pulse into a mental gearbox to change up to full torque speed, shit, if they weren't going to get started, I'd start this bloody party myself, it always worked in Yorkshire.

Without warning, I dove into the larger of the two men but they were quicker, the wooden shaft smacked into my back, forcing me to my knees and their sandal-clad feet began smashing into my folding body. I grabbed a leg and held on tight, instantly halving the number of blows. The big guy fell backwards and I scrambled on top of the writhing body and moved in quickly, I had to get one of the bastards out of action if I were to have any chance at all. WHACK! Suddenly - without warning the wooden shaft caught me full on the right temple, bursting open my eyebrow and spattering the pavement with raindrops of blood. Another swish warned me and my arms flew upward automatically to protect my face. The shaft smashed into my protective arms, knocking them back so that the shaft butted into the bridge of my nose, opening a deep gash between my watering eyes. My nose was burning on the inside, stinging and blinding as the tears welled up in my eyes. I shook my head and crimson droplets spattered the pavement. It wasn't that bad; they had worn sandals that had fallen from their feet as the attack began. Getting a kicking with good old Yorkshire hobnailed boots was one thing, getting a kicking from bare feet was much easier on the ribcage. The punching and kicking continued. I was dragged off the big guy; blood streaming from my face and speckled stars dancing before my eyes. I kneeled for a moment as more blows rained in. I feigned severe injury and collapsed disorientated on the sandy verge. The sight of all the blood streaming over my face must have satisfied my attackers. I lay on my side, protecting as much of my body as possible. The pavement was warm and slightly comforting, at least the kicking was over, and now I could go home in peace.

"That was just a warning, Mista. Now drop the case or else". He grabbed my shirt, dragged me around and tore my Walkman from my pocket

That's it, I thought, they're giving up, they must feel they've done enough to earn their payment from Sharief, they'd done their duty and were now about to depart with my Walkman for evidence.

The shaft slapped into the sandy verge and the two of them boarded the car. My vision had cleared and I wiped the blood across my face its familiar rusty taste penetrated my thoughts. Now the frustration screamed inside my head as the tears flowed down my cheeks. I could see Sharief laughing as the two men related their tale. I remembered Lyn and the Christmas with my family I had been denied. My life slipping through my fingers, day by day, with nothing to show for it but pain and heartache. I also remembered Sharief and how he was hell-bent on destroying my reputation, my home, my marriage and whilst I was thinking these things, the screaming pain stopped and the voice whispered once more, "Khowaja" I felt the rage as it blossomed through my body and flooded my veins. The uncontrollable, burning fire as the juggernaut of adrenaline smashed down the barriers of restraint. My whole body burned with hatred and the white-hot heat of revenge. I sucked in a deep, sweet breath of air, supplying the oxygen my fury so desperately craved. Wiping my eyes, I climbed to my feet as the pulsing torrent of carnal ferocity pumped into my brain. All civilised restraints disappeared, as my senses tripped into the most basic of instincts, survival mode. I snatched up the discarded shaft along with a handful of sand. I hoisted the shaft as if it were weightless and bursting with hatred; I smashed it into the windscreen of the slowly departing car. The windscreen exploded into glistening white diamonds. One of my tormentors caught the handful of sand with his face and eyes as it sprayed through the side window, which delayed his exit and the two men evacuated the car, first one then the other, rubbing his eyes and screaming, in a shower of particled glass, straight into the rage of a shaft wielding Khowaja.

"WHACK!!" already one had fallen his head jerking with the blow as a bloody red gash developed beneath tight black curls. CRACK! An arm was surely broken as it rose to protect its controller's head. I couldn't control the fury they had unleashed from within. "Com'on you chicken shit bastards let's go; let's really have a fuckin proper scrap. I slashed and stabbed with the wooden stake, flailing like a man possessed, whacking the legs from beneath the lumbering gorillas, felling the two giant Sudanese like rotten old trees. I had to make sure they were beaten, if I didn't, I knew was dead meat. I watched them crumple as they fell to the ground. I made sure they would bear no thoughts of revenge and that they would be in no position to retaliate. I spared their heads from further punishment and hammered their legs, ribs and arms. Until a pleading cry sounded,

"Please, Mista, please!"

The pitiful cry of grown men begging for mercy pierced the shroud of rage and the adrenaline-fuelled retribution slowed. The blood lust fury receded to an unknown cage within. I saw the pitiful sight that lay before me, two broken men almost crying. I stopped the punishment and crunched over the broken chips of glass to their car. I stabbed my head through the opened door and dragged out a small square carpet. Lifting the hood, I yanked the rubber fuel line from the carburettor. The free-flowing fuel sprayed the carpet and when satisfied with the soaking I threw the carpet onto the back seat of the car. I rummaged around inside the car until I found what I was looking for. As my thumb flicked the tiny steel wheel and sparked a flame to life, another cry erupted,

"Wait, Mista. It's all we got!"

I ignored them, they started this and I wanted to finish it. The flint showered bright sparks into the stream of gas from the small plastic lighter and the gangsters" jalopy flashed ablaze. The plastic and foam rubber interior fuelled the greedy flames. Breathing heavily, I wiped the blood across my face and warned the two men,

"Sharief didn't pay you enough, tell him I owe him for this little incident and tell him he'll get his dues, with interest".

I grabbed my Walkman, which had so far helped me survive this circus, I replaced the earphones, switched on the Walkman and strode away into the night. I carried the shaft under my arm for the first few hundred meters, just in case, I wasn't making the same mistake they did. Turning back to observe the situation, I realised they'd had enough and I threw the shaft of wood into the ditch. The two gorillas were limping away. The light from the blazing car disfiguring their hunching gaits. They were in a hurry to get clear before the police arrived. I knew they were probably illegal immigrants, their chosen mode of employment dictated as much. In which case, the car would be unregistered, uninsured and now undriveable. Another victim of an electrical fault or solar fire with no owner coming forward to pay for the recovery of the burned-out shell. I ached from head to foot but the sweet

sensation of an impossible victory, more than made up for the
pain.

"Jesus Christ! Bob. What happened to you?"

"I got a visiting card from Sharief, Pete. Seems he wants me
to drop the case or he's going to give me trouble".

I winced as an attempted grin rippled the stubby red and
blue pipe that had once resembled a nose and was now swollen
almost beyond recognition and sitting between two black eyes.

Pete inspected the damage, obviously sick in his stomach for
the pain of his friend.

"Where did you get the eye stitched?"

"Lyn's old place, the doctor did it on the quiet. I told him what
had happened and he said he'd keep a lookout for the two guys
coming in. He'll try to get their names and addresses from their
work permits if they had any that is before they left the hospital.
OUCH! Pete! Don't touch the stitches!"

"Does it hurt?"

"Of course, it bloody hurts you silly bastard, do you think it got
that size by playing with it?"

"The nose looks a mess". sighed Pete, "What happened to
the other guys? I suppose they ran away".

"They had to," I boasted proudly, "I burned their car". I winced
again with the pain of my grin.

"Whaaaaat!" gasped Pete incredulously.

"And they didn't run away. They were limping along like the
losing entry of a three-legged race the last time I saw them, one
blinded by sand led by the other guy who was howling in pain".

"Any other marks on you?" Inquired Pete still concerned.

I lifted my shirt and the bruises and wheals where the shaft
had connected with my flesh were angrier and redder than raw
meat.

"Jesus," sighed Pete, "Forget about the other guys, looks like
they did a pretty good job on you".

"I'll live!" I assured him.

"What happens about the case?"

226

"The case goes on as planned".

"Are you sure, Bob? I mean, even if you quit now, you gave him one hell of a run for my money".

"No!" I snapped back angrily, "That bastard's got to pay us what we're owed".

"Well, you ought to move in here, for the time being, safety in numbers and all that". stressed Pete.

"No, I don't think he'll try anything like that again. I spoke to the lawyer and he said he may get away with it once by denying all knowledge of it, but if I start looking like this on a regular basis, especially during the court hearings, he's going to be in trouble".

"You mean, you can't do anything about it?"

"I registered a complaint this morning".

"And?"

"The complaint has been registered and noted for the next hearing".

"Great!" snarled Pete with disgust, "They kick the shit out of you and you have to accept it, great! that's just fucking great!"

"I didn't say we had to accept it, Pete. Legally we must that's all".

"Well, there's not a lot else we can do by the sound of things".

"That depends on how far the Sharief is willing to push us and the risks he's prepared to take before we hit back. I've got a few ideas in mind just in case we get into serious trouble and there's no way out, we'll use a code".

"Sounds a bit farfetched to me," groaned Pete.

"Well, it's just in case, Pete. The way things are going we ought to prepare for the worst".

"I hear what you're saying," spat Pete, "Loud and clear".

We were interrupted as Hawkeye entered the room

"Holy shit! what happened to you, Bob?".

"Well Hawkeye," I began. "I was picking my nose........

The three of us discussed the situation well into the night. I stayed overnight and slept on the couch but only because by the

227

time we had finished plotting further action, it was too late to risk going anywhere.

I lapsed back into my routine of running, walking and playing night squash. By the time the court hearing came around my nose had returned to normal size. The bruising and swellings had all but gone but not from the photographs and the Sharief sat in the court with a worried look on his face. Things were not entirely going his way.

APRIL 14th LABOUR COURT

The hearing began with the judges throwing out the papers that had previously been submitted by the Sharief. They were considered worthless; no signatures were evident and they were all handwritten in Arabic which I wasn't capable of. The court had no choice other than to disregard them totally and they were struck from the records. I could not believe my ears. The judge went on to say that it was obvious that Sharief was doing his utmost to delay the proceedings and that the court would not tolerate such actions again. Furthermore, a new hearing would be attended on the twenty fourth of April, within two weeks; between now and then all accepted submittals would be examined closely. Any explanations of such material the judges thought necessary would be requested on the next court date they had set and then the judges would pass their decision.

I could hardly believe my ears, was it really ending? Was the next meeting really, in ten days" time? Shit! I could do ten more days standing on my head.

Pete and Hawkeye were well pleased with the result. At least it seemed like we were now making headway. When I received the court's decision, they would plan their notice to quit accordingly, making sure they received full award of all outstanding dues.

For my part I relaxed, sunbathing on the roof of my apartment, I also continued with my daily exercise and had the stitches removed from my brow. Things, including myself, began to look a whole lot better. I would soon be going home, my tan looked perfect and my situation had improved to such an extent that I was getting a full night's sleep.

The doorbell chirruped, I went to the sentry hole and peeped out, five armed police stood outside my door.

"Oh no!" I gasped, "Now what".

"Yes, what do you want sadiques". I politely inquired.

"We would like to check over your apartment, please. Open the door I would like a word with you".

The policeman spoke perfect English,

"Must be educated". I thought as I unlocked the door and opened it six inches.

"Yes, what do you want," I enquired again "look at the notices and see what I am involved in at the courts, you need to be aware of my court case'

They looked but seemed to have other things on their mind.

"Look we're sorry to bother you but we have a search warrant, it seems you have been reported for illegal production of alcohol".

"What!" I gasped at the accusation.

"Look". Insisted the officer, "Let us in for a look around the apartment, that's all we want and if we don't find anything we'll be gone and we won't bother you again".

My mind buzzed, "Suppose these bastards come in and plant something, drugs or anything illegal. I'm down the tubes, case is cancelled, and Sharief is in the clear and I'll never get out of Saudi Arabia in a month of Sundays".

"How many of you need to come in?" I kept the polite tone in my voice.

"Just me if you like, brewing stills are not easy to hide". he was obviously the boss.

"Show me the warrant, please".

I was shown the warrant, it was in Arabic and English and I knew I had no choice,

"OK, just you I'm willing to open the door for you".

CHAPTER 13   SAUDI STYLE   PLANS

I opened the door and the officer walked inside. He stood perplexed in the Spartan furnishings. All the personal touches had long since left with Lyn. The officer walked around the lounge, the dining room, the bedrooms and the bathroom. Finally, he entered the kitchen and with a sly wink in my direction, he opened the refrigerator. I wasn't that stupid; I'd gotten rid of the home brew months ago. The officer balked at the empty refrigerator.

"No food?" He enquired.

"Listen," I related my tale in classical Arabic, "I have a labour court case with a man called Sharief. Probably the same person that had you sent here. I have not worked for over six months; I haven't got any money so I can't afford to buy food. Now - is that a crime sir? am I under arrest for starving? I understand a good Muslim fasts at Ramadan, maybe I can do this too?"

The officer stared into my eyes as if he recognised the all too familiar predicament,

"One moment please". The officer went outside and said something to his waiting men, who began fumbling in their pockets. A moment later the officer returned with five crisp, fifty Riyal notes crumpled in his hand.

"We are sorry we had to intrude upon you like this, please take this money and buy some food". We shook hands warmly, the officer left, closing the door behind him.

I stood and stared at the money they had pressed into my palm, there was enough here to keep me going for a couple of weeks, how could they do this? they were Saudis; Saudis don't do these things. I wanted to cry with relief, tears tried to blur my vision now I was more confused than ever. One minute you hated their guts and the next minute you wanted to put your arms around them and give them a hug, one thing was for sure, Saudi Arabia had its moments and the Saudis were starting to look a lot more caring than they would have you believe in my eyes.

"I don't believe it". I sighed, "I just don't believe it". and neither did Pete and Hawkeye when I told them.

APRIL 24th LABOUR COURT

All documents were admitted and no further explanations were needed. All I had to do now was wait for the decision that would release me from the Sharief's illegal clutches. I left the court entirely satisfied. The case was concluded and now all I had to do was await the judges" decision. Just a few more weeks and I would be going home a happy man at least, that's what my lawyer had told me and Mohammed Mansouri was an honest man.

I relayed the news. The guys were almost as relieved as I was. Just a few more weeks to the decision and then we could plan our lives accordingly. Even Hangar admitted he was growing tired of the Sharief's new policies. The chopper never flew anywhere unless Sharief released it from the pad with a written authorisation or his big, wide arse was in it.

"It's getting so that a guy can't take a shit without a paper from the Sharief". grinned Hangar, "Maybe it's time we all packed up and just got the hell out of here".

I waited patiently for three weeks and heard nothing from the court,

"Why don't you visit the prince?" said the Saudis who had heard of my plight, "You can see him, he is a good and just man, and he will help you with your case". I needed to do something; I couldn't sit around watching my sanity fall to pieces around me. Eventually, I took their advice, anything was better than vegetating.

I sat with the rest of them in the prince's business office on the main Madinah Road that bisected Jeddah into two equal halves.

"Citizens in need of assistance" was their official title but I recognised their plight and gave them my own title,

"People who were being fucked over by the Saudi system, just like myself that's what I called them. I sat for two hours until finally, a shout broke the respectful silence,

"Amir, Al Amir, the Prince" up went the call and everybody dashed in the general direction of the main door.

I allowed myself to be dragged along with the eager throng. We were herded into a smaller waiting room that overlooked the entry into the main building. Once we had been assembled - with each man clutching a slip of paper. The doors swung open and the prince strode into his majlis. Tribal Bedouins flanked him, holding aloft huge gold-handled swords. Tucked into their belts, were gold-handled daggers, their handles encrusted with jewels, which sparkled and danced against their crisp white thobes. These were the prince's traditional guardians, a proud memory of days gone by. Behind the Bedouins marched two orthodox policemen, carrying black, sinister machine guns that were always at the ready. Prince Majed the governor of Makkah strode regally into the room. I wasn't sure whether to kiss his feet or shake his hand. I settled for the hand job.

"Well young man, what's your problem?" the prince spoke perfect English.

I handed over my paper, explaining my predicament in Arabic and requested my passport, that I may leave this wondrous paradise and return to my native home. The prince smiled, accepted my paper, passed along the line of the other "Citizens in need', collected similar slips of paper and disappeared into his office with a final sweep of his gold-trimmed black cape. I was impressed; I had never been that close to a Prince before, even though in Saudi, there were dozens of them.

My name was called and a small slip of paper was handed to me. Apparently, I would have to go to Makkah on the following Saturday where I was sure to receive my reply.

"I can't," I announced, "I'm not a Muslim".

"You must request this from a Saudi friend, give him the slip of paper and he can pick up your reply and send it on to you".

232

"Thanks very much" I sighed, wondering where I could find a Saudi friend willing to take on Sharief.

I eventually received my reply; a message had been sent to the labour court, everything would be taken care of as soon as possible,

"Great!" I thought, "But when".

One month after the case was concluded I was still waiting for the decision,

"Sorry for the delay" they apologised "It has to be typed up but it won't be long now".

The weeks continued to roll by and I continued my daily routine. Nothing was heard from the court, neither was anything heard from the prince. My patience ebbed and flowed. Sometimes I wondered about the inner strength that prevented me from visiting the Sharief's office and taking my passport by force. I did not have the answers, other than; I had come too far to throw it all away now. What was another week or so? or even a month at the very outside.

Pete and the guys were just as nervous as I was. I explained about my first days at the Labour Courts and it wasn't too difficult to understand where the time was going. One thing was certain, at the speed Arabic was typed; one page could easily take two or three weeks.

Another message arrived via my lawyer,

"It's nearly ready; it has been typed, the judge has checked and stamped the documents involved, we are just waiting for it to be signed.

I wondered why it could not be stamped and signed at the same time, but then, this was Saudi Arabia and you know what the man said, "Saudis - just don't do these things".

The decision was suddenly released but not quickly enough to stop the Sharief locking my passport in his personal safe and fleeing the country to London. I could not now leave, even though that was what the judges had ordered. The decision also stated I should get nothing, after all, I was the one who had resigned.

CHAPTER 13   SAUDI STYLE   PLANS

"What!" I yelled in disbelief at my lawyer office.

"They did not read the evidence; they are under a lot of pressure. We can appeal to the super court in Riyadh; it will only take one month. We will win; we have a cast iron case. We will have to go all the way; this is how things are done in Saudi Arabia. Nothing comes easy, you must fight all the way, you must be seen to be proud and to fight for what is rightfully yours, this is how it is, this is how it has always been!"

I looked my lawyer straight in the eye,

"How come I'm a prisoner here and the Sharief has run away to London and I can't get my passport? answer me that?"

"He has thirty days to appeal, Mr Bob, He can still hold you until he either appeals or accepts the decision".

"I brought the case against him, right?" I pleaded my case.

"Right!" answered my Lawyer.

"And I have claims against him, right?"

"Right again". I could sense my Lawyer felt he had to respond.

"Then please answer me here and now, how come I can't leave the country, yet he can come and go as he wishes. Since I started this affair, he's been to England, the States, the Greek Islands, the Philippines and I am being held here at his whim. Why is this? I ask you, just tell me why? Please, just tell me why?"

My lawyer looked down at his desk, his fingers carelessly toying with his prayer beads, then he lifted his eyes to meet mine and with a deep apologetic tone he answered the painful question,

"It's the Saudi Law, Bob. It's the Saudi Arabian Law".

I left him sitting at his desk, head bowed almost apologetically, thumbing his prayer beads through his fingers, I could see he was not happy with his answer. I left him to dwell on the matter; I had little else to say. It wasn't his fault he was a decent Saudi I knew this for a fact.

"Why don't you go to the Embassy?" they asked.

234

Despite knowing the reason, I decided to suck it and see.

"What's the problem?" asked the Embassy officials.

"Hey look," I began, "I don't want to bother you, but I just fought my way through eleven months of Saudi Labour court and the judges ordered that my employer must hand over my passport and allow me to go free. He has withheld my passport for the last six months or so, ever since I gave power of attorney to my lawyer. My lawyer now says there's really no reason for me to be here. The Labour Board has ordered Sharief to hand over my passport and he refuses. This means he has stolen the passport of a British subject, is there anything you can do?"

"Right! Mr King give us the telephone number of the company concerned and the name of this Sharief and we will investigate this matter at once. There are quite a few measures we can take, including banning him from visiting England until something is sorted out, leave it to us and we'll be in touch".

I left the Embassy; pleasantly surprised at the way I had been received. The consulate was going to jump on the Sharief's back.

"And I thought they were powerless," I admonished myself, "Looks like I was totally wrong about those guys".

I left the number of Pete's apartment in case the Embassy needed to contact me, they did,

"Hello - is Mr King there?"

"King speaking".

"This is the British Consul, Mr King. We've been in touch with your employer's office and they have assured us they will release your passport as soon as they receive written confirmation from the Labour office. It appears they have not yet received notification of the final decision, but as soon as they do receive it, they will be preparing your passport so that you can pack up and leave".

"That sounds reasonable, can you let me have that in writing? I need to prove to certain creditors back home that I'm being detained against my will and it would be a powerful help if I could have such a document on file".

235

"I'll have it typed up by this afternoon, Mr King. You can pick it up after two o'clock".

"I'll be there, thank you very much".

I collected the document; it would surely come in useful, proof of my illegal detention and the fact that my passport was being held without reasonable cause.

I had been born with a certain streak of independence and now that streak surfaced amongst the debris of my shattered world. Now I would sort out my problem the best way I knew how, by myself, alone - leaving no one else to blame for my failure but myself. Lyn continued to phone. It had become routine, not to mention expensive. I directed my anger and frustration to the pen, or rather the word processor, writing to every publication known to man including the daily newspapers, of the country, in which the Sharief was now illegally detaining me.

My letters began to surface in print; the Saudi Gazette's legal column, which advised me,

"The laws of Saudi Arabia are just and well established, you are one hundred percent right about your commendable actions and we have no doubt you will receive justice.

Time magazine, News week, Middle East Expatriate all expressed stunned disbelief at my present predicament. I posted letters daily and made certain - through my carefully worded letters, that if anything were to happen to me during my detention, a lot of people would want to know why. There would be no chance of a whitewash, by internal interference with commercial considerations in mind as had happened before. The Sharief, the law, the cronies and Saudi Arabia itself could do as they pleased but the truth would ultimately prevail. The finger of recognition would then be pointed and the guilty would be named.

So, it had come to this, I now had doubts about the safety of my life and I swore to myself, that whatever happened, I wouldn't make it easy for them.

CHAPTER 13   SAUDI STYLE   PLANS

I secured a new passport from the British Embassy merely to pacify the police should they decide to "pull" me in for reasons "unknown'.

"Why don't you go back to the prince?" they asked, the multitudes who knew nothing of my plight, nothing about my treatment and nothing about the police state, which they all inhabited.

Finally, having tried everything else, I decided to try it, I had nothing to lose, it would pass the time, keep me occupied and who knows, I may even strike it lucky. I delivered myself to the office on Madinah Road for the second time. The prince had arrived before me and was already in attendance. I was hustled into a reception room along with a dozen or more "Citizens'. Suddenly the Prince stood before me, I thrust my right hand forward, shook the prince's hand warmly, after all, and it wasn't the prince's fault, was it? and threw in a slight bow of the head as a measure of respect.

"Can I be of assistance?" inquired Prince Saud, assistant Governor of Makkah. A tall scholarly looking gentleman wearing gilt-rimmed Cartier reading spectacles. Immaculately dressed in white thobe and gutra headdress. Prince Saud was almost hidden from the rear by a shimmering cape of golden silk that he had positioned for maximum effect around his lean, square shoulders.

"I have a problem, your Highness," I began, "My sponsor is trying to detain me in your country using all manner of illegal...........".

"I will see you in my office in fifteen minutes," the prince interrupted my strongly delivered address.

"Thank you, sir, your highness!" I confidently replied, determined this time, to spill the total account of Sharief's extreme prejudice against my person, the way I felt about the whole issue and to hell with the niceties or the consequences.

I had conversed in some of the highest echelon offices of the business world of Saudi Arabia but that had not nearly prepared me for what I was about to encounter. A well-armed guard with a

wide, leather pistol belt that supported his bulbous belly led me
up three flights of stairs. I wouldn't have been surprised had we
suddenly passed through cloud level. At the top of the stairs, we
advanced through massive, intricately carved, red wooden doors
and I was ushered to a plush, leather armchair. They were all
here in this room, Sheikhs, Ulemas, Overlords, businessmen
seeking favour and they all turned to scrutinise the "alien" in
"their" domain.

Terse, uncomplimentary statements flowed, unaware of my
understanding.

"Infidel foreigner in the Royal office".

"Must be someone of importance," God knows that must be
true,"

"Unless he is to be punished for unholy crimes but he has no
handcuffs".

Incense burners rippled warm slivers of scented smoke into
the musky air. Enough gold existed in this room, to bring tears to
the eyes of a pickpocket. Diamond encrusted Rolex watches.
Diamond solitaire pinkie rings with diamonds the size of ice
cubes. Chunky gold cufflinks, gold thobe buttons, limited edition
gold pens that nestled snugly in gold-embroidered top pockets.
Typical Arabian faces peered in my direction to scrutinise me.
Mohammedan chin beards hooked noses and piercing black
eyes, which were hooded by dark tanned eyelids, all twitching
with curious inspection.

Tea was continually proffered in small glass demitasses,
mounted in solid gold carriers. I displayed my customary
knowledge, accepting the tea and slurping loudly from the side
of the glass. Then came the tiny eggcups of Arabian coffee. The
coffee tasted like hot linseed oil but I accepted and welcomed
the beverages with my right hand. Only the right hand would
suffice, in Saudi, the left hand was only to be used for wiping
one's arse. I accepted all with my right hand, I knew it made no
difference, as I was right-handed anyway. I drained the glass of
tea, inverted the glass and shook it from side to side, the ancient
Arabic custom for satiated thirst. I did the same with the small

238

porcelain eggcup-shaped vessel and expressed my sincere thanks in English. Preliminaries dispensed with; they watched me now with a new curiosity. Passing to each other, discriminatory comments, absolutely assured of my non-comprehension. Finally, their curiosity got the better of them and I was questioned in English,

"Who are you foreigner and what is your business here?"

I replied with an almost perfect Bedouin intonation, the most classical of Arabic,

"Who are you calling foreigner, sir? I am not a miserable foreigner interested only in your money, I am a son of this country, ten years have I dwelled in your land, building your nation, pushing your heritage onto the western world's stage. The desert of Saudi is my home; I came to see my Prince. I am being accused, insulted and abused by one who surely cannot be a member of your own. I seek my legal rights, to escape his evil, insulting clutches, he is the dung that sticks to the arse of a camel and an insult to the good and gracious name of Saudi Arabia, a country I have adopted and love as my own!"

Eyes popped wide and mouths fell open, revealing yet more of the precious yellow metal. Exclamations of intense appreciation spewed forth. My intonation and dialect had really stunned my audience. Now we conversed freely, relaxed in the knowledge that I was aware of their customs and courtesies. They grinned, joked and laughed with me, expressing their apologies for their earlier remarks and my plight. Few milk skins took the trouble to learn the language and it was a pleasure to hear my congratulatory appraisal of their rapidly advancing lands. I fed their hungry curiosity with the best lines I had mastered. In my present location, I had no choice, from this very office, men could and probably did, disappear without trace. I did not intend to become one of them and discover their deadly destination. I scanned the walls. Portraits of the past and present Royalty including the immediate heirs adorned them. I decided if nothing happened after my hearing today, I would see King Fahad himself, the custodian of the two Holy Mosques, as I knew he preferred to be known.

I relaxed into the over-stuffed leather armchair. In front of me was an Arabic teapot with the long-curved spout nestled atop a smoked glass sheet of crystal, set in a gold-plated metal framework. The prince's secretary sat behind a huge mahogany desk that sank fifty millimetres or more into the dense, thickly piled carpet. I was still inspecting the riches when the call to order echoed, down a yet undiscovered corridor,

"Robert E King!" There could be no turning back now; I was now on my way into the inner sanctuary.

I stood to attention, offered my farewells and left the room. As I left, their fading, breath-like tones announced my calling,

"Khowaja" and inwardly I glowed.

I had conversed in some of the highest echelon offices of the known Saudi business world. I had even spent some interesting moments in the office of Mohammed Binjari, RIP, secretary to Prince Saud and whom, I would later discover, was tragically killed after my visit, in a typical Saudi road accident, may God Bless and rest his soul. However, that brief visitation five minutes ago, had in no way prepared me for what I was about to encounter. I was led along a series of wealth washed corridors until we finally approached a draped curtained door where, I was instantly searched by the two anonymous guards before being led inside.

The heavy though pleasant aroma of smouldering sandalwood perfumed the inner sanctuary's air. I was led to the front of the prince's desk. The prince concluded writing on some sort of parchment document, and when finished, glanced over the top of his reading spectacles and rose from his chair. He shook my hand with a friendly welcoming grip and pointed to a seat. I sat, awed to a mystical silence. Whilst the Prince read my complaint, I scanned his luxurious surroundings. The sandal wood burners ashed in one corner - small, almost invisible wisps of smoke, spiralled slowly into the air. The windows were curtained, probably against would be snipers. Gold

240

embroidered; yellow silk curtains over delicately patterned lace hid the outside world from view.

I reclined on a pure white, leather chesterfield couch, and the thick hide was almost sensuous to the touch. A deep pile, plain carpet smothered the floor from wall to wall but was overlaid by carpets of an infinitely richer tradition, Persian silks, I guessed, embroidered with a myriad of intricately woven themes, worth thousands of pounds per square foot on the open market. Heavy, gold-plated metals supported slabs of flat, bronze crystal, which served as opulent if overdone coffee tables. As the Prince read on, I drank in the wealth. A guard stood in one corner, his machine gun at the ready. He sensed rather than watched my presence and I was certain, if that if I had attempted any unsolicited move towards the Prince, I would have been dead before my buttocks had escaped the luxurious white leather. This was not the usual clone of a half-sleeping guard, this man had maximum protection, and SAS trained, embedded in his icy features, which although appeared outwardly calm, inwardly were undoubtedly vicious and deadly. Crystal chandeliers illuminated the room, twinkling overhead like some captured miniature galaxies. My eyes returned to the prince who was obviously deep in thought. The prince sat behind a huge monolith desk of gold-plated metal and glass. He perched upon a revolving, throne-like chair of sumptuous white leather and richly-grained wood. The prince sat and studied. Behind him hung the silken flags of the Saudi nation. On his right, the national colours, green, with the gold spun inscription which if unfurled fully would have proclaimed,

"THERE IS BUT ONE GOD AND MOHAMMED IS HIS MESSENGER" On his left the national symbol, a palm tree perched above crossed Bedouin sabres, with the embroidered message instilled in Saudis from birth,

"THERE CAN BE NO PEACE, WITHOUT JUSTICE',

"Right!" I thought, "When do we start the war with Sharief?"

The prince peered over his spectacles, requesting my verbal account of the proceedings to date. I rose to my feet in respect, I took a deep breath and realised this was my one big chance to finish the quarrel. I politely gestured with open hands of my plight, warned with clenched fists about my unlawful harassment and beating, I left nothing to chance, and I revealed all, being intensely aware, that I may never get such a "golden" opportunity again. The prince listened with growing interest as I recounted the ambush and abuse in fluent Arabic; he almost sighed with disgust at the revelations of prejudice, especially involving my wife. He was genuine, he was furious he was another genuine Saudi.

The prince appraised me carefully,

"You are a very determined man Mr King and as you are aware, we hold an affinity with the name Malek (King) in Saudi Arabia".

"I know of such links, thank you, your Highness".

"I must apologise for the unacceptable actions of my fellow countryman the Sharief; believe me this will not pass without action. We are letting you go, Mr King. I can assure you; this matter will be concluded during the next two or three days".

The tone of finality, I must admit, brought tears to my eyes, I was free, at last I was free, I felt like Julie Andrews and was about to burst into song when the prince continued,

"I need a letter of no objection from the Labour Court authorising your claim about the final hearing, when the judges ordered the release of your passport. Get me this document, and I'll show you who is running this country!"

I fought to control the tears of joyous release. I left the prince's office with a smile beaming from ear to ear, a lump in my throat and a new pulsing beat in my heart. I was free; at last, I was free!

I returned to the secretary's office and bid the customary thanks and farewells. I shook hands with all powers of men, still seated there. There was no need to explain what the prince had decided; I knew they could see it in my eyes. I almost leaped down the three flights of stairs from the sanctuary on high. I knew it would be no problem to get the necessary documents from the Labour Court. I also knew that I would soon be going home to my Lyn, after all, Prince Saud, assistant Governor of Makkah had promised me as much.

I dashed by taxi to the Labour Court and for the first time since the hearings, waved my Princely request and spoke to the man in charge. I secured the required document and within thirty minutes dashed back to the prince's office.

"Yes, Mr King, you can go". the prince assured me.

I could not believe it, the words rolled like nectar over the tongue of a starving bee,

"Yes, you can go". the prince had repeated, thinking I had not heard

"I can go" I mimed, ready to burst with emotion.

It was Saturday, all I had to do now was return to the prince's office on Sunday, pick up the documents of authority and voila! Exit Visa home.

As I left the building, I recognised a face in the assembly of authoritative gathering. Sharief's brother Mohammed and he was obviously requesting an audience with the prince. A glint of recognition flashed from his beady black eyes and a definite smile of interfering mischief on his fat, spoiled and overfed, cherubic face.

"It's too late!" I thought,

"The prince said I can go, they can't do anything, the prince promised I could go!"

I left the prince's office with a new exuberance in my heart but already, the sight of the Sharief's baby-faced brother began to bleed into the colours of what a few seconds ago was a total confidence.

"Sounds great!" announced Pete and Hawkeye in excited unison,

"Looks like you could be out of here, at last, we'll handle this end of the case, should only be another month or so and you can get your backside out of here".

"You're on your way, Bob. START PACKING".

Chapter 11

ANGUISH

Sharief's baby-faced brother was waiting for me on the following Sunday. Unfortunately, the Prince was in Makkah - which was his rota they had said, "One day in Jeddah, and one day in Makkah" and today he was in Makkah. Baby face whispered sweet nothings into the ear of the Sharief's lawyer, who happened to be perched conveniently at his side. The two men obviously found something very amusing.

"Come back tomorrow". they sniggered, "We'll have everything ready for you, passport, money, air tickets, all that you are due, according to the contract, we don't want this to go any further, the prince could make big trouble for us.

"Thank you," I smiled but I knew they did not intend to keep their word; I was becoming accustomed to their ways.

The following day and for the second time, I was introduced to Prince Majed, Governor of Makkah. The awe had lost its sparkle, his authority already having been undermined by the Sharief and his corrupt clan.

"Yes, I remember you now," nodded Majed, "I will take care of it".

With respect to Prince Majed, nothing happened, I ended my day sitting in front of Sharief's brother, in the continual presence of their family lawyer, with a non-stop barrage of insults and abuse. They did not have my passport, they did not have my dues, nor did they have the decency to hide their dislike of foreigners. They were blocking my bid for freedom and causing a fair measure of distress and anguish to increase the mental agony of a man without hope. On top of it all, they were treating these events like some huge joke, specifically designed for their personal entertainment.

"Come back tomorrow," they ordered, "these things take time".

I swallowed the hatred rising in my throat; I swallowed their contempt and insulting treatment. I left the office with as much grace as I could muster a pleasant smile on my face and a maggot-ridden sickness in my guts.

"Bukra Inshallah" are the two words, around which the whole of Saudi Arabia revolves and, without these words, nothing would ever be done. A direct translation would be "Tomorrow, God willing". a fair and true statement without a doubt. To most foreigners, this was a perfectly acceptable remark. How many would have accepted the phrase having received a translation from a Khowaja? Through my years in the Kingdom, I assimilated a vast knowledge of the people and their habits and this knowledge led me to one conclusion. I now carried my own definition of the words "Bukra Inshallah" it was based on raw experience from a vast cross-section of daily events in the Kingdom. Only one translation fitted all situations and circumstances, it was the phrase that now lolled in my accustomed mind

"Piss off we're busy right now". If the new foreigners used such a translation, they would surely manage a whole lot better. Tomorrow never comes, especially in Saudi, which was why, when I returned to the prince's office the next day, I knew exactly what to expect and I was not disappointed. No passport, no money and no dues. Again, I left the prince's office with the translation fixed firm,

"Piss off we're busy right now".

I entered the prince's office on the following Wednesday. Prince Majed showed surprise to see me. Sharief and the lawyer interfered throughout the whole morning and eventually I was ordered to return after one o'clock the same day.

"Yes!" announced Prince Saud, "Most definitely you can go".

"Thank you, sir". "Shukran Al Jazeelan" I was already becoming weary of princely promises.

Immigration was now closed for the Saudi weekend, the authorities had Thursday and Friday off, and it was only the worker droids who were given one day's rest per week. I couldn't do anything until Saturday and even as I left the building, from the look on the Sharief's face, even if I returned on the Saturday, the game had not yet been won.

After a weekend of Scuba diving with Pete, Hawkeye and Hanger, I had begun to relax. I swallowed the fact that the Sharief's lawyer had been to the immigration department and blocked my exit visa with a story of me having stolen eight hundred thousand Riyals. I swallowed the fact that the baby-faced brother had now blocked my attempts to hold further talks with the prince. I swallowed the facts that nobody would listen to my version of events anymore and I had now been branded a criminal. I swallowed all these facts until my brain swelled with the hatred and poison, that Sharief had now injected into the bloodstream of my very existence.

I verged on despair, they cut off hands in Saudi for theft and although I knew I was innocent, the knowledge did nothing to console my fears. In Saudi, a man is guilty until he can prove otherwise but how could I prove anything, if they weren't prepared to listen? This had been a simple labour court case and it was now heading for a major criminal investigation, solely on the evidence of a Saudi's lies. Sharief also lodged a complaint with the prince's office through his baby-faced brother, saying that Lyn had tried to blackmail the Sharief on his last visit to London. A notice was lodged with the immigration officials of the Kingdom, that one - Robert E King was to be detained in Kingdom until further notice. Any person issuing an exit visa would be responsible for my debts, well more than eight hundred thousand Riyals. A notice was lodged with the Labour court that I would not be allowed to leave until a Saudi guarantor came forward for the eight hundred thousand Rivals. Effectively the Sharief had now sealed my exit from the Kingdom. If the court were to release me tomorrow it would take months to unravel the tangle of red tape caused by Sharief's notices. I hoped no one else in the Kingdom carried my name. If they did, the way Saudi was run, they were in the same boat and had just been entombed in the desert, along with the Pharaohs and their namesake - King. I swallowed hard as I left the prince's office for what I knew would be the last time, my miserable exit made even more difficult by the mocking laughter erupting in my wake.

One week later, Monday, I received a message to attend a meeting at my lawyer's office. I was half an hour early for the appointment; let's face it I didn't have much else to do.

"We have some excellent news, Bob". my lawyer smiled.

"What is it?" I enquired dispassionately.

"The final hearing of your case will be in the Supreme Court in Riyadh on the 28th of October.

"Great!" I replied without enthusiasm, "Only another twenty-two days for me to sit in the Kingdom with my thumb wedged up my arse while Sharief uses me for target practise".

"What's that?" my Lawyer interjected, not quite catching the despondent remark.

"Nothing!" I replied, "So I have to go to Riyadh on the 28th of October and that will be the FINAL! hearing".

"Well, you can't actually go to the hearing". mumbled my Lawyer in curiously embarrassed tones.

"Whaaaat!" I hissed.

"No! you can't go. You see, you have no work permit, no travel documents which in any case must be signed by Sharief, who has already refused and we don't want to risk you being thrown into prison at this stage do we?"

"Are you telling me I can't attend my own hearing?"
'It's not as bad as it sounds, Bob. I'll be there to represent you, you'll receive a fair hearing, I guarantee it".

"But you're telling me I can't attend my own trial, where I am the plaintiff and the Sharief is the respondent, he'll be able to throw all sorts of accusations around and you can't possibly answer the charges unless I'm there!"

"NO! NO! NO! Bob, it's finished, the Sharief can't submit any more papers, they must finalise on the evidence already submitted. He cannot add anything to the appeal court evidence. The appeal court can only pass judgement on the evidence already received during the original trial".

"OK fine; then tell me why I can't attend?"

"You know why, Bob. It's the Saudi Law".

"But if I'm not there, anything could happen; you guys could reach an agreement or settlement and I won't be there to approve it, you may even do something that I don't agree with and I won't be there to voice my opinion".

"That will never happen, Mr Bob".

"Yes! But how do I know?"

"Saudis just don't do these things!" announced my lawyer.

"Right". I acknowledged sarcastically, "I was forgetting about that!"

It was Thursday; Lyn telephoned and tore me apart. She could not stop crying over the phone, she could hardly speak. My mother refused to speak to me for the distress I was causing Lyn and, as if that weren't enough, I could hear my father shouting in the background, basically arguing that it was time I came home and stopped messing about! An English Lawyer had wrongly informed him that nobody could detain you without cause. I was emotionally wrecked; I had not realised that such a boiling pot of anguish was brewing back home. What could I do? I could not get away without an exit visa from Sharief, Sharief could give me a visa tomorrow and it would take months to sort out the computerised red tape waiting to ensnare the exit-only visa. I put down the phone and simmered for hours, trying to prevent myself paying a visit to Sharief and taking my personal property by force.

The following Monday, I called the British consulate,

"Isn't there anything you can do?" I asked incredulously.

248

"We are going to send a NICE letter to Prince Majed, we have to word it very carefully, for your sake, we cannot afford to upset anybody".

"Thanks a lot".

I did not like the sound of "We cannot afford to upset anybody', as if they knew something I didn't. I had already spoken to Prince Majed on more than one occasion and achieved nothing. The consulate was now sending a NICELY worded letter, probably written on snoopy paper so as not to offend anybody.

"Whatever happened to the roar of the British Lion?" I thought. There was a time when to be British really meant something. These days, we were all hostage to trade and commerce, although more than likely trade, with a capital "T" for TORNADO. The British Lion was obviously having a lot of trouble re-wording its meow so as not to offend anybody. What was wrong with the British? I thought, if I'd been an American, I would have been out of this mess months ago. The Americans knew how to look after their citizens, although sometimes their plans went wrong, as with the Iranian fiasco. At least they tried, at least they stood up and showed the world they were prepared to go to any lengths to help their people in trouble abroad.

28th OCTOBER RIYADH, FINAL HEARING?

I did not sleep on the night before the final, final hearing. I thought about the various decisions and what those decisions would mean. The following day, the seconds ticked by slower than ever as I awaited my Lawyers return from Riyadh. Finally, just as I was contemplating a lifetime in Saudi, my lawyer entered the room. After a few salaams and introductions I couldn't hold back any longer, my etiquette courtesy button had worn out,

"You don't look like a winner". I tried not to think the worst.

"Everything went very well, Bob". he was obviously trying to comfort me, like I said, a Saudi Gentleman.

"So, what happened?" I feared the worst.

"The Sharief went into the court, he had no power of attorney from the company, no evidence to support any of his claims and no legal documentation whatsoever that would allow him to represent OCOMA in the court, which would suggest OCOMA knows nothing about this charade".

"Fantastic!" I grinned, "So we won?"

"Not yet". admitted my lawyer.

"I don't believe it!" I sighed, already receding into a state of numbed disappointment.

"Sharief requested another hearing to present his case, seems some more evidence has come to light but it will take a few more days to produce".

"But he's already made the accusations," I yelled, "How come he can make the accusations when he has no evidence? My evidence has been with the court since day one of the court case and sixteen months later the Sharief is still looking for evidence that does not! and will not! ever exist; what is this?"

"It cannot extend beyond one more hearing, Bob. The new hearing is set for 19th November and that is it, it will be finished".

"I've heard all this before, I don't believe it for a minute, that bastard said he would keep me here forever and every time we go to court it's as if he's going to do exactly that. The same old story, The Sharief is not quite ready; we must give him more time. What is this? Is there no justice in this country? How can he be allowed all this time? are you waiting for him to fabricate enough evidence to keep me here? maybe get my hand chopped off? or how about my head? maybe he can organise that as well, I wouldn't put anything passed that snake. He's spending the months of my life like loose change and nobody is doing anything about it. All I want to know is why? Just answer me why?"

My lawyer looked to his feet, shuffled around embarrassed and lifted his head to face me,

"It's the law Bob," he sighed with obvious frustration, "It's the Saudi Arabian law".

CHAPTER 13   SAUDI STYLE   PLANS

I had already used a fair slice of my savings, which I knew would ultimately dictate that if the case was not sorted out soon, and in my favour, I had worked, struggled and saved for the last ten years in Saudi for nothing. Pete and Hawkeye were a major help, bolstering my spirit at every available opportunity but deep within my soul, the seed had already been sown. For all I knew, when the Sharief, the court and the lawyers got together, they may as well be enjoying a quiet afternoon's game of cards for all the good it was doing me, after all, despite the hearings and interventions by the Prince, the Sharief was still! submitting false evidence.

On October 28th I declared a hunger strike. I informed the British Consulate and I informed the prince's office. I informed all the relevant establishments of Authority in Saudi Arabia and for good measure I sent a letter to all the newspapers that had previously reported my case. My patience was wearing thin.

5TH NOVEMBER

I entered the prince's office. I really had no desire to do so but my lawyer had been commanded by the Labour Court to take me to their office immediately; that they might discuss the case. I was already in a weakened state. I was sure nothing would be achieved and determined to fight for my rights, even to the death if that were the only honourable alternative to the Sharief's clutches.

I was informed of Prince Majed's personal interest in the case and the Chief of the labour Court went to great pains to point out the facts.

"Listen," I began, with total disinterest, "On May 11th of this year, I came to this office and spoke to Prince Majed, that was six months ago, give or take a week, so tell me, what has he done to help me?"

The Labour Chief was stunned; he had no idea of my earlier visits; he was sure he had all the pertinent facts. Previous visits had never been in his brief. He had no idea that I spoke Arabic and he had never heard anyone speak about a Prince that way, let alone the Governor of Makkah.

"Are you sure?" He quizzed.

"Was the Prophet Mohammed a Muslim?" I had them horrified for a moment before they realised the statement was harmless and a blatant fact.

"Do you have any record of your visit?" the Chief progressed.

I opened my briefcase,

"Which visit do you want to discuss?"

"You mean you have been here more than once?" now the Chief was alarmed.

"Well, that depends on which Prince you want to discuss,"

"Well, who have you seen?" inquired the chief.

I opened my diary to the correct pages,

"Three visits with Prince Majed, and two visits with Prince Saud. They both said they would help. I never received a reply from the Majlis in Makkah, sorry, I do apologise, I did receive one reply saying,

"We have forwarded the response to the Labour Court in Jeddah but I went to the Labour Court and they deny receiving such a letter, so either the paperwork was lost or somebody is probably telling lies".

The Chief could not believe his ears; I was now accusing somebody of lying between the Court and the Prince's office.

"Can I have a copy of the authorisations?" requested the chief, a new tone in his voice, which now seemed to be softening toward my plight.

"You can keep those if you like, I have the originals safely tucked away with various copies hidden around Jeddah for my own personal use, just in case of," I paused for effect, "Accidents".

252

"You're a very thorough man, Mr Bob. I'm sure we can get this problem sorted out, now please, finish your fasting and have lunch with us?"

"Thank you, sir. But no thanks, you sort out my problem, then I'll eat, until then, I must be incredibly careful".

"You're a very determined man, Mr Bob,"

"I have to be in my Position, sir".

"Tell me, Mr Bob. What is it you need to be so careful of? Is there something else that you are not telling us about?" the Chief's voice seemed genuinely concerned.

I carefully picked dispassionately with my fingernail, at the white lint wriggling from a tear in my jeans,

"It's the Saudi Law," I offered before repeating my words with a blatant indifference and continuing to chase the lint,

"It's the honourable Saudi Law, it seems it is not intended for foreigners".

19 NOVEMBER

An eventful day for me, Prince Charles and the late Princess Diana were in Jeddah and with them came a press entourage from various English dailies. I could not believe my ears when the call came through on the contact phone. Reporters were swarming around Jeddah, noticing any story with bite. I was already top of the bill; somebody somewhere had disclosed information about my hunger strike, now they wanted an interview with photographs. I organised a meeting place and although very weak put myself at their disposal. I met the two reporters as agreed although things did not go exactly according to plan. Since their first contact they had been informed of another foreigner who had been caught drinking and was now in prison. I was a free man and they were more interested in the guilty prisoner's story than they were in my own. They snapped a few quick shots of my trim form, asked me if I knew where they could get photos of Idi Amin. I had seen him, the butcher of Uganda, doing a spot of shopping at the Jeddah branch of

Safeway. Six and a half feet of cold, clammy evil, hunched over the meat chiller. Big stubby fingers pawing the fresh meat and his massive feet bulging, around the thick leather straps of his sandals. I felt like a rabbit caught in the headlights of a speeding car. I remembered his excuse to the Saudis and why they had allowed him in their country "I only killed Christians," he had told them, "I am the Muslims friend" I wanted to pick up the exclusive" discounted offer, carving knife and stick it in his chest for all those poor people he had tortured and abused. Two guards were with him, both carried machine guns and both looked deadly serious as they pushed me aside. He stared into my eyes and smiled, but I stared back defiantly and mimed the words "Fuck You" he pointed his finger in my direction and nodded still smiling as he scuffed by. Unfortunately, I did not have any pictures and I doubted the Saudis would let anybody take any. On my negative response, Andrew Morton and his photographer hurried back to their hotel leaving me to pay for the Taxi. I had no money with me so I did the only thing possible, jumped out at the traffic lights and ran like hell, collapsing into an uncaloried heap when I was out of reach of the chasing cab driver. It took a while for me to recover. The reporters had been in such a hurry they had hardly listened to a word I had said. They were more interested in a guy that had broken the law, than a guy who hadn't and was being abused for sport.

They had obviously spoken to the consulate when the report was published; I appeared in the article to be begging for mercy. This had a positive effect on me; I quit the hunger strike,

"Fuck them!" I thought, "That's the last time I speak to the press and from now on I'll fight this battle my way, with my laws. The Saudi law obviously doesn't work for foreigners, maybe it's time I tried a law that does".

My thoughts had been confirmed by the decision from the Riyadh Court. Another hearing had been requested and awarded to Sharief. A new court date was set for December 10th, when the Sharief promised to have all his evidence ready to submit to the court. Again, I had to swallow everything,

including the burning desire to charge over to the Sharief's office and hand out a few medical complications from which it was unlikely that the Sharief would recover. Already they were heading into Christmas and again I knew there was no way I would be home in time to spend the season of goodwill to all men with my own family, that is, if I had any family left who were willing to talk to me. This would be my second Christmas in unlawful detention and nobody could do anything about it. I had done everything legally possible to secure my release and had been rewarded with insults to my intelligence. The time was drawing close when I would have to forget the legalities. Sharief had promised to make my life a living hell where every day would be filled with intense pain and suffering. "You'll have to try harder than that I smiled, I'm from Barnsley, I'm used to it".
I hoped I could maintain that level of bravado but it was getting more and more difficult

DECEMBER 10TH

All evidence was submitted on the 10th of December. My own evidence was accepted and the Sharief's was not. The judge told Sharief he was a liar. My lawyer Mr Mansouri was now extremely confident. The judge had made it quite clear the Sharief was in trouble and no way would he be getting away with a mere fine. Interfering with the legal institutions of Saudi was a serious matter.

I was not relieved; I had heard all this talk before. In the back of my mind, I found some solace; at least they were sorting things out slowly but surely. The next hearing was set for January 7th another Christmas and another New Year in Saudi. Nineteen months detained without due cause, nineteen months without work, without the comfort of close family and friends. Nineteen months of wondering where the next attack, physical or mental would emanate.

CHAPTER 13   SAUDI STYLE   PLANS

December brought with it the usual Saudi requirement not to acknowledge Christmas. Hence the Christian foreigners' usual en-mass departure for the Christmas and New Year celebrations at their home countries. The Sharief offered his usual Christmas greeting comforted by a New Year's resolution to boot.

"When are you going to learn, Bob? I kept you here last Christmas; I'm keeping you here this Christmas and I'm going to keep you here next Christmas".

"How will you know Sharief?"

"What do you mean how will I know, Bob?"

"If I'm here next Christmas Sharief, you'll be dead, I guarantee it, that's my new year's resolution to you!"........ CLICK PURRRRR.

Through the Khowaja grapevine, I heard rumours but I never saw anything, that three truckloads of Christmas mail had been trucked out into the desert, smothered with petrol and set ablaze. The Saudis had obviously no intention of allowing too much Christmas spirit to pervade the Holy Land of Islam; and after all, spirits were banned in Saudi, on "religious" grounds.

Lyn's tearful merry Christmas and sobbing, broken hearted sorrow added an unstable explosive temper to the hydrogen bomb fury now stretching my patience to bursting point. If Sharief had realised the proportions of the approaching Khowaja hurricane, he would also have realised, he had one of two choices - book a one-way ticket on the next space shuttle and park himself out of reach in earth's orbit or disappear up his own arsehole. I decided that if sheer stupidity could have been harnessed to solve the world's energy crisis, Sharief would have been in big demand. However, the world did not run-on sheer stupidity, even though Sharief was busy worming around his remaining friends in Jeddah and doing his utmost to disprove that statement on the energy crisis.

Pete made his own decisions. He could not and would not sit back and watch the cruel injustices of Saudi law as they tore away the last remnants of his friend's pride. Pete marched into Sharief's office with his notice not to renew his contract. He had decided to take his chances alongside me, working on the theory that two similar complaints may carry more weight than one. Pete hoped Sharief would not goad him about my position; he was in no state of mind to swallow ridicule. He was ushered into the inner sanctum of Sharief's office. Sharief's response stunned Pete; he could not believe his ears,

"What about my rights?" inquired Pete in no uncertain tones, as he expected the worse.

"You'll get them," agreed Sharief,

"Every cent, paid up to the minute you leave, all your dues, as per the original contract".

"You're not going to contest my claim?" Pete's mouth fell open.

"Why should I? they are your legal entitlements!"

"But what about Bob? he is only requesting the same dues, as per contract, why are you putting him through all this nonsense with the courts?"

"Sit down, Pete". Sharief motioned him to a chair with a weary sigh of regret, "Bob and I have a problem to solve, it's already out of context and I want to put things right, after all, it's merely a Labour Court problem, a difference of opinion. I have up-to-date information to suggest that you men never received the memo, I was wrong, believe me when I say how bad I feel about all that has happened. If I could only get through to Bob and put the past behind us. I'm sure if we got together, we could work something out".

"What have you got in mind?" asked Pete with no hint of suspicion, in his tone.

"Please pass on this message, Pete. I will ensure Bob will receive all his dues as per the contract. OCOMA will pay his salary up to the day he leaves the Kingdom and as a gesture of reconciliation for the misunderstanding between us, we'll add a further twenty-five percent for the unnecessary problems Bob has suffered, for which I personally feel so responsible".

It seemed too good to be true but Sharief was getting through to Pete's sense of fair play and just rewards,

"Maybe I can help, I'll speak to Bob, we're good friends. What would you like me to tell him?"

"Just the truth, Pete. That I'm sorry for what has happened and that I would like to see him, it's time we sorted out this minor problem now. I was a fool to treat Bob the way I did but I was displeased with his initial reaction threatening all manner of legal retribution. The more I think about it the more I realise, that I would have done the same in his position. Still, I could expect no less, he is a determined and principled man, fine qualities in a person don't you agree?"

"Yeah Sharief, Bob is some kinda guy, that's for sure!"

Pete could not believe it; the Sharief was just too good to be true. I could soon be free, paid up to date of departure, including all his benefits and a twenty-five percent increment on top.

"Jesus!" thought Pete, "That's some hunka money".

I was in a buoyant mood, even before Pete had related his story.

"What's up with you?" Pete queried my unusually happy frame of mind.

"I've got a hell of a piece of news for you". I replied with a grin.

"Oh! so you've heard already". sighed the belated Pete.

"Heard what?"

"About the Sharief's memo, his change of heart and your big payoff with a fat bonus to boot". Pete was disappointed he had not been able to reveal the good news himself.

"I don't know anything about that, Pete". I insisted, "Tell me all about it".

The money, the memo, the meeting. Pete left nothing out as he recounted his experience at the Sharief's office, as he brought his story to a conclusion, I butted in,

"The snake, the dirty rotten son of a bitch, I wouldn't have believed it unless I'd heard it with my own ears, the sneaky little bastard!"

258

"Why, Bob; what's wrong?" Pete was amazed at my outburst,

"It's a good offer, you could be out of here in a few days with a stack of money and a clean slate to boot, no deportation order".

I waved Pete to silence,

"Listen to this, Pete. You don't know the whole story. I just came from my lawyer's office. Seems that Sharief just fired the office boy. Fortunately, the office boy picked my lawyer, of all people, to represent him, he's given a signed statement about the cheating of employees, Sharief's interference in their personal mail and, best of all, he's more than willing to be a witness at my next court hearing".

"Jesus!" Pete whistled in appreciation.

"That's not all, Pete. You know the monthly contributions we paid to the GOSI, the General Organisation for Social Insurance?"

"You mean the Saudi Government Insurance and pension scheme?"

"Right! Well, Sharief deducted the money from every other employee in the company and pocketed the contributions. If that comes up in Court, he's in big trouble. Not only is he cheating his work workforce he's also cheating the Saudi Government and you know what that means".

"No wonder he wants you away from here in a big hurry, Bob. Now I know the full story, you ought to go down to the Sharief's office and ask for double". Pete grinned.

"Treble!" I Insisted.

"Quadruple!" Pete was ecstatic.

"Pentangle!" I laughed aloud but Pete laughed louder.

"You've done it, Bob. You've got that bastard screwed down so tight he's never going to get away with it now".

The two of us were cheering, acknowledging our future financial standing. The absolute relief almost brought tears to my eyes. Hawkeye entered the room and joined in the celebrations, he had no idea what we were celebrating but hey, he was "Khowaja" and the last thing a "Khowaja" needs, is an excuse to party. He was ecstatic when they gave him the news between cheers and whoops of delight and the familiar war cry of "Here we go, here we go, here we go'.

It was late when I left the OCOMA apartments. Hawkeye and Pete were in festive spirits. I had enjoyed a few Sids myself but did not want to get careless at this stage in the proceedings. I left them to their devices with no more than a warm glow of final deliverance radiating through my body, as I began the six kilometres back to my home.

"To Bob!" Hawkeye toasted and raised his glass.
Hangar had arrived, shortly after I had left and now the three men joined in the toast, comrades of circumstance.
"To all of us," Hawkeye began, but Pete waved his arm interrupting Hawkeye's umpteenth salute, Pete bid them all stand and after a moment's recollection he proudly declared his toast,
"Khowajas!" announced Pete, "Salt of the earth'.
"Khowajas!" echoed the two men, a proud recognition in their slurring voices.

"I must confess. I was really starting to get worried about Bob". Hangar's serious confession lowered the tone of the frivolity.
"What exactly were you worried about?" asked Hawkeye.
"Well at the end, it was no longer like he was fighting the Sharief, he seemed to be fighting the Labour Court, the authorities, the Princes and I must admit, even though I don't like to, I was starting to worry about him".
"Yeah! me too, I was getting quite nervous as to what exactly was going to be the outcome, cos it didn't look too brilliant for him at some stages in the game, how about you, Pete? What do you think?"
Pete looked up to the ceiling as if he expected inspiration from the whirling fan and paused as he tried to select the right

260

words. He took a deep breath and blew it out through pursed lips before he began with almost whispered tones, the SID lacing his voice,

"I've known him a long time. For the last few years, I've tried every trick in the book to get the better of him, in a friendly way of course. Just buddies trying to outdo each other. I've seen him stranded in the desert, acting like he was on some holiday beach. I saw him kill a shark with his bare hands and a stainless reef anchor once, which I have to admit, saved my life. I watched him windsurf with his wrist in a plaster cast and hurtle across the desert at over a hundred miles per hour with nothing but that stupid, red, sleeveless T-shirt between himself and the biggest sheet of sandpaper in the entire world. Shit! if he'd fallen, he would have had no skin left, but during all those events I've noticed one major trait".

"What's that?" his audience was hungry for the outcome.

"With Bob, it ain't over till it's over. He never gives up, he never gives in, he's got something else inside. I don't know where it comes from or where he finds it, but it's always there when he needs it and I never saw it fail him. If that ingredient could be bottled and sold, shit, we'd be millionaires in a week".

The three men fell to silent reflection; Hawkeye wobbled to his feet and raised his glass,

"Bob!" he announced with fond intonation, "The Khowaja'.

"The Khowaja!" toasted the three men.

Pete drove around to my apartment the following day, quietly nursing a massive hangover. He ran up the flights of steps to my flat and suddenly his hangover disappeared. My front door was smashed open and the contents of the humble abode had been smashed to pieces as if by some maniacal force. Blood spattered the white-painted walls and the furniture was reduced to matchwood. Bloodstains soaked the carpet amongst the shards of glass that had once been a coffee table. In the bedroom, sheets had been dragged from the bed and piled in one corner. They too were stained with dried, browning blood.

261

CHAPTER 13   SAUDI STYLE   PLANS

The sickness rose in Pete's throat as he dashed from the man-made carnage. A terrible rubbery feeling reverberated through his bones and he was sure, in fact, he told me he was certain, he would never see me alive again.

Chapter 12

TORTURE

The Shariefs had once ruled the great wasteland deserts of the Western regions of Saudi Arabia, from their base camp in the Holy City of Makkah. Now the Sharief's family had lost their power and unfortunately for them, their place in history. It had been removed by the throw of a single, primitive spear.

Bin Jaluwi, Abdel Aziz Saud's right-hand man, had launched that fortunate javelin. The point of the spear had embedded itself, deep in the postern door of the Mismac Fort. A small door set into the boundary wall, that once contained the now sprawling capital city of Riyadh. The lone spear had thudded home, narrowly missing but terrifying one man, a man by the name of Ajlan, at the time, the powerful Governor of Riyadh.

Undeterred by his inaccurate throw, Bin Jaluwi charged in pursuit of Ajlan, he forced open the postern door and dragged Ajlan to the ground. It is rumoured Bin Jaluwi had some personal reasons for hating the Ajlan, for as soon as he had he pinned the Ajlan to the ground, he took out his dagger, slashed open his garments, removed the Ajlan's liver and lobbed the dripping, bloody flesh, over the main gate into the courtyard. Witnesses to this barbarous act ran screaming in terror and informed the present occupiers of the fort, the Rasheeds'. The ferocity of the barbaric act led the Rasheeds' to believe a murderous onslaught was inevitable and they decided to yield, rather than be slaughtered like sheep.

As for the lone spear, the blade tip was embedded so deep it remains to this day. I had seen the evidence many times, despite clumsy attempts to free it, by knife-wielding, souvenir hunters. I could not help but wonder during my days in Riyadh, as I fingered the piece of metal at the bottom of the crevice, what might have been, had the Rasheed's been blessed with a bit more bottle.

Abdel Aziz Saud had conquered the Rasheed's main garrison but the Rasheeds' main force was to be found lounging amongst the farmlands of Al Dilam. With the Riyadh Fort now secured, Abdel Aziz Saud marched his warriors to Al Dilam to challenge once more the powerful army of Rasheed. Meanwhile the leading member of the Sharief family, Sharief Hussein, had proclaimed himself King of the Arabs and had begun to make inroads from the Western coastlines towards Riyadh and presumably onward from the capital to Abdel Aziz Saud, who was now firmly planted in the East.

Abdel Aziz's forces regrouped and, confident of their great leader's prowess, they headed west to meet the challenge. During September 1924, Abdel Aziz's Ikwhan forces massacred all their opponents in the Western Region town of Taif, a small, cooler town, set almost a mile above the plains, high on the rock escarpment, overlooking the parched valleys below which contained the Holy City of Makkah. The slaughter in Taif was eventually reported to Sharief Hussein.

On October 3rd, 1924, Sharief Hussein surrendered, abdicated, and fled his homeland aboard a British steamer bound for Cyprus. Although most of his family remained, none would fight against the house of Saud and its armies. Abdel Aziz now ruled the vast oceans of wasteland desert from the Red Sea to the Indian Ocean. He named the territory Saudi Arabia. It was not until oil was discovered, that the Shariefs' were to realise to their absolute distress, the immensity of the fortune they had surrendered without a fight.

The Sharief tribe were none too pleased but as the oil began to flow, even the fiercest of family prides were bought to silence with the vast fortunes of oil revenue. Positions were available for the Shariefs' tribal elders at most government levels and with salaries and benefits beyond the comprehension of western mortals, a straight jacket of commercially viable tolerance was bought.

I knew their history well and savoured a clear knowledge of what my own fight would entail. I was confident that the Law of

264

the land would ultimately prevail and even if it didn't, I could always fall back on the old proverb, "Mine enemy's enemy is my friend', which would position me squarely on the side of the ruling Royal Family, should that need ever arise.

The knocking on the door grew louder; soon they would be banging their fists against the thick, wooden barrier to my home. I had no need to think about who was responsible, it no longer mattered to me who "They" were,

"They" the Sharief's cronies hired for their muscular abilities to wreak havoc and pain.

"They" the police, acting on an anonymous tip-off.

"They" the prince's men, acting on word of paid informant. No; It didn't matter who "They" were, only that now, "They" were here, swinging on my doorbell and thumping on the door to my apartment, drawing me from the depths of a troubled, restless sleep. I pulled on my blue jeans and headed toward the wellspring of noise. I peeped out through the sentry hole and my blood turned to ice,

"Oh no!" I hissed to myself, "Not again, this is all supposed to be finished. What do you want?" I exclaimed, "It's very late".

"We have a search warrant, open the door!" an anonymous though intimidating voice replied".

A warrant was held up to the peephole but I could not read the wide angled distortion of Arabic and English, I had no choice, I opened the door slightly but kept my knee pressed firmly behind my first line of defence.

"Look! what's the problem, look at the notices? your guys came here the other day looking for booze and stuff, now your here again, why are you doing this to me?"

My visitor's response jangled a million, shrieking, mental alarms,

"Drugs! sadique, we are looking for drugs! now open this door immediately".

I never had anything to do with drugs but the mere thought of this added even if concocted complication, bathed my body with a paralysing fear and it wasn't long before they gave me something else to worry about.

"You've been drinking Khowaja!" snapped the officer, "I can smell your breath from here, now! allow us to enter! immediately if you please!"

"Oh no!" I thought, "Not now, dear God please not now, not now I've come so far, why me, of all the minions in this country why pick on me?"

My only hope was to let them in, be as polite as possible and deny all knowledge of the booze. They had no breathalysers and by the time they had tested my blood, I could be well out of tell-tale limits, I'd hardly had any drink at all and the long walk home would surely have flushed the alcohol from my system.

I opened my apartment door and left it wide open, so that the door leaf concealed the baseball bat, I kept for unwelcome visitors. It had never been used.

"Shukran, thank you," murmured the officer as he stepped inside, waving me forward. These were not the same kind of police as before and they all marched inside, without introduction, en masse. Even though I protested at the intrusion, I knew I was wasting my time, these boys were serious, of that I had no doubt.

At any time of the day or night the roads of Jeddah are crawling with all manner of police vehicles, most are distinguishable by their almost tribal coloured markings. Green stripes belonged to the traffic police and usually adorned race tuned Pontiac Bonneville's, maximum velocity had to be encouraged from these fiery beasts to out-perform the whiz kid Saudis during Thursday night speed runs in their expensive and seemingly disposable sports models. The traffic cops were also assisted by motorcycle mounted police. Sometimes the motorcycle was the only vehicle able to penetrate the traffic sludge of rush hour in Jeddah. The famous Honda, four-cylinder motorcycles were a favourite steed, capable of at least one hundred and twenty miles per hour and quite often, the death of an inexperienced rider.

266

Blue stripes belonged to the civil \ criminal police. They used a variety of vehicles and they showed a preference for the four-wheel drive Toyota land cruisers, hard-topped jeeps that could travel just about anywhere. Major city areas were patrolled by Toyota Cressida saloons although the major officers of the blue force drove around in hulking great Pontiacs. Built for comfort not speed, rather like most of the lower order of wives.

The blues were also the most prolific of the tribes, ultimately responsible for a major percentage of the foreigners now languishing in the city jails.

The Khaki green vehicles belonged to both the religious and "secret" police. The persons occupying these vehicles wore no uniform but the national Saudi costume and once separated from their vehicles, they were indistinguishable from the rest of the population regardless of creed or Nationality. All Khowajas knew very well, that if you were of foreign disposition and these guys were around, chances are they were watching you and you were in serious trouble, even if you weren't. Then came the Morality Police in their black striped jeeps, spray painting women's bare arms Black, forcing them to cover up everything but their eyes, chopping guys' hair off if they thought it was too long and viciously punishing anyone who may have stepped out of line, a very thin line at that. I hoped to avoid any major confrontation with any of the tribes. Walking was not one of the tribes" strong points and neither were the tribe so happy about venturing into the poorer areas of town to be heckled by fat old women, wanting to know when they would expel the filthy foreign influence. I had no idea to which tribe these guys belonged and they were in no hurry to tell me. Polite discussion did not seem to be on their agenda. They were untidy in appearance, with unshaven faces in poorly pressed black uniforms and their total contempt for my home did nothing to allay my increasing fears. They were obviously from some inner tribe of which, thankfully until now, I had no personal experience.

Despite a thorough search they found nothing in the sparsely furnished lounge, nor did they find anything in the bedrooms.

They did; however, find a roll of photocopied documents in the toilet header tank, a parcel of documents which received sarcastic acclaim from the officer in charge.

"Unusual bookshelves, we will have to be extremely thorough with our search"

"Go ahead "I sighed," I ain't got anything to hide.

The search was almost complete and they had moved to the kitchen, the kitchen was too small for all men present and three of the corporals moved to the lounge and sat down. They were obviously in no hurry to leave. The officer inspected the refrigerator, marvelling at its clear lack of provisions. He peered inside the freezer compartment, the freezer had been empty for weeks, and I wasn't planning on being here long enough to have to wait for a meal to thaw. The officer returned his interest to a green glass bottle in the fridge. He snapped off the wire clip retainer and smelled the contents,

"What's this?" he enquired, shoving the bottle under my nose.

"Just an old bottle, it was full of apple juice but now it's empty, I never bothered to throw it out that's all".

He looked at me with a smile and I knew what he was thinking. The bottle may have had Sid in it at some point and it did smell terrible but he couldn't discount the fact that it may have been apple juice that had festered for several weeks as the rest of the fridge was in an unfettered state.

"This is alcohol!" he announced finally and even if it wasn't, I knew in my heart, it was time for tears.

"It's just apple juice!" I told him, "Just ordinary apple juice that's gone off, look at the rest of my fridge, it's bare, there's nothing to eat, I don't use it, I forgot all about the apple juice, it must have been in there for months!"

"Then why does your breath smell of alcohol?"

He had me again but I stuck to my story and told him it was probably something I ate. I could see they were getting ready for some serious action.

"Alcohol Mamnoah forbidden!" a weedy-looking corporal announced. He was small and looked malnourished, a pencil

268

moustache was scrawled across the top of his lip, almost as if an eyeliner pencil had been drawn across to emphasise the top of his mouth. He was the smallest amongst them, he wore an untidy black uniform, black plastic platform shoes that did not make him any taller and I knew, that of all the people in the room, this venal creature was the one to watch. How could one so small create so much anguish?

"No!" I shot back.

"Alcohol!" the weed snarled his black beret almost flipped off as he snapped his head back with increasing confidence.

"No, it isn't I......".

Smack! the blow caught me full in the face, right across my cheek and for the moment I was stunned to silence. It was the weedy guy again, showing his mates how tough and brave he was, they laughed at his bravery.

"Alcohol he snapped again.

"No!" I replied, I-

Smack, again full in the face. This gimp was getting us nowhere other than entertaining his colleagues.

Smack, now he was slapping me before I even denied the accusation. I looked around the room, in my opinion, I had two choices, make a run for it and get to my lawyer's place, or stay here and get the shit banged out of me before being carted off to the desert, gang raped and disposed of. It's amazing how the human mind functions under these circumstances. I had always enjoyed a good imagination and now I hated that ability.

Smack! the weedy corporal was getting confident now and with my fear bloomed annoyance. I decided that if I got the chance, I wasn't going to hang around, if these guys dragged me out into the desert, who would know and who would care? Would they have brought a supply of K Y jelly and what would they do when they had finished with me? just let me go? I doubted that very much, I had heard about this tribe of guys before.

"Please Wait! Please, sadiques, my friends, I have a paper from the....

Smack! I tried to tell them about the paper from the courts but the little bastard just kept hitting me across the face and after each slap he turned and grinned to his mates, Smack! -Smack! - Smack! The little bully was starting to enjoy himself now and I could see he wasn't going to pack it in. He could see I was getting agitated and he worked on me even harder. His confidence grew with every slap and between every slap I summarised my options. I knew he wasn't going to give up until I collapsed in tears, he wanted his moment of superiority but all he was doing, was making me annoyed, very fuckin annoyed. I realised there were only two options available, Before the next slap came, I took a deep breath, waited for the right moment and then belted him with a left hook, it was time to say goodnight. My fist smashed into his jaw and he slumped down like a sack of spuds. I jumped forward from the clutches of the other police officers who were now in a state of shock and headed towards the door, slamming it closed on the cops outside. I picked up the bat and charged towards the intruders. The police officers outside started bashing against the door and I knew from the reverberations, it wouldn't be long before they were through to the inside. The visitors seemed stunned by my action. They didn't know what to do about the baseball bat as I dashed by them, waving it under their noses and heading for the balcony. I would have to fight my way to the balcony and jump down onto the roof of the house below. I had done it before, merely to save time, under these circumstances, I was sure I could do it again, no problem, no fuckin problem, the adrenaline rush took hold.

The banging on the door continued and suddenly the two corporals were smashing their way inside. The main door crunched and splintered, before falling from its hinges and spilling two eager figures into an already burdened room. I had to move and it would have to be fast. I swung the bat in a fearsome arc and the cops backed away.

"Stop!" shouted the officer in charge, "This is no good, you cannot escape".

"You're trying to set me up, I haven't done anything, I want to see my lawyer, that's all, I just want to get to my lawyer".

I moved towards the balcony door but as soon as I got to the door and tried to unlock it, the officer shouted, "Grab him!"

They were all over me like jackals around a fresh kill. My manic efforts to get free only managed to push the bulk of thrashing bodies back into the lounge. The human octopus stumbled backwards, somebody tripped and we all fell onto the glass coffee table. Shrieks of pain spewed forth as the body underneath the writhing mass was sliced by the broken glass and the blood spurted crimson over a boiling broth of men.

"Let me go! Let me go! You bastards!" I screamed with despair, thrashing with my arms and kicking my legs. I was losing my fight for freedom and began considering the terrible consequences. My arm suddenly broke free and I used it like a club to pummel every face in sight, oblivious to the blows now being rained upon my own body with what felt like my own baseball bat. How the situation had reached this stage I don't know, I really hadn't much choice, no matter what I said or did they wouldn't have listened, this was what they wanted, this was their "sport". On and on they came, punching, kicking, and slapping, then the batons came out, there was just no escape, nowhere left to go, and my heart was filled with utter dread.

"Let me go! Let me go! you're all the same, you're just a bunch of fucking crooks!" the frenzy, frothed in my throat. The unceasing blows to my body and head now consumed my will. Maybe I should just pretend to be unconscious, maybe they would quit, and maybe it would all be a dream. This wasn't happening to me, this wasn't a dream, it was a nightmare and slowly it began to fade from painful reality. My ribs were on fire and my kidneys were full of razor-sharp knives. Blood sprayed from my nose as fists beat into my face. I gasped and snorted and no matter how much I tried to yield, to stop this insanity, they just kept bashing away at my body and head, piling on the punishment, bash, thud bash. The pain seared into my heart and I remember gasping, probably the final gasp of a man in mortal torment, as my vision rippled and hazed to a picture-less grey, before the blackness of sweet unconsciousness swooped in mercifully to smother and hide the pain.

I slipped back to consciousness to find myself on my bed, handcuffs biting deep into my wrists, the tight metal bracelets folding my arms into an unnatural position behind my back. A hand grabbed me by the hair and I was yanked from the bed to my feet. I couldn't believe the pain that suddenly pulsed into my ribcage and almost fell as the searing, razor sharp, spasms tried to tear my flesh apart. The anonymous grip held firm and I was dragged by my hair into the lounge and thrown at the feet of the gathered throng. They sat around me on bits of furniture I had once owned. Some were bleeding - white rags torn from my bed sheets were wrapped around their wounds. The men spat and jeered, occasionally kicking me as they felt the need for revenge. The stub nose of an ancient revolver plugged into my nostril and tried to tear the bloody protrusion from my skull, I closed my eyes, I just couldn't believe this, this just wasn't happening.

"Daheen Mohdeer? Now Boss?" a vicious tone queried.

Somewhere in the room, a radio crackled

"Aiwa!" announced the responding officer,

"That's right; bring the vehicles around now. Better bring an ambulance too; we have injuries here, cutting of the skin. No! not knife wounds, some of the men fell onto a glass table during the struggle and were cut by the broken shards, we have a broken nose too but we're not too worried about that, it belongs to the infidel foreigner".

I peered through my swelling, tear-flushed eyes. My neighbours milled around outside, familiar faces, expressing more than concern, I could see them through the shattered remnants of my door

"What's he done? what's happening?" they inquired almost hysterically, "He is a good man, why are you treating him this way?"

"Alcohol resisting arrest and attacking my corporal!" announced the officer and waved their protests away, they left

272

with a disgusted expression that smothered all earlier pity, even though as neighbours in the same block of apartments, we had often drunk together during long sultry evenings. They were terrified of entanglement with this errant sector of the Saudi Law, just like everyone else. The normal police were bad enough but these guys weren't normal and nobody, even the normal police, wouldn't go anywhere near these creeps, unless they were feeling suicidal.

The barrel had been removed from my nostril, probably because the whole apartment block was now awake and tenants were asking questions. Some had seen me alive. A gunshot now, preceding my death whilst handcuffed, would surely produce unnecessary paperwork for the police tribe involved, or maybe it wouldn't, if no one had the guts to report it.

I tried to move my legs and arms, at least my own limbs were not broken, though with the nerve screaming pain issuing from my innards, I wasn't sure which I preferred.

They had me now, but it had not been cheap. As the scrum of men hit the coffee table and fell onto it, I was sure that couple of them had received serious lacerations. My arm wasn't broken either. That nice little injury must have belonged to the bloke who stumbled under the pile. I almost started to laugh into the floor, I couldn't help it, the little weasel of a bastard who had caused all this mayhem was crying, his arm twisted at such a horrendous angle, it would be a wonder if the Saudi Hospitals would ever get the bones straight again. They must have thought I was gasping or choking or something because they left me alone and apart from the odd kick or punch, I could sense, at least for the time being, it was all over. My body felt as if I had swallowed glowing embers and they were now trying to burn their way back into the daylight, unfortunately for me, they wanted to do it slowly, through my ribcage. My only consolation wasn't much help but at least the Khowaja had fought back, at least they had learned, that trifling with a Khowaja was not to be recommended. At least I had given as good as I had got, at least I was still alive, though with the pains now coursing through my body and with these daft bastards in control, I wasn't sure how long that factor would remain.

Various other police and attendants entered the room and left with either bits of my property or the injured. I was yanked to my feet and led from the apartment between two newly assigned guards of massive, physical stature. Outside in the warm, darkness of early morning, I was bundled into the back seat of a squad car with a heavyweight body on either side. In front of me sat three men. In the darkness through my watery, swollen eyes, they were hard to recognise but one was obviously the driver. The officer sat in the middle and now the third man turned from the shadows to face me and after his first sickly syllables, I recognised that unwelcoming victory-laden voice.

"Good evening, Mr Bob. Looks like you're in a spot of trouble?"

It was Sharief, his horrible, brown-toothed smile signalling his unrestrained though silent glee.

I lunged toward him, blinded by fury and desperate to sink my teeth into that face to bite off a nose, an ear, anything that would leave my vengeful forever mark, but the two hulks swung me back into the seat and began drumming on my ribcage with their fists. The pain shrieked through my innards and the cuffs bit so deep, my hands numbed and lost all feeling. When they had finished "restraining" me, the car thrummed to life and pulled out into the street. My head lolled back over the top of the seat and I stared out through the rear window at a mesmerised audience on the neighbouring balconies, then I closed what was left of the slit between my eyelids. I had no further desire to see my hopeless position. Did not wish to be present as the last moments of my life were spent. Did not wish to see my old home, where I had once lived and loved with Lyn, in a dream that now, in the darkest hours of my life, seemed so far away.

I achieved a hopeless, semi-conscious state from which I was rudely snapped back to reality as they dragged me from the car.

Half walking, half staggering between the two giants at my side. I stumbled into the station yard and was dragged along an uneven terrazzo walkway. They pushed me through an Arabic, arched doorway and manhandled my body to the front of an ancient wooden desk, to face an equally ancient policeman. It was a small consolation at this stage but at least we weren't out in the desert, unscrewing a family-sized jar of K. Y. jelly and getting our underpants off!

All walks of Saudi life stood watching, inwardly laughing at the foreigner's plight - beggars, old women, traffic violators, arrogant youths and criminal clones from every corner of the globe witnessed my treatment without comment other than knowing smiles. The charges of arrest bounced in and out of my head with almost no semblance of recognition, Alcohol, resisting arrest, assaulting police officers; the voice droned on and it appeared to be endless. My vision hazed as if I was now peering through greased glass. More mumbles droned through my mind before I was led away once more down a long, poorly lit corridor. The tops of my toes slid against the warm but rough concrete floor, grazing the skin and causing them to bleed. A metallic click pierced my mental discomfort; somewhere a key turned in a lock, followed by a squeal of well-worn hinges, obviously without oil for a considerable length of time. They dropped me without warning. Now I was falling, falling through the sky in a slow controlled glide, helplessly lost in the hands of another. My body hit the floor and my head seemed to bounce like a rubber ball. A voice inside wanted to cry out in anguish. The tears wanted to flow but within my spirit, a small spark of pride refused to yield to self-pity, not in front of these bastards anyway. Despite the pain and delirium, I concentrated on one function, to continue breathing. I was still alive, a fact proven only, by the small particles of dust that scurried and whirled as my breath crossed the warm, gritty floor. They brought no doctor and I received no medical attention - they just dropped me like a stone, made a few heroic gestures about what they were going to do to me later and after a few quick kicks and punches, left the cell.

275

Time slowed and after what seemed like hours I rolled to my back, my mind threw blurry pictures through the blood-shocked lenses of my eyes, onto the dingy white ceiling above. Mental torch light projections of a man without hope.

My mother and father, hand in hand, sobbing from afar.

Teachers from my old school, their chastising words almost ringing in my ears,

"Told you so, told you so, told you so.

I fought them away and Lotty, the girl I had abandoned, filled out the ceiling screen. She was dressed in black, almost a chador, but with her face revealed. She was crying at somebody's funeral. Bitter, wracking sobs shook her whole body and dislodged the tears from her eyes. The tears cascaded to her cheeks, sliding down her flushed skin. They dripped from under her chin and fell slowly, falling to the flowers she clasped firmly in her hands. The flowers were released and fell see-sawing down to earth; crashing against the gravestone that now bore my name.

"She still cares," I thought, "She still cares after all this time". I wanted to call her name but only managed to mouth the word that had once meant so much - Lotty. She turned and walked away, her voice fading along with her tender, young figure,

"Bye-bye, Bob. Bye- bye, Bob. Bye-bye.

"Noooo!" I wanted to scream out but the cry would not pass my lips.

Virginia's image blossomed through the clouds onto the ceiling screen. She was lovely and fresh as a morning dewed rose, smiling now; she was willing me upward to join her. I returned the smile, how easy it would be to release myself now, I was seriously considering the action, but then the flames came and as the Tri-Star burned the flames charred the flesh from her body, burning the skin from her face, her hair smouldered and began to melt producing a black sticky liquid that ran down the features of her smoke-blackened face. Now she cried out,

"Help me, Bob, help me, Bob, help me Bob help me my love!"

276

As the fire consumed her, her voice faded away and my soul was slashed once more. The tears slid down my cheeks and into my ears, exhaustion took over. Where the visions came from, I'll never know but I remember them like they were yesterday and they still fill me with dread. They say that when you're down to the last shreds of hope and sanity your worst nightmares appear, to push you over the edge. These were certainly nightmares, these were my last shreds of hope and at this moment in time, I was heading for the edge, and as usual, at the speed I was travelling, I could only have been on a motorbike.

Round and round went the innermost visions of my mind, tormenting and torturing my soul. I did not wish to view such apparitions but I was locked in the grip of a morbid fascination that I knew I had no right to own.

Lyn stood on a beach in the Philippines. Coconuts trundled up and down the shoreline as the waves ebbed and fell. It was Kandalom, her grandfather's Island. The camera pulled away, she was naked, one arm held tight across her breasts and as the camera zoomed out, it revealed the other arm, her hand clutched tight across her pubic mound. Then the sickness struck me again, for there, beside her silky upper thigh, was Sharief's sickly smile,

"Got any message? got any message? got any message? Sharief gloated and grinned, alone on the South Sea Island with Lyn. The pain became too much to bear; my heart swelled and pulsed with the enormity of the inner torment. My chest heaved as I swallowed a fury so great, I was sure I would burst my lungs.

The vision faded and the Sharief's chuckle was hidden by Lyn's pleas for mercy. I was about to give up hope when a familiar face came to me. A long-forgotten face, the face smiled,

"You got me all wrong, kid". announced the face from long ago,

"I ain't a bloody tourist, kid. I work here, I work here, I work here, I work here!"

The stranger began to fade. I saw in his eyes he was trying to pass a message; I caught his words as the vision blurred,

"Had all your injections Kid?" the stranger winked, "Cholera, Typhoid, Smallpox, Tetanus?"

"Had all your injections kid?"

"Here's another one for you!" again the Stranger winked.

"Here's another one for you!"

"Here's another!"

"Here's another!"

"Injection!"

"Injection!"

"Injection!"

The stranger faded from the screen and as his voice faded, realisation dawned.

The stranger's words pulsed the message into my brain. I chinned the shirt with the too-short sleeves from my shoulder and felt the damp spot at the crest of my deltoid, blood! I had been injected. I had no idea when or how but at least I knew their game. I had been tranqued or drugged, probably in the car, probably to make my passage to prison easy but I had also heard they did that to prisoners before they were beheaded, I couldn't remember and anyway, what the fuck were these guys doing with needles? I just hoped they had used a clean one, though, with my own personal knowledge of their habits, I doubted that very much.

"Pussy!" screamed Canadian Pete, but the vision was not sustained.

"He's made of chocolate!" spat Hawkeye in disgust.

"New Kid!" cried Virginia, her burned arms reaching out to me.

"Pussy!" screamed Pete.

"Made of chocolate!" spat Hawkeye.

"New kid!" sobbed Virginia.

"New kid!"

"New kow!"

"NewKhow!"

"Newkhowa!"

"Khowaja!"

"Khowaja!" The...

"Khowaja!" The intruding........

"Khowaja!" The intruding voice..........

"Khowaja!" The intruding voice echoed............

"Khowaja!" The intruding voice echoed along the unlit tunnels of an unconscious mind, drawing me back, to the undesired reality of my present predicament.

I struggled to my senses, my body ached and my mouth burned with the thirst of a thousand desert days but I was still alive, unless this was some sort of bitter twisted nightmare fashioned in hell.

"Khowaja!" soothed the voice,

"Drink this you will feel much better, here Khowaja, drink this water here".

I saw as the tin cup was placed on the small wooden table of previous inmate design. The anonymous, shadowy figure left the room. The door clanged shut behind it. With extreme effort I managed to sit upright. My back felt as if it had been used as a blacksmith's anvil. I was hot and feverish with a burning, blood flavoured thirst, aggravating a swollen tongue. A cup of water lay a single stride away. I moved to the table and stared at the cup, I sat there for several minutes. I tried to think before making any further moves, this had now got extremely complicated, who were these guys? They had me now, they had drugged me once and now I was suspicious of the cup. I was suspicious of everything. I reached out to the cup and lifted it from the table; I sensed them watching my every move. I remembered the harshest of my desert thirsts. How I had pushed my bike five miles, across the wastelands after the drive chain had broken whilst out riding the fool alone. The thirst ringing in my head now consumed all other thoughts. I closed my fingers around the cup and raised it to my lips. The bike! how I had pushed the bike! ten miles across the burning sands, how had I beaten the thirst?

CHAPTER 13   SAUDI STYLE   PLANS

I closed my eyes and thought about the sea, mental pictures from high in the Northern Hemisphere, I was on a drifting iceberg surrounded by mountainous seas. The wind howled into my face, smashing my body with an ice pick stinging spray. My feet were frozen to the berg's surface, my toes, cracked open by frostbite were blue and brittle as glass. The seawater drenched my body; every battering wave froze the dripping water to my skin. I concentrated hard, hyper sensing every thought. I felt chilled and as the vision turned my blood to ice, the new vision took hold and began to freeze my bones, I wished for sunshine, a burning thirst at my throat. I allowed myself back to my cage and my wish was granted. The thirst along with the iceberg disappeared. I knew the thirst was not a natural desire, I filled my mouth with the liquid, rinsed it around to dilute the bloody taste and spit it back into the cup. My arm straightened before me, pushing the cup away from my body and as my wrist slowly rotated the contents of the cup were deposited on the floor. Now my thoughts were clearing. I wanted to be able to absorb every action and plan every move, for the moment, Sharief would have to wait, my only priority now, was to stay alive. I didn't want anything from my tormentors, not until my life depended on it and I wasn't going to give in just yet, things couldn't get much worse than this - could they?

They left me to marinate in my own misery for three or more days. I sipped their offerings of water slowly and only when desperate for liquid nourishment, they weren't going to catch me out again. I ate the flat pancake-like bread and chewed on the rubbery, half mouldy, salted dates. Occasionally I would think about Lyn or my home, anything to free my mind of its present cage of pain. I thought about Pete and I knew my friends would be looking for me. So, I ate, thought about my predicament, and exercised when possible, walking in the confines of the meagre space that was almost denied the light of day. Pete told me later, what he had endured after his visit to my apartment on that morning after the arrest.

CHAPTER 13   SAUDI STYLE   PLANS

Pete thrust the photograph under the old guard's" eyes,

"Hinna sadique? is he here my friend?" he questioned politely.

"La mish mowjoud, no not here!" returned the familiar reply.

"Hinna sadique!" Pete had visited every prison in Jeddah but the answer was always the same, including the familiar grin of recognition, at the foreigner searching for his drunken, jailed friend.

"La mish mowjoud, no not here!"

Pete continued his search; he had yelled at the famous impotence of the British Embassy. Railed at the hundreds of arrogant guards. Almost begged to get inside for a chance to search the cells for what he knew would be an injured friend, but he always received the same old message,

"We are aware of it!" from the Embassy.

"La mish mowjoud, from the Saudi jailers.

Pete did not give up. He continued his search aided by Hangar and Hawkeye. He did not intend to give up the search until he saw me again, be that dead or alive.

It was not long before my healing solitude was interrupted. Two guards entered my cell, dragged me to my feet, cuffed my wrists and led me along dingy, corridors, corridors in an absolute dichotomy to the prince's office I had visited months ago. We finally strode free of the shadows and walked from the dark labyrinths into the brilliance of afternoon sunshine. My eyelids screwed tight, unaccustomed to daylight's glare. I had to squint for several minutes before I could view my new surroundings. I was in an internal courtyard; the high walls of enclosing structures loomed all around. The courtyard was bare but for a simple table like structure. A round-topped table with two small holes. I would not have given the table a second glance but for the legs, which protruded through the top by at least a foot as if a great weight had smashed the top of the table down onto the legs and speared them through the surface. There was something sinister about that table; I almost expected it to paw the ground before charging forward to pound me into the dust. This was no ordinary table from which I was about to be served dinner, the blood-spattered woodwork guaranteed as much.

"Salaamb Alaecumb, good afternoon, Mr King". The voice belonged to my arresting officer, almost pleasant with his intonation of greeting.

"Alaecumb Salaam," I replied in Arabic, I had a feeling it would be to my advantage to do so. Saudis held a faint respect for any foreigner who took the trouble to master their language and as I was practically fluent, it would do me no harm. The tiniest of gestures now could be of merciful significance later. The officer carried a handsome Arabian, young Omar Sharief like face; the usual dark moustache perched on his top lip. He had chosen not to sport the standard Goatee beard and his chin was well shaven, which was unusual. his beret covered half of his thick, short jet-black hair and perched precariously on the right side of his head. At least this man's uniform had been pressed and he looked rather more authoritative than some of the uniformed men I had observed around my present confines.

"These are rather like your English Stocks, Mr King. You put your feet through the holes, we cuff your feet and you can't run away until we have finished".

"Finished what?" I tried not to let the fear show through in my voice but I knew I was failing miserably.

The officer raised his arm and looked at his watch but before he could speak, the mullahs began their call to prayer. The call echoed around the courtyard over the omnipresent loudspeakers. At the officer's nod the two guards pushed me to the table. The table was overturned onto the four short stubby legs.

Please put your feet through the holes, Mr King. I will attend prayer and then I will return for a chat".

"What if I refuse?" I dared.

The officer pretended to draw his pistol and pointed the barrel of his finger directly into my face,

"Shot whilst trying to escape," he announced.

CHAPTER 13   SAUDI STYLE   PLANS

"In the face?" I gasped filled with disbelief at the way they just pointed their guns to kill, unconcerned about the consequences.

"Turn him around!" ordered the officer.

There was no need, I quickly placed my feet down through the holes, these vicious bastards had no respect for their own lives, why should they have any respect for mine. My feet were cuffed on the underside of the table and it was flipped back onto the four longer legs. I now hung underneath the table. The cuffs bit into my ankles and prevented me from moving or even seeing my feet. My shoulders grated on the hard-packed, hot gritty sand of the courtyard my shoulders were now burning and the sun seared into my face. All person's present were turned into threatening silhouettes of gigantic proportions. The three men strode away to prayers. I suddenly appreciated the term "maximum discomfort'. As the prayers echoed around the courtyard the sun burned down into my face. This unearthly position was a torture. I despaired at the possibilities that were about to follow. I did not have to wait long.

"Hanging around again, Mr Bob?"

Sharief stepped out from the shade of the courtyard sidewall, recognisable only, by his arrogant tone of victory and his small dumpy silhouette. My blood ran cold. Sharief rested his elbow against the table and spat down the side of my head and into the dirt. The spittle sizzled against the hot sand and quickly fried to a small dry stain against the courtyard floor.

"Maybe now you understand the term "Loss of Face?" Sharief grinned and savoured what must surely have felt like a pure sweet victory.

"Excuse me, sir! but this table is reserved, would you mind finding your own table, preferably as far away from here as possible?" I thought I hid my suffering well but inside I wanted to cry like a baby.

"Listen, Khowaja. We people of the desert stick together, we don't take too quickly to outsiders and if I were you, I'd be inclined to watch my step".

"Watch my step, Sharief? and how am I supposed to do that when at this moment in time I can't even see my feet?"

"Smart, Mr Bob, very smart, but I'm sure you'll soon regret your cocky western attitude". I noted the threatening intonation in Sharief's voice.

"Ha!" I snorted, "You're going to get your police buddies to fix me up where your cronies failed? is that it, Sharief? Is that how you intend to do it now? Well, I knew you would never be able to face me man to man, Sharief. I knew you would never face me alone, you're not man enough, you haven't got the guts of a lizard, Sharief, and remember what I told you. Whatever happens to me is going to happen to you. What goes around comes around, Sharief. So, help yourself man, get your friends to release me you know you'll be saving yourself a lot of trouble".

"Think again, Bob. These people don't care about me," Sharief lowered his voice to a whisper before continuing.

"I planted the booze. I knew you would be celebrating with your stupid friends Bob; it was easy. I sent the office boy to your lawyer, now he's disappeared back to his own country an extraordinarily rich man. You're finished, Mr Bob. Your evidence has gone. I took the apartment keys opened your or should I say our apartment and fixed up the bottle in your cooler easy. Walk in, walk out, Mr Bob. It was that simple. I could have done it a long time ago, but I gave you a chance to see the error of your ways and now your stupid pride has got you in a bit of a fix. Now they think your poisoning the Saudi youth with booze, doping and killing our kids as they drive around in a drunken stupor with your poisons of western pleasure. The only way out is for you to tell them where you got the booze".

"You know I can't do that!" I spat with venom.

"Right! Mr high and mighty Khowaja, then it looks like you'll have to suffer with the name of your supplier sealed inside your head". Sharief giggled with enjoyment at his masterful position.

"Noaaaaaa!" I screamed, writhing under the table, flinging my hand cuffed arms outward in a desperate attempt to ensnare the Sharief. The Sharief was already walking back to the comfort of the Shadows. The officer appeared at the perimeter wall and laughed for a moment with the Sharief. Then Sharief left the courtyard and the officer strode to the table, in one hand he carried the bottle, the one from my fridge. His other hand gripped a rod. I knew without fear of contradiction, that fishing, was not on his "things to do today" list.

"I have a message from the Sharief".

"Yeah! let me guess". I sighed.

"The Sharief says, "Here we go, here we go, here we go!" sang the officer, tunelessly.

"So that's when he did it!" I thought "I made it so easy for him, Jesus I left the gate wide open for him".

The officer placed the bottle beside his prisoner's feet; he gripped the rod by the thickest end and raised the tapered wispy end level with his shoulder. He then stepped back a pace or two until the end of the rod fell in line with my feet, whereupon he raised his arm quickly and scythed the air with the rod. A ferocious crack split the calm afternoon haze as the rod whacked onto the table. I realised all too clearly now, "The courtesies were over".

"Mr King! I will ask you several questions that you will answer as quickly as possible, if you are telling the truth, you have nothing to worry about. If you are telling lies - well let's not start off on the wrong foot so to speak, it's better you tell the truth, Mr King. Do I make myself clear?"

"Crystal!" I answered quickly, choking on the thought of future unanswerable questions, answers for which, I would have to provide.

"You really have an uncanny command of the language, Mr King. Such a pity you're mixed up with this, we could have become friends, discussed our diverse cultures and customs at great length?"

"Inshallah!" I sighed, "Inshallah!"

"Had you been drinking on the night you were arrested?"

"No!" I lied.

285

"Thank you, the blood tests were negative but as you appear to be willing to help with our inquiries, we'll remember your honesty".

I was almost joyful when I heard his remark, now they had no evidence from my own person and shit, they hadn't drugged me that night in the car, which was where they got the blood sample. I had been so fucked up that night I was prepared to believe anything. Shit! I thought again, they had only wanted a blood sample. All I had to worry about now was that they had changed the needle and I wasn't about to expire with AIDS.

"You know alcohol is forbidden in Saudi?"

"Yes, I know". I croaked, "On religious grounds, right?"

"Correct! Mr King, I'm glad to see your admitting the errors of your ways".

I had no love or even time, for foreigners who were caught drinking and, when deported back home in shame, told their stories to the newspapers, greatly exaggerated of course. They were warned before they came to Saudi, alcohol is forbidden. They broke the law and were punished, why couldn't they leave it at that? Why manufacture all those stupid stories for the press, who then exaggerated them once more until they were false? They were caught breaking the law and they were punished accordingly. They had been forewarned. If a Khowaja got caught, he took the punishment, three months in prison and a possible eighty lashes. A Khowaja broke the law and was punished and that was the end of it. That may have been one of the reasons the Saudis had a respect for Khowajas, we took our punishment and got on with it. The other foreigners were arseholes who were caught doing something they had been warned not to do. They got caught and didn't like it. They knew the risks, they knew the crime and they should accept the punishment, not run to the press with their monstrous exaggerations and exclamations of personal injury. A Khowaja accepted the fact he had been caught and he expected punishment and that was the end of it.

"Where did you get the alcohol?" enquired the officer.

"It was apple juice, you know it had been in the fridge ages, it must have fermented or something I really don't know anything about making any alcohol".

"It's OK, Mr King. We know you didn't make it; we know drinks can be obtained in Jeddah with little fuss. But what we want to know is where did you get it?"

"It was planted by Sharief, he must have put it in the fridge, he was the one who........!"

The terrible rod interrupted my speech as it scythed the air once more with a gut-wrenching swish followed by a loud crack as the rod smacked into the table. I watched the bottle as it rocked precariously from side to side before stabilising once more

"Listen, Mr Bob. The Shariefs are a well-respected family, they once ruled a large area of land but gave it to Abdel Aziz when he united the tribes and renamed this great country of ours".

"That's not quite what I heard but it doesn't stop them from breaking the law and using their connections to achieve their aims.......!"

"I will ask you one more time, Mr King If you refuse to answer or answer incorrectly, you will taste the old-fashioned Bedouin method of getting to the truth. I can assure you it would be better for you if you answered my question. Now! where did you get the alcohol...?!

I did not reply, I could not reply and I had no answer to give. The officer awaited my response when none was forthcoming, he nodded to the two guards loitering in the shade to my rear. My arms were now cuffed from the front to behind my back, one guard sat on my chest and gripped my nose, as I opened my mouth to breathe a handful of dirty sand followed by a dingy cloth tasting of salty sweat was stabbed and poked between my teeth. I tried to bite the perpetrator but as he stood up, he dropped a handful of gritty, salty, sand into my face, blinding my eyes which were still swollen from the beating and blocking my nose. I shook my head and snorted to get the sand clear but it was almost impossible. The rag was too big to be ejected by my tongue and made breathing difficult, especially with nostrils full of sand, grit and salt that was now carried by gasps to the back of my throat where it lodged and formed a quickly drying barrier. The guards tied a further gag tightly around my mouth to prevent the previous rag's ejection, and another handful of sand was dropped into my face and eyes. They then stood back and watched, grinning one to the other, as my writhing and facial expressions proclaimed my personal agony.

"The gag is not for you, Mr King. It is merely to prevent the other inmates from hearing your cries, we wouldn't want to upset them, now, would we?"

I jerked my head from side to side in panic, swinging under the table to rid my mouth of the gag. I was suffocating now, unable to breathe past the dried barrier of sand accumulating in the back of my throat. My torso danced like a puppet. The skin on my upper back was rubbed raw by the gritty hot sand, the salt burned my wounds and choked the back of my throat. The cuffs bit deep into my wrists and ankles but my feet did not move an inch. I could almost see again with one eye, whilst my other eye felt like it had been rubbed with a wire brush to remove my cornea. The tears flowed uncontrollably as they attempted to wash the blinding, salty debris clear. This was absolute hell and as I watched the officer pick up the rod and step back from the table once more, I realised with horror that the real torture was about to begin.

The silhouetted officer raised his arm high, so high he was elevated to the balls of his feet with the effort. Unlike the lashes, there was no copy of the Koran tucked under his arm this time; this man enjoyed maximum freedom of movement. He almost paused for breath in mid-air before his arm began its dreadful downward plunge. A loud swish tore open the afternoon calm. Then came the first contact; the whip-end of the rod cut squarely across the soles of my feet. Those strangled, upturned feet tried to grasp the end of the rod, arching skyward as the toes tried to kiss the heels. My instep muscles began to spasm and the calf muscles followed their lead. Suddenly, I lost control of my lower limbs. The blow caused no immediate pain but the relief in my face vanished before it had begun when the stinging sensation reverberated and blossomed into my insteps. Now the pain exploded from my toes to my heels and my feet were suddenly on fire. They were being plunged into glowing coals. I thrashed to free my body of the feet but the pain crashed down the muscles of my legs, burning into the calves and deep into my thighs. It drilled into my abdomen, charged into my chest and ripped at my heart before pulsing into my neck and finally flooding my brain.

I screamed, the automatic siren of a man experiencing pain beyond the tolerance of mortal beings. The gag stayed firm and it was ground between my teeth as I bit down hard screwing my features into wild demonic gestures, trying to rid my body of the terrible furnace of molten lava pain. My whole body denied me any control as the pain rippled and seared through my nerves. Finally, it began to subside, back the way it had pulsed until it was only the feet that burned as if they were resting against the hubs of hell.

The gag was removed and calm prevailed. There was an eerie silence but for the bottle of evidence, which had fallen from the table and now trundled slowly toward the edge of the courtyard. The sun's reflections danced from its surface and a tinkling; soulful melody played as it journeyed across the courtyard to escape such an unfortunate soul. We were all fixated as the bottle rolled towards the wall where it was lost in the shade and the tinkling music ceased as it rolled to a stop.

"As I said, Mr King. The old bastinado or falanga aimed between the heel and the ball of the foot methods are usually the best, would you like to answer now?"

I could not speak, my lungs sucked in the cooler air so previously denied by the gag, my heart pounded in my ears,

"Please God! no more". I prayed, I was no SAS man, I had no secret information, I wasn't trained to take this sort of punishment, so I used every trick in the book to get these bastards to stop, just to stop, I just wanted them to stop.

"Good, Mr King. You are a believer, please tell Allah who supplied the alcohol so I may hear you and it will be our little secret between the three of us".

"I can only tell you who framed me". My voice must have been riddled with a new emotion I had never experienced, cold, hopeless and absolute terror, I was ready to cry once more.

"I was framed by Sharief".

Again, the rod scythed the air, I screwed up my features in preparation for the ensuing agony, my eyes locked tight and I clenched my jaw. I did not see the officer nod but he must have made a signal. The rod did not strike again and the two guards released my feet from the table. As my feet hit the floor, my whole body tried to shrug them away, those awful feet, the harbingers of fire. I tried to stand, and it felt as if my feet had been placed in a glowing pit of well-breezed barbecue coals. The pain was too much and I fell back into the dirt, the two guards grabbed my arms and dragged me without mercy back to my cell.

"Think about it, Khowaja. Tomorrow is another day and I may not be in such a benevolent mood. No man has yet refused to tell me what I wanted to know. No man has ever received more than six strokes from the carbon fibre rod. Modern technology, Khowaja, much better than the Bamboo cane my own father used on me. Tomorrow, Khowaja, there is always tomorrow".

"Bukrah Inshallah!" I groaned, "Bukrah Inshallah!" my own personal translation ringing loudly through my head. "Piss off I'm busy right now'

The two guards dragged me back along the dingy corridors and launched me against the floor of my cell. After several well-placed platform boots had massaged my suntan, they pissed on my crumpled form, paying special attention to my head before strolling out of my cell and double locking the door. They checked the iron door's security with a shake, before chuckling between themselves as their voices faded down the corridor.

290

CHAPTER 13   SAUDI STYLE   PLANS

Jeddah is full of prisons - civil prisons, Traffic prisons, religious prisons, morality prisons, minor prisons and prisons that are not fit to be inhabited by cockroaches. Pete told me he searched each one in turn. There were no addresses in Jeddah; you found a location by its proximity to a well-known supermarket or a famous building or monument. Some prisons looked like ordinary apartment blocks, ordinary that is until you ventured inside and experienced the absolute misery such buildings contained. Other prisons were noticeable by the rotting fruit and vegetables that lay around the prison gates, thrown there by the hawkers, old stock that had failed to find a buyer on visiting day.

Pete worked his way around the holding pens of Jeddah, sickened by the grief he saw. Everywhere he went he found foreigners, who nearly always begged him to pass a message to their company or friends. Pete obliged where possible but he never saw any sign of me or received information about my whereabouts from any of them. Once imprisoned in Saudi, you are a lost cause until your company or friends manage to find you. Pete knew he had to keep searching, he thought my life could depend on it, it was that serious.

"Hinnah Sadique Is he here?" Pete pleaded.

"La mish mowjoud, No he is not". smiled the gate guards, unaware of the smouldering fury they could have so easily unleashed.

"Hinnah sadique?"

"La mish mowjoud". They joked with him, until Pete could not decide whether they were telling him the truth or merely messing him about as so often happened in these cases.

"Hinnah sadique? is he in here?"

"La mish mowjoud! No, he is not here'

The morning following my experience with the rod revealed two balloon-sized feet, blue-black in colour with an angry red weal across the soles. The normal sized toes looked as if fleshy marbles been stuck on in afterthought. I could not walk. The old guard gave me a drink and a couple of morsels of his personal rations. I lay on the wire mesh top of the cot and gazed up at the ceiling but the dreamscapes I expected never reappeared. They had obviously decided against hammering me to confession this morning. It made no difference to me; the primitive methods they were using now would have me spilling my guts if I had anything to tell them. My confession would have been signed milliseconds after the first kiss of the carbon fibre rod. Now I was at their mercy and my hopeless situation continually gnawed at my mental reserves to fight back. Tears pricked the back of my eyes but I denied them their appearance. They would beat me until I confessed or died. I could not answer their questions. Well, I could, but they would not believe me and the only thing I could look forward to, was a lengthy spell in prison and major chiropody from that evil stick.

The tears forced themselves closer as I remembered my Lyn; now I was a lost cause. The Sharief had won the day and now I would have to face the consequences. I would never see my Lyn again; I was dead meat. Even if I survived, by the time I got out of prison we would be too old to have kids. The pain of my predicament bit deep. All this was the work of the Sharief, all this over a few thousand pounds. A simple, straightforward Labour Court case that the Sharief had turned into a nightmare of pain and torture and now the mental agony was starting to invade my thoughts. Locked inside a tiny cell, my feet burning with pain, unable to walk and my thoughts on Lyn, the impossible dream that would haunt me forever. I realised I would have to think positive. I remembered all the Saudi prisons I had seen, none - I had thought at the time of viewing, could keep a determined Khowaja inside. It all seemed so easy but only when you were on the outside, it was different when you were on the inside. The trouble was, where would I go if the chance for escape ever arose?

A week passed by and the swelling had receded. I thought they had forgotten about me but I knew deep down, I had no such luck. On my second trip to the table, the officer explained,

"Once the feet swell, it serves no purpose to continue with the punishment. The feet burst like ripe watermelons," he continued matter of factly, "Surely to be infected which would mean hospitalisation for the prisoner. Very tricky if the Embassy involved visits the prisoner and learns of such treatment. We would never dream of such a barbaric act as bursting your feet. We have other things in mind for you".

I had seen the Saudis curiosity before, their idea of entertainment was watching some victim of a traffic accident bleed to death, whilst refusing to give assistance because they did not want to get involved with - of course, now I think I know, the Saudi Law.

"We would never dream of such a thing!" announced the officer as he lined up the rod for the first blow. The pain was as terrible as the earlier session but when the second blow struck home it amplified the intensity, causing a stereod symphony of blinding, searing pain. My protested innocence was ignored, much as I expected, and was once more I was dragged back to my cell gasping for air, certain I was going to die or be crippled for life. The guards dragged me around with my hair for a while before dumping me hard against my cot, and stamped into me with their boots, it was a long time before I dared move.

After the swelling of the second beatings had receded, they took me to a small, barred gate beyond which was a steel cage two metres square; inside the cage sat a guard. Suddenly, almost magically, Pete appeared before my eyes. my joy was almost too much to bear and the tears flooded my eyes. Pete's face registered the shock of disbelief and I realised I must have lost weight; I could not remember when I had last eaten a decent meal.

"Remember the code?" asked Pete

I flashed the diver's OK signal and launched into a coded discussion about the events that had taken place since he had last seen his friend. The guard squirmed in ignorance as we discussed droll subjects, interlaced with a hidden meaning. Pete returned to normal conversation with a wave of his hand.

"I've been looking all over the place; I've been here three times before they finally admitted you were here, typical non-co-operation.

"Thanks, Pete". I tried to smile but couldn't, as my lips would have split open and bled.

The two of us just sat and stared for a while, glad to see each other but lost for words until Pete spoke again.

"Hawkeye's waiting outside, they wouldn't let him in because it's not a regular visiting day. The next visiting days are Tuesday and Friday so don't worry; We'll be looking after you from now on. Hawkeye, Hangar and I have been thinking, we're all in the same boat, so we may as well go home together as soon as possible, they got us beat".

"Your leaving?" I gasped in horrified disbelief.

"No, we're all leaving, I. Just as soon as I can find your RED-SHIRT". Pete grinned at the expression that must now have been modelling my face.

The guard pushed Pete away from the cage; Pete stepped back from the bars and grinned again,

"Hope you can keep up, arsehole". Pete joked over his evictor's shoulder before he was led out of the enclosure and was gone.

"It's just a joke". I thought, "It's not supposed to be real". I thought about my friends on the outside of the prison walls,

"They'll never go ahead with it; they'll never deliver the second half of the code. It's not supposed to be real; it was just a joke, somebody could get hurt, worse than that, somebody could get killed".

I was bundled back to my cell and fell into the mesh top of my cot, one thought blotted out all others,

"Dear God, let them bring the rest!"

Pete was unemployed but his tasks became many. One of the tasks I gave him burned him inside as he had never been burned before. He was responsible for reporting my health and

294

welfare to Lyn. Lyn would not be fobbed off with excuses and demanded to know all the precise details. Pete did his best to console her but he knew there were some things he could never reveal. Saudi was famous for telephone operators who listened in on calls. Pete could not take that risk but finally passed over a clue which he hoped she would understand,

"Be careful, Pete". she had told him, her inner strength carrying her through. Pete also kept Lyn up to date of the other "interested" parties" efforts.

"We're working on it!" announced the British Consulate.

"Yes, I can see that!" agreed Pete, giving up hope that they would achieve anything through the consular channels. They had never really helped anybody and were unlikely to start now. After all, they were enjoying a substantial arms sales business with Saudi and they were not going to rock the boat for a non-taxable, non-resident, who had given up on them years ago, were they? Pete laughed at their excuses; did they really think the Khowajas didn't know what was going on? Pete knew it, they knew it, and the whole of the expatriate community knew it. The British Embassy was here for one purpose only - trade, with a capital "T" for Tornado. One could only hope the Saudis honoured their contract. They had bought an awful lot of high-tech weapons and if they decided not to pay, who was going to take it from them?

Hawkeye continued to work but he kept a low profile, he supported Pete and myself, kept us in food, and secretly supplied information. He kept a roof over Pete's head and he played out other roles that could not easily be ignored. Hawkeye continued to work, but only because it suited our "RED-SHIRT'. Hangar disappeared several times, no one quite knew where he went but he was conspicuous only by his absence. Hangar owned a villa in Cyprus, he had his own helicopter business now and was always ready to help in any way he could.

Hawkeye, Pete and Hangar visited me that week as often as possible, making sure, that I never went unseen on visiting days, although some days, I was not allowed to be seen by visitors. It wasn't due to illness or hearings as the officials often lied. my face was now rarely marked but I never walked or stood easily on the days following my absence from visiting hours.

"They're torturing him!" Pete had screamed at the consulate.

"We're doing all we can but brewing alcohol is a serious offence in Saudi". They advised him without conviction.

"That's why the Saudis' leave this bloody place, because they know they'll only get charged with drunk and disorderly, if they're punished at all that is, and there's no bloody whitewash job, like some of the reports I've read in the British Newspapers".

"There's no cause for such accusations here young man, after all, you're not even a British Subject".

"And am I bloody glad!" Pete had spat disgust, it was the last time Pete ever went to the consulate, after all, they were merely there as a supermarket for visas and to help with "Trade".

"Lyn sends her love!" Pete yelled above the din.

I nodded in acknowledgement, shifting my weight from one knee to the other before shouting across the gap to Pete,

"Are you going to the hearing?"

"Are you kidding? should be quite a circus, I want to see the Consulate's massive support for their subject; maybe their sending a card,

"To Bob, best wishes for the future'.

I had to smile; I knew exactly what Pete's words meant.

I attended the Court. It was a farce, everybody gave evidence except me. Everybody could speak except me. I was only allowed to speak after the whole affair was over. My Lawyer was brilliant as usual but he did not seem to grasp the situation as much as I did because he wasn't the guy in prison The judge asked me if I had anything to say,

"So nice of you to ask!" I fumed inside at the unfairness of it all. "Bukrah Inshallah!" I sighed, "Bukrah Inshallah!" It was the usual charade, come back in a month or so, we were still no closer to getting sorted out than we ever were and now I had the complication of being in prison for other "unrelated resisting arrest" charges which were obviously doing my character an immense amount of good.

Although I put on a brave face, I must have been visibly distraught by the whole affair. The consulate sent a man to take notes, but he must have been late for another appointment or an ice cream, because he left before the hearing had ended. As I stepped from the table, I caught sight of Sharief close by in the crowd, I couldn't help it, I almost went berserk, it was him who had designed all this suffering from nothing.

"It was him," yelled I, "Ask him about theft from the government authorities, ask him about his illegal doings. It was him, the Sharief!" I had to be restrained as I lunged in the direction of the Sharief; I was handcuffed, manacled and bundled out of court still protesting my innocence. My lawyer tried to quieten me down, he told me it was OK, I would soon be out of jail, Sharief and his mob had no tangible evidence, they were working full time on my case and had found some extremely believable potential witnesses.

The Sharief, embarrassed by the outcry and the fact that everyone in the court now seemed to be looking at him, turned and made his way to the exit. Two casually dressed foreigners momentarily blocked his progress.

"Won't be long now, arsehole". snarled Pete.

"Maybe you should have paid the insurance for yourself Sharief, looks like you're going to need it".

Sharief brushed past and left the courtroom; my two mates followed him. I couldn't hear what they said to him but he was ashen and I hoped they had threatened to tear his head off, as I would have done.

Hawkeye's contract was about to end. Hangar was on his way out of the company via an unceremonious firing by Sharief and the only ties remaining for Pete, were the tangle of legal issues Sharief was now weaving into a knot of hopeless proportions.

The handcuffs were removed when we got back to the courtyard and the two guards grabbed my ankles, one each, before dragging me back to the isolation of my tiny, Spartan cell. The skin on my back was torn to pieces as we crossed the rough courtyard and I had fallen from trying to walk on my hands in a backward wheelbarrow fashion and bashed my face against the floor. Inside the cell I saw the dark figure as it loomed over me, what was this? another kicking? An obscene laugh was followed by the warm splash of urine as it cascaded into my face, causing me to choke and gag. I spat furiously, to clear the vile fluid from my mouth and turned my face from the spray. My hair was soaked and stank, a rusty stink of human waste. I could not wash or escape the evil odour as it intermingled and obliterated the smell of sweat from my unwashed garments. At least they hadn't used me for a football, their steel segged platform shoes usually ripped the skin from my body. The physical pain had sometimes immobilised me but it was minimal compared to the mental ravages that now engulfed my thoughts. I lay in my torment and prayed for death's sweet nothing to remove my person from life's cruel hold.

Whilst trying to board my cot I fell; I must have cried out in the darkness. The old guard took pity, fearing an attempted suicide. The old guard rushed inside and saw me as I was reduced to a crawling, stinking shame. He helped me to my cot, washed the stink from my hair and face with warm water and soap and brought steaming sweet tea with bread and dates. The old guard shambled quickly; he himself would suffer if he were caught helping a prisoner, another good Saudi looking after the down trodden in the world.

He knew I was not like the rest, I had learned their language and customs, displayed knowledge of their desert ways and was a believer in Allah's will.

"If it was Allah's will that I be incarcerated here, then so be it, but there was no need for insulting my intelligence or my manhood. The old man completed his tasks quickly, and carefully locked the cell door on his way out, lest the Khowaja be fawning his pain.

CHAPTER 13   SAUDI STYLE   PLANS

I fell into that world which exists on the edge of sleep's boundaries. Sometimes enjoying a restful peace before being jarred back to a painful reality, when my body squirmed on the cot for comfort and disturbed those battered extremities. It would be a while before I could sleep through the night again, in peace.

Occasionally they took me outside and left me hanging in the courtyard for hours on end, allowing my brain to boil in the noonday sun as I imagined the consequences of the next few hours. The pain of the rod never materialised. I felt nothing, I had grown accustomed to this overworked trick and I would have gladly died rather than endure the painful, soul-destroying inhumanities, that they were now putting me through. Mentally and physically, they were breaking me down. I had nothing to tell them other than the truth, a truth I knew they would never believe. If I confessed, I could only expect more trouble, that's how things worked in out here. They forced you to confess, and then they treated you worse than before or executed you with a sword. The thought constantly ran through my mind, if they didn't kill me and this continued, I would have to kill myself, anything was better, including death, than the mental and physical cruelties I was suffering now. And so, the thoughts of suicide prised into my very existence, for the time being I shrugged them away but time and torture accultured me to the fact, that death was better than a lifetime of suffering and I made my plans accordingly. It wasn't long before they came for me again and during the humiliation of cleaning their filthy feet with my tongue, I decided it was time to get of here, one way or the other I was getting out, and if it had to be in a box, - so be it.

Chapter 13

PLANS

The tyres gripped if glued to the softening asphalt as Pete turned his car from the main road into a narrow side street. The small, white-washed corner house displayed a street-sign, a sign that until recently had meant nothing to Pete. Prison Street never did, unless a close friend or associate were incarcerated within those bleached white walls. Then, that simple nameplate became more than just a name; it became a nightmare to pierce your every waking thought. Enhanced by the humidity, the pungent aroma of rotting fruit and vegetables, wrapped the stink around you like a veil. Pete must have recognised the building at once, there weren't many buildings in Jeddah that boasted four corner towers, inhabited by police guards, cuddling machine guns as if they were newborn babies. We had all seen prisoner of war camps, whilst watching war documentaries on TV. This building could have graced any of the programmes, authenticity unquestioned.

Ruwais prison, stood out like a sore thumb in the northern sector of Jeddah, opposite the old airport site. At one time, it had been a lone encampment, far away from the bustling fishing port. The fishing port had grown with the times and now, the four-corner, masted prison lay becalmed in a sea of white-washed apartment blocks, a concrete sea adorned by dormant lighthouses, as hundreds of minarets scattered amongst the dwellings, pierced the ever-blue sky. The perimeter walls of the Prison were constructed from coral blocks, a suitable building medium that could not be leaned against. The gritty texture of the coral scratched the skin and the abrasions would itch and burn for weeks. Nobody leaned against the walls of the prison without urgent intent and such an intent could have also gotten them shot.

300

CHAPTER 13   SAUDI STYLE   PLANS

Hawkers parked their homemade barrows by the roadside. They sold all manner of fruit and vegetables, mostly to the queues of visitors, awaiting the hour when entry to the prison would be allowed. In these climes, the fruit and vegetables over-ripened and, unable to pass it off to the wary public, the hawkers simply tipped it from their barrows into the gutter for the dogs, rats and other fortunates, who survived "outside" the prison walls. If the coral had lost its deterrent factor, a few added reminders of security had been installed. Six coils of sparkling, stainless steel razor-ribbon adorned the top of the wall. A body trying to cross such an entanglement may just as well try to sneak through a mincing machine. Halting the attempted escape was unnecessary, picking up the sausage meat before it soured was all the guards would have to do. The razor wire coils traced a treacherous encirclement between the four corner towers. Each tower elevated two guards above the hustle and bustle of the daily prison rituals. They could usually be seen avoiding the sun, under the shade of a concrete canopy. These guys were in no hurry, attached to the coils were hollow metal vessels that tinkled softly if the breeze caressed their domes and positively rang out if anything other than the breeze became entangled within those deadly coils. The guards would only have to trigger their machine guns and blast the unfortunate meat from the coils, human flesh, forgotten in the gutter to complement the fruit and vegetables for the dogs and rats. Most guards slept soundly; anaesthetised by the interminable heat and the baking hot solitude of their white-washed concrete surroundings. They were comforted by the fact, that no one had ever escaped from this prison, not alive anyway. Flies and birds were the only escapees from Ruwais. After all, if a prisoner did escape, where would he go? The prison walls were surrounded by the desert on three sides and the Red Sea on the fourth, leaving potential escapees with two choices - die of thirst or drown. So far, according to records, no one had mastered the challenge. Pete briefed me later of his first encounter at the jail. He had scanned the street for a place to park. As usual on visiting day, the visitors had parked three abreast, rather than walk any distance greater than five meters. The traffic on this narrow street had been reduced to a bumper-scratching crawl. Pete lived in this place and like me, would know exactly what to look for. The main object of the exercise was to position your car so that no other car could park behind you and block you in. Saudis, he knew, would block you in for hours, before returning with an insincere smile and no hint of apology in their tone, laughing at you, as if it were some game for their enjoyment alone. Their enjoyment that is, until you blocked a Saudi car in. Then it became a war, a war of shouts, screams and offended manhood. They would scowl and rage, sometimes slapping the new foreigners around. It is against the law for a foreigner to slap a Saudi but not for a Saudi to slap the shit out of a foreigner and at that time the Saudis made the most of it. Pete considered all these factors and finally located a spot with his exact requirements. He manoeuvred into the space, much to the chagrin of the driver behind him, who continually sounded his horn and gesticulated, that this was his own personal parking spot. We had all encountered this ownership phenomenon before, every day of our lives in Saudi. Pete climbed from his car, locked the door and signalled to the irate driver that they should fight for the spot man to man. The incensed driver drove away at speed, squealing his tyres for presumed loss of pride. Pete crossed the strangled road and headed toward the prison entrance. The main gate, a huge steel latticework always remained locked, totally sealing the high Arabic archway that loomed overhead. A small pilot gate was set into the main structure. It was through this gate that everyone would have to pass. Prisoners who entered this gate were usually shackled hand and foot. If two or more prisoners arrived at the same time, they were shackled together for good measure. Pete joined the bustling crowd as they pushed and shoved, towards the crush of people squirming in the bottleneck around the tiny gate. There would be no mass outbreak through this gate. The police would have sufficient time to shave every prisoner, as he popped through the orifice on his bid for freedom, before throwing him back into the overcrowded cells. Unless of course he had been shot dead, negating the need for a shave or the return trip to his cell. More meat for the dogs and rats unless the relatives managed to claim the body before the vermin did. The pilot door was extremely small. People above a certain girth could not enter its limited opening and, the more amply fleshed prisoners would have to wait until the early hours of the morning, before being allowed to enter through the main gate, with additional security in the form of a couple of machine guns.

Pete held his position and was pushed and jostled toward the pilot door. More than once they had tried to push him from the pack. The anonymous arms that poked from below, afraid to show their dislike openly for the infidel and all they assumed he stood for. Pete wore his boots on these occasions and the pushers in sandal-clad feet could often be heard cursing, as they leapt from the throng grasping tenderised toes,

"Oh, excuse me!" Pete would exclaim as he ground in his heel and the pushers and shovers fell by the wayside.

The gate guards usually ignored him for a while and he allowed them to do so before cursing in Arabic, gaining their immediate attention and a small measure of respect. They would drag him through the door and watch in amazement at the number of visitors who jumped to one side as Pete passed, yelling in pain, grasping their toes and hopping around on one leg. A small but somewhat cooler, shadowy enclave lay on the other side of the doorway. Pete's pockets and baggage were searched. A pack of cigarettes was removed from one of the bags he carried. The guard gave him a knowing grin and Pete returned the same. Neither he nor I smoked, the cigarettes had been carried for that singular purpose - to bribe an easy passage through to the inner sanctum. A pack of cigarettes were an accepted currency in the prison and could be used to buy other goods from the jungle economy, driven secretly by the inmates inside. Pete received the customary body search that in his case always seemed to take longer than usual, he was good looking and some of the guards weren't bothered how tall he was. He wanted to kick the shit out of the owner of the probing hands but had learned long ago, not to complain. Finally, Pete was cleared for visiting, he picked up his goods and headed out of the hallway along the terrazzo pathway, which led to the westerners" section. The cells for Europeans were no different, but the inhabitants were considered dangerous. The Saudis did not want the Christians influencing other Muslim prisoners. The air in the courtyard was hot and heavy, the high walls prevented any airflow and the humidity hung like invisible steam. Some visitors were already leaving, mostly foreigners from every corner of the globe. Pete passed them by without acknowledgement; he had other things on his mind and merely wished to see his friend the Khowaja, as I had he informed me, become known in Jeddah. Pete entered the fifty-meter-long tunnel that would deliver him to the core of the visiting chamber. Even as he entered, the cacophony of yelling voices assailed his ears. He nodded to the guards in the tunnel-mouth, waved his slip of paper and they allowed him through. As he progressed the volume increased. Hundreds of human voices, speaking different languages and gabbling different messages. An entanglement of over-burdened decibels. He exited the tunnel into the light and crossed to the cage where he knew I could be seen. This time he would not be alone. There would be twenty or thirty people clustered around the bars of the cage. They would all be yelling their individual conversations to their friends or family members within. There were six such cages around the perimeter of the central chamber, totally covered by scrambling human forms, human spiders on webs of steel competing for space and voice. So many people were shouting at the same time, it became a ragged symphony, echoing around the central chamber and obliterating singular speech. The noise was sometimes so great the guards packed cotton wool in their ears to escape the verbal tide. Pete arrived at the cage. There were many people visiting today, not like his last visit where he had been allowed in alone to check on his friend and list his requirements, for the first delivery of food and clothes. On that same visit Pete had thought the bars were made of stainless steel. Now he realised, like many before him, that they were iron and had been polished smooth by the many visitors gripping and grasping there. Pete stood amongst the mass of visitors as they squirmed around the outside of the two-meter-square, steel cage. Pete began to prise his way into the human mass. It was at times like this, when he wished he enjoyed the extra six inches of height that I had so often teased him about. Pete endured the arms and elbows of total strangers until finally, the man in front of him made a move to leave. Pete forced his body into the rapidly closing vacuum, grabbed hold of the bars and pulled himself forward to secure his position. Now he stared across a two-meter gap into the pity filled faces of the unfortunates dwelling there. So many faces were squashed against the tiny, steel barred door he had to check a second time before he realised, I was not amongst them. Pete waited for a moment, and then, in what seemed to him like a lull in the storm of voices he bellowed my name. Nothing happened and he tried again. I had heard him the first time but couldn't get to the gate quick enough. The next time he shouted I returned his call with equal volume. He watched my hands grip the bars and when the other inmates gave way or left their positions, I pulled my face to the front. For a while, we just stood, nodded in acknowledgement and stared at each other. There was no need for speech; it was enough to know that the other was OK. Pete then passed a small white sheet of paper to the guard. The guard scrutinised the paper and cleared the gate by pointing his gun at the other prisoners and me. With one swift turn of a key, he opened the gate grabbed me by the arm and dragged me out before he slammed the gate shut and locked it once more. Some prisoners cheered,

"Yeah! Khowaja is free!" I had probably assisted everyone inside that hell hole, with translations and information, not normally available to them and now they were showing their appreciation. I was numbed by the unexpected accolades, seconds later the guard opened the outer gate and pushed me in the direction of the waiting Pete. Was I leaving, was I really going to leave this hole? Pete grabbed my shirt and led me back along the labyrinths to a small courtyard. He stopped and gave me the plastic bag,

"Here! get changed and let's get the fuck out of here!"

I must have been in shock and was barely able to speak to him. I pulled on a crisp pair of clean pants, a pair of jeans, which I had to tighten the waistline, by moving my belt two notches and my favourite Red Shirt. Newly ironed, crisp and fresh. I shoved my face in it, mostly to hide my joy and soak up the tears that were welling into my eyes. I got hold of my emotions, ignored any need to be overly grateful put on the shirt, stabbed my feet into a new pair of thick tube socks and then my motocross boots. I tried to ask Pete why? but he motioned me to silence and we started our journey back to the outside world, Pete's only comments, "Mansouri's complements!" It seemed Mr Mansouri had friends too and he was starting to use them. Again it proved that not all Saudis were crooked bastards but I knew that anyway. He also told me that even some of the other cops had gotten involved and discredited the evidence, they must have been the ones that visited me earlier, or maybe Faleh Muteiri had intervened as well. Overall, it seemed that half of Saudi wanted me inside a jail, and the other half were fighting to get me out. I had only one problem with this; how the fuck was I supposed to distinguish between the two?

Pete marched briskly across the inner chamber and out through the tunnel mouth. He waved the slip of paper and we passed the guards without a second glance. The terrazzo path led us back to the main courtyard where I basked in the warm, cleansing light of brilliant sunshine that warmed away the clammy feelings of dark, claustrophobic contamination. The expression on my face must have spoken a million words and I knew I could never leave Saudi now unless accompanied by my genuinely great friend. The guards gave us a brief, cursory glance and after inspecting the release paper for good measure, we squeezed through the pilot door in the main gate. Out into the freedom that I welcomed with a new appreciation born of my experience in the innermost bowels of a Saudi prison.

Our pace quickened as we approached Pete's car, I almost expected to be called back and detained. Pete slipped behind the wheel fumbled the keys into the ignition and with two quick shifts, we entered the mainstream of departing visitors. I yelled aloud, punching my fists into the roof of the car, I could hold it no longer,

"Yeaaaah! freedom! at long last freedom!"

"Hey! mind the car, Khowaja!" Pete just sat there grinning; he knew what it meant for me to be free.

The menacing towers disappeared from the rear-view mirror. The guards barely discernible as they hugged against the darkened centre post for shade. I wished them all the bad luck in the world as we turned onto the main road that launched us across town to the Cornice. Pete said we had to keep another important appointment and personally, I didn't give a shit where we were going as the prison disappeared behind us. Two weeks banged up in there was enough to make anybody crazy. I just sat there, sucking in the freedom with tears prickling my eyes.

"Fuckin pussy!" Pete acknowledged my tears with reverence, looking me over with a brotherly expression as we continued our journey. As we got further away from the prison, I recounted to Pete what had happened from leaving their apartment to leaving the prison. I could see from his expression he was not impressed, but as I told him, I had been drinking and they caught me and being a Khowaja, I had to take the lumps and bumps, no point complaining I told him, there was a lot of face involved now. I just hoped that was it and they weren't going to come for me again.

"Shit Khowaja!" you're even starting to think like them!" was Pete's only comment

We reached the Cornice and turned south. Pete drove past the Port of Jeddah and the naval base beyond. The south

307

CHAPTER 13   SAUDI STYLE   PLANS

Cornice wasn't as attractive as its northerly counterpart but held a substance we needed for our plans. A white powdery substance surrendered daily by the sea to the beds. It was here that the sea-soaked through the landlocked surface of the sun-baked beach. The rising tide level often caused small, shallow lakes to appear in-land. As the sea level receded, the lakes would be left to fend for themselves and the merciless orb evaporated their waters leaving behind the raw crusty salt of the sea. Local hands did not work the salt beds. They were inhabited by illegal immigrants without work permits, escaping their own country from war, plague, famine or death. These were, indeed, the children of apocalypse. The salt was collected into sacks and carted off to the refinery on the industrial estate. From here, in its purified form, it would be placed in silver shakers in the finest restaurants around Saudi. Vastly different from the humble beginnings where Pete now headed. The beds were small but were not more than a few desert miles apart and when worked in tandem supplied a comfortable living for the people who "Owned" them. Originally the Saudis themselves had worked the beds but since the oil wealth had improved their lives a hundred-fold, the beds were left to be worked by the Sudanese, Somalis, Ethiopians and other, seemingly luckless inhabitants of the planet Earth. The Saudi owners shared the salt wealth with the workers. Perhaps "share" is not quite the correct term to use. The workers delivered the salt to the refinery. The refinery in turn paid the Saudi salt bed owner, who in turn paid the workers. The workers received a reasonable sum as the Saudi saw fit to pay, after all, they should not be in this country. They had no work permit and no right to complain or seek recourse if they were cheated, which meant they often were. At least the workers received money for life support; they were better off here than back home. At least here, they were not being shot at every day, nor were they or their immediate family starving to death. Some Saudis were good to them, some weren't. No matter how the Saudis treated them, no one complained. Some people worked hard and some people became rich, it was the way of the world that did not make the hard workers rich and the rich men hard workers. Such is life.

Pete jumped from the car and I followed him. After the confines of the prison, it was a welcome relief to stand on the boundary, between a vast desert and the mighty Red Sea. I sucked in a few deep breaths of the salty, fresh air. A slight onshore breeze fanned my face, disguising the temperature of the broiling sun. We skidded from the road down a small, sandy embankment and although my feet were still quite sore, we headed across the crusty salt beds on foot. We made our way to the tiny wooden structure floating in the haze, which we knew would conceal the workers, as they shaded from the glare of the high noon sun. Out here, the temperatures could soar beyond fifty degrees Centigrade and though the workers were accustomed, few men managed a full working month without experiencing the effects of muscle cramps and dehydration.

The small wood and cardboard structure alleviated some of their suffering. When the noon sun soared directly above, they would move under the shade and take their afternoon siesta. Water was gulped down by the gallon and a pinch of salt placed under the tongue often helped against the cramps. The dark, shaded pile of black human beings saw our approaching strides. Brilliant pairs of white eyes now separated their shadow soldered forms. We walked head down to shade our eyes and as we first approached them, I noticed their feet. The cracked, salted skin, hard and well worn, probably more suited to the back of a Rhino. Salt ringed ankles signalled today's water level and their massive, ball-knuckled hands with pink, callused palms, transcribed the hard-laborious path, which they had trodden on life's voyage. These were men of immense tempered strength. Their backs would be bending all day, raking and shovelling the salt into conical towers. The cones of salt would be left to dry out before being scooped and bagged ready for the refinery, no-one would buy wet salt, its weight being many times that of dry.

The huge sacks would be hauled onto their glistening, sweat-soaked backs to be shouldered across the foot-sucking terrain to a waiting truck. This combination day after day, weeded out the weaklings, who left the beds for lighter work in the industrial areas, to become factory floor sweepers, gate guards and the like. Left behind were giants of men, with the hearts and lungs of lions and the physiques of world champion weightlifters without the steroids. Their diet consisted of fruit and vegetables and fresh fish, which they caught daily in their hand nets. It was a diet befitting thoroughbreds. Any one of them could have worn a full-length fur coat and fought Mike Tyson with ease. These men were not to be toyed with and the owners who cheated them were fools indeed. Pete lowered his head as he entered the shade; I did the same, avoiding a low scaffold beam that supported the plywood and cardboard canopy. The men smiled upon our entrance, mumbling amongst themselves in Arabic, sparkling white teeth and brilliant eyes toying with our unexpected appearance,

"Infidels," they mumbled, "infidels lost at sea and come to ask their way. The good lord smileth down on us, an afternoon game we can surely play. We will have sport with the unknowing ones".

Grins and smiles flashed around before Pete interrupted their mirth,

"No, you won't, turkeys," Pete's Arabic was enveloped by a chorus of whoops and laughter which shattered the afternoon calm.

"Asalamb alaecumb," continued Pete as he joined in the grinning laughter.

"Alaecumb Salamb," they chorused in return to his welcomed greeting, their pearl-like teeth illuminating the darkness of the hotbox shade.

Two small demitasses of tea were poured from a well-worn thermos and, without hesitation; we thrust the glasses to our lips taking a noisy slurping sip of the hot, sweet, golden liquid. We positioned the cups on the makeshift cardboard carpet in front of our cross-legged, seated position. It was customary to drink tea or small cups of Saudi coffee that carried a flavour, not unlike sweetened linseed oil, caused by the cardamom extract. No business ever began without the preliminaries and being a salesman, with a little help from me, Pete had mastered them well. Pete said nothing; he sat quietly, occasionally sipping his tea as he observed their curiosity swell. He would give them time; they were eager to learn the reason for our visit. They would have to endure a full measure of his ritual knowledge, so that next time, they would think twice before sporting with a foreigner again. Pete finished his first drink and his glass was refilled. I stared off into the distance, savouring my tea and felt their eyes as they probed for some sign or reason for the visit. Pete waited before finally but slowly, glancing around at their eager faces. I had laid the foundations well. Pete was now a master of tradition as he lingered on the peripheries of the reason for our visit. He made polite small talk on the comforts of their shade and the time of day. His listeners eagerly swallowed his words as they tried to cross the bridge. Now all eyes were fixed on their visitors, all attention was Pete's perspiration slid down his temple, as the tea flushed the pipes of his inner cooling system. He made no motion to wipe the drop of liquid away. A fly buzzed his face. They watched him carefully, scrutinising and appraising. Pete neither did not do or said anything. The fly did not exist. Now they were champing at the bit. We finished our second glass of tea and as Pete's glass was refilled, their curious anticipation was a joy to behold. These were their own customs and Pete had surely learned them well - he had enjoyed the benefit of an excellent teacher. He should have waited a while longer until we had finished our third cup but hey, he was just a new kid, wasn't he?

Slowly he discussed life, the weather and their current predicament, it was at least half an hour before he got around to the reason for our visit,

"How many kilos in one sack please?" he enquired.

"Khamseen, fifty," an eager voice responded.

"How many Riyals per sack?" continued Pete.

"Five hundred Riyals,"

Still, they doubted him

"Aeeeeyah!" exclaimed Pete, widening his eyes for effect and throwing his arms to the sky as he turned to myself and spoke in Arabic.

"They are digging gold from the beach, last week salt was one hundred Riyals a sack and now it is five times the price, it must surely be golden salt or they wish to play games with this poor foreigner".

Much grinning and clapping of hands followed, Pete's Arabic intonation was almost colloquially perfect and the men rolled around on the cardboard-covered floor, belly laughing with delight as Pete continued,

"I am not a foreigner, I am a son of this country, why do you wish to treat me so badly?"

Much waving of hands to soothe his hurt expression ensued; the group of workers laughed and grinned in unison, bandying the title we cherished to hear.

"Khowajas!"

We had crossed the bridge onto their territory and now the price to a Khowaja was one hundred Riyals. The normal price to friends of the workers is more than they could ever dream of achieving from the owners. Pete requested a half sack and a sack was pointed out to him; it was more than half full but he was welcome to it for twenty-five Riyals. He removed two, crisp fifty Riyal notes from his pocket, and he passed one to the sales manager who had negotiated the deal and refused to accept change. He then passed the other fifty Riyal note to the man who had served the tea,

"Buy some more tea and cake! we shall surely return to see our friends again" Pete's soothing Arabic revealed his understanding of their present situation.

We were welcomed amongst them as they leaned against the sacks of their earlier toils. Time held no urgency for our hosts, what did not get done today would get done tomorrow or the day after "Inshallah'. God willing. God ruled their whole lives and their beliefs were as certain as the sunrise. We lapsed into a lazy exchange of Arabic, detailing our differing lives before the desert Kingdom's draw. We said nothing about the fact I had come straight from jail, it didn't seem to matter somehow. We were all in the same confinement under god's scrutiny out here - weren't we?

Across the beds the rippling haze shimmered, distorting the legs of the many wading birds that, now there were no human disturbances, were feeding in the shallow pools. Herons patrolled the area for insects, crustacean and small fish but the men informed us of another sight, God's beauty to behold. Just before dawn's light the men would arise from sleep, to wash and bathe in the sea before early morning prayers. As daylight dawned and they saluted God, a pinky-red blanket of long-legged flamingos, could be observed roosting on the beds. Almost to the second, immediately after the prayers, the men would rise to their work. A noisy chatter would break the silence and whirl into a crescendo, as the birds were fully awakened and disturbed into panicked flight. The pink, mushrooming cloud of thousands of flamingos blossomed into the sky, a magical flower of life, opening its brilliant petals of reddish hue as it rose above dawn's horizon and headed down the coast in a noisy, honking cacophony. The cloud fanned outwards till it became a flat sheet of birds that flapped away into the distance and were lost to the naked eye. The birds only stayed around the beds for a matter of weeks resting and feeding as if preparing for some great flight ahead, probably across the red sea and onto the great plains and the rift valley of Africa.

The workers obviously enjoyed their company, continually thanking God for the creatures of the earth, Alhamdulillah! A fine tranquillity now played on my mind and the realisation of my freedom dawned. Although these men were not wealthy, they probably enjoyed their days to the full. The companionship, the food and the world around them. Perhaps they were right, everything was indeed in the hands of God and if they had a roof over their heads, food in their bellies and breath in their lungs, what did they have to worry about? Ozone layer, Stock market, Mortgage, Overdrafts, pensions and the greenhouse effect - they had no such worries, they owned an easy contentment and the prospect of a long healthy life. Cholesterol, Calories, Heart Disease, words and ailments they knew nothing about, words that had been invented by the fat, gluttonous nations too busy poisoning their own world to worry about anyone else's.

I remembered Juergen, what had the western world done for him?

Juergen Schnetz, held a Bachelor of commerce degree, had more letters after his name than the alphabet and was acting Commercial Manager for one of the largest German companies operating in the Middle East, let alone Saudi Arabia. Juergen's manner would have led you to believe he was a humble labourer. We had found out by accident that this young man was responsible for the finances of some of the largest, most technologically important projects that were underway in Jeddah. The massive glass and Marble building housing the Saudi Ministry of Defence, with its delicate architecture hiding the cavernous, underground nuclear bunkers. The Telegraph and Post buildings in the heart of the city. Not to mention the many other monolith-like landmarks that were scattered around the Kingdom but still under the commercial restraints of Herr Schnetz as his employees insisted on calling him.

Pete and I had emerged from the sea after a morning dive; Juergen had unknowingly parked close to our vehicle. The other foreigners had claimed the rest of the beach and of course the young Saudi lads, who were busy checking out the bikini-clad western women, who could blame them? An unusual binocular sport from twenty to fifty meters away, which ensured a close-up view of the lovely young wives of expats, something they very rarely saw, if at all. It could almost be considered as the National sport, next to World Cup football and infidel baiting of course.

314

This occurred back home or in any other country but not with the same blatant disregard for the feelings of the embarrassed young wives, not to mention teenage daughters.

The conversation had been easy. Juergen spoke English, French and Spanish as well as his own native tongue, which kind of made me feel inadequate. Juergen helped with our diving gear and later in the afternoon taught us to windsurf, a sport at which he was obviously a master. He too had commented on the fierce rivalry, and he had only known us for a few hours.

Another member became part of the team. Juergen had much in common with the two of us and he was accepted like a brother. Sometime after our initial encounter. Pete was out of the country on business. Juergen and I had decided to windsurf at the south creek. Famous for its afternoon winds and unspoiled beach. The incumbents couldn't be bothered to drive so far down the coastline and so the beaches weren't strewn with litter and sacrificial carcasses. The entire day began on a strange note, a shemal had blown up. The whole of Jeddah was socked in by a dingy orange, dust filled sky. The high humidity caused the dust to stick to warm, damp skin. By the time we arrived at the beach, even though we had travelled by air-conditioned car, we were ready for a good swim. The shemal sandstorms, rarely affected the beaches unless the wind blew offshore. Then it was hell, the hazy dust obscured the shoreline, the wind tried to blow the surfboards out to sea and more than one surfer had been accused of trying to leave the country on a small fibreglass board, despite the fact, that the unlucky sportsman had almost drowned in the process. We were lucky; the onshore wind blew hard and only picked up the sand to carry it inland, away from the wet beach. In short it was a wonderful day for wind surfing. During the trip, Juergen had discussed his plans. He was approximately one month away from a final exit visa. He was about to return home, marry the girl of his dreams and settle down to a comfortable life in Germany in the picturesque village of Heidelberg, where he had bought a luxurious home and invested substantial sums of money. In short, he was home and

315

dry. Juergen, obviously fuelled by his impending departure to his own personal utopia, rode the high winds up and down the coastline at terrific speeds. Already, several surfers had quit the gusting flurries, me included. The wind had developed into a gale and it seemed that Juergen would out ride it to the end but eventually, even he, the last able body on a board had succumbed. Back onshore Juergen complained to me about his arms aching, not unusual after what he'd just been practising. Juergen laughed it off; we ate lunch at the beach together before deciding to head for home.

On the journey home, Juergen pulled off the desert track and onto the main highway that would deliver us to Jeddah. He stopped the car and asked if I would drive, Juergen said he felt a little tired. "Herr Pussy!" I called him and he still laughed cheerfully. Just before he fell asleep, he asked me to wake him in about a month's time, preferably on the day of his departure. Halfway to Jeddah, in the middle of nowhere, Juergen yawned and stretched out in his sleep. They were the stretching motions of a man about to wake up, but Juergen did not wake up. Juergen never woke up again. I only became suspicious when I asked Juergen what he would like for dinner. Juergen did not reply, even when I slapped his leg hard and got no response. I raced to the nearest hospital, minutes from our present position. It was too late. Juergen was thirty years old and in the prime of his life. He was an athlete, and as fit as any of the men who knew him. The doctors told me that no one could have survived such a massive heart attack as the one that Juergen had obviously endured. It was obviously - "God's will'. Later as the wheels of officialdom caught up with me, I was grilled for hours and continually interrogated by the Jeddah police, who were understandably not too sure about my story and were suspicious to the point of accusation,

"Had we been drinking?"

"Had we been taking drugs?"

"Had we argued?"

"Had we been fighting?"

316

"He was my friend!" I yelled in disbelief at what they were trying to suggest with no hint of condolence.

At first, the traffic police quizzed me. Then along came the civil police. Then the religious police had a go at me, before finally, the criminal investigation department turned up and repeated the same questions constantly until I thought I would go insane. Finally, the Hospital decided to educate two young Saudi nurses in the care of the bereaved. Yes, those same females, that were not allowed to inject male patients or even touch male anatomies, but they were it seemed, allowed to ask dumb questions,

"What time did he die, sir?"

"I didn't know he had died and I wasn't looking at my watch in case he did".

"Did he say anything before he died?" they smiled but it seemed more like a giggle to me, not sympathy.

"Wake me up in a month!" I replied, my fuse now burning toward the frustration within.

"What do you think he died of?"

I stared at them in disbelief, I stared long and hard until their faces blushed around their eyes, which was all I could see of them,

"I'll tell you what he died of," I began, "He died of too much Saudi Arabia and that's probably as close to the truth as any of us are ever going to get".

"You should be happy for him, now he is in paradise".

"He was a Christian!" I replied gruffly, "And your people are always telling me, Christians do not go to paradise, isn't that true? He was a hardworking, decent, honest man and I can tell you, he loved your country. He had worked here for many years to improve your lives and provide a better country for you, not for him because he was going to leave soon, but for you. For you and your future generations, and Saudi people keep telling me, God will not take him because he is a Christian. An honest decent man, you should be ashamed".

CHAPTER 13   SAUDI STYLE   PLANS

One Saudi nurse stepped toward me, I half expected a slap across the face, her hand rested on my shoulder, which was illegal out here, and she hugged me tenderly before whispering her comforting words,

"He will surely be in paradise". then they turned and were gone, more lovely Saudis, confusing my mind and proving their real worth.

I was taken to two or three prisons and passed around Jeddah like a murderer, until finally by sheer chance I arrived at Faleh Muteiri's headquarters. Faleh listened to my story, gave me some tea and sympathy and drove me home. His parting words were of great comfort,

"Remember my friend, there is more to this life you think, and Juergen will surely be in a much better place, a paradise for all good Muslims and Christians'. He spoke with such conviction, such belief, you couldn't help but think about their religion and the five times a day prayer, what did it all mean?

I had promised to drive Juergen to the airport on the day of his departure. Juergen's departure had come sooner than expected, I went with the humble pine box to the airport and bade farewell to my friend with the silence of respect.

I eased back from my innermost thoughts to present my surroundings; I had almost dozed off to sleep and I fully expected to wake up in the confines of the prison. I was smiling again, free again, enjoying the simplest pleasures of life's voyage. The workers around us were preparing to return to the beds. One of the men motioned to the bag of salt at Pete's feet, offering to help carry the load. Pete waved away his offer and the other men turned to watch his efforts. Pete twirled the top of his sack into a rope-like handle, he lifted the bulk of the weight to test, and then he swung the sack forward and heaved on its back swing. As the sack swung forward once more, Pete heaved with his motocross arms and as the weight neared the peak of its arc, Pete leaned his shoulder under its inevitable downward

318

path. The sack pillowed onto his shoulder, but his sturdy frame did not falter, earning him the immediate respect of every man present. The sack weighed nothing compared to a motocross bike, which we had now become accustomed to heaving around the desert with our bare hands. Such practices had also provided him with a physique envied by the office-based beach bums. Pete casually turned and we bade farewell to our hosts. They all grinned their approval as Pete set off across the beds toward his car. After the walk across the dried, cracked seabed, Pete dumped the sack into the rear of his car and turned to express his gratitude in a final signal of farewell.

The inside of the car was like a furnace and we left open the doors as Pete juggled with his keys to get then into the ignition switch. Finally, the car coughed to life and we allowed it to run for a while with the ac on full blast, so that the hot, metal controls would return to an operable temperature. He fumbled in the back seat; he had brought a cooler chest and he removed two cans of ice-cold beer.

"OOOhhh! I hope that's not real beer, it plays havoc with my feet!" I joked with him and we grinned. Pete dropped the car into gear and slowly moved away but not before we blew the horn and turned once more to see the giants of the salt beds, waving in our direction before they began their afternoon toil. As we drove, my earlier thoughts returned, Juergen would probably give anything to be working alongside those men now, though who knows, how many men like that never reached Saudi? killed in the wars? killed by disease or even starvation? Life certainly was a mystery, you never knew how long you'd got, or why you were here. I knew only one thing, it was out of my control and now more than ever, I was beginning to realise, if there was a God and since my trip to Saudi I was more than ever there had to be, then everything, without doubt, was in his hands. Pete stabbed a cassette into the player; he adjusted his seatbelt and told me about his next assignment. The creek was forty-five minutes away but with the music, the Cornice and my tales of prison torture, the trip would not be unpleasantly long and that non-alcoholic can of beer I dumped down my throat, was Carlsberg and yes at that moment, it was, probably the best non alcoholic lager in the world.

Even shark was hot to the touch as we clambered aboard. Sharief had written her off, Pete and I had joined forces and funds and purchased her for what could only be described during the good times, as discounted peanuts. She had lain in dry dock for a week now and Pete had almost completed the maintenance she needed. He had completed the work himself, that way he knew he could be sure. Shark! fifteen meters long and barely three meters wide. Her twin, four-forty supercharged Merlin engines, provided her with the thrust to spray by most of her rivals on the creek. She was older now but had been well cared for and was still seaworthy to a fault. Even the rich kids in their fancy cigarette race boats still held her in awed respect. What would they say if they knew what Hawkeye's mechanics had done to her now? She still enjoyed a low profile and being black she was almost unnoticed amongst the multi-coloured ego-trip speedboats on the creek, unnoticed that was until those Merlin's roared. It was then that colour and paintwork proved nothing and raw power decided the race. She was still black, all black but for those freshly painted, bright red eyes staring almost menacingly from her bow.

Pete stowed the salt in the hold and glanced around. The emergency dinghy was well packed, her two motors bulging from their sealed rubber housings. Fuel tanks were full and the spare tanks strapped in position. The floats, which he had checked a hundred times were still showing full, pressure. "Tomorrow", he told me, "Shark would be back in the water, faster and wilder than ever before. Hawkeye's master mechanics had promised to see to that. All that remained," he said, "Were the salt tests". He checked the locks securing the hold making sure that the register pin was carefully in place, the pin would signal unauthorised entry, when satisfied, Pete glanced back along the deck; everything was in well waxed shape. Tomorrow we would

320

start up the engines and, after a careful fettle and adjustment we would take her out to sea for the final preparations of Red Shirt.

I remembered leaving the creek but with so many things for my mind to dwell over, the return journey had somehow eluded me. Suddenly we were on the edge of town, awaiting a green light. I knew the sun had only just disappeared as the wailing calls to prayer floated into the early evening sky. The green light appeared, bringing with it the usual blast of car horns from the impatient drivers behind us. Accustomed, Pete ignored their impatience, some drivers would wait for no one, some Saudis, would line up six abreast at a left turn and hope that four of the cars in line would drop out to allow two cars to continue into the opposite junction. They would bring a major highway to a tyre screeching halt, just to be at the front of a traffic queue. I could barely remember overtaking a Saudi and not see him a moment later flashing by on the outside lane, risking his car, his life and his family, just to retrieve his over-valued face. The risks they took were unbelievable but this life meant nothing, it was the next life they craved. Pete crossed the intersection as the light turned to red but he watched in his mirror, as we always did, just to see how many cars would still ignore the red light. We counted six before a screech of tires, signalled the end of the red runners" charge, their stampede, fortunately, cut off without accident. Little respect was given to traffic lights in Saudi, not by the Saudis anyway, traffic lights were for foreigners and quite a few Saudis paid the price.

The compounds built by Arabian homes were one of the few, well prepared housing projects in Jeddah. They had been constructed long after the first oil had been pumped. This assured the tenants of superior quality. The first compounds consisted of Porta-cabin style buildings surrounding the oil rigs. Times had since changed. Arabian homes were built from concrete and breeze blocks, modelled on the same lines as Spanish villas, although the Arabs probably exported that fashion to Spain during their days of conquest. The Arabs had influenced the Spaniards anyway, so they were merely recovering a design that was rightfully theirs. Wooden pergolas abounded, covered by climbing plants and lush green vegetation, technologically watered daily by auto sprinklers. Tennis courts, swimming pools, squash courts and well-manicured lawns were all included in this expat paradise.

The original camps were designed for single men and little or no emphasis was paid to their creature comforts. Now whole families were catered for and the higher management demanded the best. The bigger companies had sited the bulk of their top personnel in the luxury and style that these compounds had to offer. The tenants often organised their own entertainment. Their lives revolved around late-night barbecues, elegant dancing and social evenings, which was the term used in such circles for a good old-fashioned piss-up. I remembered my first living quarters; I had discussed the same subject with Pete. It appeared we had endured the same initiation, steel army cot, no mattress Spartan furnishing and the only electronic device that worked regularly was the battery-operated alarm clock that snapped you from the sweetest of bachelor dreams. Now, when the new foreigners came to Saudi, they were housed in elegant, computer-designed compounds, with every modern amenity known to man. These were the very same people that were often heard to moan, in complete sincerity,

"Jesus! life is so tough in Saudi!"

Pete parked his car outside the compound wall. We checked in through the guardhouse and swapped pleasantries with the Indian gatekeeper. The freshly hosed gravel crunched underfoot as we headed along the pathway to Pete's friend's home, his friend had gone on leave and was not coming back because of a rift with his Saudi Sponsor and so Pete now had the run of the place.

There would be a barbecue tonight; I could smell the paraffin-based oil that had been spread onto the coals in preparation. The coals were not yet lit, they did not have to be, I knew that smell so well, my mouth began to water. Now my thoughts switched to succulent, American rib-eye steaks, with crispy edges, fresh gulf shrimps as big as bananas, baked to a deep pink mouthful of tender juicy flesh. Well-cooked sausages, jacket potatoes and of course chicken, the Saudi staple.

"Jesus', I thought, "life is so tough in Saudi".

My stomach ached; it seemed like I had not eaten for years. I hoped we would be noticed; surely someone would see us and invite my cavernous, empty stomach to the evening festivities. I hoped it was someone we knew. I hoped they would see us before it was too late,

"Why doesn't someone see us?" I thought, as we rounded the swimming pool and crunched up the gravel path in the yard. Pete inserted some keys into the door, disappointment vividly painted on the canvas of his features.

"Hey, Pete!" the voice called out and Pete winked at me.

"OK thanks for the invite, Jim, yeah eight o-clock will be fine; OK we'll get showered and changed, Jim. Thanks a lot, that's great I just fancied a barbecue tonight, you saved my life".

I grinned at our luck, tonight we would not have to cook a meal, no snails and best of all, we would not have to wash the dirty dishes. We had enough time for a hot shower, a quick drink, non-alcoholic of course and a close shave, probably in that order. Jim had informed us that there would be a bus full of Stewies from Saudia City joining the party later. This usually signalled unaccompanied females on a one-night layover in Jeddah, the bachelor foreigners readily accepted anything that had the merest hint of singular female species. Females were as rare as elephant shit on the polar ice caps and a true Khowaja would plan to any lengths to fulfil his earthly desires. It was widely known that imprisonment was the penalty for carrying unrelated females in a vehicle. Those men found guilty could be separated into two groups - Group one was the men who accepted being caught and were resigned to their fate. Group two was the miserable bastards. The difference between the two was simple, group one was caught taking the girl home after a night between the sheets and group two were caught taking the girl home for a night between the sheets. The moral of this story is, if you must get caught by the police, make sure you're not a miserable bastard. Pete would suffer no such dilemma, Jim had already explained, the girls were being delivered by minibus tonight and would be picked up tomorrow morning after staying the night with a married friend.

A true Khowaja spent most of his allotted time in Saudi with two major questions rolling around his head, where are all the girls and who's got the booze. I remembered the infamous "Prince" a true Khowaja of immense notoriety. Other members of his ilk bestowed his title. Prince was of Irish decent and held more than a faint brogue in his accent. His incredible good looks were well matched by an impeccable education that went a long way to earning him his title. Everybody knew him by the name Prince; an artist formerly known as Khowaja and his love of the drink was matched only by his passion for the ladies.

Prince became emotionally, followed by physically entangled with a young maid from the Orient. She happened to be staying at the Thai embassy. Apparently, she had come to Saudi to work as a housemaid but her employer had expected other performances unrelated to housework. She refused his advances and he tried to take her by force. Fortunately, she managed to escape his clutches and bolted in tears to the Thai Embassy. She was not alone; the Consular grounds were full of beautiful young women who had suffered the same fate at the hands of their employers. Not all of them had escaped the physical advances and were reduced to a miserable departure home, followed by an even more painful reunion with their husbands. Ruined marriages, if not ruined lives followed and all for the sake of a verbal promise of prosperity from some Arabian overlord. In their home countries, they would have been offered fabulous salaries and marvellous conditions. When they were collected at the Saudi Airports, their contracts had been reworded accordingly and the maids slept on the balcony of the Saudi family home innocently wondering, what other disappointments lay in store. Such an unfortunate caught Prince's eye, he was literally swept off his feet. She was not married, had not been raped and was the apple of his doting eye. His love or his lust, finally overpowered him and one night after a few uncle Sids he decided to visit his love at any price. He was chauffeured to the Embassy compound that was protected by the usual machine gun carrying police and soldiers. Prince scaled the three-meter wall under the noses of the guards, slid across the lawns on his belly and was soaked - they were being sprinkled at the time, scaled the ramparts to the fourth floor and entered through an open window. His love's specific instructions led him to her bed and they spent the whole night muffling the cries of their rampant passion. Before the light of day, Prince left the building the way he had entered. I had seen the whole episode, once more; I had been promoted to chauffeur. Prince's neck was blue with bites, his clothes were soaked and grass stains covered his knees and elbows. Prince revelled in the formidable respect his foolhardy escapade had generated. A respect which lasted for a whole month before Prince was deported after being caught perpetrating a ghastly if not heinous crime - smoking in a toilet during Ramadan, the holy month of fasting. Prince was deported but stays a Khowaja legend in the hearts of those who knew him. (RIP Prince)

We stepped out into the heavy night air, eight fifteen precisely. Pete's attire consisted of loose canvas pants, a light cotton shirt and docksiders with no socks. I still had on my original clothes; after all, I'd hardly worn them. Tonight, I would try to relax and forget my present troubles. I glanced upward to the heavens beyond the glare of the compound lighting. I assumed it would have been an open sky had it not been for the misty, fog-like ribbons a hundred yards above. This was not the misty shroud of Mother Nature; this was the smoke from the burn-offs around Saudi. It wasn't unattractive to look at as it reflected the city lights and the aroma produced was not unpleasant to the senses. The mist carried a warm oily smell and on balmy nights, it added a touch of comfort to know that the wells were still pumping oil into the refineries despite the rumours and undercurrents.

The pool shimmered turquoise in the underwater spotlight glow. The barbecue bathed the immediate surrounding area with a pinky-red hue. Already I could smell the steaks as they sizzled alongside the shrimps on the blackened grill. The smoke curled upwards into the night and over the tops of the breeze rustled palms. My stomach groaned in anticipation of the feast to come. Jim had built a small drinks bar between the palms and being a regular at such gatherings, Pete and then I was welcomed amongst the elbows with a quickly mixed Sid and Pepsi with ice. At least Khowajas had some style, I thought. At one point I wondered if the Sharief had planned all this but it wasn't his compound, we had not been followed and he probably had no idea yet that I was out of prison. Despite my nervous reservations "Fuck him!" I thought and got on with my life.

Usually, the main parties were held on Thursday night but as Jim had explained earlier, tonight was the only night the girls could make it. Strangely enough, not one man present disapproved of that beautiful little explanation, not in the least.

I unconsciously tapped my foot to the beat of the music by Kool and the Gang,

"She's fresh! Exciting; She's so exciting to me'. A slow slackness warmed over me, and I recognised the symptoms at once, they were usually caused by Sid on an empty stomach and boy was my stomach empty. I watched Pete as he mellowed into the party atmosphere and then it came to me - that wonderful, never to be equalled sound, of high-heeled elegance on warm terrazzo. I turned, just in time to see a bevy of beautiful girls clatter confidently between the palms. They all presented fresh lipstick smiles and once the Hijabs were removed, silky sensual clothing.

326

"Thank goodness for the airlines, and may they always hire the pretty ones," I thought, enraptured by the incoming, fragrant femininity. The girls settled into the wicker chairs positioned around the tables by the side of the swimming pool. Some foreigners jumped in with old, well-worn lines and offers to dance.

"New guys" I whispered to Pete and we nodded in unison, "Silly bastards haven't got a bloody clue".

Pete would wait, as with business etiquette, certain ladies demanded a certain courtesy. Stewies were no exception, they at least deserved time to sit down, collect a drink and relax, not dragged up by some guy two weeks away from his wife and desperate to assert his manhood.

"Foreigners!" "Whatever happened to the days when men were Khowajas and the women were glad of it? I grinned to myself. I noticed too that Pete had not gone unnoticed. Saudi was an alien territory for women too and they would need a darn sight more respect and understanding than they would back home. Pete gave them time. The food was ready and people were bunching around the tables; some were picking at the salad bar, some eagerly forking huge rib-eye steaks onto slightly inadequate paper plates.

"Hoy! you eat now".

A small voice sang by Pete's side. He turned to discover it belonged to a willowy Malaysian beauty. I had learned how to differentiate between the beautiful girls of the world with whom I had so far, fortunately for myself, come into contact. She pushed a paper plate into his hand and motioned him to the tables. In the seconds when his eyes caught and locked with hers, I remembered what I had told him,

"You were on the tracks and you knew the train was approaching but you couldn't get out of its way. When the train hit you, it knocked your life inside out and there she was, I could sense it, trouble with a capital "T"

My words had not meant much to Pete until now, but I knew he was now on the tracks and he struggled to be free.

327

CHAPTER 13   SAUDI STYLE   PLANS

"You live here?" she quizzed him with her breathy voice as it left those pert lips. Her hair was black as the night sky and was complemented by a skin tone I could only describe as perfection.

"Yes, I live over there, the house with the bikes on the yard".

"My brother have same type bike, he a little crazy but I bet you crazy too, I can tell, I been here a while and I know the difference". She smiled revealing near-perfect teeth. Pete was being tied to the track he knew the train was coming but he could not escape that face. Her classic Malaysian features, swept-back, jet black almost flowing liquid hair cascading around her shoulders, attractive smiling eyelids with a hint of coloured make-up surrounding those deep fathomless pools of her eyes. Her small hands were well-manicured works of art. She was as delicate as a flower, as tall as Pete in her heels and had managed to develop a figure that could be complimented from her head to her toes, full breasts, trim waist and a sculpted bottom perched above long strong but slinky legs.

"I like bikes, I ride my brother's when he not around, drive him crazy if he finds out".

Pete's body just would not behave itself. She was driving "him" crazy let alone her brother. Didn't she realise this was Saudi? didn't she realise he had not been out with a girl in months? Didn't she realise he couldn't breathe? As we collected plates, he told me he was in love and he had become worried she would disappear in a puff of smoke. Pete carried the two plates whilst his nimble companion piled the food on one plate and added sparingly to the other. She finally topped off the huge serving with a chunk of steak that rode above salad, shrimps, sausages and a huge jacket potato. Her eyes twinkled as she took the larger helping and left him holding the weight watcher's minuscule portion. The mischief in her expression was prominent as she left him and sat down, where they had met earlier, with her back to the palms overlooking the pool. I watched as Pete hurriedly, if not embarrassingly topped up his portion of food before sheepishly walking across the terrazzo to join her. I sat a few meters away, not wanting to spoil their fun

328

but I had a good rendition of the full conversation and the feelings now being swapped

"Everything is not as it seems?" she grinned.

"I thought that was for me". Pete smiled.

"You should not assume anything in Saudi, are you knew kid? just arrive in this country?" now she was laughing at him.

For a while they ate in silence though I watched Pete, as between his mouthfuls, he studied this vision of beauty that had entered his life without warning and would ruin it forever if she ever left. She complemented our hosts and finally revealed her name, Katherine, her friends called her Katy or Kate.

"I'm not your friend!" Pete announced but when her happy expression melted to what could only be described as the beginnings of embarrassed hurt, he stopped it,

"I want to be different, Katherine. I'll call you Kit if I may?"

Kit it was. Kit explained how she had become a Stewie with Saudia airlines. Her home was in Pahang in Western Malaysia. This was her second year with the airline and her first attempt at liberation. She had become sick of being a choice of others and decided this time she would be the chooser and when the right kind of man appeared, she would do the choosing. She had attended many functions of this nature and had been danced till her feet ached by would be suitors with gropy hands. She had become aware of the Khowajas through a friend's teachings. They had told her to look out for the Khowajas who were exceedingly rare, but you could still find them occasionally. Khowajas were bronzed but did not go overboard with the suntan routine. They wore little jewellery; unlike the nugget carrying flash Harry's who spent so much money on trinkets they had little left for living life to the full. Pete laughed at her description of himself more so when she explained her first perusal,

"I see you over here, you in no hurry to jump on girl, you relaxed, dressed like you going to fall asleep. Not much jewellery especially on the wedding finger, though some foreigners hide wedding ring as soon as they leave airspace of wife back home, you do this thing, Pete?" she enquired with a troubled tone.

"No, I no married," announced Pete, forgetting the T and imitating her broken English before she continued with her appraisal.

Strong body, healthy looks but a bit short, but not bad for Miss Wong".

Pete remembered me, he had introduced me to Kit and now he looked in my direction as Kit related her tale, I guess he wanted to get his own back, for the occasion when Ginny had been giving him the full SP on me.

"Now I can sit here with you, Pete, and eat in peace, the other guys will leave me alone, you look like you give them trouble if they disturb us".

I could see Pete was stunned, she was beautiful, endowed with a fabulous figure, sparkling personality and extremely intelligent to boot what had he done to deserve such a prize?"

"Please don't get wrong idea, Pete. This does not mean I want to sleep with you," Kit paused before continuing, glancing in my direction to see if I had heard, I pretended not to have and she continued

"This simply means I rather sit here with you, who I quite like, than be danced all over the floor with every male at the party because it impolite to refuse, hope you understand?"

Pete nodded, his mouth too full to speak, his brain still enraptured, his heart pounding in his chest.

"If you not want to talk to Kit, no problem, you just walk away, I understand, this is the first time I done this sort of thing and I hope you not offended by my approach to you?"

Pete watched discreetly, as she devoured the steaks followed by everything else on her plate. They small talked under the palms for a while before Kit stood and headed to the tables to collect dessert, refusing to allow him to stand and go with her. This time she prepared three portions of equal size, and as the desserts disappeared, we were well into our past, present and futures, though mostly not mine. The party continued around us

330

completely unnoticed. Kit ceased drinking the Sid when she had achieved "The happiness" as she called it, merry but in complete control would be the European equivalent. We discovered Kit held a business degree, but she could earn four times the salary back home by working for Saudia Airlines and so here she was. The music slowed and the chatter lulled as the evening passed them by. Kit stretched to her feet and pulled Pete upward onto his cramped legs, they held each other close and swayed in time to the music. Pete pushed her away at arm's length, staring deep into her eyes, his reaction stunned her,

"Hoy! what's wrong, Pete?"

Pete reeled his arms around her and eased her in close, bent his head slightly and whispered in her ear, I don't know what he said but it worked.,

I knew what was happening from my own experiences. When it hit you, you felt bad, you did not want to lose sight of them, you were ready to throw away everything just to keep them by your side. Pete must have felt the sickness and he knew I had been right, now he knew for sure that my accident had been self-inflicted, shit! I could see Pete would have thrown himself under a bus just to keep this lovely creature in his life. Now he dreaded the hour when she would have to leave him. The revellers began to drift away, a few couples lingered on the dance floor and the hardened drinkers propped up the bar. Most of the girls were staying in one house, the married friend who had promised Saudia she would take care of "their" girls.

Pete savoured her every word as if each one might be the last, finally he found the courage, somewhere in that trembling shell of a frame, to ask if she would like some coffee? Kit lowered her head almost ashamed, raised it slightly to glance over to where the girls were staying the night and, in that moment, when he thought he had lost her, she retrieved her bag from her friends and click-clacked up his yard. Pete fumbled his key into the lock, at that moment it was the most erotic action he had ever performed and I tried not to think of what the night held in store for him, I waved him away and told him straight, "get on with it! After what I've been through, I can sleep anywhere tonight, even out here in the open gazing at the stars, you get on with it Pete I'll be fine".

Kit had insisted on preparing coffee for the three of us. As they huddled close on the sofa and the conversation mellowed to intimates, I knew I had to be going. Pete offered his room if she would like to stay, he was a gentleman and would sleep on the sofa, she refused.

"I unexpected visitor, I do not take your bed, your home your bed, always so in Malaysia".

Kit collected the coffee cups and padded barefoot into the kitchen, her tanned athletic legs, swelling a long-forgotten fire in my veins, I was still human after all. Pete followed her into the kitchen, he could not bear to lose sight of her loveliness and when he tried to help with the washing-up, their bodies rubbed together in friendly combat over sink space. The static exploded between them, then their eyes locked, followed by their arms and then their lips. Pete felt the train as it thundered through his heart and disappeared down the tracks forever, taking with it the last remnants of his self-confirmed bachelor hood. Kit extracted herself from the overheating clinch, requesting some sheets and a pillow for the sofa. Pete obliged, unwillingly, though he would never deny such a fragile delicate face. At this point I left, I was no gooseberry and besides, Pete would give me the low-down tomorrow, we usually swapped outline notes, which is why I can continue.

Pete moved to his room, it was the correct thing to do; he had no desire to spoil something he wanted to last forever. Pete showered in the en-suite before falling longing into his pillow. Every move Kit made seemed to be amplified in the darkness. The other bathroom door opened like a castle gate, her clothes fell to the floor with a crash, the shower sprinkled over her nakedness like hail on a tin roof, the burning fire tore into his heart; there would be no sleep tonight.

CHAPTER 13   SAUDI STYLE   PLANS

The silence boomed in his ears, at least a year had passed since he had climbed into bed, or so it seemed. He wondered if he could just sneak in and see her face once more, just to make sure she was real and that he had not dreamed up this vision of loveliness whilst in a drunken, Sidney stupor. He did not want to wake up and have to go to the store for a packet of dog biscuits for her breakfast. A noise alerted him, movement outside his door. Slowly the door creaked open and shyly he feigned sleep; the lower bed sunk under the prowler's weight, was it her? was it Bob having a laugh, with a bucket of ice-cold water, again? or was it some burglar about to murder him? He prayed for the obvious and, he told me, he also prayed that it wasn't me doing the dirty on him with the bucket of ice. The new warmth entered by his feet, a heavenly, silken chin pressed tight against his leg, riding along the contours of the million-mile limb. The chin delicately crossed his loins, closer and closer, riding up his belly, rubbing onto his chest. Their bodies drew level and she entwined her arm and leg around him, squeezing an embrace of hot, tight, naked flesh and in the merest of moments when their lips were not welded tight, her hot breath tingled in his ear,

"You nice man, Pete. I changed my mind".

That was all Pete would tell me, for which I had only one response,

"You lucky bastard Pete - you lucky, lucky, lucky bastard!"

Chapter 14
LIMBO

Throughout the torrid passions of the night, Pete and Kit continued their embrace. Neither must have slept; Pete was extremely fit and Kit's physique gave the impression she could have worked him to a frazzle. The early morning prayer call wafted across Arabia, barely audible above the incessant hum of air conditioners. A warm contentment must have mellowed my expression as the prayer call lulled me into a comfortable but light doze. I had spent the night on a massive air mattress in the pool; it was probably the best snooze I can ever remember. Pete gave a brief review of what happened when he awoke that morning, he told me he had reached out to caress her form but she was gone. Jolted from his easy pose, he was about to leap from the bed and call out. There was no need, the smell of fresh coffee floated into the room. Chinking cups signalled her return to the love nest and she floated through the doorway clad in nothing but a pair of skimpy, deep-blue, silky briefs. Pete watched closely as she brought the tray to the bedside. Kit's hair was so black; it shone blue where the early morning light pierced the window shades before caressing her head. Her breasts were full and rosebud nipples protruded from a light amber skin, like small, dark cherries on a large scoop of vanilla ice cream. Her hair bobbed forward in unison with her breasts, as she bent to place the tray on the bedside table. She caught Pete's approving glances and in a gesture of sudden embarrassment, skipped quickly under the strewn sheet. They cuddled for a moment before squeezing their bodies into a tight, well-sculptured bond. Then their lips met followed by the other more intimate parts of their bodies and the coffee, never poured, turned cold. I asked him why he hadn't brought the coffee out for me but he asked me if I would have done the same for him? I shut my mouth.

They showered together in the en-suite. Kit was ready when the doorbell chirruped. Her companion, Marriane, had noticed

Kit's departure and inserted a mental location of her partner's whereabouts, just in case, the Stewies always looked after their own. A final hug in the kitchen broke the spell and Pete opened the door to Marriane and me as I followed her up the driveway. I entered the room with a sly grin. I couldn't help it; he looked washed out and knackered. Pete could not help wincing under Marriane's scrutiny as she eyed him head to toe. Kit collected her belongings, dropped them into the small flight bag and with a gentle brush of her lips against his cheek they headed outside. Marriane smiled,

"Do you have any friends?"

Pete nervously glanced at me before answering,

"Yes, I have, of course, I have, why?"

'Good, you should invite them over next time we're here, single friends though, no drunks or marrieds". Marriane acknowledged my wedding ring with a gentle nod,

"If they look as good as this guy, no problem" I felt myself blush as she continued, "Kate was right, my feet are killing me. I must have danced with every fellow in the place last night and none were really my type. It would have been nice to eat, chat and," Marriane paused for effect whilst looking Kit up and down,

"Fall in love?" a wicked grin split her sly expression.

Kit swung her bag playfully and bumped Marriane's backside,

"Hoy! don't embarrass me".

The two girls crunched across the gravel, which was no longer white. It had been dampened by the early morning sprinklers and now looked a little grey but the sun had begun its work and already, away from the shaded areas, patches of brilliant white were drying through. Kit glanced over her shoulder many times before she finally boarding the Saudia bus. She waved from the bus as it left the compound. Pete returned her gesture with a smile; he knew in his heart he would see her again.

Shark's engines finally coughed to life. The fuel had taken a while to force its way through the lines but they had been

335

completely drained and so we expected the delay. The Merlin's had previously been run for a few hours at the workshop to ensure smooth operation and balance of new parts. Now she was back in the water, free of the dry, dusty dock and the unwelcome drying and cracking effect of the constant heat. The fuel lines were completely bled free of air and Shark once more breathed the raw power of life. The yard hands cast off the lines that automatically recoiled into their stainless-steel sleeves. Shark nosed cautiously from the pier, we did not want to damage her now, the repercussions could be really frustrating. I cruised Shark down the creek toward the open sea and allowed the engines plenty of time to warm to running temperature. Fuel gauges registered both tanks full, oil pressure signalled a well lubed high, and so it should, that new-fangled oil pump had cost an arm and a leg. The Merlin's turned sweetly with a smooth heavy throb, almost as if begging to be released. It felt good to be on the open water again, away from the dust and smells of the humid desert township.

Shark was eased into the creek side and nudged against the coast guard station. I steered her alongside the concrete pier and gently squashed the rubber tyre bumpers. The coast guard recognised Shark and her crew from earlier days and we exchanged good morning courtesies in Arabic. Pete explained we would be trying her engines after their recent overhaul. The coast guard logged her registration, he had seen her in dry dock, and he had never known the black Khowaja boat spend so much time, tied up on dry land. He knew the Khowajas well, and he also knew, it wouldn't be long before they were back to their regular if not routine sea trips. Pete waved his thanks as we pulled away from the pier, fortunately the guard had not requested my Iquama, work permit, hr knew me but I no longer had one and what I was doing now was illegal. The temperature gauges still registered normal, oil and fuel were OK. I gave Shark a quarter throttle. Her engine note changed to a powerful thrumming and Shark's bow rose into the air. The water surged at her stern and she skipped across the creek like a flat tossed

336

rock, with her engines barely labouring. Pete listened and scrutinised carefully but there were no abnormalities in her powerful tones. What a great day to be alive, I thought, standing behind the wheel of such a craft. I marvelled at the new strength that her engines possessed and hoped the mechanics hadn't botched the intricacies of a complete overhaul.

Shark approached the mouth of the creek, buffeting slightly over the swell of water, where the waves broke over the outer reef. Once clear of the creek, huge chrome throttles were palmed forward. The effect was stunning and immediate. The engines growled to a new unrestricted tone. The overhauled supercharger whistled as it kicked into the mid-range rev band. Shark rose upward from the water, higher and faster than she had ever done before. Pete was forced back into the passenger seat as Shark accelerated from the confines of the estuary and thundered out to sea, smashing down the waves that had dared to cross her bow. I eased her upward to seventy percent of maximum power with tender care and the effect was almost ecstasy. The awesome power, vibrating from the deck reverberated up my legs and through my bones. The sheer force of acceleration, lifted her from the vacuum of the sea, skidding her across the top of the swells, bouncing her from crest to crest as the jet wash spumed free at her rear.

Pete popped a cassette into the cockpit tape deck. "Everybody wants to rule the world" blared out suddenly from the inboard speakers. A more fitting song could never have been written for my present emotions, as we raced out to sea, heading due west. Our legs flexed and bent beneath us to absorb each rolling wave and our shirtless bodies, bathed luxuriously in the fine, salty spray, pulsing over the prow. Arabia fell away behind us and finally disappeared. Soon we were alone but for the occasional gull as it tried to match the speed of the slingshot Shark. The spray caught the sun and rainbows arced over the bow; the engines growled smoothly creating their own throaty symphony.

CHAPTER 15   SAUDI STYLE   EXIT ONLY

Five miles out, well inside the twenty-mile limit, we slowed, allowing the engines to climb down evenly from their powerful driving revolutions. When satisfied with her condition I swung her around and cut the allegro whine. The tape deck cut with the ignition and the silence was immediate and complete, but for the tiny wave crests that slapped against the bow. Shark lay becalmed, shrouded by a hot, shameless silence. We were suddenly alone. Immediately the heat began to build. The sun danced against Shark's chrome work and flashed distorted sparking reflections in the rippling sea. Pete took out the binoculars and scanned the horizon. He saw nothing, nothing but the heat waves, a slight swell and the silence. Confident in our solitude, he disappeared into the hold and dragged out the sack of salt. Then he brought out a small length of nylon line and a plastic float. He weighed out five kilos of salt, placed it in a small hessian sack and sealed in the salt securely. The float was attached to the sack along with a non-return depth gauge, Pete checked over the connections and when satisfied, he dumped the whole bundle over the side of Shark. The package sank without trace. The result seemed to please him and, as the last surface ripple disappeared, we turned and went below deck into the hold.

The twin outboard motors weighed in at fifty kilos. The rubber inflatable weighed twenty-five kilos. Pete had squeezed every air pocket from the inflatable, to ensure it would pack as small and tight as possible.

"How the fuck did you do that?" I asked him.

"I put it under a board on the sand and ran over it a few times with the car!"

"Say no more sport!" I congratulated his efforts I had never seen the dinghy folded so small. Ten freshly charged air tanks lined the walls of the hold, five per side to effect balance. Diving regulators, although unattached, hung over two of the tanks. A recent service had left them in a shiny condition, the silicone spray still undisturbed by a voyage into the depths. I sucked on mine, the air flowed smoothly and the regulator's mechanical

338

actions were barely noticeable. The temperature rose rapidly in the small confines of the hold and the heat began to smother everything. We passed a final glance over the equipment before climbing into the merciless sun once more. Up on deck, despite our acculture, the sun prickled naked shoulders. Pete leaped exuberantly from the deck, over the small chrome handrail and into the sea, instantly refreshing his clammy body. My body hit the water before Pete's spray had crashed onto the surface. Swimming here was in total contrast to the hot, humid gloom of the hold. Cautiously I followed Pete, he swam to the jet outlets where the new rubber seals were compressed behind the stainless-steel backing plates. The old steel backing plates had been replaced and the housings were now free of the rusty red stains, caused by the oxidisation of unprotected metal.

Pete swam around the craft at least twice and I followed in his wake, checking and double checking and, when he was sure there was nothing extraordinary to be found, he hoisted himself to the deck once more. He probed around in the cooler and extracted a non-alcoholic beer, He threw a can to me, and it hit the water and disappeared. I dove and followed the can down, remembering to surface as quietly as possible where Pete could not see. Ten minutes must have passed and I knew he wasn't looking for me. I hauled myself aboard and went around the deck and stared at him, he was lying across the deck, soaking in the sun.

"I could have been drowning man, why didn't you look for me?"

"I've been in the sea with you before Khowaja, I was more worried about the fucking marine life from your pollution than I was about you!" he grinned and I accepted the compliment in silence, after I'd emptied the contents of the ice cooler all over him that is. I snapped back the ring pull and threw the contents of the small aluminium cylinder to the back of my throat. Twice, I tried to lean back, with my shoulders pressed against the fibreglass top deck, and twice the broiling heat had sizzled the sweat from my skin. I eventually got comfortable by sitting up upright, with my backside protected by a beach towel and sunglasses shading my eyes, reflecting the brilliant glare of sun on crystal sea. Pete dozed to contemplation. Time to dwell - what were we doing here? were we crazy? did we not know the penalty? were we really going to go through with this? Questions I could not answer, eventually time would supply the solutions but by then I knew in my heart, it would be too late. While we were soaking up the sun, another Khowaja was doing his bit. I received full details from the horse's mouth and this is what Hawkeye disclosed.

Hawkeye scanned around from his lofty perch; it was a sad day for Sharief. He could remember the days when the yard had been empty and the customers were constantly screaming for the tankers to deliver. Today things were different, hundreds of grey-bellied road tankers simmered in the heat around him. A herd of mechanical hippos, no water or shade, to cool their paint-blistered backs. SHARIEF painted in large blue letters, was once emblazoned on their sides. Now they sat, huddled together in a desperate search for impossible shade. The dust had settled over their scorched backs, disguising the lettering completely, leaving only the bottom half of the letters to read like some stone-age tombstone. The commercial parade was over and the projects created by the oil boom lay like the tankers - massive mouldering carcasses, redundant in the dust. A sorry sight to behold. Even sorrier was the view to his rear, the refinery in all its glory, billions of dollars" worth in mint condition, now barely holding her own. Her suckling children had deserted her and now she sat alone, swollen breasts, with unlimited milk but her children had grown up and having found their own food supplies, had left the uncomfortable squabbling of the parent's" unhappy home. The squeeze was on and the West's, newfound oilfields were returning the commercial favours of OPEC hard-liners with gusto.

340

CHAPTER 15   SAUDI STYLE   EXIT ONLY

Rivers of perspiration ran down Hawkeye's body. The heat did not concern him despite the fact, that to climb up onto the tankers, he needed leather welding gloves. The ladders and crawl-way steelwork were frying pan hot. No - the heat did not bother Hawkeye; he had something else to think about. He was wondering how much of his carcass would remain to be posted home if Pete had been wrong about the chemistry with which he now dabbled. Hawkeye trusted Pete: they had known each other for a long time. I had once prevented Hawkeye from almost ruining his future. That was one of the reasons Hawkeye was here now, sitting atop forty thousand gallons of high-octane petro-sludge. The average temperature around him he guessed would be more than fifty degrees. He carried no metal about his person or on his clothing, no zips or metal buttons. A spark now would reduce the requirement of an air ticket home, for he was certain, if he made a mistake now, some parts of his body would probably fall on England anyway. Some may even break gravity's hold and float off into space. Hawkeye moved carefully, opening the package he had removed from his pocket and lowering the small plastic cube into the belly of the tanker and leaving the receiver visible from space. When the lines were secured, he closed the vent lid onto its rubber seals. Hawkeye stood atop the tanker and removed his face mask and ventilator, his eyes streamed with tears,

"Jesus! Pete," he thought aloud, "That's some stink of a mixture".

Hawkeye turned, unaware he caught the vent flange with his foot. The errant foot wedged tight and Hawkeye was flung forward and down. His body slammed into the crawlway and he opened his eyes in time to watch the sand shovel, break loose from the top of the emergency tool rack. The sand shovel cascaded down the side of the tanker in a shower of chipped metal sparks, before finally slapping into the compacted, oil-blackened sand below. The tanker echoed like some ancient, Chinese funeral gong. Hawkeye lay rigamorticed with fear; the sweat pearled across his forehead as his bowels prepared for release. Only when the monotone echo dissolved, did Hawkeye's heart start to beat and a small, breathy exclamation of courtesy escape his lips,

"Alhamdullilah, thanks to God!"
He retrieved what was left of his composure and slowly clambered down the rear ladder of the tanker; he had four remaining rides with fear before he could leave this graveyard to the fortunes of oil. He moved to the next tanker in line and checked which pocket held the small packet.

Hawkeye patted the huge, hollow metal cylinder on the rear end,

"Khowaja!" Hawkeye announced loudly, "This bastards for you!"

Hawkeye clambered aboard the tanker, replaced his facemask and ventilator, opened the breather vent, and continued with his perilous work.

The seascape lay becalmed, caught between transition from offshore to onshore breeze almost as if it were unable to decide. The breeze had stayed away; Mother Nature was having sport with the yachtsmen of Jeddah. Pete swilled another non-alcoholic into the back of his throat, in a useless attempt to quench his thirst. His thoughts had obviously returned to Kit, and I wondered if anything would develop. My senses were suddenly disturbed and I turned my face to the tiny disturbance of sound.

"Shit!" I thought, "We didn't need them now, not now, not here!" my thoughts were anything but complimentary. The slight buzz grew to an incessant droning. Propeller driven planes produced the same monotonous whine. I knew who they were and what they were looking for. They were looking for the whisky smugglers who plied this area, unloading their cargoes to the depths of the sea to be picked up by divers later, though usually during darkness but in fast boats, not unsimilar to Shark. Her black paintwork ideally suited to night-time rendezvous with fear. Operations of such nature were extremely profitable for small time smugglers who had no desire for apprehension whilst

342

smuggling drugs. Whisky held you in purgatory for months but in Saudi, drugs could hold you in a near death grip for an exceptionally long time. They aimed straight at Shark, the Saudi Coast guard, blades howling, and spray flying. The hovercraft could be heard approaching miles away, when would they learn? We could have disappeared at once on catching the noisy, airborne beast of the sea. But we dare not take the risk; someone may have caught sight of us through binoculars. Today we had little to fear we would take a good percentage chance and stay put.

The massive propellers slowed as the ungainly, seemingly uncontrollable, coast guard hovercraft circled around Shark. The ballooning skirt drafted and sea spray filled our immediate airspace. They were breezing us purposely. Finally, the beast's engines ceased and she settled on her skirt, which slowly sank and reduced her size by almost fifty percent. The craft nosed forward to nudge against the Shark, the front gull wing door slued open. John Wayne himself could not have matched the poseur now standing on her prow. A small well ribboned man in uniform, hand on hip; beret tilted to one side of his slicked back, greasy hair. Mirror spectacles obscured undoubtedly inquisitive eyes and a large root, used for dental hygiene in these parts, protruded between nicotine-stained teeth. The poseur's hand rose to his glasses and slid them above his hairline. He turned to his men, flicked his head to one side in a smug gesture and turned back to confront us. We were surprised to hear the English language. The coast guards dealt mainly with the locals and it was rare, unless smugglers were apprehended that English was a requirement. I bid him good afternoon and the captain of the vessel responded, striding to the bow of his vessel and speaking to his men in Arabic,

"Foreigner!" he called back to his crew, "Watch carefully, men. I'll show you how to put the fear of Allah into these people, and then we will find out what they are up to".

Pete decided to play along and clamped his mouth shut. The captain stepped aboard Shark and passed a cursory glance around the top decks of Shark,

"See how innocent it looks, men?" he announced.

His men nodded in agreement, mumbling and insulting the foreigners. "Always go below decks, men. That's where they usually hide the girls and you never know what else you might find down there eh?"

"May I look below?" he questioned me in English.

"Yes sir! Of course, sir". I replied in the same language.

"See how he calls me sir," switching back to Arabic, "He must have something to hide - whisky, drugs, naked ladies would be a bonus". He grinned to the approval of his beady-eyed, eagerly nodding crew.

I was tiring of the game and the insults to my intelligence, the crew were now watching me with slightly less credibility than a camel with sunstroke. I turned to his crew and announced in Arabic,

"Hey, chaps, while we're below, the cooler chest is full of non-alcoholic beer and soft drinks. Grab yourselves a cold one and have a drink on me".

First, they were stunned, and then they grinned, whoops of laughter exploded as they leapt across the decking where Pete handed out cold drinks and the sergeant, aware of his mistake, shook his head in acknowledgement,

"Khowaja!" he sighed, "I should have known". and was now grinning in unison with his crew. They had been right, learn the language, it made a huge difference and earned lots of friends.

Pete handed the captain a can of Vimto with a relaxed smile, he had to be seen to be obeying the law, non-alcoholic or not. In these climes" drinks were rarely, if ever refused. Especially ice-cold beers on a burning hot deck. Now Pete and the Captain stood chatting in Arabic, as the crew of the hovercraft ogled us with surprise at our command of the language. Pete explained our trip, we had come out of Jeddah creek to check repairs performed in dry dock, we had a minor problem that we were sure we could fix.

"We know all about you," smiled the officer, "We already checked with the creek coast guard by radio, your story checks out, can we offer you a tow back to the creek?"

"No sir, if you can give me one minute of your time, I am sure I can fix the problem".

"What do you want me to do?"

"Well sir, stand in the cockpit and, when I give you, the signal just turn on the ignition".

Pete dropped below as the captain assumed his position, a moment or two passed before they heard his voice again,

"Turn the key, Sir!" yelled Pete.

The engines whined but did not fire,

"Once more sir, please!" yelled Pete from below.

Again, the whining but no sign of ignition. Pete returned above deck, turned over the pre-heat switch and eased the throttles forward a touch. Pete dropped below with new purpose and reconnected the wires he had removed on his first visit below.

"Once more please Sir!" yelled Pete.

For a moment, the whining returned, before the twin Merlin's thundered to life. Pete's grinning features stabbed above the deck and the captain smiled glad to be of help.

"Mind if I look?" I hoped the worry did not show in my expression,

"Of course not!" I announced, "Help yourself".

The captain dropped below the deck he was below for a few minutes, we hoped the heat, would discourage him from a lengthy exploration,

"You keep a well packed boat". it was a question.

"Yes sir! she belongs to this guy and me, we like to dive and fish at the weekends. We keep the dingy, just in case of - well, I'm sure I don't have to explain the reefs out here to a man of your position?"

The captain appreciated the compliment, especially from a Khowaja, especially in front of his men, especially as he had taken a likening to these Khowajas and had decided to let us go. He didn't need the hassle either and he knew it would have been more trouble than it was worth, to put a foreigner in his cells who had such a command of the language.

"If that had been real beer, you would have been in deep trouble, Khowaja. I would have thrown you in jail, despite your efforts to appreciate this fine country of ours".

"I would have expected nothing less from a man as dedicated as yourself, sir". Again, the compliment, I played this fish like a well-practised angler.

We hoped they would piss-off before the floats popped up. How were we going to explain that? Finally, they jumped back aboard the hovercraft. As the aero engines screamed to life the captain pulled the glasses down from his head to shade his eyes. I caught his words just before the engines drowned out all other noise,

"Thanks for the drinks, Khowaja, maybe we'll meet again someday?"

"Yeah maybe, Inshallah!" I answered quietly, "You never know what the future holds, Inshallah"

The gull wing door hissed closed. Already the skirt around the base of the craft was half full size and rising. Then the spray returned, the craft skipped up onto the cushion of air and defied her pilot to whirl around in circles, before heading off towards the creek. Moments after their departure the bright luminous float popped to the surface. Pete felt relieved, grabbed the float aboard and checked the depth gauge. He made notes in his sketch pad as I palmed the gear into drive and accelerated into the wake of the hovercraft. Shark caught up with the coast guard in minutes, reeling her in like some overfed puffer fish. We blasted by them, our own wake causing them to wobble in the troughs, I smiled and waved politely as we roared by, my gesture was pleasantly returned.

346

We reported to the coast guard pier. They had already received word of our self-inflicted misfortune. It had caused them to smile and chastise the Khowajas in a friendly tone, before handing back our documents. I nosed the Shark down the creek toward her moorings and made further notes as the loading ramp at the creek side slid by. It was five hundred meters from Shark's berth, Pete had paced it out on an earlier occasion and now the distance was noted in his book. I reversed Shark into her berth and secured her with two mooring lines. I had to juggle the hot metal fasteners onto the dollies; it had been yet another normal, paint blistering, Saudi day. With all security measures taken, we left. The swell lapped at Shark's belly whilst the afternoon sun still played with the chrome on her deck. She looked almost relaxed, glad to be away from the dust and oily diesel stench, so prominent in the dry dock. The fishermen of Jeddah were heading to sea for the night patrol, their motorised dhows and canoes chugging up the creek. Excited chatter bounced from opposing creek shores as they discussed the night fishing to come. The sun slid towards the West and the first pangs of hunger invaded my stomach.

Now I thought about the barbecue and Pete's thoughts returned to Kit. A Jumbo groaned overhead, almost too slow for flight,

"Where is she now?" I could see Pete looking skyward and wondering. Pete tried to squash the memory of Kit, but her haunting good looks tormented him and as we drove back to the compound, he re-played the joys of yesterday's nocturnal union and spared me the intimacies, which I've already discussed so I won't go over it again. Hawkeye meanwhile was leaving the compound across town.

Hawkeye trundled the bulbous beast of a bowser truck up to the checkout gate, the air brakes hissing and squealing as he stopped and parked. He jumped from the cab and entered the hut,

"You're delivering this one as well, sir?" enquired the gate controller.

"Special delivery, almost next door to my home. I'll take her out tonight and return the tractor in the morning, no point in disturbing a driver, it's hardly worth the effort".

"Jeddah?" enquired the clerk.

"Hey! I ain't going any further," grinned Hawkeye.

"OK, sir. You're booked out, weight has been checked and the release papers are signed. See you in the morning".

"See you in the morning," grinned Hawkeye as he left the gatehouse, hauled himself aboard the tractor-trailer and pulled away from the refinery weigh bridge. The giant diesel truck growled towards the hot asphalt highway. Daylight was fading quickly. Hawkeye lit up the running lights and pumped the accelerator, eight tyres squealed for purchase in the loose sand, before throwing the tractor onto the main highway north. As the diesel rumbling returned to a more sedate cruising tone, the call to prayer penetrated the open windows of the cab,

"Allaaaaaaaah Akbar!" echoed the call,

"God is truly great".

"He truly is," responded Hawkeye with deep sincerity,

"He truly is".

Whenever we arrived in town, the prayer call always sounded. Now all the stores would be closed, denying us the opportunity to buy snacks or drinks. We decided to go straight to Pete's apartment where we would shower, grab a Chinese take-away later, and relax with the in-house cable video. As Pete heaved himself from the car in the parking lot, we discussed the sunburn on our shoulders, it had been a long-exposed day. We strolled through the compound to the sound of splashing water from the pool. A skimpy, blue silk bikini caught my eye and so did the body it enveloped, skin stretched tight like a drum skin, Pete would recognise that voluptuous figure anywhere. Kit hurried towards him droplets spattering in her wake,

"Hoy!" she teased him, "Remember me?"

348

Pete threw his arms around her and pulled her fresh, wet body to his own,

"How could I forget? what are you doing here Kit?" he could not contain his delight to see her again.

"Re-routed to New York," she smiled, "The flight is long haul type, and they give me extra day off and said to get some sleep, maybe I look like I need it, Yah?"

Kit's sultry intonations gripped his loins, he squeezed her tight and grinned.

"Well, you came to the right place, Kit". he squeezed her knowingly, "You certainly came to the right place for sleep".

A strange fullness swelled up inside me. I realised he did not want to let this girl go and was on his way to ditching bachelorhood.

"Just when you least expect it" I had warned him and it looks like I had been right. In the middle of everything that was going on, Pete had fallen in love. It was obvious, Pete's mind was made up and the night was his for the taking. Kit told me sometime later what she had thought during their first encounter.

Kit had waited for the evening prayers. She had slept during the day to recover from her newfound love. Dare she think that? She wasn't quite sure but she had a strange feeling about this man. Insecurity had suddenly crept within her very bones. She wanted to share the rest of her life with this man. She had never had such a feeling dominate her thoughts but something inside gave birth to a great caution. This man was different in more ways than one, of that she had no doubts. Perhaps it was the intoxication of the caution, that an unknown entity was enticing her. She realised it may also lead her to a great sorrow of which she wanted no part, but tonight he would be hers and as they entered the door to his villa, the world had nothing to offer, that would have induced a change of heart and me, I was sleeping in the garden again and had to remember to turn the sprinkler off this time.

The dawn prayer dragged Pete from the depths of a sleep borne of sheer exhaustion and he rolled over to find Kit, lost in a deep blissful slumber by his side.

"Alhamdullilah" he whispered to himself; it had not been a dream after all. The trace of a smile graced Kit's mouth and all at once he was totally captivated by the beauty of her delicate, almost fragile porcelain features. The urge to encircle her with his arms came upon him, he wanted to squeeze her with a force that was sure to cause pain, to weld her to his side, that she would be his forever more. But just as I used to resist the temptation with Lyn, he would have resisted the powerful instinct, settling instead, to drink his fill of the innocent beauty of his absolute infatuation.

Pete told me he wanted to tell Kit everything, there was so much he would have liked to explain to Kit but feared he had already revealed enough. The new thoughts broke the bewitching spell and deciding to prepare breakfast, he eased from the close-up zone, and was about to raise his weight from the bed, when Kit's eyes blinked open and delivered their early morning smiles. Kit politely yawned, stretched her limbs the full length of the bed with elegant, feline poise and smiled,

"Hoy!" she announced, pulling up the single sheet to cover her chest, "What time now?"

"Five thirty," replied Pete; secretly wishing he had been able to get to the bathroom to brush the sleep from his mouth.

"Where you go now?"

"I was going to cook your breakfast, Kit".

"What you cook for miss Wong?"

"Imitation bacon with eggs sound, OK?" he smiled.

Any kind of pig meat was forbidden in Saudi and by the Muslim faith. The pig is considered a lowly animal, dirty and unfit for human consumption. Foreigners substituted bacon with smoked beef. It was labelled breakfast beef in the supermarkets but in no way did it substitute for the real thing. A true Khowaja's first breakfast outside the Kingdom would be hot bacon sarnies, washed down with, and forever destroying their macho man sophistication, Vimto

"I'm not sure I like bacon and eggs this morning" Kit purred, "I prefer early morning roll with coffee".

"Coming right up ma'am". grinned Pete.

"No, I think you not understand clearly," Kit giggled, dragging Pete back into the bed, "I like my roll now, we can get the coffee later".

Their warm bodies collided in the tangle of the straggled single sheet. Pete could not resist her, any part of her. From her fragile womanly grace to her delicately sculpted oriental features.

Later, in the shower, the hot water welded their bodies together under its powerful jet. Kit pulled from the lovelock and began to wash him down. She washed his face neck and ears and rubbed his chest tenderly with her fingers. She massaged his shoulders and ordered him to lift his arms so she could scrub his armpits. Pete had never enjoyed such personal attention. Kit was driving him wild. Kit knelt at his feet, subservient as if in prayer. She placed each foot in turn on top of her thighs, meticulously scrubbing them clean. Slowly she worked the soap upwards from his ankles towards his knees. Kit scrubbed his calves and worked upwards to his thighs, massaging each muscle as she progressed with her delicate stroking fingers. Pete tried to ignore her attentions but was failing fast. Kit then positioned Pete so that the forceful flow of water sprayed away the soaps of her labours. Pete closed his eyes and the blood boiled through his body. Her lips slid upward across his belly; her teeth nibbled into his neck as she drew up to face him. Kit leaned against him, pushing his shoulders against the warm tiled wall and encircled her arms about his neck. Assured of his stability and without words, she hoisted herself upward, climbing his hot, wet body. Kit curled her legs behind his thighs and locked them against his belly. Kit breathed heavy with the effort whimpering small endearments, interspersed by cries of delight as the docking manoeuvre neared completion. NASA would

351

have been proud. Kit relaxed, her legs and torso now hung in ecstasy, bayoneted by his male flesh. Pete's desire swelled up inside and he rotated his body, changing positions and pressing Kit against the warm misted ceramics. Kit sunk her teeth into his shoulder to smother her cries; her body shook with the spasms. Unconsciously he sensed her tender acknowledgement of his undying strength. In an all-consuming moment of passion, the final thrust was delivered, pressing kit against the ceramics with nothing between them but the power of eternal procreation and Pete finally announced his love for her.

As their strength ebbed, along with the urgency, Pete encircled her tight. Neither spoke, it was not necessary and words could not have described. They preferred instead to languish in the smouldering bond of fire. Forever he could have held her, had it not been for the passing of man's immortal enemy - time. He dried Kit with his huge, terry towel, tenderly rubbing her, until her skin glowed almost ashamedly. He cocooned her with the towel, hoisted her into his arms and carried her into the bedroom. Kit squealed as he flung her through the air, bounced her onto the bed and fell upon her once more in a final gesture of compliment, to the intimate depths of bond they had so quickly managed to achieve.

"Kit," Pete began later.

"Hoy! you have many things to do today, make sure everything complete, your friend relies on you now. You keep your promise and when we meet again soon, we make all our decisions".

"Your right, Kit". He acknowledged, "When all this is finished, I'll send for you, or come for you myself and we'll make our plans together".

"Until then we wait?" she could not hide the sadness with her smile.

"Until then we remain friends?" he announced.

"Close friends?"

"Very! close friends". Pete emphasised the word: very.

"We almost," she stopped as their eyes met.

"Lovers". Pete finished her statement,

"Not almost, Kit". he assured her,

"We are lovers".

Kit squealed with delight, pulled him close and squeezed. Finally, they released their hold and the bond had been sealed. They dressed as all lovers' dress, hurriedly; to make up for the just one more kiss and cuddle routine. For the first time, Kit wore her Airline uniform before his hungry eyes. Her incredible beauty stunned him as she turned from the mirror having applied her "flight face'. He was almost tempted by his desire but it was too late, he had no wish to ruin her career with deportation in shame. Nor did he wish me to have to race last minute, through the early morning rush hour traffic of Jeddah. It would suit everybody concerned far better if he placed his animal instinct back from where it had risen and allowed me to deliver them to the airport on time. As the car slowed in the airport park, they did not share a farewell kiss or hug. In the privacy of the car, Kit slipped her hand into his own and he squeezed tight, she returned the concealed embrace,

"Hoy! you take good care of my Pete now!" she warned me.

"Hey, don't worry about me, Kit," Pete responded. "I'll be careful, extremely careful, unbelievably careful from now on. I've got somebody incredibly special to share my life with and I'm not going to let her down".

She fluttered those eyes, those sensual eyes that spoke volumes, but now she fluttered them to fight the tingle of approaching tears.

"You no forget? you forget and I get very drunk off with you!"

"Kit," Pete grinned, "The word is pissed off with me". I had to smile; she was wonderful at these literary slips.

"No matter the word, you not keep promise, Pete. I never come here again, I quit Saudia, I go home and you never see Mistress Wong again, not ever again".

Kit did not smile and I'm sure Pete believed her. She gracefully exited the car and straightened her skirt before bending and bidding him farewell through the side window.

"Bye my Pete, please take care". her voice trembled.

I watched her walk away toward the aircrew building, a slight breeze pushed her hair over her shoulder, and her body crossed the asphalt as if it were the catwalk of international fashion.

"Dumb laws!" Pete hissed, and I knew then that he loved her, and as she walked away all remaining doubts disappeared. He told me he wanted to shout her name and tell her the truth, just in case, I asked him why he didn't and fixed him with a stare that would have melted steel. Now she was nearing the terminal building,

"Dumb fucking laws!" he hissed once more before jumping from the car and calling out her name,

"Kit!" he shouted as he ran toward her, Kit turned suddenly, her cheeks glistening with the tracks of her tears. She dropped her flight bag as they collided into a fierce embrace,

"I love you!" he announced, "I really and truly love you!"

"I know this," she cried with joy, "I know this is true".

It seemed as if the whole of Jeddah had turned to witness their expression of love and strangely, no one seemed to care, as if their observers understood the incredible importance of that one single embrace and, understanding the magnitude of the occasion, the whole of Jeddah turned and looked the other way. They obviously thought they were married. Except me of course, I sat there with a tear forcing its way to my eyes. "Shit!" I thought, "This place must be getting to me'.

I gunned the car to the North Creek, now Pete was at peace with his affirmation to Kit. Now he would keep his promises. First to Hawkeye, then to me and finally to Kit and I could already hear wedding bells tolling in the desert sunshine.

Early Thursday morning and already a few weekenders were out on the creek. Most, if not all schools and government offices were closed and some were already making the most of their Thursday and Friday weekend off. Pete was feeling better. Kit was well out of the way and he carried about his person the letter from the labour board which even the police, would not question unless he was caught engaging in criminal proceedings, which at this stage we were both frantically trying to avoid. He chastised himself for his recent breach of law. If the civil or religious police had stopped him with Kit in the car, to whom he was not married or related, they could have locked us up for six months. With me getting another 50 years to life!

"To hell with them it was worth it". he grinned as he remembered, "At least I wasn't a miserable bastard!"

Kit would soon be in New York. He was, for the moment at least, stuck in Jeddah with distance, visa complications and me likely to cure the most fervent of his romantic ardours.

Shark's external appearance had not changed since we had last seen her; Pete saw nothing to arouse his suspicions. He disappeared below deck and checked the contents of the hold. When satisfied he returned to the pilot deck, where I had begun to clean and fettle the various gauges and controls. I sighted the huge vehicle before we heard the deep resonance of its engine. A large corkscrew of pluming dust and sand had signalled its approach. It drew up alongside the road in line with the pier and parked cleanly with a hiss and squeal of air-assisted breaks.

Hawkeye squinted, adjusting his eyes to the brightness, which existed on the outside, of the shaded, air-conditioned world of his cab. Finally, he sighted us, as we were purposely hiding from Hawkeye's view in the rear of Shark's pilot deck. Hawkeye waved his single middle finger in recognition of the childish prank and headed over to the pair of us.

"Asalaamb alaecumb," greeted Hawkeye as he mounted the steps.

"Alaecumb salaam," we returned the Saudi greeting and threw Hawkeye a Vimto non-alcoholic. Hawkeye guzzled the contents and threw the empty can into the trash bin by the side of Shark, whilst issuing a loud burp.

Hawkeye grinned snapping back the ring-pull on his second beer and raising the can in salute to his lips. When his thirst was satiated Hawkeye got down to the real nature of the visit.

"I filled six tankers with the exact mixtures you requested, Jesus, Pete. My eyes are still watering from the stink of that stuff, scared me to death every time I walked past one of those big-bellied bastards". Hawkeye gave us the details of his tasks.

Hawkeye pulled a small, plastic, waterproof bag from his pocket.

"These are for you. The colour coding is idiot proof, jade green for jail and red for refinery. I hope you can remember that? because if you don't the show will be over with a capital O!"

Pete took the small cigarette size boxes and separated them. He dropped the box with the red tape into the chart drawer; at this range, it was worthless anyhow. Then he stuffed the green taped box into his pocket.

"What happened at Sharief's office?" Pete broke into Hawkeye's nervous stare as the boxes were treated with such disregard. Hawkeye revealed the full story. His anger and disgust were barely contained as he unfolded his tale. Hawkeye had met the Sharief, who had shaken his hand and congratulated him on his wise decision. Hawkeye had smiled and accepted the two months" pay. A mere tenth of what he was really owed. The Sharief had announced his pleasure at dealing with someone with the common sense to know what sort of financial constraints the company was now enduring.

"What did you say?" interjected Pete.

"I wanted to break his bloody neck with my bare hands".

"You and me both mate. You, me and Bob included".

"I gotta go!" Hawkeye was obviously disturbed, "I got a lot of packing to finish, I want to check all the connections just one more time for my own satisfaction so don't go messing around with the boxes just yet, you may cause me some unbelievable hair loss". Hawkeye grinned as he dropped down the ladder at the rear of shark. A jumbo grumbled overhead and Hawkeye stabbed his finger skyward, tracing the path of the lumbering silver bird,

"Won't be long now, guys?" a serious expression clouded Hawkeye's words as he turned and headed back for the truck.

"See you tomorrow, don't be late". I called after him.

"I'll probably be a few hours early". Hawkeye had to shout as he climbed into the cab and the big diesel engine barked to life. Hawkeye slammed the door behind him and wound down the window, before purposely slipping the clutch and spraying a shower of dust into the air, which drifted over toward Shark and subsequently dusted her passengers. Pete leaped up from his perch and shook his fist in mock anger. Hawkeye glimpsed Pete's signal in the rear-view mirror, laughing to himself and replying with a similar single finger signal of his own, the big tractor grumbled away followed by a lengthening trail of whirling dust clouds.

We continued fettling of Shark's controls. Noon burned into our shoulders as the orb climbed the eastern wall of the sky and blazed directly overhead. I opened another beer from the cooler-chest, greedily sucking down the contents from the alloy cylinder. A faint pattering caught my attention, the pattering increased in volume as the seconds passed by. Pete scanned the blue backdrop until his eyes sourced the increasing sound. The chopper scudded low, barrelling toward us at a fierce angle, before pulling away at the last moment. It circled the area twice and slowly fell to earth, settling on the spare ground, to where Pete now stared with interest. Already a gaggle of kids dared the dust to take a closer look. I caught sight of the Greek cap, the mirrored glasses and the jaunty approach, though I knew the identity of the visitor as the first sounds invaded my ears.

"Pete!" growled Hangar, "How the devil are you?"

"Still here, Chief". Pete responded as Hangar climbed the rear ladder.

"Permission?" requested Hangar, an avid sea fairer and follower of nautical etiquette.

"Granted!" I grinned, unaccustomed to such formality.

Hangar dropped into the pilot deck with his familiar salute, a whistle emanated from his lips,

"If she runs as good as she looks, guys, her belly is rarely going to touch the sea. I never saw her looking so good. It's amazing what a coat of paint and a good polish will do, how you doing Khowaja?"

"I'm Ok mate, expect to go to court in a week or so, expect a sentence of fifty years plus life, expect a couple of batterings between now and then but other than that, I'm fine!"

"Bastards!" grunted Hangar, "Shower of illegitimate fucking bastards, I'd like to overfly that place with a Huey and give them a piece of my mind".

"Yeah!" but you ain't got a Huey, this ain't a war zone and you ain't John Wayne".

"I have a Huey Pete but it's in Cyprus. I fixed it up myself, going to use it ferrying sightseeing tourists when I eventually leave this place. In fact, that little bird is where most of my funds have gone. You say this ain't a war Zone? try telling that to the Khowaja here, war Zone ain't going to describe how he's feeling about this place and thirdly, your right, I ain't John Wayne".

"When are you leaving, Hangar?" I enquired sympathetically, acutely aware that he had no real desire to leave this place.

"Officially today. I was just returning to base with the chopper and I thought I'd take one last ride over here to see you, before I hand over the keys. You want to come with me for a last spin, I got something for you?"

"Not much left to do here," Pete replied, "We've got to do something to kill a little time".

"OK! let's go, I don't want the air jockeys over at the base to miss their little bird, they tend to get a trifle panicky".

"We're right behind you," we chorused, locking up Shark's hold and removing all items from the grasp of prying little fingers".

"You about ready?" inquired Hangar as we strolled to the chopper.

358

"Everything done but the waiting".

"It's always the worst part," declared Hangar, "Waiting for something to happen".

We followed Hangar through a throng of excited kids, who had gathered around the helicopter, Pete warned them in Arabic to stand far away, the sand could be blasted into their eyes or their heads cut off by the blades. The kids moved back nervously but a few stubborn adults stood their ground.

"There's always a hero," I declared, as we boarded.

Pete had flown alongside Hangar before and we both strapped ourselves into the seats - tightly. The turbines whined to life and the blades flicked by above us. The observers" Nightgowns were blasted against their skin, head scarves had to be chased and grabbed tight as the die-hards retreated from the downdraft. The dust obliterated everything from view and suddenly the chopper lurched skyward, rose from the sandy fog and into the clear blue sky above. Hangar headed due east toward the hills, we asked him no questions. Hangar knew what he was doing and we trusted him. Hangar had offered to help and it was not an offer to be taken lightly.

The chopper buzzed between the dunes, swung low into the mountains and hugged against the floor.

"Jesus! why so low?" Pete squirmed in his seat.

"Radar!" Hangar boomed above the noise.

The chopper skipped across the rocks below them and I was certain a few were dislodged as the chopper whistled by.

"What radar?" Pete did not look up from his inspection of the ground as it rushed by below us.

"They got a radar post on the highest peak, we gotta stay below it or they will call us in. We ain't got no excuses to be out this way so if we stay below their range, we won't have to answer their stupid questions, as they say, guys, out of sight, out of mind".

"I hope so Hangar, I fucking hope so, what the fuck sort of explanation have I got for doing this if they catch me?" I enquired solemnly.

Hangar looked at Pete and Pete looked at Hangar and after a brief pause,

"Pussy!" they chorused together.

We had no idea where we were going, Pete attempted conversation to soothe his fears but it was almost impossible in this noisy bird. We had no idea who this man really was who now sat beside us, only that there had to be something more than Hangar had told us, you could tell, he was that sort of guy.

By the time Hangar dropped us back at the Shark, my mind had folded into thousands of inquisitive creases at what I had just learned. We loaded the new supplies aboard Shark, I was terrified that someone would see us and walk over for an inquisitive chat. There could be no possible excuse for what we were now loading into the belly of Shark and if we had been caught, it was a certain date with cassation for all of us.

I could not concentrate on the drive back to the compound. How had we gotten ourselves into this situation? The original plan for Red Shirt resembled nothing like the one now being contemplated. Who was Jerry Hangar anyway? Jerry had revealed himself to be a total stranger. A man we thought we knew, had suddenly turned out to be someone else. Pete still shook his head in wonder, to clear his mind of the nagging doubts within. It was too late to worry; Hangar had thrown us completely off balance and we had gone along with him. Now we sat on a train of events, the train had accelerated to such a speed, jumping off was no longer an option and would only result in death. To stay on the train would mean a journey into hell. What worried me the most, was the fact that I now feared I had purchased a one-way ticket and there would be no return trip if we were caught.

360

Chapter 15

EXIT ONLY

The moon hung suspended in the early dawn sky. The Orb had not yet tipped its arc over the horizon but the orange glow, heralding sunrise, had tinged the moon into a golden surrealism. Shark bobbed and swayed in the orange creek as Pete climbed aboard. It was five o'clock in the morning, we were early. To be late would have added more tension to an already burdened day. Today we had enough worries to keep ourselves busy, even the minor details had kept me awake all night.

Pete paced around the pilot deck, not quite knowing where to start. I could hear other mariners on the creek, probably preparing for a long day's fishing. Today was Friday, the Holy day, a day of rest for all foreigners and Saudis alike. I checked the fuel gauges; both tanks registered the same full capacity.

Now I dropped below deck, to scrutinise the rosewood shutters, which led to the hold. The check pin remained in place, undisturbed, revealing no unwelcome intrusions. The key turned easily in the well-lubed lock and I entered the hold where the lights sparkled, a sure sign of fully charged batteries. The air tanks lined the walls; I picked up a pressure gauge and measured each one in turn. None had leaked; all contained eighty litres of pure sweet air. In well-trained hands, eighty litres would fill up a telephone box and provide a competent diver with at least one hour of underwater exploration, providing he stayed within fifteen meters of the surface and did not unnecessarily exert himself. I screwed the valves down tight and replaced the protective plastic covers to the bottleneck valves. The regulator breathing hoses still shone like new, the silicone oil Pete had applied during their service sparkled as the hoses flexed and coiled with the swell, catching the light from the small, overhead lighting.

CHAPTER 15   SAUDI STYLE   EXIT ONLY

The dinghy, along with its outboard motors was stowed in good balance with a fifty-gallon drum of fuel. The total package held together by a medium diameter nylon line that ran through the eyes of brightly coloured sea floats, which in turn were pressed together under two tightly woven cloth bags. Everything was in decent shape; we had checked them a hundred times. I took three air tanks from each side of the hold, fed them into a triple harness and secured them with quick set toggle clamps. When six tanks had been prepared in two sets of three, I lifted them above the sacks and secured them to the package. I shoulder charged the large bulk of equipment to assure myself they were secure and well balanced - they were. When completely satisfied, I returned to the pilot deck. The early morning sun peeped over the desert horizon, turned in my direction and almost at once, the wailing call to prayer drifted across the creek from the recently constructed mosques. We savoured the moment of tranquillity, blessed by the early morning prayers to God. We stood transfixed, unwilling to disturb the salutations to the Holy one. There was no need to hurry, all the coast guards would be at prayer, and it was time for brief respite while the opportunity availed itself. We knew that the future would hold no such luxuries. As the dawn prayer echoed to silence, I watched them as they left the mosque, over on the far bank, the worshippers - stabbing their feet into the pile of leather sandals that they had carelessly deposited outside the main doors. No man entered the mosque with footwear and it was not unusual for a pilgrim to leave his spiritual duties wearing someone else's badly worn sandals. His own new pair on the feet of a fellow worshipper who would never again pray at this mosque, until the purloined goods were worn beyond their newness and easy recognition.

Pete cast off the keeper lines and I fired up Shark's engines. They burst to life almost instantaneously and coughed up a blue rope of twisted mist from the water level exhausts behind the pilot deck. The new batteries were performing well. I checked the instruments with the care and precision of a brain surgeon

362

and nosed Shark slowly from the dock. This was a critical day and a good start would help achieve a good finale, or so I hoped.

The temperature gauge crept evenly up the dial as Shark burbled up the creek. I eased her hull against the coast guard jetty. The duty guard came out to meet us and offered morning courtesies. I explained we would be taking her up and down the creek once or twice to check out the faults that had recently arisen after repairs. I assured the coast guard we would not be going out to sea and would merely perform one or two low-speed passes and perhaps a final high-speed pass later in the evening when the creek was empty and the faithful had gone home to their beds. I had no wish to disturb the citizens on their Holy day. The guard waved us on without interference and logged our number,

"How considerate!" he must have thought, "Khowajas can sometimes be more considerate than my own countrymen". The coast guard offered a smile and a wave before returning to his morning, Turkish coffee and newspaper.

We cruised up to the estuary before turning and heading back to Shark's berth. The old guard waved from his chair as we passed by the end of the pier. Shark's engines were barely audible at the steady cruising glide. A slight splash disturbed the morning stillness but no one saw the ripples as a heavy object fell from the rear of Shark and see-sawed into the cool, silent depths. It was not an unusual sound on the creek and no one paid much attention. Shark picked up speed and we performed a few quick passes, making sure to wave to the guard on each broadside of the official outpost. Finally, I edged her back to berth and left her as we had found her, bobbing and swaying in the morning light. No noticeable changes other than a slight variation in weight and the heat radiating from her engines. We left her secured in anticipation of our next visit.

By the time the hands of his Rolex toyed with eight o'clock, Pete had pushed his breakfast of scrambled egg on toast at least twice around his plate. I had gobbled mine down with an eager hunger, for I knew that there would be no bacon and eggs where we were going. I swilled the last mouthful of cold coffee into my stomach and, almost refreshed, set off to the office of an expat friend, to where we had re-directed mail and communications. The fax had worked overtime during the night; a lengthening ribbon of type awaited the operator. Pete glanced quickly through the commercial Jargon, mostly from suppliers in different time zones of the world, hence their overnight arrival. The smallest of messages caught his eye, he grinned with appreciation as he read the contents to me,

ATTN. PETE V.
        NEW YORK IS EXTREMELY DULL, REMEMBER YOUR PROMISE. KATHERINE, KATY, KATE, KIT, SUIT YOURSELF. XXX

He tore off the top copy and stuffed it into his shirt pocket, leaving the ribbon of copy messages whole. He didn't want them to think he had removed something not belonging to himself. He sat down on the polished wood surface of the reception desk, wedged the receiver between his shoulder and neck and tapped in the code numbers transport,
    "Hawkeye please". he requested as the line clicked open.
    "Hawkeye here, can I help you?"
    "Did you get the red shirt and sneakers?"
    "Sorry I didn't". replied Hawkeye, "I had them delivered".
    The line cut dead. Pete replaced the receiver and ticked another item from his checklist, so far so good, everything was going to plan. It was ten o'clock before we left the office, carefully locked behind us and pushed the key through the letterbox. We would no longer need it and we had left a message of thanks where we knew it would be found. Our next stop was overseas express, to confirm that two steel trunks, holding our personal belongings had been delivered to the airport for tonight's flight. Pete signed the customs and excise declarations that the trunks held nothing but his personal belongings; he waved thanks and good-bye to the express

364

employees and ticked off another task from the rapidly diminishing list. Now we headed across town to pick up Hawkeye.

The merest hint of a breeze tried to cool the morning heat but failed, midday was fast approaching and then the breeze would disappear, forcing the temperature well into the hundreds and beyond.

At this stage I was physically and mentally well prepared but in the depths of my mind, a startled bird fluttered skyward at the approach of unknown danger. I paid it no heed, concentrating on the tasks ahead. Today would be a turning point in my life and I decided, though with little choice, should anyone challenge me today, I would brush them away like the bothersome flies and pay them less attention.

The noon prayer call soothed the three of us as we headed toward the airport. Once we had been a team, now we were fragmenting and the sorrow revealed itself in our reflective tones. Mostly we discussed the old times. No matter what happened now, the adventure had been worth it, that even though the Sharief was burning us, it had been a good life while it had lasted. The constant flow of wealth had relieved us of any financial values. We had once spent money like water without a care in the world. A Khowaja bought gold for close family, for his wife or his girl but he himself wanted no such symbol of wealth, such symbols were beacons for muggers, pickpockets and thieves and a Khowaja desired no such encounter. A simple tidy neck chain, occasionally supporting a crucifix, announced his calling and between himself and God, it was all he had, it was all he would ever need.

We had all learned from experience and, it was not too long before a Khowaja took stock of his situation and the wealth he was pouring away. As the Saudi work week took its toll and the hard-earned cash no longer numbed the pain. The material world was elbowed to one side and suddenly major chunks of Khowaja cash found its way into the stocks, bonds, gilts and Far Eastern funds. It got to the point where a Khowaja merely had to think about investing money and the financial advisors were bugging his phone.

A final act of self-indulgence would then temper the man. He would head downtown and relieve himself of eight thousand Saudi Riyals, procuring a final purchase before Khowaja-ism took control, a Rolex submariner. He would not purchase all gold models, not so much a beacon as a magnet to muggers. He would settle for stainless steel with just a hint of the yellow metal thrown around the crown to enhance the day-date-diver's watch, accurate and waterproof to depths of one hundred and fifty meters.

The watch would never again leave his wrist; it would dive with him into the deepest, darkest depths of the Red Sea. Rattle against his wrist as he traversed the desert on a motocross bike. Windsurf; squash and tennis with him and ultimately, it would not look out of place as his hands caressed the curvatures of the most beautiful girls in the world. It was guaranteed forever and if the promise held good it would last a lifetime. If the promise failed, a Khowaja would be on the next flight to Geneva with a pocket full of rockets and enough abuse to shame them into supplying a replacement, as they had once replaced mine, no questions asked.

Pete, Hawkeye and I discussed the past as we entered the airport and found the familiar short-stay car park, positioning the car where we would not be blocked in. We marvelled at the Saudia fleet as the planes lay basking in the afternoon sun. As the doors of the car were flung open, a hot wave of air rushed inside, smearing the air-conditioned chrome work with fine misty dew. Beautiful clear blue skies welcomed us, a marvellous backdrop to behold as the great alloy birds droned in and out, especially, if you were about to board one of the great alloy birds and drone out. Hawkeye said little; this was quite an occasion for him. His last exit from a country he had almost grown to love. A country that had delivered unto him - a Hotel in Spain, a beautiful wife and not a small amount of financial stability, despite the Sharief's attempt to curtail his legal entitlements.

366

Now he was glad to be leaving, as were most of the Khowajas. The oil bubble had burst and unemployment and harassment rippled in its troublesome wake.

The Saudis themselves loved to get away from the place. No real freedom existed in Saudi, too many irksome rules, too many petty restrictions and too many arseholes eagerly enforcing them. It was a multi-police state - full stop. As we walked toward the departure terminal we were greeted by a familiar smell, dry piss on hot asphalt. It was created by the unfortunates without money who camped on the airport grounds awaiting a flight home and during the night, relieved their bladders and sometimes their bowels, between the parked cars, watch out for that one! Jet fuel and urine are the most potent smells at the Jeddah International Airport carpark and it is debatable which is the stronger of the two. As we stepped onto the pavement outside the departure lounge, a familiar droning voice announced the flights, as if he were speaking from the bottom of a long and windy tunnel. Automatic doors sliced open as we approached and our bodies, having acclimatised to the hundred plus temperature of the outside world, we were soaked in a swath of condensation as the cold mechanical environment welcomed us inside.

We serpentined the small islands of baggage, passing by family groups who were crying their tearful good-byes. Entire families and their possessions were constantly swallowed into the cavernous bellies of the massive jumbo jets. Occasionally a twin-tone horn would sound followed by a sharp announcement, which was in turn followed by a translation, neither of which could be clearly deciphered. Information boards continually clattered to announce incoming and departing flights. According to the clatter-boards, Hawkeye's flight was dead on time, or so they would have you believe. Passengers cluttered the check in desk; half were still completing passport formalities as Hawkeye dropped his suitcase at what appeared to be the end of the human chain.

The three of us conversed briefly, a total nonsense to any intruding ear.

"Everything is in place". breathed Hawkeye.

"I know, Hawkeye". replied Pete, nonchalantly scanning around.

"I checked things over and over till I was blue in the face".

"I knew you would, Hawk. that's why you got the job".

"Thanks, guys. I hope everything goes OK; I just wish there were more I could do to help".

"You've done your bit, Hawkeye; we could never have got this far without your help. Whatever happens now is out of your hands, it's up to us to complete the rest".

"You two guys must be close, not everyone would help out a friend like Pete's doing now".

"He'd have done the same for any of us, Hawkeye. You know that".

"You know, I always felt strange when I was with you two guys, as If I was intruding into something special. Everything was a contest between the two of you and there was no second place".

Pete interrupted him, we shuffled the baggage forward and loaded it onto the scale, the electra digits flicked around to forty-five kilos before suddenly flicking back to twenty-two, Hawkeye was stunned.

"That's twenty-two kilos, sir. You're two kilos overweight, but we won't charge you for the extra two kilos, special discount to you".

"Special Khowaja discount". I interrupted, nudging Hawkeye's elbow and motioning to the scale. Hawkeye had been puzzled at first, but now the game was clear. My foot was wedged firmly under the scale. The attendant tagged and labelled the bags, pressed his control panel and the case disappeared down the luggage chute. There remained little else to discuss. We dragged our feet over to immigration and tried to think of conversation pieces. Hawkeye checked through with his passport and hand luggage. He turned and offered his right hand, changed his mind and threw his arms around his friends in a hug, not without a flush of embarrassment. We returned the hug with the same crushing force, we wanted to break a rib or something but we let go when he cried out with pain.

"Good luck bastards look after yourselves!"

"We will, Hawkeye". assured Pete, "You can be sure we will".

"You guys never failed to amaze me, I lost two daughters because of Saudi and what kept me going was the fact that Saudi had given me two sons. I guess that's it, all I can say now is...".

Hawkeye trailed off, it had already been said, without words, so many times before.

Hawkeye collected his belongings. Neither of us betrayed much emotion but for the prickle of tears behind our eyes, tears that we knew would never be allowed to flow. Hawkeye passed through the X-ray followed by the body scan and with a final wave of his middle finger he said good-bye, the Rolex submariner signalling his calling as it glinted in the overhead spotlights.

We sidestepped the waving throngs; I needed to get away from this place as quickly as possible. The aura of happy departures had begun to destroy my resolve. We were soaked once more as we left the man-made, mechanical environment and were bathed in the broiling heat. The stench of broiled piss assailed our nostrils once more and I personally hoped, it would be for the last time, at least in Jeddah's International Airport anyway. It was almost noon; we planned to pass by the creek once more before for one last check. Hangar had gone, Hawkeye had gone and suddenly I felt very alone. Then I thought of Pete and how it would feel once we were away from this place. The time was fast approaching when indeed, God alone, would decide our fate and I prayed that my fate, would hold at least enough time to see Lyn once more, if only to say good-bye.

The many weekend sailors and windsurfers burdened the creek as we boarded Shark. Nothing was amiss. I warmed up her engines and made a few steady runs up and down the creek. Pete made sure to catch the eye of the coast guard during every pass. At each pass, the coast guard fell into the routine of wave and smile, wave and smile. I allowed Shark fifty percent power on her last run down the full length of the creek, her motors burbled smoothly; she was ready and eager to go. As I docked Shark against the jetty, I forced myself to admit the truth. Our work was finished at the creek; ahead lay more important tasks that had to be completed. I clambered down the ladder, patted Shark on the stern and whispered a silent message of future hope.

The loading dock was crammed with fishermen, their rods bristling in the sunlight like the spines of a porcupine. The water lay becalmed, half a kilometre did not seem such a great distance at this time of day and I hoped that by nightfall, that same half a kilometre had recovered its true and lengthy guise. Then a bolt from the blue struck me. What if the fishermen dredged something from the bottom? It was too late; there was nothing I could do. I tried to reassure myself as I stared out across the creek, my eyes momentarily locked in a stare of hopelessness but the glare from the rippled creek forced me to avert my gaze elsewhere. It was too late to worry now; the wheels were firmly in motion and I had already discarded the brakes. Pete clambered into the car beside me and we headed back into town.

During the journey back to town, something gripped me inside; it had a presence that did not intrude; yet for a moment it would not leave my guts. It was a feeling almost unknown to me, but most people could have explained the phenomenon, it was the slow crawl of impending fear as it spread a widening net to ensnare me.

We were stopped by the traffic cops on the way back into town. They wanted my documents and would not accept the bit of paper I offered them; Pete was OK and he got away with his paperwork. They said they would take me to Ruwais prison until they had checked things out with my sponsor Sharief. I tried to put on a brave face but I wanted to be sick. Pete stood his ground and informed me as he left me outside the prison gate,

"Don't worry mate, everything goes as planned".
Then we were parted and I was dragged off to the Euro-cell once more where I awaited my fate and despaired at the unfairness of it all.

Dilating rapidly, the pupils of my eyes searched frantically for a base mark, in the dim enclosure that they had thrown me in. I almost collapsed with disbelief when they told me they knew who I was and what I had been doing. In Saudi, prison meant prison, Saudi prisons were no comparison, to their luxurious European, hotel-like counterparts. In Saudi, they were not the hotels that the West were using at a formidable cost to the taxpayer. The Saudis did not pander to the whims of child killers like Brady and Hindley either. Hindley was currently costing the taxpayer a fortune with her education to degree level. Her special treatment and her cosy, Lord Longford-like friends. I had plenty of time to dwell on such subjects. There could be errors of judgement of course, but in cases of such brutal murder where there was no doubt, the Saudis had the right idea. As long as there was irrefutable proof, let the victim's families decide the fate of murderers and child killers. There was no deterrent in the UK and that was the root cause of the problem. Chop off the heads of child rapists and murderers then stand back and watch the crime rate fall. It worked in Saudi; it could work elsewhere. I smiled to myself,

"You could never get the do-gooders to agree to such a punishment". I mused to myself, "Unless it was "their" kids who had been raped, tortured and mutilated that is!"
Only a brutish determination along with the knowledge of my innocence had previously saved me from insanity, and as I slept on the steel cot that night, I wondered how much more I could take. The rising prayer call flooded the building, heralding the deliverance of dawn and the rising of the orb. Darkness blended

into to greys, revealing the Spartan furniture of my cell. At the foot of the steel framed cot, a solitary scarred wooden chair, no cushion to grace your buttocks, but a small piece of damp chipboard would support any behind. I traced the crack between the floor and the wall. A rusty red cockroach scuttled into the crack, distracting my gaze as it stopped, as if to bid me good morning, waving its antennae in salute before disappearing into the secret cavity. A fibre board tray with soft plastic utensils lay by the cell door, strong enough to serve their purpose but useless as a digging instrument, or when absolute desperation craved, weapons. A tin pot stood in the corner I used it as a toilet during the off hours when the guards were hypersensitive and the hole in the ground was blocked solid and needed cleaning – by hand. It was obvious the decorators hadn't been in since my last visit.

I had learned during previous incarceration to void my bladder after the evening prayer and the stinking rusty pot was mostly ignored, unless of course I could not walk more than a few steps on bruised and swollen feet, or the guards wanted me to drink from it. A small table leaned against the peeling whitewash on the damp plaster wall.

The rattle of a key chain disturbed my thoughts. The guard was about to deliver my early morning tea, heavily sweetened with no milk. I had grown accustomed to such taste and did not mind, I had drunk this beverage many times, before becoming a guest of his Majesty the King. A piece of flat Arabic bread and a few dates were included, a fine breakfast indeed and I loudly thanked God for the food, as my tray was delivered to the bottom of the bars, where a gap existed for such purposes, the old guard smiled and nodded at my exaltations of thanks to Allah.

I stretched out on the cot and the muscles in my body ached, not from any beating, though I had received them often enough, from the increased targets I had set myself as I exercised daily. I sat upright and inspected my feet. They were strong again and I hoped they didn't start with that shit again. Although a dull ache sometimes persisted, I could walk and run without much trouble. I ate the bread and drank the tea. I threw the dates into my mouth one by one and savoured their sticky flesh. The empty cup chinked when I spat the date stones into it,

"A fine breakfast indeed," maybe they had decided to leave me alone, I secretly prayed, to finish this minor incarceration in peace. I knew Pete would be out there doing everything he could and I knew he would not let me down.

They could also be playing their games as they had done so many times before, comforting me, lulling me back to a comfortable existence so that when they dragged me outside once more, the torment would not have been numbed by its continuity. Maybe that's why they had released me for a few days, to add to the torment. They may have even followed me, Oh God, I hope not, what if they were searching Shark at this moment, Shit! If that were the case, I would be dead in a day or so for sure.

The old guard bade me good morning; he had a big smile on his face when he saw me as if he were genuinely pleased to see his old friend. As soon as the door closed behind the guard, I pushed my head and shoulders under the bed to perform press-ups. The full weight of the steel cot bounced against my torso above my pumping shoulders and arms. I breathed a smooth heavy rhythm in time to the rising and falling of the cot, until my arms could push no more. I wriggled from under the cot, rolled onto my shoulders and cycled to no-where for thirty minutes until the clatter outside signalled the time for the Friday morning shower. Friday was a good day, we could shower twice for religious purposes and maybe have a shave, before being thrown back into the cells for another week. Cold showers did not exist, even in the prison. The water was pumped from the underground tanks to the massive fibreglass holding tanks on the roof. There they caught the full broiling heat of the noonday sun. I enjoyed the high-pressure soaking that was spoiled only, by the leering prisoners, it reminded me of my first day in Saudi and the old apartment block, I had no regrets I loved Saudi and what she had given me, you couldn't blame Saudi for the actions of one man.

The morning rolled slowly by. By eight o'clock I was back in my cell after a brief walk around the central chamber, my official exercise period. As I walked around the central chamber I chatted with the other prisoners. Most were short termers from the European section. Guys who had been caught drinking, partying, fornicating or even the heinous crime of carrying a female passenger in a car, who was not related by marriage or blood, most were looking deeply sorry for themselves. I did not see any other Khowajas; I knew they weren't that stupid. Quite a cross section of foreigners were present, drunks, fornicators, racing drivers and the odd hit and run merchant. All due to receive eighty lashes of the cane before deportation in shame and a heroic newspaper article back home. I had no intention of going to the newspapers, I had my own story to tell and did not want the truth to be twisted by some half-baked typist who had never journeyed beyond the shores of London let alone the UK. My thoughts still dwelled on the aspects of Saudi law, not unusual considering the amount of spare time I had on my hands now.

I did not agree with all Saudi Laws but some were worth considering. There weren't many murders in Saudi, not for lack of weapons. It was the cassation that deterred most criminal clones and rightly so. Thoughts turned to Pete, and what - according to Saudi Law, was Pete risking. After all, today was Friday and Friday was the day when public sentences were performed, be that lashings or hand or head chopping. The sentences were conducted before the public eye, usually outside the main mosque after prayers. Would we be here next week? I thought, awaiting the final swing of the sword? or would we be back home, probably in bed with our partners making up for lost time. I did not need to think about such matters, I knew exactly where I preferred to be and I hoped it would soon be a reality.

In Saudi, we had been a team, a team that had promised to stick together and help each other during our allotted time in this foreign land. Even to the point of discussing various problems and scenarios, should they arise. Invasion by Iranians, or maybe and more likely by the Iraqis, Nuclear attack by the Jews, Russian advances for oil, or perish the thought, caught wearing Bermuda shorts in a supermarket. Human curiosity knows no bounds when lubricated by a stiff Sid. Pete had once laughed whilst quizzing me before,

"What do you want me to bring during visiting hours when you are caught doing the Tango with Lyn?"

I had wrinkled my brow in thought before replying to such a laden question,

"You can bring me my motocross boots, red tube socks, canvas pants and of course my sleeveless red shirt".

"Why the red shirt?"

"Easy, Pete. Every time I wear my red shirt, I beat the hell out of you whatever we're doing, it inspires me. I'd be out of the slammer in a flash".

Pete had jumped on top of me and we had rolled around thumping each other and wrestling for ten minutes before Pete's lip was "accidentally" burst open on my fist and we had to stop to clear up the bloody mess. Across the front of the red shirt, I so loved to wear was a simple Saudi message, "I ain't a bloody tourist, I work here". I had printed the shirt myself at one of the local "T" shirt booths. A month later, hundreds of similar logos were noticed around Jeddah. I had blown a fuse, furious that my design had been poached by the "T" shirt people and no royalties were forthcoming. I cooled off when I realised that the phrase was not actually my original design. After all, I had received it from a very special foreigner, a stranger who since my insertion into Saudi I had never seen again.

So, the red shirt had become a signal, code and conveyor of our quest for justice and freedom. Neither of our group ever expected to use the code but at this moment, my feelings could not be put into words. We had long since discussed and prepared in case of such an occurrence taking place. discussing such things had been easy with a glass in one hand and barbecue fork in the other. Now reality had bludgeoned those comfortably planned fantasies and I experienced what can only be described as second thoughts. The call to prayer echoed through the prison, it was ten fifteen am. Chatter pierced the bars of my cell, the staccato voices emanating from the communal washroom as the Muslims purified their bodies before an audience with the one true God. Again, my thoughts turned repeatedly in my head, taking me back to that night, more than a decade ago, during my first years in Saudi......

........I was sure I was asleep but then I wasn't sure. Although I could not see anybody, there was a presence in the room. I wasn't really scared. The fact it could have been a burglar, mugger, murderer or worse never crossed my mind. Just that I was asleep or wasn't asleep and that somebody else was in the room. The ac humming in the corner suddenly died, and absolute silence reigned. I lay still, the single sheet covering my naked body, the silence imploding into my ears, I had to speak I felt commanded to do so,

"Who's there?" the whisper escaped my lips almost without sound.

"Your father". This was no ordinary voice and neither was it, my father, the voice reassured me, in a way my own father's voice could never have done

"My father's in England". I did not labour the point.

"That's right, I'm his father too; your father, his father, his father's father, you could say I'm everybody's father". the voice was obviously pleased

"God?" I had not wanted to use that word but the effect stunned me. Almost as if I had opened a door, there stood a man beside the bed. I could not see his face, no matter how hard I strained, I just could not see beyond the light covering the man's face. I relaxed, somehow aware that I had nothing to fear. It wasn't necessary to see the man's face, my heart soared within my chest, and I had no need for further identification. I studied what there was to see. Perfectly formed well-muscled

376

arms protruded on either side of a long white robe. These were not the arms of the meek and mild so often depicted in religious scriptures. The robe cascaded from impressive shoulders and covered the whole of the body, only the arms were visible and the outer perimeter of the face. The words did not emanate from the face it was as if the voice was the room and everything in the room spoke with the voice. The whole tone of the conversation changed from strangers to close family,

"My son".

"Yes, father,"

"I came to see you, to let you know".

"That I am here for you and all men".

"I know that father".

"But you had doubts?

"I ....

"You had doubts, so I came to relieve you of your indecision".

"But why me?"

"All men will receive me at least once during their lives, many will deny it, many may not receive me until the very end, but every man will, all my children will receive me, not all will believe it is I but everyone will be given the choice".

"The choice?"

"To decide between good and evil, right and wrong. Let no man say he did not have the choice. And now my son the choice is yours".

I did not speak. my mind was strangely emptying of all its earthly problems. A freshness filled my lungs and new blood surged through my veins. Now - and only now, was I alive. The feeling was completely overwhelming. Tears prickled my eyes; I reached out for my God,

"It is not yet your time," the voice continued,

"Enjoy your earthly years as they are nothing compared to your true existence. They are but the merest drop, in the deepest of oceans".

I heard the single drop as it hit the surface of a massive body of water, a musical note, resonating across the vastness of time rippling toward eternity.

"Father".

"Yes, my son".

"May I speak my mind? I wish to ask...".

"Proceed with your thoughts, I understand".

"The wars, famine, the leaders, who in your name persecute, torture and kill.....".

"You are not the first. I can answer your questions by saying this. Supposing your world was perfect, no wars, no famine or death and harmony amongst all men. I could have made the perfect world but then what? how would you distinguish between right and wrong if you had never known or experienced either? A perfect world would require no choice and there must be a choice if you are to continue. Just as you have the choice, so have other men. Always there are false interpretations; always there are those who would turn to evil. They exist as a lesson to you all. Men do not kill in my name; men kill for power over other men. For their own greed and selfish satisfaction, do not be fooled, as I am not. Observe each situation closely and remember my words".

"I will remember".

The huge arms swept down to the side of the bed and the figure rose upward with ease. Voices seemed to be calling from far away.

"I have to go now, there are others who need me," an arm swept down to my shoulder. The hand gripped with a tenderness and love I could not describe. The whole wall of my room raced away from my sight until it became a small spark what seemed like aeons away, the figure became the light, which had hidden the face from view, accelerating down the tunnel where the wall had once stood. Now the wall returned with a furious rushing thump. The ac chimed loudly back to life and a new voice reverberated around the room,

"Allaaaaaah Akbar!" God is great!

I sat bolt upright in sheer astonishment, the feeling of belonging to a greater existence was still with me but my life's problems were flooding back. The feeling mellowed and as the minutes passed, I thought it would disappear altogether but it did not. I was left with a feeling of energy. As if starting out on a new life. I no longer felt tired. I was refreshed, almost as if I had slept away the years of tiredness, toil and worry from my bones.

"That was some dream!" I thought, and as the last word rolled through my mind and a familiar voice punched through the walls and into my bedroom from the nearby minarets,

"AllaaaaaaaaaH oooo Akbar!" God is truly great!"

"He truly is!" I answered with tears" "He truly is!"

A long time had passed since that night so many years ago. I had discussed the event with Bryan Jackson RIP or BJ as we labelled him, a co-worker at the site but BJ had not taken it seriously and treated the event as a joke but then probably BJ had not received his own personal visit. I hoped he would one day and that he would experience the feeling I now carried with me. Whenever I helped a fellow man, whenever I made the right choice. The feeling blossomed within and I was glad of the experience. I remembered the night as if it were yesterday and I drew strength from the visit, dream or not.

Now it was Friday the Holy day. During the afternoon, around the city of Jeddah the Mullah's could be heard delivering their sermons. Usually concerning of the rights and wrongs of the external world outside of the Muslim faith. They would order their flock to seek forgiveness for their earthly sins. The prisoners received the same sermons, and some, whilst incarcerated, became almost fanatical in their beliefs. Pakistanis, Indians, Turks, Indonesians, Arabs, all the worlds" Muslims, brothers in their beliefs in God.

Why did religion cause so many wars? Here in the prison, they were attuned to each other's needs and bonded by their beliefs. Back on the streets they would be back at each other's throats in a matter of hours and all in the name of religion. God must surely despair of his squabbling children. My thoughts turned back to Pete. Pete would be visiting this afternoon and I would finally discover what my brother had achieved.

Three o'clock was the start of visiting hours in Ruwais prison. Visiting normally continued through to five o'clock although on some occasions had been extended to five thirty. I prayed that Pete would show and I hoped there would be no misunderstandings. Prisoners who signalled some intention of escape, through conversation with visitors or the purposeful slip of a malicious tongue, were clapped in leg irons until their day of release. I now thought about the leg irons, how they peeled the skin from the ankle bones causing bleeding and infection. I thought I had enough to endure; I wanted no part of such a garment. I thought about failure and the sweat ran from my temples to the stubbled shadow of my jaw. This was not the sweat caused by the noonday heat. This was the cold clammy liquid, of the fear of the unknown.

At midday, I paced up and down my cell. Midday brought lunchtime and a choice of fruit I had received from friends. A cold, half cooked fish complete with head and tail on a bed of brown rice, flecked with bits of camel meat on a rusty tin plate. One of the guards had pissed in it, of that I was sure, but I did not complain. My only complaint was that if the guard did not collect the uneaten fish soon, the heat would sour the flesh and the aroma of rotting fish and urine would stink up the cell for days. Here in the confines of these solid windowless walls, the heat had a way of encouraging the best of stinks, not least, in some of the dirtier prisoners who were known by their odour and not by name. They could be smelled approaching long before the need for sight arose. Even the guards gave them a wide berth, which was probably why they allowed themselves to reach such an aromatic condition in the first place.

The hands signalled one thirty on the face of the well-worn clock that hung above the cell block exit. I had finished my fruit, now I lay on the cot and listened to the sounds around me. Most noticeable was the constant humming of air conditioners from across the main yard at the guards" quarters. The drone of ac's never ceased unless a power cut intervened. A fly buzzed around my face; an occasional shout erupted from a nearby cell to be acknowledged by trailing laughter. Though what there was to laugh about in a Saudi prison, I had yet to discover. A guard clacked along the corridor in his high heeled boots. I knew the guard well, without seeing him I knew exactly how he looked, down to his high heeled boots that he wore to make himself appear taller than his four-foot six frame would allow. He was a mean little bastard and appeared to blame everybody else for his lack of height. He delighted in proving to the taller prisoners that height was not an advantage, especially when you were shackled to the floor and he was jumping on your head with his boots whilst trying to hold onto the plaster cast, neatly immobilising his broken arm. I knew he would not forget that in a hurry.

No screams were evident today. They did not beat up and torture the prisoners on a Friday; it was against their religion. The whole prison appeared to relax in this knowledge before the afternoon onslaught of visiting hours began. The calm before the verbal storm. Faint sounds of freedom also stole into my enclave, a car horn from some distant road, a police siren wailing to some emergency close by, probably at cross-roads, with traffic lights and probably between the fearless and the brave. The occasional pigeon fluttered onto my breather hole ledge in a search for shade from the blistering afternoon. The pigeons and doves cooed softly and I often wished I could fly to freedom with them. I had caught a dove once, trained it to visit my cell for scraps of food, but the guard with the boots had found the pet and served it to me for dinner the following day. I did not eat it and was beaten black and blue but I would not eat the bird that had brought a brief respite from the monotony. Finally, the guard gave up, after he had minced the bird meat and stirred it in with the rice. I expected such a tactic and did not eat meat for a few days, surviving on fruit and vegetables alone. Other than that poor fowl, the birds around the prison were free to fly away. Not so on the outside world, where it was the birds themselves who were trapped and imprisoned as pets, never to see the light of day. The regular schedule of jets rumbled overhead and I knew they would shortly fall to earth on the shimmering ribbon of asphalt to the north of the prison. All that remained was the silence but for the cot spring squeak as I twisted and turned in anguish, searching for the comfort of womb.

Echoing shouts jolted me from my doze. I rubbed the stiffness from my cramped limbs. Three o'clock was heralded by the cacophony of the first visitors, as they called to caged relatives or friends. Pete would soon be here. I rose from my cot and paced around the cell. I stood up and sat down again. Now I rubbed my head in my hands, everything was moving so slowly. I rested my head on folded arms, with my elbows pressed into my knees. I sat with my hands clasped in prayer as the hour jangled through my nerves, second by second, minute by minute. The prison echoed with noisy voices now, no particular words, just a wild frenzy of voices, all trying to pass messages of hope and small comfort

Three-thirty and there was still no sign of Pete. I sat down from the task of hopeless pacing. It was early, I told myself repeatedly. There was plenty of time for Pete to appear between now and five o'clock, which would signal the end of the visiting period. Now I wished I smoked, bit my nails, or did anything that would relieve the nerve twisting tension building up inside my guts. What could have happened? Had something gone wrong? Where was Pete, he was already over an hour late!

Three forty-five, and my every glance was mockingly returned by the old clock, daring me to turn away that the minutes lost would be added back on. Where was Pete? He should be here by now, where was, he? he had always been punctual on earlier visits, where was he today? what had gone wrong. Something had gone wrong, hadn't it? I thought, or he would have been here by now. Perhaps they had been following us and he was now dead?

Four o'clock laid me on my cot with a hopeless resignation, something had happened to Pete, it was all over. I covered my eyes with my hands. I had no wish to see the four walls of my new predicament now closing in around me. I prayed for the shout that would release me from the mental torment that was rooting and sprouting from the implications of Pete's delay.

Four thirty finally crawled onto the hands of the clock. I wanted to vomit, I stood up and I sat down. I breathed deeply, so that the sickness in my stomach would pass. Claustrophobia crept around my shoulders, shadowing my eyes before probing into my ears.

The cell grew smaller by the minute, solid concrete walls, eased inwards to crush the life from my body. Wild thoughts rushed through my mind. Pete was in another prison, caught drinking or fornicating or both. Pete was dead, drowned by the sea, killed at the traffic lights, murdered by the Sharief. Why wasn't he here, why wasn't Pete here?

At four forty-five, my thoughts were adrift in a sea of explanations. My hopes slowly drowning under that very same sea. The minutes dragged on and five o'clock turned me into a shell of spent emotion. Pete had not arrived, it was over. Cold feet, cold heart it mattered not. Without that shout, I was doomed to years of Saudi prison. It would add thirty years to my life, it would kill me. I was finished, who knows how many long and solitary years, without a friend, without a hope.......

"Khowaja!" at 5-35pm the voice of deliverance shattered my despair, defibrillating my heart to a new beat and smashing open the claustrophobia of my previous vacuuming thoughts,

"Here Pete, I'm here!!!" My voice was choked with relief. The guard escorted me to the visiting cell, where I thrust myself against the bars and there was Pete. He was covered head to foot in dried blood; a slimy coating that was caked to his body in smeared clots.

"What the hell happened to you?" I gasped.

"Camel!" grinned Pete relieved to manage the deadline.
"Didn't have enough time to go home and get cleaned up, the

383

car's a mess but nothing else has changed, everything stays the same".

Pete passed the duty guard the plastic bag; the guard checked the contents but without interest. An old pair of boots and a couple of items of clothing were not considered dangerous. I received the bag and grinned to Pete, studying him closer now as the tensions of the past hours drained away. I thought I caught an air of uncertainty about Pete's person, but I pushed it from my mind. Pete had just endured one of the most common accidents in Saudi, he had the right to look a little messed up and uncertain.

Pete was here, despite wrecking his car; despite of a coating of blood from head to foot, he was here, grinning through the bars. The prison guards began to clear the other visitors, side-stepping the Khowaja who would be allowed an extra minute or so. They knew how such an unfortunate accident could occur and probably had a near miss themselves. We exchanged nervous glances for a while until the yelling visitors bellowed their farewells and disappeared from the central chamber.

"Relax Khowaja, Make sure you read the washing instructions; you'll have to wash your own clothes from now on. I'm going on leave for a while".

"OK, Pete. I'll try, don't forget to come back. I don't want to starve to death in here".

The guards re-entered the chamber and signalled to Pete.

"I gotta go," grinned Pete, "I wouldn't want to go to a leaving party looking like this would I?"

I forced a smile as Pete released his hold of the bars and with a final wave of his middle finger, disappeared from the central chamber. Pete was allowed plenty of room with minimal searching; nobody needed bribes covered with camel shit and guts. I was escorted back to my own private enclave, where I relived my own encounter with a beast of the desert.

It was night, I saw it at the last second or so, I had ducked with milliseconds to spare as the great beast hurtled into and imploded the windscreen. Had I hesitated; a wooden overcoat would have been my next choice of garment. I did not own the strength to push the beast off me and climb out the beast wedged me onto the long front seat and leaked body fluids over me all night It was claustrophobic and dark. I knew someone would find me in the daylight and prayed it wasn't my blood dripping all over the front cockpit of the Plymouth Fury. When daylight came, I perceived my rescuers as they struggled to remove the carcass from the top of my vehicle, excited whooping shouts that could only mean Bedouins. I was wet, a warm dampness prevailed as the blood flowed from the dying, but still twitching beast, as it smothered my body with a stinking, brown slime. I felt no pain, I wasn't sure if I was hurt or not. My hopes were confirmed as the steaming carcass was pulled from above me and I climbed out of the ragged, peeled-back roof of the Fury, out into the sunshine and the exclamations of delight from my rescuers,

"Alhamdullilah!" they cried, "Thanks to God a miracle".
I hitched a ride on the back of the Bedouin truck. Even the Bedouins, who rarely had the facilities to bathe, would not allow me to sit in their vehicle. I had to ride on the flatbed with the goats. I offered them my sincere thanks and of course payment for their dead camel as they dropped me off at Sharief's garage, Jeddah Automobiles, where I begged for a pickup from some of the guys I knew. I had quickly covered the driver's seat with a plastic sheet so as not to ruin the upholstery and sped off home to get a hot shower and a change of clothes, I seem to remember I had a date that night.
"Alhamdullilah" I gave my thanks to God and gunned the car home.

Back in the cell, I removed the contents of the package and placed them on the cot. First my canvas pants, newly ironed and crisp to the feel. I read the washing instructions.

"Hang on to the bars of your cell at midnight". Heavy-duty woollen tube socks followed the pants, which in turn were followed by my soft, well-worn, leather biking boots. They were enclosed in a separate bag. Pete had obviously polished them and had not wanted the polish to stain the newly washed clothing. New laces had also been inserted into the brass eyelets. I placed them beside the pants with tender care and stuffed the red tube socks inside. I unfolded the bottom legs of the army-style canvas pants, the brass buckles to tie pockets and leg bottoms had been meticulously polished and sparkled like new. The buckles were tied around the boots to prevent rocks and debris from entering the pants as we rode through the desert. And on more than one occasion had saved me from the ravages of the scrub-brush spikes. I checked the thick webbing belt, locked in position around the waistband of the trousers by the heavy-duty straps. When satisfied I rolled up the pants and returned to the bag. I reached inside; touch alone predicted the discovery of a much-loved red shirt. I held it in my hands and pressed it to my face, breathing from its fibres the newly washed scent. My old companion that I had worn on many occasions, riding across the desert plains on my bike and even to the bottom of the red sea on various dives. I checked the label, small words of comfort inscribed within,

"Lyn sends her love and prayers and awaits your safe return".

The red shirt of freedom. I opened out the folds and smoothed the shirt flat. A new operation came to light. The original message had long since faded with the constant washing and passing of time. Now a new message was clear. Branded onto the front in small leather letters, across the chest the first new line the same as the old,

"I AM NOT A FOREIGNER". and below it, in place of the old line in the same neat leather lettering,

"I AM A KHOWAJA'

The change caused me to smile through my present, nervous disposition, I folded the shirt to conceal the message and lay it atop the pants. As I gazed fondly at my garments, the knock came,

"Aiwah!" I signalled; I would be taking my Friday evening shower. I left the cell and escorted by the guard with the plaster cast, we walked along the dingy corridors out into the yard.

"I'm sorry about your arm". I apologised.

"It was God's will," he replied, "I knew it was not your intention which is why I signed your release and dropped the charges of assault!"

There they go again, being nice to me, I held out my hand and he took it, I gave him the customary loose but warm handshake and he responded with the same enthusiasm.

"Good luck Khowaja" he wished me well.

"May your arm heal as straight as an arrow, alhamdulillah" I returned the tidings.

I undressed, threw my dirty clothes onto the floor and passed through into the warm steamy mist of the dancing spray; secretly hoping it would be for the last time.

I lay on the cot, the full weight of my body pressing the steel mesh into the flesh of my back. My eyes alone betrayed the stillness as I gazed to the ceiling in a silent, final prayer. I watched the fan in the corridor as it spun freely around, gently drafting the corridor and even a small whisper of a breeze, slipped into my cell. Round and round went the fan, like the blades of a helicopter. Round and round, I was getting dizzy, I was tired, round and round, round and round, now I was falling, falling through the sky in a slow controlled glide, falling through space down through the darkness, down into the abyss that welcomed me into its caress once more.

I rose suddenly, the mesh squealing at the instant loss of tension, I strode around the cage with the impatience of an expectant father. Again, I checked the Rolex, the only personal item allowed by the guards, just in case, they hoped, I needed to use it for a bribe. They wouldn't steal it, the law worked for them too and they didn't want to lose their right hand. Eleven forty-five glowed back into my eyes from the luminous dial, the second hand slowly pulsing around the black oyster's face. I sat down once more to make infinite, though unnecessary adjustments, to the straps of the boots. Bending and flexing the ankles to assure a comfortable, painless fit.

"Jesus!" I thought,

"This is worse than the rod!" my mind interrupted and corrected the wrong. "No way, stupid". I grinned, "No way at all".

I rose once more and moved to the bars in practice. Hugging the thick blackened rods of metal, so unlike the visiting cells where the bars were polished to a chrome-like sheen. High heeled footwear clacking against the terrazzo scraped the frayed nerve endings in my ears; the Rolex signalled eleven fifty-five, the approaching footsteps twisted my thinking inside out and gave rise to a sickness that was well below the depths of despair.

"Not now!" I almost cried out, "Please, not now! not today, not after all the effort, please pass me by, pass me by!"

The key kicked into the lock, the lock, and the door to my cell squealed open. A uniform entered and as my eyes adjusted to the new light, I recognised the guard who had so often assaulted me, one minute they were wishing you well, the next they were trying to fuck you over. Another man entered the cell carrying a small black bag. He in turn was followed by the officer who had carried out my interrogation to date, and as if that weren't enough, another guard brought up the rear. The officer voiced his approval of my fresh attire.

"You have a date tonight, Mr King?"

"Yeah!" I tried to remain calm, the poker player without a hand,

"I invited some girls over for a drink, they're due any minute, we're going dancing".

The bluff fell to unconvinced ears. The officer was not in the mood to play games, he smiled, laying my neatness to personal hygiene and began his brief introduction.

"You will be glad to know; we are giving up on the rod. However, we would like to continue with our questioning, allow me to introduce Doctor Faraz, Doctor...".

The doctor moved toward me, and tried to soothe me with some sort of reasoning,

"It's OK, Mr King. This will be easier for you, no pain, just a mild drug that will loosen your thoughts and hopefully your tongue. All we need is a little information, a small injection tonight will help you to relax, put you to sleep for a while, prepare you for tomorrow's questions. I can assure you it's quite harmless".

I wanted to glance at my watch; instinctively I knew it was the wrong thing to do,

"I already told you," I insisted forcefully, I recognised the terror lacing my voice. My outburst was waved to silence by the officer,

"Doctor Faraz will perform the injection; it will be a painless experience compared to our normal modes of questioning and merely serves to loosen the tongue. However, I must warn you, Mr King. If used over any length of time the effects can be quite devastating. So, I ask you, please speak up, I would hate to see such a brave man reduced to a chemically controlled vegetable".

The officer grinned with a trace of unfettered malice, nodding to the guard, who having moved to my rear, now grabbed my arms to restrain me, locking them behind my back where, unaccustomed muscles could not shrug them free. The Doctor snapped open his bag and produced a syringe, hermetically sealed in a plastic sandwich. The seal was broken and the syringe removed at least they had made some progress since my last injections. The Doctor stabbed the needle into a small capsule that he discarded when the contents had been sucked into the transparent, plastic barrel. Now the Doctor checked for air bubbles, lightly tapping the barrel with his fingernail, before squirting a small amount of the drug and any trapped air, from the barrel towards the ceiling.

CHAPTER 15   SAUDI STYLE   EXIT ONLY

"It's new, Mr King. This is my first time too," the doctor approached with intention. I began to struggle but the guard held on with a firm grip. Desperation twisted into brain and my eyes fixed unerringly on the needle's approach.

"Really, Mr King". the officer interrupted, "We've been through together these past few months and now, I find out your terrified of a needle. I wish I'd known earlier; we could have saved ourselves a lot of time and trouble". His inflection of disgust was not concealed.

"It's Friday," I spat, "You don't do this on a Friday!"

The officer looked at his watch, "It was Friday Khowaja, it was Friday but now it's Saturday, only just, but it's Saturday.

I almost cried out with desperation at the untimeliness, I struggled wildly, almost frantic with a singular purpose, to avoid the drugging needle. The Doctor was at my side now, about to raise the needle. As he grabbed my shirt at the shoulder, I caught sight of the doctor's watch, midnight precisely. I had to do something, I could not let them inject my arm, the drug would surely destroy any controlling senses. I reared my head back feigning terror and as the doctor moved in for the strike, I snapped my head forward with immense force, smashing into the bridge of the doctor's nose. The Doctor dropped the syringe and fell to his knees with a pitiful cry. The blood sprayed the floor as the Doctor wailed with pain, covering his nose with his hands and trying to stem the flow. I danced on the balls of my feet as the guard kept his grip from behind and the second guard fronted the officer and advanced with menace. I kicked and butted but within seconds the two uniformed men aided by the officer had wrestled me to the floor. I yelled like some wild beast at the unfairness of it all,

"Why me? Why me? Leave me alone. I haven't done anything, leave me alone you fuckin bastards"

Pete had loitered in the shadows beneath the dark foreboding guard tower, the luminous dial of his Rolex leaving midnight behind. He checked the two metal beasts that lurked beneath

390

the wall. The fear in his guts delaying his immediate action, second thoughts gnawing at his dwindling courage.

"I could turn around and leave here," He thought, "Get on the next plane and be long gone, there's no need for me to be doing this".

His conscience immediately responded,

"No, you couldn't you chicken shit bastard. How could you hold Kit in your arms and explain why you'd run away? How could you leave the Khowaja to these bastards? did he ever let you down? did he leave you for the sharks?"
The debt was remembered with some emotion and brought with it a swirl of fortitude. Pete glanced around once more to make sure he was alone and then turned his attention back to the metal tankers stranded beneath the wall. The doubts returned,

"What if it doesn't work, what if nothing Happens, what would Khowaja do if he were here?"

Realisation dawned, if the Khowaja were here, he wouldn't hesitate, he would never show fear in front of him, he would never hesitate with such an important task as he was doing now. He would look me in the eye, see the old familiar grin of persuasion and the job would be complete. Pete caressed the small box in his hands, the Khowaja's words would undoubtedly be ringing in his ears by now,

"Com'on Pussy, are you going to do it or what?"

Now Pete eyed the transmitter, Jade for jail, that's what Hawkeye had told him. My image goaded Pete's thoughts once more. Pete scanned the heavens as if in silent prayer, twinkling stars spattered the dark spacial canopy.

"Com'on Pete" He heard my whisper, "Why the hesitation? what the fuck are you waiting for? a medal?"

Pete thrust himself as deep as possible into the cover of the wall where the loose wind-blown sand had drifted; still grinning he spoke aloud,

"What fucking hesitation?" his arm snaked around the corner of the wall, once in position his thumb stabbed the activator and an eerie infrared glow winked from the small perspex dome. The infra-red beam scythed across space, across the metal skin of the tanker and transported its deadly message to the receiver. Pete awaited the response and surrendered to my absent encouragement.

I was now involved in a furious struggle with the officer and guards but I was losing the struggle. The past months spewed up inside, the cheating, the lying, the mental and physical abuse, it boiled within my guts and I lost control as the blood rage began to flow; they had me pinned down,

"What would Pete do if he were here now?" I thought.

The recognition flowed into my own mind too, without Pete, there was no one to impress. If Pete were here, Pete would have leaned against the wall and seen my plight and added the following words,

"Com'on Khowaja, there's only three of them, I could have ordered them an ambulance by now if you weren't so bloody slow!" and me, unwilling to lose face in front of Pete, would have exploded into action and knocked these bastards out cold. Face, that all-important Arab face, I realised that we too, were now locked in its grip.

The pressure inside my eardrums swelled with a straining fury. I was on the verge of hopeless surrender when my eardrums were pierced by a brain-stunning thunderclap, almost as if lightning had struck the bars of my cell, against which we now struggled. The floor danced beneath us and the walls visibly shook. Sand and plaster debris showered from the ceiling above. The bellowing roar continued, stilling the guards with an impotent terror.

"Earthquake!" yelled the officer but the sudden daylight glow was about to prove him wrong. The massive ball of flame still mushroomed skyward. Having reduced the tankers to shards of metal, it now tried to suck the desert dust and inner-city debris up its spiralling stem. Hot liquid fire now rained down on the prison compound. Shrapnel and twisted metal forms that had once resembled cars fell from the sky like rain. The prison wall,

392

or what remained of the wall, glowed in the eerie light of a spluttering oily blaze, the flames licking furiously in the billowing thermal updraft. The guards were running everywhere, assuming they were under attack.

Pete poked his head around the side of the wall; he shook it to clear his ears, still ringing with the force of the pressure wave.

"It worked Hawkeye," he voiced, though he could not yet hear it, the pain in his ears had numbed his senses. "Bloody hell, Hawkeye it worked".

"Hold him!" ordered the officer rushing from the cell to inspect the damage outside. Half the prison wall had disappeared and two concrete guard towers had slumped to the ground as if made of sand.

"You men!" screamed the officer, "Get to the wall, form a human chain, do not let anyone through!" it was all he could think of, as pools of burning oil flared and sputtered everywhere,

"Napalm," he must have thought, "We've been napalmed!"

He stared with disbelief, "Was this war? who were they fighting? Aliens, Jews, an attack by Iran?" Questions flooded his mind but they were questions for which he had no answers. Some of the more desperate prisoners were already seizing their chances, charging against the wall of guards, in the hope of breaking through to freedom. One wall of the communal block had collapsed and the prisoners raced into the yard yelling with fear, their faces distorted by the sputtering flickering light.

Pete threw himself into the driving seat. He wanted to reconsider but time would not allow it. Already the massive diesel engine had barked to life. The tubular framework surrounding his body shuddered as the great beast vibrated into action. Plumes of sooty black smoke erupted from the giant exhaust stack. He slammed the shifter into gear and slowly but surely the great machine began to move.

"Get off me, you dirty bastards!"

I screamed at the two guards, one perched on my chest and pinned my arms, whilst the other sat with my full weight pinning my legs to the floor. Somewhere in proximity the doctor now

393

searched for the syringe. He was wild with rage; his nose had been broken in the struggle and he was determined to stab the contents into my body by any point available. In fact, he had decided, he would stick the needle through my eye, such was the hatred now boiling in his veins.

I did not want to be here; I did not want the needle in my eye. I knew Pete was close by; the explosion could only be Pete. The doctor voiced his glee as he recovered the needle and headed towards the tangle of bodies struggling on the floor. I caught sight of the doctor's approach, thrashing my restricted limbs against my tormentors without success. Their joint strength and weight just too much for me to conquer and break free. I relaxed; it was useless. The doctor was already upon me, grabbing my hair whilst lifting the needle like a dagger, aiming to plunge it into what seemed like my eye. The blood from his injuries spattering my face. I closed my eyes in anticipation of the murderous thrust. Now the walls shook anew as the ground trembled beneath us. The whole room appeared to sway from side to side and a grinding, crushing overture began. The doctor must surely have plunged the needle home, was this some drug-induced hallucination? Or did I really open my eyes to see the massive teeth before me, chewing through the wall of my cell, crunching through the coral and cement with formidable force, revealing the night sky, peeping into the cell through a massive, jagged orifice?

Recognition flashed to my brain as Pete's form scythed through the dust and into the cell. I stared wide-eyed as the Doctor's arm accelerated toward my face, but the needle never reached its intended target. Pete's motocross iron grip clamped onto the doctor's wrist whilst his free hand broke open the doctor's fingers and snatched the syringe free,

"Just a minute, Doc!" snarled Pete, as he plunged the needle into the neck of the guard whose weight was crushing my chest, palming the plunger and voiding the contents into his jugular. The stunned guard, already weakened by shock, now experienced the first crawling, numbing effects as the drug took hold. He released his grip on me and fell face first into the dust as if pole axed. Pete did not release his grip on the doctor as I; now free of the weight turned my fury on the high heeled guard still gripping my feet, mercilessly battering him until I finally broke free.

"Your fucking late!" I snapped jumping to my feet.

"You seen the shit storm outside?" returned Pete without apology.

Suddenly we were together, fear disintegrating as the rivalry gripped us in its unyielding embrace.

"Yallaaaah!" screamed the doctor as he rose to his knees trying to mobilise the two unconscious guards. He was too late; we had already scrambled through the jagged orifice and down the broken remnants of wall. Once down to ground level we sprinted across the outer yard and clambered through the hole in the perimeter wall where seconds earlier, the massive caterpillar tracks had launched the excavator through and over, the felled concrete structure and sent it charging to the centre of the prison compound.

"Follow me!" hissed Pete as we ran through the darkness where the streetlights had mysteriously failed. Two hundred yards farther on Pete turned into a small, dark alley, took hold of a large green tarpaulin and dragged it clear of two motocross bikes, which leaned against a wall. Seconds later we were aboard, slamming down the kick-starters to fire the bikes to life. I revved up my engine,

"Take it easy!" yelled Pete; "We don't want to seize the bastards now!"

I returned a quick nod of acceptance and the two bikes lurched from the alley.

The bond had been revealed our spirits were now released. The wailing sirens shattered the normally tranquil evening. Fire trucks raced across town to the scene of devastation. Observers flung open louvered doors; Olympic size obstacles were leaped in a single bound in order that they were the first witnesses on the scene. Tower blocks around the prison were suddenly ablaze with lights, groups of sightseers hung over balconies, witnessing the carnage by the light of the flames. More cars exploded as petrol tanks could no longer tolerate the strain of massive thermal expansion. Women screamed, but not as loud as the men, whose cars now melted in the furnace of uninsured heat.

Two heads poked through the opening in the perimeter wall and caught sight of two bikes as they screamed from the alley and headed north; excited chatter swelled the already burdened airwaves.

"PRISONERS ESCAPING ON MOTORBICYCLES, HEADING NORTH
REPEAT: PRISONERS ESCAPING ON MOTORBICYCLES HEADING NORTH! ALL AVAILABLE VEHICLES BE ON LOOKOUT FOR
MOTORBICYCLES AND PREPARE TO INTERCEPT".

The white-painted houses around the prison were now bathed in an eerie amber glow, occasionally flashing to a brilliant white as yet another explosion ripped open the night,

"Jesus! did we do that?" I yelled as we throttled away.

"Hawkeye!" Pete shot back, "Hawkeye, a tanker and a few chemicals I asked him to load".

"Bloody hell, Pete. I thought the whole of Ruwais was going up in flames".

"Nah!" Pete hissed, "That was just a small diversion!"

"Red Shirt?"

"Red Shirt!" replied Pete as our two bikes accelerated from the centre of Jeddah's attention. We had no time to wear helmets. The speed wind caused tears to flood our eyes and stream along our temples into free flying hair. I began to laugh, I was free and my exuberance could no longer be contained, they would never recapture me now, I thought, not alive anyway, never in a million years. Pete's features remained set with a

396

determined silence. We may be out of the prison but we weren't out of the woods yet, not by a long way and he had volunteered for this mission, I had been given no choice.

Although the two bikes were now heading out of town, we ignored the direct route. Pete led me into the poorer sections of the underdeveloped township. Along this route, the roads were narrow, the street lighting poor and at best, a car could just about manage a wary crawl. Pete hoped, that by sliding through the humble back streets we could avoid major confrontation with any of the tribes. Walking was not one of the tribes" strong points and neither were they happy about venturing into the poorer areas of town to be heckled by fat old women, wanting to know when they would expel the filthy foreign influence. Within moments of the explosion, I had no doubts, that every police authority in Jeddah was summoned by the airwaves to be on the lookout for a pair of desperate criminals, as we would, by now, have now been labelled. Green stripes parked at least one vehicle beside every major crossroad in town. Every guy on a motorbike was arrested, his bike confiscated and the luckless rider thrown into a waiting van for identification purposes later.

Blue tribe was out in force. They had abandoned their usual supermarket patrols searching for the improperly dressed and were now racing northwards in the hope of cutting off, or at least sighting our fleeing bikes. A massive vehicular clamp was thrown around Jeddah in minutes and everyone on the streets that night agreed it would not be long before the murderers would be caught. For it could only have been murderers that would warrant such a finely meshed net. The blue strobing lights of the police cars sparkled around Jeddah and their sirens joined in the desperate choir. To the north of the city a new collection of beasts joined in the search. Their turbines had whined to life as soon as the column of flame had climbed into the night sky and now, the civil defence helicopters took to the skies. Huge twin rotor "Flying Bananas', as they were called, lifted off from the helipads to begin their search. The drones were taking to the skies to protect the hive from intruders. These impressive machines fanned out and spread across Jeddah, causing more than one near miss on the roads below as the drivers gazed skyward to identify the increasing swarm of U.F.O's.

Eventually we crossed a small intersection and inevitably, a warbling siren pierced the usual city symphony. Frantic shouts spewed from the motorcycle mounted traffic cop, who radioed his location after the chance sighting. The attention of every tribe was quickly diverted to the surrounding area. The two of us knew we had to shake off this hound or the shit really would really hit the fan. We powered away from the alerting whine and red flashing pursuit strobes. The police bike gave chase, hanging on to our path, where no car could match the serpentine pace. This bike cop knew how to ride, dodging back and forth between the traffic with one hand, whilst continually relaying his position through a microphone held in the other. Heads stabbed from the open windows of cars, shouts and yells filled the night as the three bikes twisted, skidded and turned amongst the tightly packed vehicles.

"Follow me!" yelled Pete, "We'll get rid of him".

Pete led the chase to the main road. The traffic sludge thickened at the constant red lights. Roads began to snarl up as the police took control of the signalling systems and slowed down the pace of the traffic to hinder our escape. Cars were nose to tail, no room to manoeuvre, which is just what Pete had expected. He mounted the pavement and headed straight for the pedestrian bridge. We braked suddenly, our engines revving wildly. Clutches were slipped once more and our bikes shot forward, front wheels lofting and pawing the air. We mounted the wooden steps of the pedestrian bridge, standing astride the foot pegs to effect immediate balance, the rear tires clawing up the many polished steps. We had no fear of colliding with pedestrians, the bridges were never used. The pedestrians preferred to stop the traffic flow and jam the intersections for miles, rather than walk up a few steps. We crested the staircase, sliding sideways as we turned to cross the main walkway span that was suspended by wires, hanging from the main arch of the

398

bridge. Police bikes were much heavier than motocross bikes. They had to carry radios, lights, and boxes of equipment, protective shields, sirens and all types of equipment necessary for the task of patrolling the highways. The cop should have known better but was probably fuelled by the excitement of the chase. Now his lack of experience was about to reveal itself as he headed straight for the steps. He did not loft the wheel nor did he slip the clutch. his front wheel slammed into the woodwork, rammed the front wheel rim flat and bent the front forks back into the exhaust pipes. The forward momentum flung the rear wheel skyward, launching the cop over the handlebars and into the higher steps, where his outstretched hand was slammed into the timber stair treads. Our bikes bumped down the steps at the far side of the bridge. The motorcycle cop hoisted himself to a seated position to check over his twisted bike, in doing so he caught sight of his mangled arm and broken fingers and realising the extent of his injuries, passed out cold. I hoped the guy was OK, our fight was not with him, and he was a biker like us and had performed admirably on such a limited machine. We darted into the side streets and headed for the northern sector alleyways, hoping for concealment in the labyrinths of poverty under a dark, Jeddah night.

A helicopter battered the air overhead, drawn into position by the transmissions of the luckless cop, who was now surrounded by unhelpful but curious, blood-thirsty citizens. The pilot saw the crowds in his floodlights, all fingers pointed in the same direction; it could only mean one thing. He turned his machine and headed off on our trail. The dark, unlit and unmade roads that had once been our friend became enemy. The dust trail, stirred up in our wake, guided the chopper to its source and ultimately our bikes. Spotlights scythed along the backroads and finally we were bathed in the sudden wash of electronic daylight. The chopper thundered overhead and the two of us strained as the brakes locked the wheels of our bikes. A sudden turn through ninety degrees led us into a warren of alleyways where the poor own no cars. Our bikes surged on, zigzagging through the maze of tightly packed, single-story dwellings. We strained our eyes with a single probing scan. Now we had to be alert for women and kids who inhabited these concrete and crinkly-tin buildings. Heart stalling moments did not slow our charge, as we hurtled through the darker shadowed areas, where a woman, clad in her dark "Abayah" or chador, could stray into our path unseen, only the light from her eyes to distinguish her from the blackness. Almost no chance of avoiding her, in the unlit streets of poverty's domain. Occasionally a dingy yellow lantern light spilled from a doorway or window guiding our trajectory through the concrete maze. We had no choice, but to speed, somebody may have already died. The least we could expect now was life in prison, or the sword of justice after Friday noon prayer, as it fell to relieve us of our desperate criminal heads.

The labyrinths disappeared, as suddenly as the finishing tape in a major race. A brief relief from the nerve-jangling darkness eased my straining eyes. We launched onto a newly constructed dual carriageway. Within seconds, the chopper screamed overhead once more. The spotlights lancing into our progress and the airwaves confirming the sighted hare. All over town the hounds turned once more. Blocking traffic lights, cross-roads and intersections as the net tightened further. The chopper shadowed our rear, he had us now and there would soon be no place to run. Now the chopper switched off his searchlights, they were no longer needed, the roadside city sodiums revealed its prey. I could feel their victorious eyes burning into my back and I knew what to expect if I was caught.

"Bob!" Pete shouted again, "Bob!"

I turned to Pete who pointed out the direction. I signalled my understanding and the two bikes slithered to a tire smoking stop. Almost at once the engines screamed once more, as we accelerated to a furious speed, bouncing over pavements and sidings, at ninety degrees to our previous path and out across the open desert. The chopper's blades strained with the pressure of the sudden directional change; searchlights flashed below to keep the bikes in view.

Again, a change of direction, the two bikes bumping over newly laid paving stones, their engines screaming as our clutches slipped and burned. Thrusting us forward, lofting the front wheels as the immense torque channelled through the rear wheel and threatening to turn the bikes over backwards. The chopper slued around in mid-flight and was quickly back on our tail. The roadside sodiums now mocked our flight once more. The chopper drew ever closer washing us in the down draft of its twin rotors, hoping for a mistake that would send one or the other of us crashing into the ground. Closer and closer the chopper descended; the pilot's abilities were rapidly consumed by the chase. A professional glance at his instruments saved his life. He heaved back on the cyclic stick; the belly of his aircraft missed the arched canopy of the underpass by inches but his landing wheels were smashed from their mountings. As the aircraft rattled into the steelwork, dust and debris were blasted into the sky and shocked the pilot back to his sense of safety. The chopper slued around the heavens before he finally achieved control and his damaged ship steadied and stabilised,

"Alhamdullilah!" I bet the pilot breathed, "Thanks to God!" though how he was going to land it I had no idea.

The chopper continued to follow the path of the road that was now buried deep below the underpass. The pilot knew our bikes would appear one and a half kilometres further along. The pilot wiped his brow and smiled,

"We have you now, Khowajas. We have you now!"

The chopper slowed as it reached the exit, pulling up sharply and hanging in the sky, its wheels dangling precariously on broken steel tendons. Our two bikes never showed the disappointed winged predator had lost its earthbound prey.

We had braked furiously in the underpass, sliding onto the shoulder with both wheels locked. We turned around and headed out the way we had come in, much to the chagrin of the drivers in the oncoming vehicles. Their blaring horns voicing disagreement with our near suicidal turn. We exited to shrieks of screaming rubber as dozens of tyres slid and screeched along the highway to stop the mass of metal cars above, still trying to avoid the chopper's undercarriage. Scrambling up the slip road embankment we crossed the concrete pavement and accelerated across the open desert once more. The chopper could be seen far behind our newly chosen path, harrying the exit of the underpass, stroking the surrounding desert with searchlights in the hope of retrieving its prey. Now we were between the main Madinah Road north and the Cornice, heading northwards as fast as our screaming engines would allow, occasionally slowing to a crawl to bounce over the obstacles of postponed infrastructure, the concrete and trenches of civilised man. The Cornice sparkled to our left, a ribbon of welcoming glow, almost haloing the star-spangled night. Madinah road lay to our right, alive with vehicles on a northbound charge, blue lights flashing and sirens wailing to warn of our approach.

Now the fairgrounds on the coastline slid by, brilliant ferris wheels of multi-coloured light. One for women and children only and one for the men. The Albilad Hotel fell by to our side to deliver us parallel with the newly constructed British Consulate. I smiled to myself as we powered on by. "If only they could see me now," I thought,

"I'm working on it," I voiced to myself, "I'm really working on it".

I knew in my mind, if I ever saw the consular officials again, they would be my last vision before whatever the Saudis were about to do to me.

Ahead now lay the globe, a huge steel and glass replica of the earth, exact in every detail. It was lit from the inside by a powerful bank of lights, a bright multicoloured ball against the dark night shroud.

We slowed, our engine notes calming. This spot was notorious for the police as they waited to pounce on unsuspecting camera wielding foreigners who, upon trying to photograph the magnificent globe would have their cameras confiscated for redistribution amongst friends and family of the arresting force.

We were now bouncing over the pavements of the minor road, on the far side of the globe, suddenly realising we were not alone. Police vehicles of every tribe swarmed around the intersection, blues, greens, and specials the works. Behind the police, some three kilometres away, sprawled the airport, the Haj Terminal glowing in the dark distant night. An alerting cry filled the night, we had been seen.

"Get to the road!" I yelled, "We'll never outrun them on the rough!"

The bikes accelerated from their sedate pace. The cops around the globe leapt into their vehicles as doors slammed, engines chimed to life and anonymous voices yelled encouragement as the various police tribes joined in the chase. The once calm, languid air was shredded by sirens of all intonation, flashing red and blue lights and the screeching of rubber against asphalt as the cars charged into the fray. Our bikes sailed up the sand embankment, left the ground and were volleyed some fifteen meters across space, before landing on the asphalt with a rubberised squeal as our tyres bit home. The speed wind had now dried all tears, pushed all our hair to the back of our heads and laid flat the hair on our unclothed arms. Ribbons of blue two-stroke mist traced and scented our path. The luminous globe fell rapidly behind. We were five kilometres from the creek. Ahead lay one more traffic roundabout, which would have to be crossed before we could join the creek road. Flashing lights were already plentiful in the distance as we hurtled towards our goal. Behind us a swarm of angry hornets who were determined to lose their stings. We approached the circle and all appeared lost, the East, West and North exit from the roundabout had been blocked by a line of police vehicles. We were entering from the Southern Road and would shortly be delivered into the trap. Pete glanced at me; his face tinged with uncertainty. I dispelled my uncertainty and signalled Pete to pull in close. Our two bikes were now travelling at more than seventy miles per hour and Pete moved to within inches of my position. I pointed us straight towards the roundabout without deviation. I prayed to God that nothing had changed since our last visit. The roundabout had no pavements yet; it was deemed too far North for immediate work. Currently, it was merely a ring of asphalt around a hollowed sandy bowl. The swarm was gaining now. I adjusted my velocity and Pete followed my lead. Pete had no idea of my intentions but having no alternatives himself, he stuck close like glue. The police at the roundabout stood ready to close the trap, cars nose to tail in horse-shoe formation with the swarm following up behind pushing the riders into the waiting net. Our bikes crackled as gears were changed, sixth down to fourth in two swift moves, increasing the revs and powering us dagger straight into the centre of the circle. I aimed carefully and the two bikes bucked as they left the road. Plunging across the embankment into the sandy bowl, falling into the depression with a dust-swirling thud, both bikes centrally bisecting the hollow, full throttle across fifty meters of hard-packed rubble. Sharply accelerating towards the far embankment, a gradual slope of sand. Just as we had always done, we hit the slope together, the front wheels thrown skyward, as we charged up the slope and exited the bowl skyward, at some eighty miles per hour and, at least three meters above the asphalt,

"EEEEyaaaaaaah!" my voice boomed out in fear as we flew over the barricade of vehicles, half expecting to crash and burn. A finely controlled trajectory, arcing across the far side of the circle, not as difficult as the loose sand banked wadis but at stake, much more. Yells of stunned amazement erupted from the police. Intermingled with cries of sheer appreciation from the other citizens halted at the roadblock. Our bikes hurtled through space, some forty or fifty meters. Backlit by the Cornice halo, before falling to earth with the merest hint of a squeal, some twenty meters beyond the blocking vehicles. Pete sucked in a large gulp of breath, this had been our finest jump, out of the jaws of certain death and away. If only we could survive I thought, what a tale we would have to tell. The police were in shock, some jumped into cars and fumbled with keys, unprepared for what they had just seen. Before any of the stationary cars had moved the chasing swarm charged into the traffic circle. Wheels locked tight were skidding and sliding, their bodywork sparking as it connected with the chrome work of the other cars. The cops leapt out of the way, as the swarm careered into the bowl spraying skyward a shower of dust. Mechanical crunching and tearing issued from the clouds of sand. Cars poured into one end of the dust cloud, but nothing vehicular emerged from the other side. Lights twinkled blue and red through the carnage-filled dust cloud. Brakes squealed in vain and only when the last car slithered sideways into the bowl did the dust begin to settle. A traffic cop's nightmare, or instant junkyard, not one vehicle exited the bowl under its own steam. Officers were screaming blue murder; drivers were climbing out of their overturned vehicles through broken windows and twisted metal doors. The halted citizens on the other approach roads were having the time of their lives,

"Just like American movies!" A voice yelled in Arabic.

"Excuse me, sir. What film is this? Where are the cameras?"

"Aish el Kalaam!" impossible and un-believable.

The police barricade was already accelerating onto the path of our bikes, grateful to be leaving the mayhem. In their wake, a tangle of metal that would take enormous amounts of paperwork to explain and they did not wish to participate in the aftermath. Every car in the bowl could now be seen, none had escaped maximum damage and all would have to be trailered back to the station yard, it had been an expensive evening.

We did not follow the creek road that would take us around the soft sucking tidelands. We left the road and would have no problem crossing the tidal sands of the creek. A new crow flight path would take us directly to the creek and hopefully the waiting Shark. Once more the dry dust trails were picked up in the chopper's beams and the pilot radioed position and direction. The following hounds accepted the call and the wailing sirens pierced the night once more, again they were closing in on the hares.

The bikes cackled along at full speed, shrieking engines now filled the surrounding voids and drew attention to our flight. Our presence betrayed to a wary ear. The green stripe hurtled along the north sector highway, charging up the creek road and finally relayed the position of the fleeing bikes. Now the warbling sirens converged, surrounding their victims, once more closing the gap. The hounds were rushing in for the kill. The supercharged green stripe reeled in the two fish. Now the loudspeaker crackled to life, a message of impending doom,

"KHOWAJAS! STOP! OR I WILL SHOOT".

"THERE IS NO ESCAPE!"

"KHOWAJAS! STOP IMMEDIATELY OR I WILL SHOOT!"

I glanced at Pete, my thoughts brimming around the edges of an over-burdened mind,

"Pete, my friend Pete, you tried to help me and now you're going pay the price".

Pete glanced back in anguish as if reading my thoughts. I watched the Shark as she flashed by on my right, the police green stripe now only meters from my rear,

"KHOWAJAS! STOP! THIS IS YOUR FINAL   WARNING!"

"KHOWAJAS STOP OR I SHOOT!"

"YOU ARE HEADING INTO ONCOMING POLICE VEHICLES, STOP OR I SHOOT!"

Ahead of us blazed a myriad of headlights, the gap snapping shut like a trap. I tried to think but could not, what was the point of all this? We were already dead, was Pete going to drive full speed, head on, into the oncoming traffic? Why didn't Pete tell me what to do?"

Pete turned to me and flashed a quick signal and our two bikes suddenly skidded sideways, changing direction and charged up the loading dock road. One police car managed to execute the sharp turn before the pursuing hordes arrived and continued the chase as a mass of vehicles swarmed for access to the pier to my rear. Pete turned to me flashed another hand signal and completely disorientated my perception of what I thought we were going to do,

"Had Pete gone mad?" I thought, "His brain muddled by the blazing sun which had blown him out of his tiny mind?"

Now it was Pete's turn to lead the chase with me knitted to his side and the green stripe harrying our rear. Seventy- eighty- ninety miles per hour, dust obliterating the ground as if we were sailing through a dusty cloud.

"KHOWAJAS STOP OR I SHOOT!"

Finally, the traffic cop wound down his window, thrust out an arm at the end of which was gripped a black revolver and loosed off a few wild shots at the bike tyres, crack! crack!

I felt the vibrations, as the front wheel of my bike mounted the loading dock timbers, charged up the ramp and launched me once more into the sky, out across the water where the only place left to hide, was in death. The green stripe braked, its wheels biting into the planked surface, which spun the car sideways, slammed it into the end of the pier and ripped off the supporting rail. The green stripe hurtled out over the creek rolling over sideways in a rapidly, spinning plunge.

The green stripe hit the surface of the creek first and a massive arc of spot-lit spray exploded from the surface of the creek and fanned skyward, to the underbelly of the over-flying helicopter. The body panels slapped the surface of the inky black creek, creating a mini tidal wave that now headed back to the shore. Our two bikes, revving in unison smashed into the surface of the water, a moment of flailing arms and legs ensued and then silence as the three vehicles and their drivers were lost to the depths below. Already creek-side vehicles were disgorging their excited passengers who ran to the end of the loading dock for a better view, headlights rippled across the surface above us. Steam and bubbles hissed from the chase hot engine compartment of the green stripe, moments later the car totally disappeared and then the driver bobbed to the surface. A wild ecstatic cheer erupted from his colleagues.

"Mabruk Ahmad, Mabruk!"

Other cars were converging around the scene and their occupants running to see the watery end of the chase. The creek side was awash with vehicles, flashing lights and human shadows running back and forth. They had followed the flashing green stripes all over Jeddah and were determined to inspect whatever carnage followed. Ahmad, the driver of the car turned submarine was hoisted from the water, the backslapping cured his slight cough and the cheers lifted his dampened spirits,

"Alhamdullilah!" he repeatedly announced,

"Alhamdullilah, thanks oh merciful Allah thanks!"

Cars were cheap in Jeddah, especially for police heroes who could expect a new vehicle instantly and possibly a commendation from the King himself. Excited gabble filled the air. The helicopter hovered overhead, keeping a wide-beamed search for Pete and myself, after two minutes the chopper's external speaker gabbled to life,

"MAFI KHOWAJAS! THEY ARE SURELY DEAD!"

"MORTE! THEY ARE DEAD!"

For more than ten minutes the chopper hovered over the point where we had entered the water. The driver of the car was safe, but it was obvious, to the cops, the Khowajas had gone to their deaths.

"THEY ARE DEAD, IT WAS GOD'S WILL, THEY RECEIVED ALLAH'S PUNISHMENT, THEY DID NOT SURVIVE, NO SURVIVORS, I REPEAT, NO SURVIVORS, THE KHOWAJAS ARE DEAD!"

Along the creek side the police nodded in agreement. More than one face showed a trace of remorse at the heroic attempt to find freedom.

"Dead?" inquired the sodden driver.

"Must be!" replied a colleague,

"No one could stay underwater for such a length of time without drowning, it was God's will my friend, you were doing your duty and God took his revenge on the sinners".

408

"Aiwah walahe! they could surely ride the motorbicycles though!"

"God knows that is surely true".

The surface of the creek returned to its normal placid guise, the ripples and spray from the down draft ceased as the helicopter pulled away from the creek and headed to a nearby landing site with a final announcement from its speaker,

"KHALLAS FINISHED THEY ARE SURELY DEAD!"

"Attention stand clear please we have no undercarriage'

The chopper moved over to waste ground where it slowly descended to earth. The crew jumped clear and ran as the pilot hovered low. The pilot moved to a safe distance and slowed the engines. When the rotors could carry the weight no more the chopper slewed over and the rotors smashed into the sand. When the rotors had smashed themselves to pieces, the pilot jumped clear and ran to the gathered throng of police, another helicopter arrived, the crew deplaned and hurried to the site where their friends had crashed and the Khowajas had perished. Excited Arabic filled the slightly remorseful atmosphere at the Khowajas unfortunate demise.

"Khowajas, they are dead drowned in the creek!"

The final announcement stilled them to reflection as if explaining all, and then the usual explanation crept in.

"Khallas they are gone it was God's will".

"They are dead, it was God's will".

"Khowajas!" morte Khowajas!"

The Foreigners are dead!

Chapter 16
NIGHTMARES

The impact had numbed my senses, disorientating all perception of earthly direction. My eyes strained through the blurring vision of darkness. I was desperate to keep Pete's body within view as we descended into the ink-like, liquid shadows, at the bottom of the creek. I had followed what I thought to be Pete's instructions but now, as my body was slowly dragged deeper, my reasoning became very unsure. Our bikes had smashed into the surface of the creek, their rear wheels spinning free and scything into the water. Slamming us forward over the top of our machines, over the handlebars, into the boiling spray and swallowed up by the creek beneath us. The impact had slung my body forward with such force that the wind had been pummelled from my lungs and I had barely been able to draw breath before the weight of the bike had pulled me down. Pete had signalled me to take a deep breath and hang on to my bike but I had managed only a desperate gasp before the waters had engulfed me. Now the bike see-sawed into the murky depths and I held on tight as instructed. At this moment in time, it was preferable to being shot dead by the Saudi authorities but that faint, almost irrelevant preference, was fading fast.

I pinched my nostrils with my free hand, forced air into my blocked nasal passages and equalised the pressure in my inner ears. The painful ringing faded with the pop of relief, clearing my mind in suitable time, for some rapidly advancing thoughts of desperation and panic. As I descended further, the pressure compressed the air in my lungs and the gasp of air at the surface was now failing to prevent their collapse. The chopper harried above us, no sound could be heard, but the searchlights provided us with distinguishable greys rather than total liquid blackness.

Pete's shadow was no more than two or three meters away but that did nothing, to console the fear now mounting in my brain. A brain whose thoughts now switched into survival mode and began to instruct all the supervisory senses in my body, to surface at once. My dread fear of death by drowning did nothing to help the panic. Although I had heard it was a pleasurable way to die, nobody who had ever died under water had ever returned to confirm this fact. Death held no foothold in my mind and I knew I could never surrender to a watery grave. I peered upward from a depth of twenty meters and once more equalised the pressure in my ears. The minute pearl of air in my lungs, now struggled to support a fading life form. As the bike continued its descent, the tightening fear continued. I had to decide; in a few seconds it would be too late. I would never be able to reach the surface alive. The drag against my wrist ceased, as the bike struck the bottom of the creek. The halt of an endless descent brought me no relief, for as the bike gouged into the bed of the creek, it disturbed a blossoming cloud of slurry and silt. A particled soup, which now, tried to wrap itself around me, clouding and dimming further, my near blind vision. Panic stabbed into my body; I could not hold out much longer. The desire to breathe was now a burning fire in my lungs, a fire that would be quickly extinguished if I opened my clamped mouth. In a few moments, the chopper would move on and a silent imploding blackness would rule the depths once more. I would then have to make the choice, death by drowning or death by bullet.

Pete had not reckoned with the silt and now that lack of knowledge must have confused and disorientated him. He rose above the silky particled cloud, eyes straining furiously in this deep, dark and silent world. The rods and cones of his eyes worked overtime, craving for sight and the small but sparkling vision of life. He rotated slowly; he knew it was here somewhere. It had to be here; surely the fishermen had not dragged it away and reduced his chances to a flat useless zero. Had he not been twenty-five meters below the surface, Pete would have cried out with relief, there it was, suspended by a plastic bubble of air. A mere speck of brilliant lime green in an otherwise dense and colourless void. Pete relinquished his hold of the bike and swam to the pin prick of light, where he found the equipment, he had deposited earlier in the day. He clutched the valve stem and gripped the armoured rubber pipe. Savouring the moment as he released the valve and the pipe stiffened, with the three thousand pounds of air pressure straining to escape. Pete traced the pipe to his mouthpiece and after what seemed like an eternity, grabbed the regulator between his teeth, purged the water from within and sucked in a mouthful of pure sweet air.

By this time, I was near to screaming point. Pete had disappeared and the silt had begun to fold around and smother me. I was all alone, wrapped in a silted shroud of eerie silence at the bottom of the creek. My brain demanded air and used every trick in the book to satiate that craving. Hallucinations, panic, sweet memories of my past, my family, my friends and now my girl. Lyn,

"Please don't die" she begged in my ears, almost as if she were beside me. My nostrils were now filled with water from the lack of air pressure within my lungs, the nasal passages between my eyes burned like fire and my oxygenation system began to fail. If I did not breathe soon, I knew it would be closed for good. The water penetrated every available orifice, fully intent on prising the life from within my human shell.

"My God!" I panicked, "I'm going to drown".

My head gyrated for some sort of bearing but it was useless, all I could see was the swirling silt, the black floating sludge particles dancing against a grey shroud. My own personal shroud which now awaited my immediate and certain demise. I searched for Pete, but no sign of my friend remained. What if Pete was already dead? hit by a bullet. Again, my mind tried to reason with me, I wanted to cough but that would signal the end. I wanted to scream but that was impossible. I wanted to cry out in desperation, but before I could do so I would have to break the surface and be shot. That was it then, better to be shot than endure this lingering hell much longer,

CHAPTER 16   SAUDI STYLE   NIGHTMARES

"Better to die by bullet like a man, than drowning in the depths to be eaten by the fish like a maggot. No burial, no cremation, no funeral, torn to pieces by the scavengers of the deep"

'Funeral!" the word rang in my waterlogged ears like a gong, the significance all inspiring.

"I'm going to die if I stay here," I thought, "I must get to the surface now, it must be now. I don't want to die. Sorry, Pete, must get to the surface now".

I wanted to gasp or choke or anything to relieve my clamped jaw but I knew the inrushing water would destroy the rapidly fading control of my oxygen starved senses. I had to go now; I had to push myself away from the bottom and I had to do it now. I would never reach the surface without first sucking in water, but my second breath would surely be pure sweet air, followed almost certainly by a bullet.

"At least it will be over quickly!" I thought as I slammed my feet into the silt, propelled myself upward with my legs and surged toward the surface. Progress did not continue as quickly as I would have wished, something was holding me down. I thought my clothing had caught on the bike. Something had gripped my leg and was hauling me back into the silt. A shark? my heart stopped, my eyes bulged and as I opened my mouth to scream a regulator was jammed between my teeth. I purged the valve and swallowed a mouthful of salty water. It choked into my throat and was about to cause convulsions when the pressurised air flooded my windpipe and fully inflated my lungs. I coughed out through the mouthpiece, pulsing a stream of bubbles through the open vents. Deep pure breaths followed, filling and stretching my burdened lungs. Pete held onto me as tightly as possible. With the amount of air, I was sucking in, I was blowing up like a balloon. I finally got hold of some control and slowed my gasps for air. Pete signalled me to hold on to the bike. I passed the regulator back to Pete who took a few sweet breaths before disappearing once more into the murky shadows. I followed closely behind Pete and was led to the green speck of chemically induced light. Pete fumbled with a second tank, within seconds the regulator was gripped between his teeth and operating smoothly, he passed a face mask to me, and I now suckled the regulator like a newborn at its mother's teat, gulping in the basic ingredients of life: sweet pure air.

I positioned my facemask and exhaled slowly through my nose, tilting back my head, so that the expanding air pushed out the water through the bottom of the mask's rubber seal. Suddenly I could see again or see as much as the inky blackness allowed. The world was no longer, a foreboding place of darkening greys and threatening shadows. The chopper still droned above us, allowing faint visibility at the bottom of the creek. Pete waited until I had settled to a more normal rate of breathing, but we both knew we would have to move soon. We did not want the exhaled bubbles to betray our presence. The escaping bubbles from the sunken vehicles would soon disappear and as the down draft from the helicopter moved on, our own bubbles would reveal our position to our pursuers. Pete signalled me to hold onto his arm. Pete circled the fishing line with his thumb and forefinger and inverted the chemical light that fudged into the darkness. He then led me away, following the minuscule nylon line that he hoped would lead us farther down the creek to Shark. The alternative plan had served us well. We had practised night diving on many occasions and were no strangers to the overpowering blackness as the chopper, whose crew now presumed we were dead, changed direction and slowly moved away.

Tracing the guideline to Shark was a cinch, compared to some of our earlier night dives, where the curious beasts of the deep had nudged and nipped our trembling limbs. I raised my head and peered up to the surface, all was black but for the slight silvering of ripples atop the moon-washed creek. I grinned instinctively, a reaction of pure relief. The men above would now assume us dead and we were totally invisible to their desperate searching eyes. Pete turned to face me and I noticed the grin at the edges of the exhaust vents, I had no choice but to grin back, despite the mounting fears that now ravaged my confidence. If he could still grin, I thought, so could I. One question pierced my burdened mind,

"What the fuck is he grinning AT?"

"NO SURVIVORS, THEY ARE SURELY DEAD!"
The final announcement crackled, over the loudspeaker. Help was on its way. The crane would soon be here to winch the car from the creek. Divers were on their way; a police launch was heading in from the sea to help with the recovery of vehicles and bodies. The launch had divers aboard and a massive underwater spotlighting system sealed into its hull. The creek side was crowded with chattering police, all reliving their night of adventure - the chases, the crashes, the police car in the creek and of course the two dead criminals.

Within fifteen minutes the creek was bustling with trucks and recovery equipment. Almost every policeman within a hundred-mile radius was on duty by the creek tonight. All of them were chatting and applauding their hero officers, making as much of the event as their otherwise boring existence would allow. They were so engrossed in congratulating each other, that nobody heard the slight wash of ripples as Pete's head broke the surface of the creek. He signalled all clear and I silently surfaced behind him.

"Drop the tank but keep hold of the regulator," whispered Pete, "They'll make too much noise if we try to climb in with them".

The air tanks slipped silently from our backs and see-sawed into the depths from where they had been recovered earlier. Pete checked the immediate surroundings for any sign of life that would raise alarm, there was none. He hauled himself aboard Shark and slipped silently below her deck. I shadowed him into the cabin the only sound we made, was the sudden shower of water from our clothing onto the bone-dry deck. Pete produced two large towels and we quickly stripped and dried, before pulling on a set of clean dry garments, almost identical to the wet piles of sodden material that lay on deck.

"Sorry I couldn't find any boots!" hissed Pete.

"Don't let it worry you, Pete. My feet have been getting used to a bit of rough treatment lately".

We tried to dry our boots with the towels and when we had done all we could to relieve the boots of the moisture, we pulled them back on over a thick pair of warm, dry, tube socks. Pete produced a thermos of hot coffee, opened a cold box and pulled out a large packet of prawn salad sandwiches.

"You made sandwiches?" I hissed in disbelief.

"Yeah, I don't like travelling by boat on an empty stomach". Already the refusal to show any fear began to wedge itself between us.

After our narrow escape, we feasted heartily. I sipped my coffee, my third mug. Now, at last, I was free. I had a belly full of prawn sarnies and I felt better than I had for months and now I threw a chastising comment to Pete,

"No dessert?" I mouthed in disgust.

Pete tossed me a small bar of chocolate from the cooler,

"Especially for you!" Pete whispered.

I studied the bar in the moonlight,

"Animal bar?" I announced as if offended.

"You said it!" Pete grinned.

I munched the chocolate between sips of hot coffee. Compared to what I had just left behind, this far from Utopian existence was almost luxurious. We relaxed as much as could be expected in the Spartan comforts of the hold, moving around as smoothly as possible without the use of light and trying to make no sound. A discussion decided we would have to move before morning, darkness alone would now have to conceal our chosen way. Pete moved to the cockpit and checked the gauges; everything was as we had left it earlier, full fuel tanks, full charge in the battery and Shark, fully prepared for whatever the future would hold.

CHAPTER 16   SAUDI STYLE   NIGHTMARES

We were hoping the police would leave the area but as time passed, it became obvious. The police were going nowhere without two bodies to show to the world. The Saudi law sat around on blankets, drinking hot, sweet tea and coffees between torrid discussions of self-awarded bravery. Around their jovial gathering stood the public, wanting to know what was going on and receiving a greatly exaggerated response. More people appeared as the crowd grew and as the crowd grew it seemed that more people were attracted to its growth. Pete and I slid around Shark like the ghosts of snakes, until all that remained was time. Two thirty was the deadline and police or no police, that was the time when we would have to leave.

The police launch cruised up the creek at a leisurely pace, dead bodies were not in the habit, of escaping custody. She was in no hurry and even took the time to warble her siren as she broadsided the creek, reversed her engines and slowed her forward motion to a halt. As the anchor fell into the creek with a splash, a sudden blaze of light flooded from her hull, the creek below her belly glowed green as her engines turned smoothly to generate the power for the underwater probes. A creek-side winch had been secured to the rear axle of the car-turned-submarine and now, as the car was hoisted clear of the water it swung like a giant pendulum. The hoist did not have the height to lift the car clear of the creek wall. It would have to be lowered once more and hooked up sideways, before leaving its liquid tomb, much to the amusement of the surrounding crowd.

The police divers on the launch were quickly dispatched and within minutes a new commotion filled the air. Already the police were jumping to their feet from their relaxed pose and began shouting and running along the creekside. One of the divers headed to the side of the creek. He swam with one hand, he had to - clenched in his other fist was a brilliant speck of luminescent green, signalling the end of the Khowajas" supposed demise and the immediate start of an intensified search. Pete knew they would be able to follow the tell-tale tracks through the silt and he knew that those tracks, would eventually lead to Shark.

417

"Bob!" hissed Pete, "We got to get moving now!"

"What happened?"

"We've just been resurrected by the divers. They just found the crystal light and it won't be long before they find the tanks and then they'll realise we ain't at the bottom of the creek".

"Shit!" I spat, as I lifted my eyes above the sidewall of Shark's deck and peered toward the commotion. Through the constantly bobbing pleasure craft I saw a gaggle of police surrounding the sparkling speck of green, it was obvious what was on their minds.

"What time is it?" I Breathed.

"Two o'clock, why?"

"Just checking my watch before the start of the race". I sighed, "Get the motors fired up as soon as I give the signal, I'll get the lines".

Pete crouched behind the control panel and flicked the ignition key over to pre-heat the plugs. Pete left the heater on longer than necessary to assure himself of an immediate start. I slithered across the deck and joined him.

"All set?" hissed Pete.

"Let her rip!" I replied in the same breathy tone.

Shark's starter motor whined across the creek but her engines did not fire. Pete tried again, and then again. The whine was picked up by the police, who having realised the Khowajas were still alive somewhere, were suddenly alerted to the distant whirring of a starter motor. As the police turned to inspect the source of the noise, the engines fired-up and forever destroyed any doubt in anyone's mind. The Khowajas were leaving. Pete nudged the throttles forward and the mighty Merlin engines roared to life. Now the police launch targeted every available top-deck spotlight in the direction of Shark, suddenly revealing her in a blanket of daylight, her red eye, gleaming defiantly in their searing beams.

"GO! GO! GO!" I yelled.

Pete gave her half throttle, although her engines would still be warm from her earlier run, he did not want to overload her now.

418

Shark responded. She bucked forward some two or three meters and suddenly jerked to a stop. Her engines roared in vain and two spuming jets of white-water foam, climbed into the sky from her stern. Shark, for no immediate reason, was going nowhere.

"The keeper's jammed in the pier!" I hissed as the sabres of light lanced across the creek to plunge white hot holes into Shark's body. An excited shout echoed around the creek side,

"Khowajas, shuff hada, Khowajas!"

Shark's engines roared in vain and the turbid waters frothed at her stern. Her jets pulsed the silt from the bottom, mixing it with the phosphorescence of the boiling stern soup. An eager shot rang out, somebody was determined we would not escape again. Pete quickly ducked below the level of the top deck as my shout reached him,

"It's the rear keeper, Pete! It's caught in the pier! I'll go and free it! Get ready to make a dash for it!"

I jumped upward onto the deck and was fired upon by a scatter of small arms. The bullets scythed overhead. The police launch revved up her engines in preparation for turning and the unusual smell, of hot diesel and spent black powder invaded the creek. We were pinned down, any attempt to rise above deck level brought with it the indiscriminate pistol fire of the creek side police and now the launch was moving into position to cut off any escape. I tried and tried again to reach the stern; it was hopeless. I hammered my fists against the deck and cursed in my hopeless frustration.

"I can't reach the fucking keeper, Pete. I can't get the bastard free, every time I try to stand up, they're fucking shooting at me. Pete, I can't reach the keeper, do something to distract them quick!"

Pete dropped below deck and returned within seconds, in his hands a roll of greased paper and cloth. Unrolling the cloth revealed a pristine AK-47 assault rifle. A standard issue to most bearers of arms legal or otherwise, in the Middle East. A cheap but reliable product from the Eastern Bloc and standard equipment - to the world of terrorism.

419

CHAPTER 16   SAUDI STYLE   NIGHTMARES

"Jesus! Pete, do we have to use it now?"

Pete fumbled the banana magazine into the belly slot and drove it home with the edge of his fist,

"You remember what Hangar said?" Pete retorted, "Don't be afraid, if somebody is shooting at you, you HAVE! to shoot back, it's the only way to survive.

"Jesus, I knew there was more to that guy than he ever let on".

Pete held the rifle up to my face and made urgent instructions,

"Safety catch, magazine lock, auto feed, single shot, got it?"

"Got it!" I replied, the macro lesson was over.

We looked each other in the eye. We realised we had no choice, we were being fired upon and to escape we would have to return that fire but in doing so, would guarantee our death if we were caught. I managed to voice my acceptance of the situation,

"We have no choice Pete, God only knows what they'll do to us now if they catch us, we ain't got no choice".

"Are we going to discuss this all night?" hissed Pete, "Or do you want me to distract those bastards?" acknowledging his acceptance of the situation and confirming his stand beside me.

"Ready when you are, Pete!" I snarled, remembering the ritual duel, as we jumped above deck into a hail of bullets.

Pete ran forward of the pilot deck crouching as low as possible, I ran in the opposite direction but was soon pinned down by the constant though inaccurate pistol fire from the police.

"Pete!" I could not move any further; to do so would have been suicide. My call to Pete was a desperate plea for urgent action. Pete heard the cry as he was pinned against the decking which now left him with but one choice. Pete turned to me as I lay in the stern,

"We're going to die! Pete!!!!" my voice was laced with absolute desperation, leaving Pete in no doubt about what we had to do. Pete rolled from his side onto his belly he had

420

endured enough. He pressed the warm stock of the assault rifle to his ribs and squeezed the trigger. Suddenly, his whole body shook with the thumping vibrations as the bullets spat from the muzzle of his weapon, the end of the gun barrel flashed alive with brilliant spearheads of white-hot flame.

The effect was immediate. Where there had once been a mass of armed police, not a single figure remained. Every single body had launched itself behind solid objects and the whole Saudi police force vanished in an instant. The impressive power lifted Pete's spirits; he was no longer the hunted, helpless prey. He could now bite and he would use those teeth to good measure. Hangar had been right; it was the only way to survive, we didn't want to kill anybody we just wanted to escape. Pete turned his attention to the patrol boat, raking the spotlights with fire and reducing them to shards of smoking, tinkling glass. The patrol launch's shadows devoured her crew and now lay silent, Pete crawled back to the pilot deck where he jumped below the sidewalls and turned his attention to the spotlights on the shore. The flames spurted from his weapon once more. Mini explosions erupted on the creek side as the bullets smashed home, raking the cars, pulverising their metal bodywork and shattering every windscreen in sight. Tinkling glass chips peppered the police and warned them against hasty action.

"Get down! get down! they've got a gun!" the new Arabic command echoed along the creek side, as the civilians continued their flight to safety and the police reloaded their weapons.

I perched precariously on the stern tugging at the keeper line. Shots rang out, the shock of Pete's return fire was wearing thin and the police, having reloaded their weapons, were keeping their heads down but were now finding the courage to fire back. The shots fizzed around my ears until Pete slammed home another magazine and emptied it in the direction of fire. A car exploded into flaming debris, lighting up the line of greens, blues and specials now parked alongside the creek. Pete was hypnotised by his own power. He turned to me and, as more

421

shots rang out, he gasped with horror as I was shot in the stomach, buckled over and fell from the stern with an almighty splash.

Shark surged forward, now free of her mooring lines and powered across the creek towards the far bank. Pete had no choice; he lunged to the controls, grabbed hold of the wheel and at the last moment turned Shark towards the sea, avoiding a collision with the bank by a hair's breadth. The patrol launch was already moving into position to cut off his escape. He had to go now, there was no way he could return for me, he thought I was dead anyway and too far behind to return and pick up. Shark blasted forward as Pete increased her speed, slamming down the throttles to maximum torque. He wedged the wheel with his knee and emptied the second magazine towards the launch, screaming my name in a hopeless wail of mournful grief.

"Khowaja, your stupid son of a bitch! all this way for nothing, you should have stayed in jail; you should have stayed in jail! Your stupid arsehole! You should have stayed in Jail".

Shark careered along on her belly; the whole of the creek erupted to life. Gunshots exploded from every available weapon, all pointing in the direction of the fleeing black missile. Shark bucked and tossed, rolled sideways onto her belly and as Pete threw the wheel over, she rammed sideways into the launch, rebounded deep into the creek and soared into the sky completely out of control. She hit the water with an almighty smash as her jets sucked an overload for full thrust and catapulted her down the waterway. Police cars wailed sirens and the pursuing strobe lights danced down the creek road towards the sea. Some police gave chase on foot firing pistols at Shark, their cars were now ablaze, or in the eager hands of others. The patrol boat lumbered compared to the nimble shark. She was too big a craft for tight manoeuvres and now all her efforts were concentrated on making the turn that would point her back out to sea the way she had arrived. A helicopter rose upward from a cloud of swirling sand and the air was electrified with the urgency of the chase. The creek glowed green with the

422

phosphorescence of turbid propellered waters, continually stroked by chasing searchlights. The glow from the burning vehicles tinted the wash with orange and the smell of diesel intermingled with the smell of burning rubber and gunpowder. Pete steadied his flight, locked the wheel and grabbed fresh magazines from the storage box. The sights and smells exciting his adrenalined wrath. Never had he experienced such an overpowering feeling of hatred, increased in savagery by the loss of his closest friend, who now lay dead and buried at the bottom of the creek. Hangar had taught him how to tape the magazines together for easy turnaround. Pete threw the empty clip over the side and rammed a double home. He had hoped the need would never arise but now it had done so with a vengeance and the death of his friend would cost them dear. The chopper was above him. Pete careered shark from side to side dodging the metallic rain from the side door of the aircraft above, Shark's stern spumed furiously as she thundered along the creek.

Within minutes Pete turned toward the coast guard shack and the Shark screamed right on by. Pete raised his hand in salute as he passed. The old guard, already accustomed and primed for the high-speed pass returned his salute with a smile, realising his mistake too late. The Khowaja boat hurtled by him, the spray drenching his uniform as Shark flipped over to her opposite sidewall and skimmed away from the coast guard to the far side of the creek. Above the Khowaja boat a police helicopter, searchlights slashing the black boat and crossing the water in the path of their prey. Guns and pistols blazed from above, thunderous roaring replied as the Khowaja returned fire. The coast guard's mouth dropped open as the spectacle roared down the creek. His mouth snapped closed like a bear trap, as the patrol launch hurtled past, his arm flung to his forehead in salute as the spray drenched him for the second time and the thoughts danced for attention in his mind. He had heard the escape over his radio; he had no idea we would be heading in his direction. The last message he had received was that it was all over. The Khowajas had been killed in their attempt to escape, he had not realised it had been his Khowajas, his personable friends,

"They said they would not disturb anybody!"

"They said this is the holy day, a day of peace!"

"I should have known better, those camel dung Khowajas, more trouble than four wives heavy with child. Khowajas! Huh! I should have known!" The coast guard returned to his shack, picked up the half bottle of Jonnie Walker's whisky and stared into the golden liquid swilling the bottle sides, and then he remembered the Khowaja, skiing on his belly in the dead of night, followed by helicopters and patrol boats,

"Nah," he hissed, it can't have been, it must have been ". he paused for silent reflection.

"They warned me about this!" he thought and flung the half-full bottle, out through the open doorway into the creek

Pete's knee gripped the steering wheel locking his course down the centre of the creek, his whole body shook as he raised the rifle and blasted his pursuers in the sky. The noise almost deafened him but above the mayhem, he was sure he heard a voice call his name; Pete halted his firing to check his direction,

"Yes!" he thought, "There it was again",

"Pete! I screamed at him, for God's sake hold your fire until I get into the boat!"

Pete refused to believe his eyes, there at the stern was the head that once belonged to me, poking above the aft wall and being pushed onto Shark by the rest of my body. I clambered over the stern and fell exhausted into the cockpit of Shark, a sodden crumpled mass of flesh and torn clothing. A surge of relief washed over me as I crawled in Pete's direction and pulled myself up alongside him,

"What the hell happened to you?"

"I forgot my fuckin skis!", I did not want to show my sickening fear in front of him I took the rifle from Pete's grip,

"Steer the boat Pete, I got a few scores to settle, it's my turn now!"

424

CHAPTER 16   SAUDI STYLE   NIGHTMARES

Pete steered Shark, stunned by the evening's events, completely oblivious to the fire raining down from above. I yanked out the empty clips and bashed two more in place, yanking back the auto feed and staring skyward at the pursuing chopper before yelling my command,

"Let the bastard get close, Pete! Drop the engine speed and make him overshoot before you open her up again!"

Pete did as I requested. The chopper overshot Shark and thundered overhead. Pete palmed the throttles forward and gave chase, now the chopper had become the prey. I wedged my legs into the side rails as the Shark accelerated, absolute determination must have etched my features as I lifted the hot barrelled assault rifle and opened fire into the chopper's belly. Seconds later I yanked out the magazine reversed it and slammed the fresh clip back into the breach before continuing the merciless metallic spray. Sparks riddled the underbelly of the chopper as the bullets smashed home. Suddenly a trail of smoke broiled in her wake, flooding from the aluminium engine cowlings now riddled with torn holes, sparks and brief bursts of flame. She stumbled and twisted in flight as the hot steel poured into her shell. Dipping and twisting from her crow flight path as the Shark accelerated beneath her belly. Now she was falling from the sky and already the crew were jumping from her doors some thirty meters into the creek below. The chopper burst into flames, drifting sideways towards the creek bank, where she smashed into the swaying palms and exploded into a thousand flaming fragments, lighting up the sky for miles and colouring the creek with an orange blood tint. The launch ignored the chopper's crew and continued her pursuit. They would have to swim to the shore or be picked up later; the patrol boat's skipper had more urgent things on his mind.

I wobbled back to the cockpit where I jumped in beside Pete,

"That's it Pete, whatever happens now, if they catch us, we're dead men and no amount of pleading from anyone is going to make much difference, from now on it's us or them!"

Pete voiced no reply, merely nodding his head in acceptance of the fact, a sad recognition of hopelessness washing his features.

Pete approached the sea estuary with caution. He cut the corner of the outlet as tight as he dared and steered Shark over the tip of the coral breakwater. He headed south, pushing the throttles to maximum; the power unleashed lifted Shark from the water and bounced her across the wave crests with a tremendous force. Straight out to sea would have served no purpose the pursuing launch would have radioed positions and help would be on the way. We had to lose our pursuers amongst the night reefs.

The police launch turned a tighter circle hoping to cut the lead of the escaping Khowajas. Police cars were screeching to a halt on the jetty, a few shots were fired but the Shark was soon out of range and all that was left, was to cheer on their fellow pursuers as they sped by on the launch. I eyed them carefully. I pointed out the reef line to Pete, the patrol boat was taking an awful risk as her pilot cut deep inside our phosphorescent wake.

"If he makes it, he's going to be on top of us in no time!" I yelled above the roar of the thundering engines.

It was a fact; although the reef line was clearly marked it had no set depth. Many a deep-hulled cruiser had floated over the razor-edged reef without so much as a scratch, followed by a rubber dingy a few meters to one side that had been torn to shreds on the coral heads. We followed the progress of the police launch as it thundered alongside to head us off.

"Shit! he made it!" I spat as I ducked to avoid the bullets now smacking into Shark and whining over my head.

"Look!" yelled Pete with relief, the patrol launch was slowing, her thin-skinned hull descending into the sea. The reef had sliced open her guts and now she wallowed on her belly as the water flooded her cabins below decks.

The distance yawned open between us until the luckless craft was a mere speck of desperate searchlights against the dark backdrop of horizonless sea and sky. When she finally disappeared, Pete slowed the Shark, allowing her engines to spin as quietly as possible, keeping the noise and the phosphorescent wake to an absolute minimum. As Shark burbled along on the outer line of the reef, Pete whispered to me,

"What happened with the keeper line?"

I answered in the same whispered tones,

"I never touched the keeper, Pete. As I approached the stern it suddenly broke free of obstruction and the force of Shark yanking on the line whipped the loop into my belly. It whacked me with such force I was winded but managed to grab hold of the loop as I fell over the stern headfirst. It was bloody hard work hauling myself up that line to Shark, even more so when you were blazing away at the boat with the rifle and throwing Shark from one side of the creek to the other, hitting every obstacle in sight!"

"I thought you were a gonner!" Pete interrupted.

"So, did I, But I was determined to get back aboard this boat and punch you in the mouth!"

"Punch ME in the mouth?" he was surprised.

"Punch you in the mouth," I repeated myself, "I'm struggling for air, hanging on for dear life, sprayed by the downdraft from the helicopter and all I can hear is your voice yelling

"You're an arsehole, Bob!"'

Pete remembered and grinned, thumping me on the shoulder,

"Sorry, mate. I thought you'd become fish food and was upset that you'd ruined all our plans for getting out of here".

"Where are we going now, Pete?"

"Take the wheel!" he commanded as he dropped below into the hold and returned seconds later with a small plastic bag that he handed to me.

"This is for you, Bob. Hawkeye and I with a good deal of help from Hangar planned a little going away party, you know, a Khowaja always leaves with a bang and the rest of it. Hawkeye sends his best regards and apologises for not being here in person. He felt he owed you one for helping him out when he needed it".

I tore open the small plastic bag, inside was a small red box, "What the hell is this for?" I asked incredulously.

"Remember Sharief?" I nodded, "Remember all the money he cheated us out of?" I nodded again,

"Remember how he detained you, framed you, had you locked away as if it were sport?"

I remembered and suddenly the bile of hatred rose in my throat, I hadn't had time to think about the Sharief but now my thoughts turned to the subject and my thirst for revenge dried my mouth as the blood rage swelled within my body

"Well, Bob. We're going to pay a call on Sharief and this little box is going to take back all that we're owed, with interest and damages".

Pete's explanation was interrupted as a helicopter reached out behind us, walking on light stilts across the sea for a distance, before returning to search the shoreline. The noise from its blades barely audible above Shark's burbling engines. Within seconds another sound assailed our ears,

"You hear it?" hissed Pete.

"Hovercraft!" I replied with concern. "Keep your bloody eyes open!"

Shark headed south at a smooth accelerating pace as the two of us urgently scanned the forward expanse of sea.

For the first time during the night, we noted Shark's condition. Tattered, shattered fibreglass abounded, where the bullets had ripped into her upper deck as she had lain trussed up at the creek. Her engines sang sweet music on the warm and heavy sea air. Her black paintwork, now suddenly perfect, concealed her against the many shoreline watchers, no lights shone from her body and even the control panel lights had been screened from surrounding view. Pete throttled back as we rounded the headland and were caught in the glow of a million explosion

428

proof arc lamps, heralding the steelwork of the monstrous metal refinery. A massive swollen tanker lay at berth well down in the water, obviously full.

"It's one of ours!" I hissed.

"Good, it'll be a bonus!" returned Pete in the same hissing whisper, which did nothing to hide the malice of his intonation. Shark burbled along slowly, her engines still idling smoothly. More choppers appeared to the South. They had not reckoned with Pete slowing the speed to avoid detection and were now strobing the seascape at the south creek. Another chopper swung out over the refinery, its pattering sound reaching us to animate the sighting.

"What's wrong with you?" I inquired of Pete's sullen features.

"I was just thinking". Pete forced a grin.

"What's so funny at a time like this?"

"Our future!" Pete replied.

"What about it for Christ's sake?"

"Well, Bob. If ever we work for the same company again and you decide to leave, please give me a month or so notice".

"Why what's wrong?" I inquired naively.

"I want to get as far away as possible before the trouble starts".

We stared at each other in the darkness. It was a few moments before I replied,

"Pussy!" I spat and the two of us, despite our circumstances almost broke into laughter.

Shark progressed down the reef edge before Pete angled her in towards the tanker lying at berth in the deep dredged water. The tanker lay offshore, suckling on the end of the massive umbilical cords that were now loading her belly with the Saudi Arabian light crude, and by the look of her plimsoll lines, she was due to be weaned. We could hear the burn-offs clearly. We had seen them a few miles away, on their approach but now, we could hear them. Flaming flags, in the breeze blown thermals of massive waste-gas flames. We could almost feel the heat as the reflections danced across the sea and caressed Shark's body. Pete reversed Shark's engines, halting her march inland,

"Open it!" Pete pointed to the plastic bag.

I pulled out the small red box,

"What's with the red colour?" I asked

"Hawkeye's idea, he figured we may forget which one to use so he colour coded them, red for refinery, jade green for jail".

"Hawkeye was right," I whispered, "Only a pair of dummies would be cruising down the coastline when the whole of Saudi Arabia is out looking for them".

"Wait I want to get this on record!" hissed Pete, "Are you telling me your scared?"

"Who me?" I smiled lamely for effect, hoping Pete hadn't noticed.

But Pete I could see was sure he detected unease in my voice and was determined to probe further

"What are you worried about?"

"I just hope you got the colour coding right that's all!" I replied as nonchalantly as possible.

I took care not to disturb the activator. A chopper swung over the refinery striding on light beams, marching outward over the sea. A third beam scythed from a side door, bleaching the sea around shark, pinning her in the glare of bright electronic daylight. Bullets smacked into the water around us. Pete slammed the throttles forward and Shark surged away, dancing on her belly across the waves and out to sea.

"Hit the switch!" yelled Pete.

"For all the poor sods hurt by Saudi," I whispered as I thumbed the activator.

"Hit it! Hit it!" yelled Pete.

I pointed the transmitter at the refinery and repeatedly thumbed the switch whilst Pete zig-zagged the Shark to avoid the fire from above.

"Bastard doesn't work!" I yelled.

"It must work!" Pete responded.

"I just told you it doesn't!"

430

"Grab the wheel!"

I grabbed the wheel as Pete took control of the transmitter, Pete thumbed and fingered with a wild desperation but nothing happened, he cursed his luck aloud,

"Shit! Shit! Shit!"

"Wrong colour?" I offered,

Pete stabbed a glance at me,

"No way, Bob. No way, it's the right colour OK, the bastard just doesn't want to work that's all, the bastard just doesn't want to work, maybe we're out of range?"

Pete was almost sick and raved in his desperation,

"That bastard has escaped!" he cursed with unrestrained venom, "The bastard has got clean away!"

I suddenly realised how much Pete hated Sharief and how much of that hate was channelled on my behalf.

"Pete, it's OK!" I yelled in consolation, "There'll be other times".

"Fuck other times!" snorted Pete furiously, "I want that bastard now! I want him burned now! The way he burned us all! I want him to suffer Bob and I want him to suffer now!"

Pete raved like a man possessed, thumbing the transmitter, totally consumed by his desire for retribution,

"All my calculations, all the work, all the effort by Hawkeye and Hangar, how are we going to tell them we failed? the invincible Khowajas failed! we never fail! Khowajas never ever fail!"

Pete threw the transmitter into the deck with a furious, temper.

The transmitter smacked into the deck with a crack. Milliseconds later a thunderous, bellowing roar, ripped open the air around us, swallowing all other sounds and sucking in the surrounding voids. A brilliant flash of light accompanied the mighty roar, as six pillars of fire lit up the refinery and mushroomed into the heavens. Six mountainous clouds of upward curling, furious inferno, suddenly delivered daylight

431

where night had reigned supreme. Burning gasoline sludge rained down from the sky to smother the refinery below creating liquid pools of napalm-like fire. Spreading and fuelling the maelstrom as the greedy flames devoured the supplies of fuel with a massive, unbridled appetite. Vast areas of the refinery were instantly ablaze, explosion after explosion spattered the night sky with a million reversing meteors.

Now the feed wind rushed into the epicentre, sucked into the inferno by the rising, spuming, oil-fired thermals. A massive tower of oily-black cumulus rose upward from the buckling steelwork, fanning inland as the accelerating clouds piled into the cooler air above. The once onshore breeze had suddenly become a wind, blowing the dense oily canopy over Jeddah as if it were some beast about to devour the entire Petropolis.

I powered Shark around the stern of the tanker, thundering westward, out into the open sea as the flames erupted even higher. Pete was overpowered by the crescendo of his satiated lust for revenge. I flung my arms skyward, clenched my fists and shook my arms with a nervous spasmic rage,

"Yaaaaaaaaagh! Sharief, fuck you and your cutbacks, take that sucker to the bank!"

It did not last; Pete was reduced to a stunned silence by the impressive, billion-dollar fireworks of his own design. Now the inferno's reflections licked the sea, reaching out to Shark as if trying to consume her with their fearsome wrath. Explosion after explosion carried the uncontrollable fires towards the sea, where they danced along the umbilical pier to the nurturing tanker's breast. Gobbling up the fuel lines and spawning a blazing, furious snake. The chopper ignored the Shark and hovered erratically in the sky. An insignificant insect against a swarm of blazing angry bees. The orange escape boats plunged from the rear of the tanker with only seconds to spare. The flames had reached the ship. The blast wind rocked the Shark like a tiny cork as the ensuing explosion ripped through the air and billions of gallons of burning oil spewed skywards, before falling to earth to smother the sea. Within seconds, the broken-spined tanker

432

was seen rolling in her final death throes and sinking into a spuming froth of bubbling burning oil. Pete stepped backwards towards the wheel; his eyes could not disengage from the scene, he spoke only when he bumped into me,

"My God Bob, did you see it?"

I did not reply I was choked by the obscene destruction before me.

"Bob!" Pete's sharp cry broke into the spell. "What the hell was that?" I couldn't avert my eyes from what had once been the refinery, the pride of Jeddah, almost a child of my own creation that was now consumed by an inferno, the likes of which I had never seen before.

"We did it, Bob. We did it! that will teach that son of a bitch Sharief a lesson he's never going to forget".

"My God', I breathed "Oh my God!"

"Like you once told me, Bob. A few chemicals in the wrong place and whoosh! up she goes".

"Jesus! even the sea's burning," I gasped.

The two of us were stilled as if in mourning,

"What about the guys inside there?" I whispered as if unwilling to break the spell.

"Hawkeye told them to be ready to leave at a moment's notice. He warned them there would be a fire alarm drill and that they should be prepared for the worst. Hawkeye was confident they'd be Ok, he didn't put the trucks where anyone would be working, not at this time of the night anyway and all the men should have got out OK. Besides, at this time of the night there would only be a skeleton crew anyway, don't worry, Bob. Everybody should be OK, and the sea barriers are on alert, minimal pollution maximum damage".

I pointed off to the left behind us,

"At least we know the tanker crew got away Ok look, there they are".

A small flotilla of orange lifeboats bobbed on the sea about five hundred meters behind. The helicopter hovered over it; all the men were standing on top of the fireproof deck. They were safe now; they had climbed from the internal fireproof cocoon and were watching the fireworks. The explosions had all but finished. The whole of the refinery was ablaze and as we watched we were lulled into a false sense of security. Only minutes had elapsed from the first explosions to the inferno that now raged before them, Shark still surged westward as I turned to the controls,

"Yaaaaaah!" I screamed, wrenching the wheel around, throwing a suddenly shocked Pete onto the deck in a hopeless attempt to avoid the oncoming hovercraft. She had sneaked in from the sea, her noisy engines disguised by the roaring inferno and now she was upon us. Pistol cracks filled the air as Shark skidded in a tight curve, rolling over onto her sidewall to effect maximum turn. Phosphorescent spray arced skyward. Showering the hovercraft with a curtain of water as Shark ploughed into the rubber skirt, her belly slamming the hovercraft sideways as she bounced from the cushion of air and continued her way, still reverberating with the sudden impact. I already cradled the AK-47, locking the wheel with my knee and screaming to Pete,

"Get the wheel, Pete! Get the wheel!"

Pete snake bellied across the forty-five-degree angle of the deck, Shark was locked into a tight forceful turn and angling away from the hover craft as Pete grabbed the lower rim of the wheel and pulled himself upright. I staggered to the bow and locked my legs into the side rails as Shark turned through three hundred and sixty degrees; thundering once more, into the path of the police hover craft.

"Pass down the left-hand side!" I screamed. I had noticed the rear end of the rubber-skirted beast was now swinging to the left. The crew were fighting for control after the unexpected collision, I opened fire, my scream obliterated by the roar of the weapon which pumped hot metal slugs into and through the rubber skirt before I raised the fiery muzzle and sprayed her engines with a swarm of buzzing hot steel. I dragged the empty clip from the

434

breach, flipped it around and stabbed it home with the edge of my fist.

"Round again, Pete. We've got to stop this bastard now!"

As Shark skidded around on her sidewall the police struggled to their feet and return fire, ducking down once more as Shark's bow came around and I opened fire.

"Go! Go! Go!" I yelled. Pete instantly threw the wheel to the right, flicking Shark from her turn, planting her upright on her belly and slamming the throttles to full speed where-upon, she lifted from the water and roared away from the Hovercraft. Smashing across the wave crests and out towards the sea with consummate ease.

"The captain of the hovercraft watched us fade from view, he had seen that boat before and as his ship lost power and slowly sunk into her deflating rubber skirts, his memory tripped to recognition and a single word of remembrance whispered from his lips,

"Khowajas!"

I staggered back to the cockpit, almost falling as I jumped in beside Pete. Ahead lay the open sea. We now commanded a good lead and it was unlikely any of the other boats would be able to match our speed. We were miles from the shore but even so, the inferno seemed closer. It was about to swallow the sky and tore at our souls as Jeddah's usual night halo took on a different guise. I broke the silence of respect,

"What do we do now?"

"We head west with Hawkeye's best maintenance job ever, he figured we may need the extra power".

"He figured right!" I pointed out to the stern, the helicopter was on our trail, and it followed our wake for a while before turning off and heading back to land. He had obviously run low on fuel and was unprepared for ditching in the sea at night. Pete throttled the boat to a fuel conserving seventy-five percent power and as Shark raced westward, the inferno still coloured the sky. Bleaching the Horizon with an eerie yellow glow. We were lost once more to the dark, murky anonymity of seaborne night.

ENGLAND.

The wet cup slipped through her fingers and shattered against the ceramic floor tiles. Her eyes widened at the scene before her. She stood transfixed, hypnotised by the newscaster as he flashed his message from the small box that graced billions of homes around the world.

"Good evening, ladies and gentlemen, this is the world news in detail, brought to you from the news service of the BBC".

"Reports are now flooding into the studio on the refinery disaster this evening at the developing city of Jeddah on the Red Sea coast of Saudi Arabia. The fire is still out of control. Our reports from the area suggest the facility is ablaze, including a tanker that was loading oil at the outset of the tragedy. Burning oil is said to be contained and of no threat to the coastline other than in the immediate vicinity of the refinery. We have no news yet, to what may have caused the catastrophe but we are informed that terrorism has not been ruled out. A total news blackout has since been affected by the authorities concerned and as the fire rages out of control, the Saudi Government now looks to lay the blame".

"Lyn!"
"Lyn!"
"Lyn! are you OK?" Bob's mother had been alerted by the cup as it fell to the floor. She had rushed to her daughter-in-law to discover what had happened. Lyn's eyes brimmed with tears; she wiped them away with the towel clutched tightly in her hand. Deep in her body her heart had twisted. She knew that she had just seen and heard something that concerned her husband. She struggled to halt the flow of tears to deflect the questions that would surely follow.

436

"Yes! oh sorry, Mum. I dropped a cup, I'm OK, seeing Jeddah on the TV made me think of Bob. I miss him so much. I half expected to see him on TV".

"He'll be home soon, Lyn". soothed her mother-in-law, unaware of the exact nature of her son's predicament and his subsequent flight to freedom, now out of everybody's hands but his own.

Lyn knelt to retrieve the fragments of the shattered cup; she dropped them into the small plastic pedal bin and continued to dry the utensils from the early evening meal. When she had put away the last cup, she called to her mum in the living room; her voice betrayed the grief she felt inside,

"Excuse me, mom. I think I'll take a shower".

"OK Lyn, I'll make a hot cup of chocolate before we go to bed, it should help us to relax and sleep".

Lyn almost dashed from the kitchen, dragged a towel from her bedroom and entered the bathroom, taking care to lock the door behind her. She undressed quickly, spinning the shower taps to full flow so that the noise would drown her sobbing. Once inside the steamy cubicle, the tears flowed freely. The water had a soothing effect and as she turned her face into the spray her tears were lost - but not the pain.

NEW YORK.

Swathed in towels from the bathroom, Kit slinked into her hotel bedroom. It was early morning, one towel hugged around her breasts and draped towards the floor, stopping short at the crease in her flesh where her legs supported her buttocks. She unwound the towel turban from her hair and rubbed it vigorously against her sodden black tresses.

The massage ceased abruptly at the familiar name, she moved to the TV and increased the volume of the early morning news service.

CHAPTER 16   SAUDI STYLE   NIGHTMARES

"Satellite shots show the extent of the damage. As you can see from these excellent pictures. Here we have the massive black clouds of smoke moving inland across the city of Jeddah, almost obliterating our view of the city. News is scarce since the Saudi government blocked reports of the major disaster on the coastline. The sea is awash with burning oil, after a super tanker, loading oil at the time, was caught in the fire, exploded, and sank. Earlier reports suggest the work of terrorists but with the news blackout coming into force it is unlikely we'll get full details of the cause until the Saudi government releases the information. And so - as the multi-billion-dollar refinery burns out of control CBS news hopes to keep you informed with an up to the minute report on the developments at the disaster on the Red Sea coastline".

Kit switched off the set; a sudden fear of recognition caught her breath and filled her being. What was it Pete had said before she left for New York?

"We have no choice, Kit. We must help Bob; we all owe him and he'd do the same for us without question. One thing is for sure, we're going to take back what we're owed with interest and I mean billion-dollar interest!" Kit shrugged,

"Don't be silly," she thought aloud, "They not do something like this, it not possible, surely it not possible".

Then her thoughts turned to Pete, his conviction to his close friend. How Bob had saved him from the sharks, the bond, that she knew existed between them. They were like brothers, what was it that bound them so close? She did not yet understand the bond between them or the depth of that bond's hold. Then the realisation dawned, it swelled upwards from her heart, choking its ascension in her throat.

"Oh my God!" she whispered aloud, "Oh my God!"

Kit fell onto her sofa and hugged the towel to her tearful eyes,

"Pete!" she sobbed, "Oh Pete, what you done? Oh God! I can't believe such a thing, Oh my God! I never see my Pete again".

CHAPTER 16   SAUDI STYLE   NIGHTMARES

SAUDI ARABIA - Somewhere on the Red Sea.

"Try her again!" I stabbed the order to Pete from inside the engine inspection hatch that was presently devouring my head and upper torso down to my waist. Pete turned the ignition keys to heat, gave the plugs a few moments to cherry up and then spun the engines over. The engines whined and then stopped, whined and then stopped in time with Pete's completion of the ignition circuit. Pete twisted the key over one more time but the same result prevailed.

The water had seeped into Shark's innards during the night, oozing through the crazed holes where the bullets had pierced her fibreglass hull. Now the salt water had reached the engines, entered the fuel system and caused the engines to sputter and die. Since first light of dawn, we had manually pumped the water clear by the hand pump above the deck. The hand pump normally served to clear the rain or storm water and the occasional wave that smashed over the bow and into the open hold. It had never been used in Saudi, where there wasn't that much rain to speak of. We never went out during high seas and being previously unused, the pump had performed admirably. The water level had fallen rapidly and as I worked on the engines, Pete patched the insides of the hull with neoprene, water-resistant cement. All had gone well but now the engines were refusing to fire. The seawater had invaded the fuel system and was now providing me with all sorts of problems.

Pete: having concluded his patching assignment now sat in the cockpit, grinning at the repertoire of my verbal mechanics,

"Shit! this bastard's still full of water!" I hissed with alarm as I unscrewed the filter and primed the fuel pump. Observing the greasy globules of water as they slid through the glass tube in the fuel observation line. I replaced the filter once more and rapidly primed the hand pump to flush the impurities from the system, and then I tightened down the bleed valve and yelled topside to Pete.

439

"OK, Pete. Let her rip". The engines continued to whine and die, whine and die,

"Again, Pete!" whine whine whine-whine whine whine.

"Shit" the bloody water's still coming through!"

I repeated my earlier filter removal and line pumping routine, "Again! Let her rip!"

The engine stubbornly whined, - but did not fire!

"The battery's going to be dead in a minute,". Pete warned.

"Fuck the battery. These fumes are going to kill me in a minute if this bastard doesn't start - OK Pete, try her again!"

Whine whine whine!

"OK, One more time I can't hold my breath much longer!"

"Gee Bob you mean you've been holding your breath for the last hour or so?"

"Spin the engines, arsehole and quit the chat, I can hardly breathe down here, let alone pass the time of day chatting with you!"

Whine whine brrrrmm!   Whine whine Brrrrrm!"

"She's rolling!" yelled Pete........

ROARRRRRRRRRRRRR! The roaring thunder exploded into my ears and I jumped back from the engines assuming they were about to explode, almost crashing through the sidewall of Shark.

"Get up here! Bob. Fast!!!!"

I was on top deck in three urgent strides but the sight I beheld made me wish I had stayed below. I stood and stared in hopeless disbelief,

"F-Sixteens!" croaked Pete.

The two planes glinted across the sky as they caught the early morning sunlight. Banking against the blue-sky backdrop in a full three hundred and sixty degree turn before heading back towards Shark.

Jesus! check out the markings!"

Saudi Airforce". I groaned as the sight of the ultimate Khowaja killers, howling around the sky in a full banking turn sickened Pete.

Get below quick!" ordered Pete.

Maybe they'll think she's deserted". We fell over ourselves in our efforts to avoid being seen. Diving into the hold in the hope that we would not be recognised. You can't park an F-Sixteen on water, Pete; maybe they wouldn't see any signs of life just go away.

Eyes of Allah! Eyes of Allah! repeat over!"
Eyes of Allah! Eyes of Allah! repeat over!"
Control this is Eyes of Allah, we have small power boat in sight, black in colour, registration on close up scope is as follows, CR-30-Shark, over!"
"Eyes of Allah! Eyes of Allah! repeat over!"
"Control, black power boat, registration CR-30-Shark! over!"
"Eyes of Allah! Is anyone on board? over!"
"Control! co-pilot informs, looks like two men dodged below deck on our approach! over!"
"Eyes of Allah! Await further instructions! over!"
"Understood, Control! will await your further instructions! Over".

The two planes banked around Shark in a wide thundering circle. It was a few minutes before the radio crackled back to life and a desperate voice cut through the static and delivered their instructions.

"Eyes of Allah! Eyes of Allah! do you read? over!"
"Control! reading you loud and clear! over!"
"Eyes of Allah! destroy the vessel and any passengers! over!"
"Control! did you say destroy vessel and passengers? over!"
"Eyes of Allah! you heard correctly, destroy the vessel and passengers! over!"
"Control! I will repeat! men on board! over!"
"Eyes of Allah! we understand, destroy the vessel and any passengers on board! over!"

"Control! understand your message to be destroy vessel and passengers over!"

"Eyes of Allah! Affirmative! over!"

"Control! beginning attack run now! over!"

"Eyes of Allah! Allah be with you! over and out!"

The two F-Sixteens roared out of the long banking turn and snarled down the sky towards Shark. As the screaming turbines blasted them closer to their target, canons opened fire at each side of the nose cones. The shells ripped apart the decking, spraying hardwood and glass fibre shards into the air. Shark bobbed and bucked under the merciless onslaught. She was no match for the ultra-fast species of technological advancement. One by one they sprayed her, pulling out of the fearsome attacking dives and hurtling around the cloudless blue sky. Shark was defenceless; she and her occupants were totally at the mercy of the attacking machines. The Khowaja spirit stayed with her as the final attack began. Her bright glowing eyes blazed from her hull in fierce defiance of the murderous onslaught.

Now came the missiles, spitting from beneath the wings of the leading plane, mirrored exactly by the shadowing aircraft, four missiles in all and, as the planes pulled out of their dive, Shark exploded into a million fragments of fibreglass and wood. The sea around her a spuming mass of flaming flying debris.

As the air cleared Shark was no more, almost totally vaporised. Bits of driftwood and fibreglass were all that were left, bobbing and swaying on a smouldering sea. A small part of the sidewall remained and as the technological sky chariots passed overhead, a blazing red eye stared upwards from the surface in absolute defiance, as if denying them the victory of an easy kill.

"Control! this is Eyes of Allah! Over!"

"Eyes of Allah! reading you loud and clear! over!"

"Control! target is destroyed, I repeat, the target is destroyed! over!"

442

CHAPTER 16   SAUDI STYLE   NIGHTMARES

"Eyes of Allah! Any survivors? over!"

"Control! no one could have survived such an attack, men and vessel destroyed! over!"

"Eyes of Allah, these are not men, they are Khowajas, are you sure? You must make sure, over!"

"Control! I repeat! target is destroyed! there are no survivors, I repeat, there are no survivors! This is Eyes of Allah we are returning to base! over!"

"Eyes of Allah! we read you loud and clear, no survivors! over and out!"

Nothing remained but the smouldering debris, rolling and bobbing with the slight swell of the Red Sea. Shark's solitary eye of defiance winked and weaved in the rising sunlight, tribute to a gallant attempt to chase freedom. The sea calmed as the noonday orb rose high and from a distant shore, the noonday prayer echoed faintly across the particled surface of the water as if calling the spirits to life.

ENGLAND.

"Good evening, ladies and gentlemen, my name is Richard Simms and we're here at the BBC news desk bringing you an up-to-date review of today's international news. Reports have confirmed the refinery disaster in Jeddah as an act of terrorism. This morning, F-Sixteen fighter aircraft of the Royal Saudi Air force searched the surrounding coastal waters and discovered the terrorists making their escape in an armed powerboat. The terrorists are said to have sunk a police launch, and a coast guard hovercraft, a helicopter was shot down and various police vehicles were destroyed as they made their escape. The report states that the F-Sixteens were fired upon by the terrorists with heat-seeking stinger missiles leaving them with no choice but to return the fire killing more than a dozen armed terrorists in the boat. It is believed all men involved in the action against the refinery are now dead. Police and army patrols are still combing

the area whilst the Saudi navy are reportedly searching the area with helicopters. We hope to keep you up to date with any future developments".

Lyn rose awkwardly from her seat, switched off the TV set and padded defeatedly into her bedroom, flinging herself onto the bed as the wracking sobs issued from her throat. Lyn hugged the pillow to her face suppressing the sounds of her heartbroken grief. She prayed that the pillow would smother her, that she may join her Bob once more. The pillow was crushed in a tightening embrace, soddened by the tears of hopeless desperation. Now she was alone, there was no point waiting for Bob to arrive. She may as well go home and forget about him, her mind protested at this inflicted torment,

"You lied to me Bob, you lied, you told me not to worry as you would soon be home. Oh, Bob how could you do this to me? How can I tell your mom? what am I going to say? how can I tell her I knew all along? Why did you lie to me? why Oh why Oh why......."

The telephone interrupted her mourning; she held her breath and picked up the receiver, a satellite link clicked, it was long distance,

"Lyn?" a strange American voice drawled her name.

"Yes, this is Lyn, who's speaking?"

"A friend, just to let you know, don't believe everything you hear or see on TV, we'll contact you when we know for sure, one way or the other Lyn, we'll let you know. One way or the other, can't say anymore, there may be ears, just remember, we'll be in touch".

CLICK PRRRRRRR!

A tiny glimmer of hope now stemmed the tearful flow. She had no idea who had called but the fact that they had called reassured her. She would wait and until they called again nothing she read or saw, unless it was Bob's body would make her believe he was dead. She did not wish to believe what she had seen on TV and now the voice had strengthened her resolve; she bit her lip and awaited further news.

NEW YORK:

"But you can't do this to us!" he snapped. The small, chubby little man in the silk suit, waving his arms for emphasis. Stubby cigar gripped between equally stubby fingers. Five feet four inches tall in his well-heeled shoes. An uninteresting, cherubic sort of man, with a thin black moustache, constant dark sunglasses, greasy slicked back hair and dark olive skin. He was well known amongst the employees. He was a toucher, an excitable little fellow who loved to grope. He considered the girls to be his property and tried every trick in the book to get them into his bed, even to the point of threatening them with the sack. But even that threat had not carried much weight against his pudgy little features. His threats were bravado but some of the new girls had almost been caught out, had it not been for the old hands who had warned them beforehand of his schemes.

"I can do this! - I do this now! you bring relief hostess, I not go back to Saudi. I never go back to Saudi!" Kit's eyes were red after hours of crying. She trembled as she spoke to the Saudia manager of the New York office, who was rapidly losing the battle and therefore turning nasty,

"You're breaking your contract, Katherine. This is not fair, neither is it allowed, you can't just walk out on us like this, it is illegal, we can punish you!"

"What can you do to me now to hurt me anymore? Same you did to Pete and Bob? Throw me in jail? Maybe you give me lashes? Torture Kate hah, maybe you make me sorry for leaving your Saudi Airline?"

"You can't leave, I will not allow it, you cannot leave this office without the check hostess. You will go back to Saudi Arabia and then we will see!" The manager smirked with self-important, arrogant satisfaction, almost choking on his cigar as Kit finally released the pent-up emotions and exploded,

"Fuck you! I never go back to Saudi. I sick of Saudi. I sick of Saudi men feeling up my uniform on plane. I sick of Saudi stewards pawing my body. I sick of your Saudi laws. I leave now. I quit!"

"I'm warning you!" squealed the supervisor in silk, "You must return to Saudi, there are laws........

"Yes, I know Saudi Law!" interrupted Kit, "Forbidden to drink alcohol, forbidden to kiss in public, forbidden for girl and boy to date, everything in Saudi is forbidden, unless you are Saudi. Then it seems to be all ok! Well, this is America; this is free country. I can do what I like and I want to leave now. You try to stop me; I scream so loud every cop in New York come to see what is going on. Your law took away Bob and because of this Pete now dead. You take your Saudi Law and think about it next time you in disco looking for a woman because you drunk and horny, you think about your Law then and you see what Kate mean, when I say I put it all in newspaper of how you behave with the girls. I go now, Good-bye!"

Kit slammed the door. The Saudia airline aircrew manager stood in disbelief,

"She would never have got away with that in Saudi," he thought as he stubbed the cigar into his ashtray and winced with the pain as his fingers were singed

"I would have had her in prison immediately until she surrendered to my wishes or received a pardon from the King. It would have been different in Saudi; she would have been in real trouble that's for sure".

Kit marched along the corridor; dropped thirty floors to ground level in the express elevator and headed to the entrance of the building. Her plane would depart in two hours; stop over in London for a further two hours and then on to Malaysia and home. Pete had been right, sometimes you just had to speak your mind and to hell with the hypocrites. Kit sobbed openly as she skipped down the hotel steps and hailed a taxi, her sorrow turning her thoughts upside down.

446

"OH Pete! I miss you already, I for sure we in love. I for sure you're the man for me, now I not know which way is up or down, I only know I lost you, Pete. Oh! Pete, you make me so unhappy. I knew this would be. Now I understand the caution feeling when we first met. You made me so unhappy, Pete. Oh, so unhappy, I never see you again. What I do now, Pete? What I going to do now?"

"Taxi! Taxi Mr Please!"

"Where to young lady? my, you look upset, are you OK miss?"

"Yes, I OK thanks, just a bit upset I have to leave my relatives behind, take me to JFK and please hurry, I have a flight to catch".

SAUDI – THE RED SEA

Crudely manufactured from a lady Stewardesses stocking, the tightly compacted ball sat in ignorance of its vital role. The toe section had been packed tight and the leg of the stocking knotted tightly behind it with a firm sealing knot. If Kit's toes had been present in her stocking now, she would have undoubtedly been a corpse. Human beings rarely survived at the bottom of the Red Sea, in this case, some one hundred meters below the surface amongst the shadowy monochrome depths.

Scavengers roamed the seabed, a species of fish not normally associated with the appetites of man. Unless he happened to be drowning at the time with his semi-conscious body still attaining the sense of sight. At such a depth, a single breath from a regulator returns to the sea as mere pear-like bubbles. That same breath, when closer to the surface, would explode from the regulator into a mushrooming cloud of carbon dioxide gas.

Originally the toe had measured the size of a tennis ball but the tightly packed salt had slowly resalinated and the Red Sea welcomed its return. As the ball of salt was further reduced, the small spring pushing against it slowly expanded. After thirty

447

minutes, the valve at the end of the spring had opened sufficiently to allow a small stream of bubbles to escape from the attached air tank. After one hour had passed, the air had rushed into the orifice and had now ceased. An evil red eye swelled upwards from the darkness and now gazed toward the surface from the seabed. Large sacks of salt continued the resalination process and as their weight decreased, the beast with red eyes, began to rise.

The devil eye rose upward for three meters and halted. Two bulky objects had ended its immediate ascent. Finally, when enough salt crystals had disappeared and the weight vanished along with the salt, the beast eye began to rise once more. Slowly at first, with the two heavy objects trailing behind, dragging and delaying the beast in its silt-streamed wake. The ascension quickened as it left behind the silent grey seabed. As the beast rose faster it expanded and as it expanded it increased its speed. Rising quickly and free of the crushing pressure below. The beast eye rose through the thirty-meter mark, rapidly unfolding to its true shape, expanding air filling and swelling the air pockets. The red eye surged towards the surface, gliding silently through the twenty-meter mark. The form continued to swell, accelerating to speed. At fifteen meters it was almost full size, hurtling towards the surface at an accelerating velocity, the two heavy outboards could no longer hold. As the rubber cavities swelled to full size, streams of bubbles erupted from the overpressure valves and they whistled and screamed their warning overture. At ten meters, it boiled passed Pete and myself, suspended in the ocean at neutral buoyancy, powering upwards towards the colouring light of day. The overpressure now blasted from the overworked valves. Upward the dinghy charged, five meters, three meters, and one meter, smashing through the surface of the sea and continuing its upward momentum into the sky, before falling back to sea level. The true gravity of the outboards ending its wingless dash to flight. The dinghy slapped into the frothing surface, overpressure escape valves hissing and singing in the warm sunshine of day.

448

Thirty minutes later it lay becalmed on the afternoon seascape, bobbing and swaying with the swell. Tiny hisses emanating from the valves as the Orb radiated the rubber, heating and increasing the pressure inside the burdened skin.

The Rolex submariner glowed luminous-green in the sunless depths. A signing signal was executed, the downtime was re-checked and in silent agreement, the two of us began to rise. We ascended slowly, staying well behind the bubbles of our exhaled breath. Allowing our physical functions to return evenly to a more normal state of earthly pressure. Slowly but surely, we rose upward. Strapped to our backs were three, eighty litre tanks of air that would support a regular diver for up to three hours at a depth of ten meters.

My head pierced the surface first; I checked the sea and skylines before passing the signal to Pete, who rose through the surface with barely a sound. The two of us swam ten meters or more before grasping the line, which had been strung around the main flotation bags of the dinghy. We spat out the regulators and gasped in the natural easy breathing air. I threw my mask inside the inflatable, unscrewed the regulator and removed my harness, allowing the tanks to see-saw into the depths, lost for all time. I tossed the regulator into the dinghy and pulled myself aboard.

"Yaaaaagh!" I screamed in mortal agony, leaping back into the water with an almighty splash and disappearing.

"Jesus what happened to you?" gasped Pete as I reappeared a moment later.

"The fucking rubber's red hot!" I squealed.

Pete tried not to laugh but after what we had previously endured, the relief was just too much to hold back. He coughed as if sucking in a breath, before grinning with his teeth clamped firmly together. Finally, he could hold back no more and he laughed out aloud as I began dousing the surfaces of rubber that had been exposed to the full glare of the sun.

"Are you going to get aboard?" I hissed with embarrassment, "Or are you going to swim home?"

CHAPTER 16   SAUDI STYLE   NIGHTMARES

"I'm boardin, I'm boardin". grinned Pete, as he gingerly hauled his body over the warm rubber cylinders and declared,

"Watch out the rubber's hot".

I followed his example and once inside the inflatable we removed our shirts and pants and laid them out to dry. The night was sure to be cold after a long day in the sun. We lounged in the belly of the inflatable, luxuriating in the hot sun. Enjoying the pleasant warmth of mammalian life after the hours spent under the sea, in the soundless, weightless womb of cold anonymity. Now we were able to breathe without sucking on rubber. Communication was easy as Pete opened a plastic container of orange juice he had stored in the pocket of the dinghy. We drank and dried out. Two hours underwater was a long time, regardless of the shallow depth and it would be a while before our skin lost the prunish ripples and stretched back to a normal elasticity.

"Pete, where the hell is your face mask?"

"Behind you" replied Pete,

"Why?"

"Put it back on!"

"What for?" queried Pete taking the hook line and sinker.

"You look shitty without it!" I grinned, the warmth and the juice breaking into the sombre mood. Pete stuck his middle finger in my direction and when certain I had received his message, he collapsed onto the belly sheet and we soaked up the sun in silence for a while.

"What gave you the idea to move the window, Pete?"

"I thought we might need a back door, you know, an alternative just in case".

"Like our tanks at the bottom of the creek?" I noted.

"Like the tanks at the bottom of the creek," Pete replied nodding as he did so.

"I took out the viewing window inserted a fast action crank for the doors and sealed them from both sides; worked really good, eh?"

450

"Our sitting here in one piece is proof of that, Pete. No doubt about it you saved our lives. When those missiles hit, I was glad to be thirty meters down. God only knows what would have happened to us had we been aboard Shark, or even just a few meters below the surface. That shock wave still knocked me sideways at thirty meters".

"Wooden overcoat for sure!" warned Pete, "With an exit-only visa nailed to the side".

"More like fish food, we would have never found our bodies out here. The sharks would have had us for dinner, that's for sure. After the tanks at the bottom of the creek, the escape hatch in Shark, the drum that went through the doors first was full of fuel for the outboards and we're just waiting for it to pop to the surface now aren't we, Pete?"

"You think I'm going to piss in the outboards to get them going?"

"Right Pete, sorry I asked the stupid question".

After a brief respite, we removed the rubber housings from the outboards and cleared out any water that would prevent them functioning, we were soon ready for the arrival of the fuel drum. Pete removed a compass from a stored pack and took a basic reading. I was satisfied that the pressure had not damaged the outboards and they would run perfectly as soon as we had the fuel. I knew the drum would be popping to the surface shortly but I still took pleasure in ribbing Pete.

"Supposing the drum doesn't arrive, Pete?"

Pete unhitched two paddles and threw them at me.

"It's a long row to the other side, Bob. So, you had better pray the drum appears soon because you're the first on the list for paddle duty".

"How did you rig the drum?" I inquired.

"Simple; I filled it so there was no expandable air left inside. Liquid doesn't expand and contract. I attached buoyancy floats to prevent it from sinking and then I added enough salt to keep it down for at least two hours, it should be here any time now".

"We should have hung on to the air tanks," I added, "We could have used them for a sea anchor so that we don't drift too far away".

"You and your hindsight, mate. It's always perfect!"

Thirty minutes later the fuel tank broke the surface around seventy meters down-wind. The reason for the delay became obvious, one of the floats had burst and filled with water, leaving the single float to do the job of two including lifting the weight of the waterlogged float. By the time the fuel was loaded and the drum stored behind the outboards where it would cause little drag it was four-thirty. The sun had ceased its fiery midday blaze and was now descending westward to the horizon. I yanked the starter chord on one of the engines, it fired to life on the third try. The second outboard took a while longer but with a few choice words of French encouragement; I had the twin set thrumming sweetly.

I waited for the temperature to rise evenly in the motors. I received a heading from Pete and the inflatable cruised away in the direction of the slowly sinking sun. Now all we had to do was wait and hope the water and the fuel would last the course. Both of us donned our stiff, sun-dried shirts. The salt had baked into the material, almost like a starching agent and spoiled the otherwise comfortable fit. Pete scanned the Horizon for shipping, constantly checking the compass as I tended to the motors continually preening and adjusting, to squeeze out maximum mileage from the fuel.

"Won't be long now, Bob?" smiled Pete, "It won't be long now".

Both of us were slowly accustoming ourselves to victory. The Saudis would have stopped the search when the Shark was destroyed. We had enough fuel to reach our destination and now it was only a matter of time before we were home free. Old rivalries surfaced once more as we re-lived the past hours. An incredible relief washed over us, now we were both certain it was only a matter of time and we would surely be home free

452

Chapter 17

DESPERATION & DEATH

The twin outboards droned steadily for at least an hour, before finally stuttering to a fuel-less respite. I crawled to the stern of the dinghy to refill the empty tanks. I juggled with the fuel drum until a cry of desperation hissed from my lips,

"Oh shit! I don't believe it!"

"What happened?" quizzed Pete, eager for a response.

"The fuel!" I sighed, "All the bloody fuel has gone".

"What!" cried Pete in disbelief.

"All the bloody fuel has gone!" I cursed and sunk dejectedly into the belly of the inflatable as if all life had drained from my body. The drum had been positioned across the rear of the outboard motor support and during the journey, the vibrations had rolled the drum steadily around its fixings. Those same vibrations had worked the cap free, depositing the fuel in our wake.

"I know I secured it, Pete!" my desperately apologetic tone unconcealed.

"I know! I checked it!" spat Pete, I was more afraid we wouldn't be able to get the cap back off, you screwed it on tight, Bob. like I said, I know, I checked it!"

"What do you think, Pete?"

"Vibrations did it, I thought the dinghy was riding high in the water but I never gave it a second thought!"

"So, did I, I thought it was due to the fuel used by the outboards. I screwed that cap on so tight I almost cut accidents my bloody palm open. Would you believe it, just as we are making some real progress, we get another slap in the face!"

"Just unlucky," there was no hint of consolation in Pete's dejected tone of voice.

"I don't suppose you've got any alternatives to this?" I knew the answer before he'd asked the question.

Pete threw me the small plastic paddles,

"Better get your personal weapons systems working, no point in discussing the barn door now that that horse has pissed off long ago".

"All the way across the Red Sea?"

"Just keep going straight, we're not dead yet, we've got a date remember? There's sure to be shipping out there somewhere'

I cut the ropes and rolled the drum free. It bobbed around for a while before sinking without a trace but for the slight rainbows of surface oil, slowly drifting aft. I assumed the position on the rowing board and began to row, slowly at first until my muscles warmed and acclimatised to the work. I rowed for five or six minutes before I stopped,

"What's wrong?" Pete queried the curses.

"I swear I'm losing my mind, Pete". I replied as I moved back to the stern, hoisted the outboards clear of their mounts and dropped them into the sea. When I assumed position once more and began to row, the dinghy appeared to fly compared to our earlier rate of speed. We grinned in unison and even in the depths of uncertainty the rivalry sustained our spirit.

"Bob!"

"Yeah, what do you want?"

"We don't want to turn this into a contest; let's forget the contest for the moment, we should each pull for one hour then rest for one hour, you agree?"

"I'll buy that". I agreed.

"That way, we'll conserve our strength and the water. I don't want you to work up a raging thirst and demolishing what's left of the water supply, the Red Sea ain't big enough, just give the fish a chance".

"I heard you, Pete. You'll get your share of the work don't worry about that".

"Resting man holds the compass and the heading is west to freedom".

"You got it!" I grinned, "West to freedom, just one more thing".

"What's that?" queried Pete.

CHAPTER 17   SAUDI STYLE   DESPERATION

"I bet I can row a lot farther than you in an hour".

"I give up," groaned Pete, "I just give up".

After rowing for only thirty minutes, we swapped positions, as usual, I had overestimated and one-hour rowing was a non-starter, I had never rowed before and it wasn't that easy, so thirty-minute stints it was.

The two of us settled down to the journey ahead confident that, by sharing the workload as we had always done, we would eventually achieve our goal. I removed my sun-baked shirt - I was warming to the efforts of rowing and I would need a dry shirt later, when the sun had gone and the sea breeze cooled the night. It was four forty-five. I squinted into the backlit shadow of Pete's face, as he took his turn at the oars. We were approximately three hundred kilometres south of the tropic of cancer that threw the arc of the sun over to the left of our heading. I sat - dry, warm and comfortable in the rear of the dinghy, I was just about to doze off to sleep when Pete broke into my slumber with his words interspersed with grunts of effort as he shouldered the oars.

"By the way, Bob. You were right for a change".

"What about?"

"Umph! being on the railroad tracks".

"Which railroad tracks?"

"You know, Umph! when you meet your girl for the first time".

"Hit you did it, Pete?"

"I'm telling you, Bob. Umph! there I was standing alone, Umph!"

"As usual!" I interrupted.

"As soon as I saw her, Umph! I felt sick, Umph! I wanted to grab her by the, Umph! waist and never let her go, Umph!"

"You're hooked, Pete. You can kiss your bachelor arse good-bye. You're even talking like a hooked fish. I bet she'll have you down the aisle in a flash when we get out of this mess".

"Umph! which brings me to the main topic of the conversation, I need you to do me a favour, Umph!"

455

"Of course, I'll be the best man, Pete. I'm always the best man, aren't I?"

"You're an arsehole, Bob. Umph! that's what you are, Umph! and you just ruined my big speech".

"You were best man at my wedding, weren't you?"

"Right! Umph! but that's not the point, Umph!"

"OK, Pete. You tell me what the point is?"

Pete did not have time to explain, a faint sound broke into our immediate conversation and reduced the two of us to a desperate silence.

"Listen!" hissed Pete.

"I can hear it, I ain't gone fuckin deaf!" I replied in the same panicked whisper as if blaming Pete for the sound.

We flung ourselves face down into the belly of the inflatable, below the level of the side floats. Slowly raising our heads until our eyes peeped cautiously over the rubber float.

"Twin rotors!" my voice was troubled.

"I ain't blind, Bob. I can see the bastard!"

"In this light, they're sure to spot us!"

"Who the fuck are they? that's all I want to know?"

Pete unzipped the inside pocket of the side float; he emptied the contents of a waterproof housing onto the rubber belly sheet before him.

"Jesus! what's that?" I knew before I'd asked the question.

"Flare gun for friends, handgun for enemies".

"Jesus! Pete. You think of everything!"

"They're coming closer". whispered Pete, trying to prevent his voice betraying the sickness now welling up inside his body.

"Yeah, I see them," I acknowledged, as the knot in my stomach tightened into a ball of increasingly strained proportions.

"Can you make out who it is?"

"Just that it's the silhouette of a double rotor banana, swinging off to the left and coming in fast".

"The Saudis have double-rotor jobs,"

"I know that! that's what I'm bloody afraid of, maybe they'll pass us by, maybe no one's looking in this direction".

"And maybe they ain't Muslims, Pete". The sarcasm laced my faltering voice.

As the chopper drew level, a mile south of our dinghy I was first to recognise my worst fears.

"Fuck! it's the Saudi coast guard, what are they doing this far out? OH shit! now he's seen us and he's coming over to check us out, oh no! Please no! Not now, not now! You cruel bastards".

"There's no justice in this place," Pete moaned, resigning himself to his fate,

"All this bastard way for these arseholes to get lucky and pick us up, there's just no bloody justice at all!"

"Control! Control! do you read? over!"
"Control! Control! do you read? over!"
"Border Guard this is control, we read you! over!"
"Control we have a small inflatable in sight, heading due west, I am making a pass to check them out! over!"
"Affirmative Border Guard, awaiting your report! over!"

The chopper moved in closer and circled the small inflatable dinghy. Boats of this size were very rarely seen this far out to sea unless they were the survivors of some larger craft involved in an accident. A suspicious inflatable on an infamous salty sea. The chopper descended closer, tightening its circle of observation, kicking up spray and mist with the down draft and drenching the two occupants of the rubber craft.

"Control! Control! do you read? over!"
"Go ahead Border Guard, we read you loud and clear! over!"
"Control we have small inflatable in sight, two men aboard, registration CR-30 I repeat registration CR-30! over!"
"Border Guard! repeat immediately! over!"
"Two men aboard a small inflatable, registration CR-30! over!"

"Border acknowledge, coral-reef-three-Zero over!"
"Control that is affirmative! over!"
"Border are the occupants alive? over!"
"Affirmative control, occupants are alive! over!"

Pete fumbled with the pistol in his hands; it was warm to the touch almost as if it were alive. An instrument of death with a life of its own. He checked the ammunition; the pistol held a full clip. He checked the flare gun and passed it to me,

"Just remove the pin and pull the trigger". His instructions carried little encouragement and I accepted the flare pistol without words.

"This gun's warm," I thought, "Everything in this land is warm but for some of the people who exist here. They're a cold bunch of uncompassionate bastards who care about nothing on earth but the life they expect to lead in the paradise here-after no matter how many sins they commit".

"Bob," Pete's voice almost disappeared with the effort,

"I don't know about you but I don't want to get my head cut off. I'd rather get it over with here and now, to hell with dying in front of a bunch of bloodthirsty arseholes. I'd rather finish it now, quick and painless".

"I'm with you, Pete". I croaked, "I'm with you all the way".

"Any suggestions?"

I toyed with the flare gun in my hand squeezing the grip firmly,

"I saw a movie once," I began, as I rose from the dinghy, thrust my arm towards the helicopter, yanked the safety pin clear and aimed the flare gun, into the side door of the helicopter and squashing back the trigger. The flare gun popped and fizzed, spitting a few dampened smoking shreds, into the sea below my outstretched arm. I looked at the useless object in my hand, stared over to the helicopter and turned around to face Pete with a shrug of resignation.

"They ain't shooting back, maybe they thought it was a distress signal".

458

CHAPTER 17   SAUDI STYLE   DESPERATION

"It was". sighed Pete, "Believe me it was".

"It was supposed to blaze across the sky into the cabin and explode into a million pieces. The bloody thing must have gotten damp on the seabed or its sell-by date had expired".

"I know how it feels," voiced Pete, hopelessly. "Hey, I ain't going back to Saudi!"

Pete's voice was filled with the dread of what would happen if we were taken back to Saudi.

"Neither am I, Pete. But what's the alternative?"

Pete raised the barrel of the gun to his own head, a wild hopeless expression on his sickly, pale face.

"Wait, Pete! Jesus is that the only choice we've got?"

"Unless you know of a better Idea?" the words were almost lost in Pete's dry throat.

I dropped into the dinghy beside him and took the gun from his hands. A terrified sickness took hold of me, as I removed the gun from Pete's grip causing me to wretch and vomit over the side of the dinghy. I recovered what was left of my composure and slid in the belly of the boat beside Pete.

"Are you scared, Bob?".

I stared Pete in the eyes before delivering more bravado in answer,

"No, I think the prawn sandwiches were off".

Pete could not stop the grin that spread to his lips. If I had not been present, we would have been reduced to sobbing, wrecks, desperately pleading for our lives and once again, I realised the strength of our bond.

"Heaven is full of beautiful hooris according to the Muslim faith, Bob".

"Yeah! Only if they let us in".

"I'll be fine, Bob. It's you I'm worried about".

"Well, if I go downstairs, Pete. An awful lot of my friends are going to be there to meet me and I'll have a lot of fun greeting the ones that follow me down and besides I met someone once……..".

The spray had become a thick drafting rain as the coastguard chopper moved in closer. My resolve to go down fighting was weakening but Pete's tormenting voice spurred me to life,

"You ain't got no fuckin friends man, everybody always said you were an arsehole".

"That's funny, Pete. Because everybody always said the same about you too, that makes us a pair of arseholes, eh?"

I stared into Pete's eyes which betrayed our true feelings for each other. A warmth of camaraderie fell between us; there was no need for spoken words.

"Border! Border! come in Border!"

"Control this is Border Guard, reading you loud and clear! over!"

"Border! this is control, you must destroy the dinghy and occupants, leave no trace, destroy all evidence! over!"

"Control! occupants signalled with distress flare! over!"

"Border, forget the distress signal, you must destroy them! Over!"

"But control they signalled distress....

"Are you refusing an order, Border? over!"

"Control they are helpless! over!"

"Border! it is they who destroyed the refinery! it is they who escaped from the prison, it is they who machine-gunned the Jeddah police forces and shot down one of your comrades! over!"

"Control reading you loud and clear, destroying dinghy and passengers! over!"

The pilot's voice carried a trace of alarm, he was not trained to murder helpless men in perilous situations on the sea but he had to obey the command, the consequences of ignoring it would be severe indeed and no foreigners were worth such punishment.

CHAPTER 17   SAUDI STYLE   DESPERATION

"What do you think they're going to do, Bob?"

"They ain't here to save our lives, that's for sure".

"I'm not going back to Saudi for beheading, Bob. For God's sake shoot me now!"

I turned to Pete, the pistol warm and heavy in my hand I could not believe what he was asking me to do,

"If I shoot you, Pete. What am I going to do?"

"You're an arsehole, Bob. You can shoot yourself".

"I can't do it, Pete. All these years we spent together, I feel like you're my brother man, more than just a friend, I just know I can't do it....

I was cut short as the chopper drew in closer and the winchman was lowered from the side door, hanging over the sea as if he was going to rescue us, we knew he wasn't, he had a pistol clutched menacingly in his free hand as his other hand steadied his descent by gripping the taught cable handle.

"Give me the gun, Bob. I ain't going back to Saudi, I'm going to finish this now!'"

Pete reached for the gun; I had no time to release my hold of the instrument before a shot rang out, zipped by my head and into Pete. Pete's body arched upward from the belly sheet in a frantic contortion and the blood sprayed from the wound in his upper thigh,

"Bob!! I'm hit! Shit, I'm fucking hit'

I watched the contortions of pain. The sight of my friend twisting in agony pumped adrenaline through my veins; seconds later my fear had been anaesthetised and I rose to my feet, with the pistol gripped firmly in my hand. When I reached full stretch my finger pressured the trigger and the weapon jumped in my grip

"Com'on you fuckers," I whispered into the boiling spray,

"Now we'll find the hereafter together!!!!!" CRACK! CRACK! CRACK!

Shots were exchanged; I almost watched the bullets travel to their target as they left the gun and ripped into the glass panels around the pilot's cabin. The chopper staggered in the sky, throwing the winchman sideways and deflecting his aim. As the pilot slumped forward with blood pulsing from a gaping neck wound, the co-pilot took control of the staggering chopper. The winch man was lucky, as the chopper stumbled around the sky, the bullets intended for him smashed into the chest of the doorman, slamming him back against the fuselage, before the chopper rolled once more and dumped him headfirst into the sea. He was dead before his body had hit the water.

My finger continued to squeeze off the shots until the gun was empty but the finger, unconsciously controlled by some inner blind fury, continued to smack the firing pin against the empty breach. The air around me was ripped apart by supersonic metal slugs. The chopper finally steadied and the winch man found his mark. Suddenly an invisible force slammed me backwards, the intruding metal probe smacked into my shoulder and spun me around, before bouncing me face down into the belly sheet. Now I lay beside Pete. A searing rod of white-hot steel poked through my shoulder, blood poured from my nose and a whispered prayer that it would be over quickly, released the droplets of blood from my lips. The remaining chopper crew now had the upper hand. They had seen me fall and now, the winch man was lowered in for the kill. The winch man had seen me drop the weapon, he knew we were unarmed and suddenly he was feeling very brave.

"Shoot me!!!! For God's sake shoot me!" gasped Pete, "I ain't going back to Saudi'

Pete saw the blood running down my shirt

"We're done for," Pete sighed hopelessly,

"They've got us, Bob, they've finally fucked us over just like everybody else in the Kingdom!"

"Just you wait," I began, adjusting my pain-wracked body for comfort, "I'll pretend I'm hurt really bad and when they winch us aboard, I'm going to kick the living daylights out of the lot of them". I spat over the side, as if to underline the ridiculous statement. Pete smiled that knowing smile before falling to that semi-conscious state before the blackness rules over.

462

CHAPTER 17   SAUDI STYLE   DESPERATION

"Pussy!" Pete spat, as he dizzied, tipped, and fell to unconsciousness, tears in the corners of his eyes.

As I turned to face my friend another shot rang out. It pierced one of the airbags to my side, the bag hissed and collapsed, as the pressure was lost. I prayed they would shoot. I hoped they would not sink the dinghy and let me drown. I hated the thought of drowning.

"Why couldn't they just shoot me and be done with it?" I thought,

"Why did they always have to resort to torture, even to the bitter end?" I pulled myself close to Pete squeezed my good arm around his shoulder and whispered a near-final word.

"Together Pete, just like everything else". The hissing airbag coupled with the noise from the helicopter drowned my words. I closed my eyes; I remembered Lyn and my life. Silent tears flowed down my cheeks. It was over. There was nothing I could do but pray it would be fast. Lyn's vision crossed before the front of my mind's eye and I whispered my final choking words,

"Good-bye Lyn: I'm sorry my love, Good-bye".

I heard the shots explode from the gun. I felt the dinghy shudder as the bullets raced home, first one and then the other. The first must have been Pete's and the next was surely mine. I could almost feel the bullet, as it spat from the end of the barrel and accelerated towards me. Billowing into my brain tissue and shattering my whole-body system. A tremendous thrashing clatter pierced my ears as my nervous system collapsed. The whole inflatable shuddered and strained, as if under some immense force, now pushing me down the path of misery to eternal darkness. The sea around me rose upwards. A solid sheeting spray smashed my body downward as the great black shroud of death swooped over to engulf and smother me, crushing my body with a tremendous blasting pressure wave. Suddenly I felt no more but perceived the presence of others, certain that in my struggle for life I was no longer alone.

CHAPTER 17   SAUDI STYLE   DESPERATION

My thoughts replayed the words as they were dredged from the bottom of my memory and projected into my brain by that same, all-commanding voice,

"IT IS NOT YET YOUR TIME"

Slowly I opened my eyes, half expecting angels or even demons. First, I saw the winchman, still suspended from the side of the helicopter. The pistol was no longer in his hand, which along with his arm, his leg and half his torso had been ripped away by some ungodly force. Now he hung suspended, like a half beast carcass at some primitive Saturday morning meat market, still-warm blood dribbling into the sea. A carcass shredded beyond immediate recognition of previous human form.

Behind the winchman, a black whirling fist pulsated across the blood-red sky, groping against the sea breeze, passing over the sinking Orb and its lukewarm glow, swinging around the sky on an invisible chord of air. It slowed before pulling up to hover, directly in front of the Saudi Coastguard. It was another helicopter, all black in colour; even the windows were tinted black. All black but for a familiar blazing red eye, staring defiantly from the engine cowl. It hung in space directly in front of the Saudi aircraft, not even the merest hint of instability could be perceived in its conquest of gravity.

The co-pilot was shocked by the death of his captain and stunned by the chopper that a few seconds before, had hurtled under his belly and over the inflatable, in a near-impossible manoeuvre. Was now feeling very alone on an increasingly hostile sea. He slapped the transmit switch of his radio, his unrestrained fear echoing in his urgent call,

"Control! this is Border! over!"
"Go ahead, Border. We read you loud and clear! over!"
"Control! this is the co-pilot, pilot is dead, two of our crew men are dead, I wish to report unidentified aircraft directly ahead".
"Repeat Border! over!"

464

CHAPTER 17   SAUDI STYLE   DESPERATION

The co-pilot could not spit the words from his mouth fast enough but the response was not encouraging.

"Border! assume standard intercept procedures, keep control informed of the outcome, I repeat, keep control informed of the outcome! over!"

The co-pilot was losing his nerve,

"Control! we need assistance! I repeat we need help! over!"

"Border, use the standard intercept procedures; we are doing all that we can! over!"

The loudspeaker crackled to life under the flying banana, words were gabbled quickly in an excited chatter of Arabic.

"This is the Royal Saudi coast guard, you must leave this area immediately, these men are recently escaped criminals whom we are taking back to Saudi for questioning".

The black Huey made no move, until very slowly but purposely, it began to inch forward toward the Saudi helicopter. Now the Saudi co-pilot spoke in English, repeating the same speech, though his strained voice lacked any real conviction as the black Huey crept ever forward.

"We are protectors of the Saudi coastline, you must leave the area, you are in violation of Royal Saudi Airspace!"

Still, the Huey crept forward, the blades of the ghostly craft sliding slowly towards the cockpit of the inexperienced coast guard, who, on the verge of hysteria, now screamed into his loudspeaker microphone,

"You must acknowledge! you are in violation of international boundaries; you are trespassing Saudi Airspace! I repeat! you must acknowledge!"

The strange unconcerned voice invaded the co-pilot's earphones,

"Check your instruments, you are twenty-four miles out and way outta line, these are international waters. May I suggest you retreat gracefully and take what's left of your winch man with you? I repeat, these are international waters, those men in the dinghy you tried to murder are my charges and I politely request you back off gracefully".

The co-pilot stared as the winchman, or what was left of his winch man, was drawn upward, his captain still lay beside him, the blood from his head-wound crawling across and smothering the digital readouts. The co-pilot was rapidly losing his nerve, he slammed the discharge handle and the winch man was unceremoniously dropped into the sea as the cable was disconnected by a brief explosive charge, the cable and its contents were swallowed without trace.

"This is murder!" screamed the co-pilot.

The co-pilot slowly rotated his helicopter until they were side on to the Huey's nose cone. Two uniformed men stood in the open doorway of the Saudi banana, machine guns at the ready, menacingly pointing in the Huey's direction. The co-pilot's voice was quick and to the point.

"You have five seconds to leave before my men open fire!" Now, he was sure he held the winning hand, confidence returned to his voice and he was determined to make them, whoever they were pay the full price.

"No shit!" returned the calm voice.

"Who are you? Where are you from? What are you doing here?"

The black Huey gave no acknowledgement.

"Prepare to accept Allah's judgement!" warned the co-pilot with confidence.

"Roll em, It seems we have a slight difference of opinion here!"

The small hatch doors flicked open on either side of the Huey and from the inner enclosures slid two evil-looking cylinders - one black cylinder per side, they would suffice. Each cylinder, the pilot knew, had a capability of two thousand rounds per minute. Two such cylinders mounted on either side of a chopper would enable it to fly through a forest at ground level, both puffs, as they were tagged, blazing furiously and they would never hit a single tree. The forward timbers would be reduced to

466

matchwood as the chopper proceeded unhindered, right on through the timberlands. Suddenly the co-pilot was unsure, he had never seen such weaponry,

"Control! Control! we are under threat of attack! over!"
The control centre had no idea what our man was facing but they were quite prepared to transmit the order to attack,
"Border! you may use any force you feel is necessary! over!"
The co-pilot was not convinced,
"Control, unidentified craft appears to be heavily armed! Over!"
The controller relayed the final message with a fanatical intonation, he knew who the men in the dinghy were, and that they had already mocked attempts to apprehend, capture and kill them. Now the controller wanted these men dead, with a desperation bordering on suicide - as long as it was somebody else's suicide.
"Border you must shoot them from the sky, kill them all, the men in the dinghy and the men in the aircraft. I order you to kill them all, in the name of Allah I command you. KILL THEM ALL!
The co-pilot acknowledged the command, he signalled to his men without heart, now they were ready. All they had to do was, kill the men in the dinghy and blast the opposing aircraft from the sky. Then, they could rid themselves of the captain's body. His spirit had ascended to Allah and he would have no further use for the empty shell. It was Allah's will. Everything was Allah's will and if they were to perish here too, well that was Allah's will also and there was nothing he, nor anybody else could do about it.
"Control! message received and understood, over".
The Huey positioned itself with a calm born of experience, even in the face of two men carrying machine guns, its flight remained true. The Huey resembled a painted shadow, smeared against the evening sky. Hangar's concentration now centred on his trigger finger and the loudspeaker of the Saudi Helicopter. Hangar could hear every word uttered by the co-pilot and his Arabic bordered on terrestrial. Hawkeye sat in the rear of the

CHAPTER 17   SAUDI STYLE   DESPERATION

Huey, feet against the alloy deck plates, pushing his body into the rear jump seat between the huge metal boxes of ammunition. He checked the porthole,

"They got the dinghy, Hangar. One of her floats is collapsing!"

Hangar did not reply, he was somewhere back in Vietnam, out on another mission, lost to the world of mortal acceptance, his steely gaze riveted to his foe with a fanatical, unblinking stare.

"Hangar the.........".

Hawkeye's words were cut short as Hangar's co-pilot waved him to silence. The Huey held position as the co-pilot checked the ammo, keeping his fingers well clear of the rattlesnake release of the auto feed. Hangar's mask remained set, slight creasing of his brow, those piercing probing eyes, searching for the weakness of his immediate foe. Hawkeye could have sworn they had landed, the Huey sat in the air like a heavy rock on a hard place. Hawkeye turned his eyes back to the front of the Huey and through the bubble screen, he saw the three men turn with guns at the ready.

"Where's the dinghy?" snapped Hangar.

"Rear and clear!" immediate co-pilot response.

Although weakened from the loss of blood, I could hear the threats issuing from the Saudi loudspeakers. Now the Saudi co-pilot launched into Arabic as he prepared his men to fire on the Huey. I hoped the Huey and its crew understood, there was nothing I could do to warn them.

The gunners in the Saudi helicopter yanked back the auto feed on their automatic weapons and poised ready to strike as the co-pilot hissed in Arabic,

"I will ask this foreign dog one more time to leave the area, on his refusal you will fire immediately as I give the word, be ready for my signal!"

"These are the territorial waters of Saudi Arabia; I ask you for the last time to leave the area at once. These are my prisoners and we are taking charge. You must leave the area immediately!"

468

CHAPTER 17   SAUDI STYLE   DESPERATION

Hangar squeezed slowly, he voiced no response, he had no time, he knew of the order to the three gunners. The co-pilot had not switched off his transmit button and still assumed they would not fully understand his Arabic. Hangar squeezed and waited, not for the enemy but for the trigger, to reach that certain point of lock where nothing remains between right and wrong, nothing but the release, as the firing pin escapes the catch and right and wrong are decided in seconds. Only at that hypercritical moment did Hangar speak,

"These are international waters...!" drawled Hangar, before being cut of in mid-sentence.

"FIRE!!!" screamed the Saudi co-pilot, cutting Hangar short and attempting a surprise action.

The dinghy turned and twisted like a leaf on a breeze-blown pond, now I was in full view of the proceedings. Pete lay unconscious, the blood oozing from his wounds and pooling in the depressions of the reinforced, rubber belly sheet. I thrust my fist against the shoulder wound, to stem the flow. I turned back once more, to the confrontation above. The Saudi crew members pointed their machine guns and opened fire as the final Arabic command left the loudspeaker. As the first puffs of flame ejected from the Saudi guns, a terrific crackling scream obliterated all other sound. The space between the two choppers became a black seething mass of swarming, steel hornet fury.

The sea around me was peppered with spent metal cartridges that rained from the Huey like hand thrown gravel on a flat surfaced pond. The Saudi helicopter buckled and already, the solid metal skin leaked daylight through a thousand spattered tears. I stared in disbelief as the banana began to fold and was torn to shreds. The fuel tank suddenly exploded, showering the sea with smouldering scrap metal. The hornet swarm passed through the broken twisted structure almost unhindered as the twin rotors leaped high into the sky suddenly released of their weighty burden. I watched the chopper, or what was left of the chopper as it smashed into the sea. By the time it hit the water it seemed like every square inch of alloy had received a murderous measure from the Huey's weapons.

The broken wave from the death plunge washed over me. Now only the Huey's motors remained. Hawkeye gaped below at the oily froth where the chopper had disappeared under the sea.

"Hangar!" Hawkeye's voice broke the verbal silence.

"Hangar!" Hawkeye increased the volume.

"Hangar!" Hawkeye broke the power trance, and as Hangar turned slowly to face him, he revealed his concern,

"You used all the ammunition, every shell, it's all gone, two thousand rounds, not one single shot left".

Hangar did not reply immediately, he released his hand from the trigger and checked his aircraft for damage. A few bullets had crazed through the screen above him but other than that his baby was OK and he turned to Hawkeye to speak,

"Yeah, Hawkeye that's right," he drolled, "I didn't want to have to take any back may as well use it up as take it back"

"Two thousand shots!" returned Hawkeye.

Hawkeye slumped into the jump seat mesmerised, by the empty steel canisters that seconds before had been full. Hangar grinned at Hawkeye's bewilderment and swung the Huey down from the heavens towards the rapidly sinking dinghy.

I clutched Pete's clothing. The inflatable had lost one of her flotation bags and was now sliding below the sea level. I did not want Pete to roll into the sea where I could not swim after him. The wash from the rotors of the Huey did nothing to help, spinning the dinghy around as it approached from the rear, skimming the surface as it came. Hawkeye, strap tied to the Huey balanced one foot on the dinghy and one foot on the Huey's skid as he tugged Pete into position and with the help of another guy, hauled the limp body aboard and strapped it to the mesh cot.

I waved Hawkeye away, rolled over onto my knees and tried to stand on the flooded belly sheet. As my good arm pushed me upright into a near-standing position, I turned towards the door of the Huey and a strong bronzed arm reached out to help me. I

470

stared in disbelief and for a few brief moments, time stood still. He smiled before I held out my arm and the voice at the other end of my reach spoke,

"I see you got rid of the luggage new-kid!"

There before me, stood the stranger. Same cut sleeve shirt, same gold chain, same carefree attitude, my soul soared,

"Well don't just stand like a bloody tourist," I almost sobbed, "Help this old new kid aboard".

The two outstretched hands met across space, same tanned skin, same muscular tone. Similar in strength and not least, similar in the warm bond of kinship that flowed from deep within. The side door of the Huey slid home and was locked. Hangar hit the toggle switch and the guns and ammunition boxes were ejected into the sea.

"Where we're going, they won't mind the crew but for sure they won't accept the guns, mine enemy's enemy and all that". It was all the explanation that was needed.
Hawkeye closed the hatches while the stranger tied Pete's legs together to steady the bleeding thigh. Hangar leaned the Huey forward and we headed from the smoking, oil-stained water directly Westward into the path of the orb.

Hangar tuned into the frequency that had led them to the dinghy's position, he pressed the transmit button and spoke,

"Control! control! do you read me? over!"

"We read you, identify yourselves! over!"

Hangar continued the conversation in Arabic as I conversed with my saviours,

"I didn't think we were going to make it; Pete never told me we were going to meet you guys. He just told me we were going to be picked up by ship. No wonder the bastard was so calm when we ran out of fuel, he just threw me the oars and told me to row. I turned to Pete who was regaining consciousness,

"Sneaky son of a bitch, thought he'd pulled one over on me, I bet". I attempted to smile with affection but the pain in my shoulder nipped the grin short. The stranger moved toward me and stabbed the morphine injection sachet into my arm,

"You never said you were a doctor!" my voice tinged with pain.

"You never asked!" the stranger smiled, "I told you to get your injections didn't I?".

"But you never even told me your name!"

"Hangar!" replied the stranger with a grin, "Alex Hangar to be precise".

"You're Alex Hangar? his brother, the battlefield medic?" I stabbed my good arm in the original Hangar's direction.

"All these years I knew he had a brother, he always talked about you but never had a single photograph. All these years it was you, Alex Hangar, the stranger. I don't believe it; I just don't believe it".

Alex stabbed the morphine sachet into Pete's leg and worked on his wounds, he spoke as he worked.

"Missed the bone, tore away a lump of flesh but with a bit of luck he'll be OK in a month or three". As the morphine numbed the pain, Pete regained some sort of groggy consciousness,

"We going to make it?" He croaked from the cot.

"Yeah, but you won't be no dancing tonight!"

Pete slumped back to the cot too exhausted even for conversation.

"Yeah, we're going to make it, Pete". My confident voice assured him,

"We always make it remember?" My good arm squeezed Pete's shoulder as I continued,

"We always make it, Pete. We're Khowajas!"

"Khowajas!" whispered Pete as he fell to unconsciousness,

"Khowajas!" spat Hawkeye, clenching his fist to his chest in salute and savouring the glow of comradeship in the Huey's womb.

The radio barked and crackled t life:

"You must identify yourselves! over!"

"I repeat identify yourselves! over!"

472

CHAPTER 17   SAUDI STYLE   DESPERATION

The controller still demanded some form of identification as he screamed over the radio.

The Huey scudded low across the darkening seascape directly tracing the path of the mighty Orb. The Huey a smudged silhouette against the blood-red sky. Behind us, far to the rear, the first call to evening prayer echoed across the water but it never reached our ears. The Huey's pulse drowned all but its own mechanical vibrations and Hangar's final words as he responded to the interrogators before killing the traceable transmitter,

"You must identify yourselves! over!"

"I repeat identify yourselves! over!"

"Khowajas, my friend. Just ....". Hanger glanced around at us before the final words issued from his lips.

"Khowajas!"

Chapter 18

KANDALOM

The small dugout canoe carried two passengers; occasionally it rocked from side to side onto its outriggers, nudged by the small waves on approach to the tiny inlet. A dugout with an outboard motor was considered a luxury by the natives, whose main source of income was from fishing the clear turquoise shallows behind the reef, which held at bay the rolling Pacific swell.

She watched as the small vessel entered the shelter of the channel, when the small boy cut the engine and allowed the canoe to glide, she rose to her feet and strolled down the grassy bank to meet them. The dark-skinned, native boy grinned as he held out a letter. She read the address, folded the letter neatly in two and placed it inside the breast pocket of her loose cotton shirt, a shirt that barely concealed her bikini top.

'Lyn," She stuck out her hand and released a warm friendly smile,

"Welcome to my grandfather's Island".

"Katherine," announced the beautiful young passenger, accepting the hand of friendship and returning the friendly smile.

"Bukas Ma'am? Tomorrow?" enquired the boy eagerly.

"Bukas," smiled Lyn, giving him a friendly wave as he padded down the grass and skipped into his canoe. He started the engine and sputtered out of the cove with a friendly wave of his own.

They talked as they walked along the golden shore, intermittently shaded by the overhanging coconut palms. Some coconuts had fallen and now littered the beach, continually in motion as they trundled backwards and forwards with the hydraulic of the waves that curled into the tranquil bay.

"It's beautiful," Kit complemented her surroundings.

"Mabuhay sa Philippinas - welcome to the Philippines," returned Lyn.

CHAPTER 18   SAUDI STYLE   KANDALOM

Lyn guided Kit along a small dusty path, which led them from the beach into a shaded coconut grove. They crossed a grassy slope and entered a small nipa-hut. A small native dwelling manufactured solely from various parts of the coconut tree. Extremely primitive but ideally suited to the typhoon blasted islands. A perfect place to shun the race and relax into oblivion. Lyn carried Kit's bag into an adjoining lean-to.

"Better if you change now, it will soon be night and we can go for a swim to freshen up".

Kit changed into a petite, blue-silk bikini, covered by a flowing shirt and the two girls chatted and squealed like sisters before they ran down the beach and into the sea. Once refreshed they perched on a warm dry grassy knoll that fringed the beach and overlooked the bay. The sun caressed the Horizon as Lyn spoke with serious tones,

"He waited, Kit. He did not want you to see him until he was healed," Lyn was almost apologetic with her tone.

"This I expected from him".

"You too eh, Kit?" Lyn nodded with a knowing smile and Kit blushed with her embarrassed reply.

"Look!" Lyn pointed out to the reef, "Here he is now".

My head and shoulders rose above the surface some hundred meters out from the shore. They must have heard me cough as I spat the regulator from my mouth, before removing my facemask and shaking my hair in sudden release from the tight rubber straps. I sank back into the water reaching for my flippers and then regained my full height to lob the flippers over my shoulder and out of the way.

The water swelled around my chest, as I started progress toward their grassy outcrop. Then I caught sight of them and raised my free arm in a wave of recognition. I leaned forward into the water and created a small cresting wave that ran before my progress. Behind me now, another head pierced the surface, spat out the regulator and copied my earlier movements by removing the mask and flippers. As soon as the regulator left his mouth he was complaining,

"Bob! wait! you know my knee's still bad, help me with my tanks, wait, com'on Bob, please! Some help you are, my knees bad, my thigh hurts, these tanks are……".

Suddenly he was silent, his eyes struck the grassy knoll and the two female figures perched on top. Pete waved his arm and accelerated his walk to the shore. A large wave formed in front of his chest as his legs pumped hard against the weight of the sea. The water level had fallen to his waist and by the time he dashed by my side, the tops of Pete's knees were now visible above the frothy surge.

"I see your knees all better then?" I quipped as Pete splashed by. I received no reply, eager lips tell no tales. They connected like a perfect jigsaw, Kit was sobbing, tears streamed down her cheeks, and she squeezed Pete until her arms could squeeze no more. Lyn and I watched them from the knoll as Pete tenderly carried Kit up the beach. The tanks were still on his back, his gear still clutched in his hand and a sixty-kilogram female snuggled against his neck supported by his forearms.

"Well, Pete. I guess your knee miraculously healed?"

"Sure did, just in time too," replied Pete.

We walked along the beach together, up the sandy path and into the nipa-hut. Pete formally introduced Lyn to Kit as we removed our tanks and gear.

"I feel I know you so well already," smiled Kit as Pete chipped in,

"Yeah, there ain't much to know, Kit. You could write Bob's life story on the back of a "small" postage stamp".

I stared at him with disdain!

The sun had now gone and we lay on the grassy outcrop under a burning sky. The aroma of smouldering coconut husks wafted across our position as it surfed the night breeze. I studied the letter and when I had finished, I spoke,

"The Amazons, Pete! We've been accepted on our terms!"

476

"Lemmee see! Lemmee see!" Pete's excitement was hardly concealed.

Pete read the letter and exploded,

"Great!" he yelled, "Magic, now we can stop sending those dumb resumes all over the world".

"Yeah, Pete. Looks like we're off to the Amazons".

Pete felt Lyn's finger as it dug into the flesh on his back and a silent signal of warning flashed from her face.

Pete turned to Kit, took her arm and stroked it tenderly with his free hand.

"Will you come with me?" he enquired affectionately.

"Hoy I can't just disappear into jungle with crazy Canadian, what I going to tell my mom?"

"Tell her you're going with your husband!"

Kit shrieked with joy and leapt into his arms,

"Hoy! we be very happy together, I sure! I sure!"

The foursome divided in two, me congratulating Pete, Lyn and Kit discussing wedding plans. The sea reflected the sky and glowed like the breeze fanned embers of a winter blaze. The four of us sat together, staring across the velvet-calm Pacific Ocean, an ocean now reflecting a scatter of pin-bright stars in a sultry night sky. The fire crackled and popped as the music of the sea graced the shore. Four souls lost in Paradise, no cares in the world. I gazed into the deep pools of Lyn's fathomless eyes, they seemed inquisitive and unsure.

"Penny for your thoughts?" I inquired.

"I was just thinking," she began, as the firelight glow danced across her golden skin tones,

"What if they don't stick to the contract and try to cheat you when you get to the Amazons?"

A silence veiled the gathering. Pete glanced into Kit's eyes, and then he gazed at Lyn for a while before finally, he turned to me, I gave him the look, and the shadow of that familiar smile was already creasing into place, answering the question without words.

CHAPTER 18   SAUDI STYLE   KANDALOM

"Oh please, Lyn. For heaven's sake No!" pleaded Pete in
mock dismay, jumping to his feet and heading off down the
beach as if he were going home to his mum.

"Don't set him off before we even get there, anything but
that," he moaned.

Lyn tried to stifle a laugh but it broke free, Kit joined in the
laughter as I politely smiled. Pete eyed me up once more and his
face lost that desperate expression. The two of us understood,
at last, we were finally free, gazing into the heavens from the
safety of our private retreat, drinking the night wind of the salty
Pacific Coast.

"Amazons," I whispered mostly to myself.

As if telepathic, I saw Pete pluck the breeze-borne whisper
from the air, he turned to face me and in the depths of our being,
the restless spirit stirred.

Printed in Great Britain
by Amazon